FIRESTORM

RACHEL GRANT

JANUS PUBLISHING

Books by Rachel Grant

This one is for Elisabeth Naughton.

Amazing author, fantastic plotter, and dear friend. Our daily messages keep me grounded.

I'm sorry Luc had to suffer, but it was the right thing to do.

Thank you for helping me navigate this crazy, wonderful world.

Chapter One

Camp Citron, Djibouti
Late May

Savannah James didn't bother to look up from her computer screen to see who'd entered her office without knocking. A tingling in her neck told her Sergeant First Class Cassius Callahan had arrived. The physical reaction was triggered by something subliminal and unknown. His scent? The sound of his footsteps?

Whatever the cause, the reaction irritated. "I take it you've spoken with your XO, Sergeant. For the record, you weren't my first choice, so don't whine at me."

He pulled back the visitor's chair and dropped into it, then propped his feet upon her desk in a clear demonstration of disrespect.

Lovely. He was going to be a joy to work with.

She closed the lid of her laptop and finally met his gaze, and there was that small, maddening flutter in her belly that always followed the tingle in her neck. He was the most achingly handsome man she'd ever met. He had the deep, dark brown skin of his Congolese mother combined with the tall, thick build of his Irish American father. Heavy brows capped warm brown eyes. His broad nose and square jaw could give several Hollywood heartthrobs a run for their money.

"You spooks just can't help lying, can you?" He held her gaze. "According to my XO, you only asked for me."

She smiled. She was a professional liar for Uncle Sam and would never apologize for that. He couldn't goad her by calling her what she was. But in this instance, she'd spoken the truth. A CIA operator would be easier to work with than the handsome sergeant who was congenial and charming to every person on this damn base but her.

"I asked the CIA to send a Special Activities Division paramilitary officer, but SAD can't send someone right away, and timing is crucial, so I was forced to go shopping in Camp Citron's Special Operations Command catalogue."

"Am I to take that to mean I'm the right color and gender?" His voice held a hard edge.

"Exactly. Plus you speak French and Lingala."

His eyes narrowed, lowering those thick brows. His head was shaved bare, and he sported a trim beard. He effortlessly exuded masculine energy that triggered a hunger she couldn't bury deep enough, no matter how hard she tried. He was her only option. He was here, spoke Lingala, and SOCOM said she could have him as long as he agreed to the mission.

"I'm not the only one at Camp Citron fluent in Lingala. I can think of two other guys who speak it, and one of them also speaks Swahili, which you also might need in the Democratic Republic of the Congo, assuming that's where your mission is headed."

Lord, she hoped they wouldn't have to go into DRC. "But they're both intelligence officers. Glorified translators. I need an operator."

His full bottom lip caught her attention. He signaled he noticed her stare by flashing perfect white teeth. "You saying you need a real man, Savvy?"

She rolled her eyes even as her belly fluttered at his use of the nickname. She ignored the ridiculous reaction. It wasn't as if Savannah was her real name, so the nickname shouldn't feel intimate. "I need an operator with native fluency."

He dropped his boots to the floor, grin firmly in place. He obviously knew how handsome he was and that even she, coldhearted spook that she was, wasn't immune. But then, he'd never lacked ego.

She stared at his perfect smile, her confidence in her plan fading. He'd never pass. His teeth would give him away. Too much orthodontia, too little khat. "You need to grow a longer beard. You need to look less like a broodingly handsome Luke Cage and more like an unkempt, hostile drug lord looking to enter the diamond trade."

"Seems like my body armor—not my beard—will give me away."

"No body armor, no Army uniform where we're going. You'll be sheep-dipped and trade in your M4 for a Kalashnikov."

"You want a covert operator, grab a guy from Delta."

She stood, walked around her desk, and closed the office door. It was time to tell him what she figured many on base suspected but few at Camp Citron knew for certain.

"What I'm about to tell you is classified. I'm not a CIA case officer. Nor am I an analyst."

He snorted. "No kidding."

She couldn't help but smile. She'd done little to protect this secret with Special Operations Command. It hadn't been possible or necessary. She crossed back to her desk. "I started as an analyst, went through case officer training and was one for a while. When I find someone I think would make a good asset, I let the case officer at the embassy know."

"It's Kaylea Halpert, isn't it?"

She didn't miss a beat and just rolled her eyes. "You think you're the first person to try the guessing game on me?" He wasn't, but he was the first to guess it in one try. Most assumed the case officer was a man. Few soldiers looked at Kaylea and thought she was CIA. Usually they were too distracted by the beautiful black woman's curves.

Unlike Kaylea, whose cover as an embassy employee hid her true job, Savvy worked directly with SOCOM and, like the soldier who sat before her, was prepared to deploy on special ops alone or with a team at a moment's notice.

Savannah James's official cover was civilian public works liaison for Camp Citron, which gave her access to Djiboutian ministers and the right to come and go as she pleased from the base. But she wasn't Savannah James, and she was hardly a public works liaison. She worked with a degree of autonomy that was rare in the intelligence community but completely necessary to be able to react quickly when opportunities arose to gather intel on particular individuals or organizations.

"I don't run spies, but I'm privy to the intel they provide. I handle top secret tech like subdermal trackers, but that's not my main job either. My actual title is paramilitary operations officer for the Special Operations Group within SAD."

Cal looked skeptical. "I thought SOG officers were recruited from the military? Special Forces, SEALs, Delta. You aren't military."

She wasn't, while he was US military through and through. He probably bled Army green. Worse, Sergeant Callahan had more than made it clear he was no fan of the CIA.

"Most do come from the military, but a few are recruited from within the CIA—especially the women." She flashed a smile. "Special forces isn't exactly a bastion of equality, and some jobs—like this one—require a woman."

She cleared her throat. "Unlike other special units, SAD/SOG operatives are trained to operate with limited to zero support. When I'm working a covert op, I don't carry or wear anything that connects me to the CIA or US government. If compromised, the US government will deny all knowledge of my existence."

Special Operations Group was considered the US government's most secretive special operations force, with good reason. Missions—conducted by teams or singly—included raids, sabotage, and even targeted killings, hence the need for the US to have plausible deniability of their covert operatives' actions.

She rested her hands on her desk. "I won't force you to help me in this operation. You can say no and return to your A-Team. But I want you to know, I wouldn't ask for your assistance if this weren't important. The intel we recovered from Nikolai Drugov's operation is time sensitive. We have a chance to strike a major blow for Team Democracy and take out the kleptocrats and warlords who have been preying upon the Democratic Republic of the Congo since before Mobutu changed the name to Zaire."

This part made her nervous. If Cal said no, she was screwed. He didn't like her, but his mother was from DRC. She'd left the country when it was called Zaire under the rule of Mobutu Sese Seko. For Cal, this could be personal, and she would appeal to that.

His lengthy silence had her sweating, despite the air-conditioning being set to frigid.

Finally, he said, "Seems like I should know what I'm agreeing to before I commit."

She nodded. "I have intel collected from Drugov's yacht and found information that another Russian oligarch, Radimir Gorev—a rival of Drugov, but also a business partner—is hosting an event on *his* yacht in Dar es Salaam next Friday. A gathering of warlords, drug smugglers, corrupt government officials, and wanna-be oligarchs. A nasty, old-fashioned cabal. Drugov compiled quite a bit of information on the other guests, including the fact that Jean Paul Lubanga will be there."

"Who is that?"

"In my opinion, he's the biggest threat to the relative peace of DRC."

"Then why haven't I heard of him?"

"Lubanga is quiet. Stealthy. And shrewd. After witnessing the mistakes of Mobutu, he's doing his best not to draw attention to himself." She grabbed a file from her desk and pulled out a picture of the man. "At present, he's a government minister, the ultimate power in DRC's vast mining and mineral rights industry. Analysts believe he's working toward gaining the loyalty of the military, and once he has that..."

"He's planning a coup?"

"It's our job—*my* job—to find out. I think Drugov hoped to get Lubanga out of his rival Gorev's pocket and into his own. The oligarch who can bring Russia the riches of DRC would be the second most powerful man in the country."

"And why do you need me?"

"You're my ticket onto Gorev's yacht. Into the heart of the cabal. It's an evening of business negotiations, sex, and drugs. Sex and drugs give him the kompromat he needs to keep his associates in line, while the business deals keep everyone rich."

"And how do I get you ringside seats to this shitshow? Because I'm assuming you don't plan to watch from the sidelines."

"Warlords and oligarchs will never accept a woman at the table, unless she's there as a toy." Her gaze flicked down Cal's perfect, soldier's body. "You're the businessman. I'll be your sex toy."

Savannah James, his sex toy. Now there was a thought that should turn Cal cold. *Should* being the operative word.

He studied the woman, finding it all too easy to imagine her in nothing but kinky strips of leather. He had zero interest in sadomasochism, but he had to admit, the accoutrements were sexy, and on Savvy, that kind of getup would be pure hot sin.

"What's the timeline?" he asked, returning his focus to where it belonged.

"We head south the day after tomorrow. The meeting is Friday night, but before we can get invites to the party, we need to connect with some of Gorev's associates on Thursday. They'll extend the invite if you pass muster. If I don't get everything I need at the party, we'll stick around for as long as Lubanga is in Dar es Salaam. All told, it should take a week."

"You hope," Cal said.

"Yes. I hope." She dropped back into the chair behind her desk. "I've gotten intel from Morgan's crew on artifact trafficking." Morgan was Dr. Morgan Adler, an archaeologist who'd sought protection at Camp Citron two months ago. Cal had met her when her car blew up two miles from the main gate.

"What does Morgan have to do with this?" he asked.

"We'll use artifact trafficking to get that invitation. Gorev has a fondness for antiquities. You've got goods to sell and want to use them as your ticket to the big show, because precious metals and diamonds are where the real money is."

He cocked his head. "You've got artifacts to sell? From Morgan's project?"

She gave a sharp nod. "And another source."

"Morgan's not going to like that."

Her eyes flattened. "Morgan is never going to know about it."

True. At least, she wouldn't hear about it from him. "Was Nikolai Drugov involved in artifact trafficking too?"

"I haven't had a chance to delve deeply there. Connecting the dots takes time."

When Savvy started playing dot-to-dot, she drew murals. Cal, he connected the same points and came up with a hangman every time.

"I need you, Cal. These men aren't exactly feminists. An American woman dealing in artifacts and precious metals will be noticed in a way that a cowed sex slave would not."

He snorted. "I doubt you can play cowed convincingly."

She shook her head, her disappointment evident as she tsked. "Typical chauvinistic military asshole bullshit."

"Typical spook." She had no respect for military personnel who got the job done. He stood. "Find someone else to play master. I only work with trained soldiers."

She tsked again. "Taking your toys and going home at one slight? I expected better from you. I'm slighted constantly—by you and everyone on this damn base—but I don't whine about it. And for the record, I've had as much training as you. Plus, I'm trained to work alone."

She stood and leaned on her desk. "I'm versed in special weapons and tactics. I can fight and kill unarmed. But unlike you, I'm expected to fuck to protect my cover. And if I don't, and my cover is blown, our government will disavow me." Her eyes hardened. "So yeah, I can *act*. My very life depends on my acting ability. It doesn't matter if I can't run ten miles carrying rocks like Special Forces, when my fate can turn on a badly delivered lie."

She circled her desk to stand before him. "I can do everything you can do, Sergeant. Backward, while wearing high heels. So you can take your chauvinistic attitude and shove it up your ass."

Standing before him was the fierce woman who hid behind a cold façade. There was far more to Savannah James than he'd imagined. And he could—and had—imagined a lot.

The woman was sexy as hell and pushed all the right buttons. She was danger and desire in one scary, beautiful package. "When we're in public, you'll be meek and subservient?" he asked.

"I never break character."

"And when we're alone?"

She ran a fingertip down his chest. Her eyes turned liquid with desire.

And damn if his heart didn't react to that.

"If I think we're being monitored, I will stay in character." She traced his neck upward from Adam's apple to chin to bottom lip, her nail finding the skin under his short beard. "I will do whatever is necessary to get the job done." She leaned close, bringing her mouth a breath away from his. Her scent was soft, sultry. Sexy. "My job is everything. My reason for living. And I protect it at all costs."

Only now, when they stood so close, did he see the true emotion in her eyes, the lie of this husky-voiced seducer. She was showing him one facet of her acting, making him wonder if the surreptitious looks he'd received from her during their months in Djibouti had also been an act.

He'd egotistically believed Savannah James was attracted to him, and now he couldn't help but wonder if she'd been playing him all along. Setting him up.

But why? It couldn't be for this. No way could Savvy have foreseen the path that took them here.

Except she was a spook, and the way she connected intel was freaky. And in the case of Drugov, she'd been on the money. Savvy was the unsung hero of that op. She'd identified Drugov as worth watching. She'd convinced SOCOM to send one of Cal's teammates to Morocco to help trap the man. No one would ever give her credit, but her work had stopped a genocide.

And she did it all without leaving Camp Citron.

"So, Cal. Are you…"—she let out a soft, throaty laugh—"in?" Her sex-kitten voice combined with her scent would haunt him when he tried to sleep tonight. Her finger traced a straight line down his chest, over his heart, heading south, stopping just short of his belt.

He could so easily picture her popping open his combat uniform buttons on the trip down. His erection caused his pants to bulge.

She was acting. He, clearly, was not.

In one fast motion, he lifted her and set her on her desk, planting himself between her spread knees. He slid a hand behind her neck. Her breath warmed his lips as he rocked into the cradle of her thighs.

His erection brushed against her, and her breath hitched, telling him what he wanted to know. The sound, the flash of heat in her eyes, those were real. If anything, she wouldn't want him to know she was aroused. She'd have masked it, if she could.

But the queen of control hadn't been able to hide that reaction.

Satisfied, he released her and stepped back. They were equally exposed. Vulnerable. Heated up.

A level playing field for a game in which she would almost certainly always have the upper hand. She was the spook. He was a simple soldier.

Like her, his life was the job, the job his life. And also like her, screwups meant death—for him or his brothers-in-arms.

"I'm in." And he was, no hesitation. But then, he'd always been in, and it had nothing to do with Savvy's sexy plea. His XO had made it clear he *couldn't* turn this assignment down, not without pissing off his command. SOCOM wanted a mole in Savannah James's operation. They wanted to know what the hell she was up to and why she operated unfettered by superiors in the CIA.

When Savvy asked for Cal's help, she'd unwittingly elected him for the job. She was a spy for the CIA. He was a spy for the US Army Special Operations Command.

Chapter Two

"Pretend I'm one of the guys on your A-Team, Sergeant. Let me have it." Savvy circled Cal on the sparring mat with fists up, looking for a gap in his defenses. He protected himself well, but he was holding back on throwing punches. Going easy on her. That would never do.

This mission wouldn't work if he saw her as less capable than him. He couldn't be soft on her in any way. He'd expressed worry over her acting abilities, but really, *his* were the issue. He would have to treat her as his property—to use and abuse—and softness toward her could get them both killed.

He took a swing, and she dropped her guard on purpose, taking the blow from his ungloved hand on the chin.

"What the fuck, Savvy?" His words came out in an angry growl. Anger was better than concern, at least.

"Will you look at that, I'm not made of glass. I didn't shatter. *Bring it*, Cal." She followed up by taking a jab at his face, which he blocked, but didn't follow up with another punch.

She took another swing at his head. He ducked, then popped up, sweeping her legs out from under her with his. But even as she fell, he caught her and followed her to the mat, cushioning her landing.

"Dammit, Cal. *Fight me.*" She pushed at his chest as he lay beside her on the floor, glad she'd commandeered the gym for this training session. An audience would only make this more difficult for him.

"What's the point? I know you can fight. You know I can. There's no reason for us to do this."

"To maintain cover, you might have to hit me."

His gaze turned hard. "You want me to beat you? That's a hell of a thing to ask of a guy."

She tucked her knees beneath her and sat up. He was going to hate this, and she didn't blame him. She lifted his fist from the mat and guided it to her chin. "Punching me in the face isn't even the worst thing you might be required to do."

His palm opened, and he cupped her chin before dropping his hand as if her skin burned. He might not like her, but he was attracted to her, and she was counting on that to work in their favor during the mission.

"You're going to have to kiss me, touch me," she continued. "And at times, I might not appear willing. You'll need to be rough, to show the others you're teaching me a lesson. You need to treat me as an object. Not a person."

She saw the moment her meaning registered. His dark eyes lit with a hard, angry fire.

"This isn't a game, Cal. I'm not talking about playing at sadomasochism or bondage for fun. I'm talking about maintaining cover to save our lives."

"You're saying I might have to rape you."

"Not rape. I'm giving you consent right now to do what you need to do. It wouldn't be rape. Not for me." But what would it be for him? She didn't want him walking into this mission naïve about what they faced. What they might have to do.

His role meant he had to be a savage master. Brutal to his core. That wasn't Cal. He was a congenial buddy or hard-ass Special Forces operator, but never cruel. He needed to tap into his darker side for this mission. Fortunately, she tended to bring out the worst in him.

He bolted to his feet and paced a large circle on the mat. "This is fucked-up."

"Hopefully, it won't get that far. But the sexual nature of our cover is going to push us to the limit. These are Nikolai Drugov's associates. The event will be a sex party with enticements of forced sex and drugs for all the guests. Drugs are out, so we'll use sex. But you aren't a fan of sharing or screwing random sex workers, so you brought your own. This gives you an excuse not to partake of Gorev's offerings, and it protects me. I'm your property."

"And you expect no one will grab you the moment my back is turned?"

She climbed to her feet and gave a slight shrug, not wanting Cal to know how much she feared that. "So you won't turn your back."

"What you're asking is impossible." He stalked toward her, his handsome face a hard mask of anger.

She took a step back, retreating before she had a chance to think better of it.

He kept coming, driving her back to the wall. Her pulse jumped as he took a lock of her hair and rolled it between his fingers. "You think they won't take one look at you, with your soft, silky hair and those wide brown eyes, and they won't want you for themselves?" He ran a thumb along her jaw and over her lips. "You think they won't take one look at your full lips and have X-rated fantasies about what they can do with your mouth? Fuck,

Savvy. You're one of the sexiest women I've ever seen, and you're going to walk into a den of thugs acting as my whore. You'll be a magnet for assault."

Her heart raced wildly from the moment his thumb touched her lip. It was possible she'd miscalculated in choosing Cal. She'd thought the attraction would make it easier to be close to him, as this job required. But she hadn't factored in that with one touch, her focus was shot.

She gripped his tight Under Armour shirt and pulled him even closer, turning his weapon back on him. "Then you're going to have to be very jealous, Cal. Hurt the first man who touches me. Send a message. Because this"—she took his hand and slid it down her side, starting at her breast and ending on her ass—"is yours. And only yours."

He cupped her butt and pulled her against him. His mouth hovered above hers. "There's one thing you need to know." His voice was a low whisper. "Anything that happens between us on this op is an act. My body might respond to you, but I don't trust you. You lie, manipulate, and bend people. So don't start thinking it means anything if we screw."

His words sent ice through her body, as she knew he'd intended. "Hit me," she said in a hard voice. "Give me a black eye. The uglier the better. Split my lip so no one will have fantasies about my mouth." She flashed a cold smile. "Shouldn't be too hard, given that I'm a conniving bitch."

He pushed back from her. "Sonofabitch. You're doing it now. Manipulating."

"*Hit me.*"

"No."

With a sharp kick, she swept his legs out from under him. Caught off guard, he went down. "Then don't bitch about thugs wanting me if you aren't willing to do anything about it."

He grabbed her ankle and pulled her down. In a flash, he had her beneath him, arms pinned above her head, his body pressed full length to hers. He supported his weight on one elbow, using that hand to hold her wrists together. "Stop baiting me, Savvy. You might have mad super spy skills, but I'm bigger and stronger, and I've had more physical training. My whole *life* is training."

She rocked her hips, stroking the growing erection he couldn't suppress. "I can kill with guns, knives, and my bare hands, just like you." She let her body go soft and compliant. "With my hands is my favorite. Get them up close and hard. They never saw death coming."

He released her hands and laughed. "I gotta hand it to you, Sav, this mission won't be boring. Dangerous as fuck. Possibly suicidal. But watching you in action won't be boring."

Admittedly, she'd fantasized about seeing Cal in action, but she wasn't about to give him that satisfaction. She shoved him to the side and rolled to her feet. "Sparring is over. Shower and meet me in my office in thirty minutes. We need to go over the details of our cover story."

He stood and nodded. "Yes, ma'am."

At least he wasn't fighting her over command. This op was hers from beginning to end. It was good he understood that.

Cal studied Savannah. She was all poise and cool control, sitting behind her desk. What would it take to break her icy self-possession? In the gym, she'd been turned on as he pressed close to her, but she never so much as flinched, not even when he insulted her.

Instead, she'd twisted his own weapon against him. She had the upper hand during their sparring match and knew how to wield it, how to push his buttons. Worse, she hadn't been baiting him just for kicks. She really *had* wanted him to hit her. And in so doing, she'd exposed a weakness he might not be able to overcome.

He stared at her face—which he'd pictured in far too many sexual fantasies in the last few months—and tried to imagine throwing a punch that would blacken one of her beautiful, intelligent brown eyes.

The thought made him sick.

She wasn't a blonde bombshell like Pax's girlfriend, Morgan, and lacked the glamour and polish of Bastian's girlfriend, Brie. Savannah's beauty was subtle. Understated. She tried to fade into the background, like any good spy, but her eyes and those full lips were a car alarm that went off for no reason and couldn't be silenced.

She'd never go unnoticed. At least, not to him.

If she wore makeup, it was understated and imperceptible, and he couldn't describe a single outfit she'd worn in the months he'd known her—except for the workout clothes, which didn't hide her full bust and perfect, round ass—because she dressed for invisibility. But no matter how much she downplayed, he saw her. He saw her understated beauty and her keen intelligence.

He saw her passion for her job and her allegiance to the CIA.

He couldn't deny it, her intellect scared him. Not that he feared intelligence—brains were always a turn-on. What he feared was how Savvy used her mind. She made connections invisible to others, then she used what she saw to twist and torment intel out of people. She'd pushed Bastian to get close to Brie without a care for what it would do to the couple when Brie learned the truth. For Savvy, the ends always justified the means.

No matter how attracted he was to her, that was the sticking point. He'd spent the better part of six months with his emotions on lockdown around her. She would never use him as she had Bastian. And now SOCOM was sending them on a covert mission together.

Fucking great.

There wasn't a person at Camp Citron he liked less or a woman he wanted more.

She opened a file on her desk, revealing the headshot of Jean Paul Lubanga she'd shown him before. "Operation Zagreus is an intelligence-gathering mission, and this is our primary target."

"Zagreus?"

"Lubanga's code name. Zagreus was a minor Greek god. From the underworld."

Of course Savvy would know the origin. But then, she'd probably assigned the code name. "C'mon. There's more to it than that. Zagreus isn't a common name from Greek mythology."

"In Greek, a hunter who captures living animals is called *zagreus*. Lubanga captures children and makes them dig for diamonds, or he sells them." She shrugged. "And we've already used the better-known deities." She pulled a blue passport from the file and handed it to him. "Your name is Mani Kalenga."

He took the booklet, which appeared to be genuine. He approved of her selecting the common Congolese surname that started with K-A-L. He presumed she'd done this because he wasn't trained for covert work, which was fine with him. Less room for error if he could go by Kal.

"Your father," Savvy continued, "left Zaire in the early eighties when he married your white American mother, who'd worked in Kinshasa for a US mining company."

This was something of a reversal of his real parentage. His mother was from the Democratic Republic of the Congo—then called Zaire—and his father had met her when he worked at the US embassy in Kinshasa. They'd settled in the US not long before Cal was born in the mideighties. He nodded acceptance of this cover story. While he was fluent in Lingala, he was unmistakably American. He'd visited Kinshasa along with the village where his mother was born and the rainforests and jungles in the area, but he could never pass for a local.

"You were working for Drugov's organization in South Sudan," Savvy continued, "providing private security, when you heard the oligarch was dead and decided to move into his business. You'd done some translating for him, which is how you knew about his plans to cut a deal with Lubanga for a diamond mining claim."

Again, he nodded. There were Lingala speakers in the southwest part of South Sudan. If Drugov had been seeking to get into the diamond game, it was easy to believe he'd take advantage of muscle that spoke the language of the capital of DRC.

"I'm a merc, then. Former US military?"

Savvy nodded. "Yes. Not Special Forces, though. We don't want anyone digging in that direction. And they'd never trust you if you claimed to be Delta. We'll leave it at soldier and dishonorable discharge."

Cal winced, but he knew it was necessary. His character was anything but moral and upright. Better they believe he was greedy enough to get caught—but not so sloppy he'd served time. He didn't worry that the men he'd be dealing with would question his lack of patriotism. These men were loyal only to money and power, and found it easy to accept those traits in others. "Okay, then. Now tell me about you."

Savvy pulled out another US passport. "My French accent is too American, so I'm a tourist. I was a companion to an octogenarian on a Tanzanian and Kenyan safari. He'd always dreamed of going on safari, and I'd always dreamed of inheriting his money. Unfortunately, his children hired a private investigator to watch over us, and the investigator found me in bed—with you. We met at a hotel in Nairobi before the safari started, then you showed up at Amboseli National Park, which is where we were caught in bed together. I was dumped from the tour with nothing but my passport and clothing. You promised to buy me a plane ticket home from Dar es Salaam but are stringing me along. I have nothing and am completely dependent on you."

He nodded. That worked. "Your name?"

"Jamie Savage."

"Smart. So if I call you Sav, it will make sense. James too."

She nodded.

He cocked his head. "What's your real name, Sav?"

She answered him with a look, and he couldn't help but laugh. Two weeks ago, when Morgan Adler visited Camp Citron, he'd joined her and Pax in Barely North one evening. Savvy had been there too, and Morgan commented that she was more comfortable with being called Savvy than Savannah and asked why she'd chosen an alias she disliked.

Savvy had replied, *"I didn't choose it. It was assigned to me."* It was one of the few times Savvy let any real emotion show, and he figured she'd been pissed about the alias. He'd spent too much time wondering why. But it wasn't the sort of question she was likely to answer. Ever.

"What's our next step?"

"Tomorrow we fly to Nairobi. From there we'll buy a truck and drive to the park. We'll spend the night there, then head to Dar es Salaam, which will take a day, maybe two. On Thursday, we'll meet with Gorev's associates. Friday is the big event."

Cal flipped through his passport, seeing stamps from all over the region. Savvy was thorough. "How the hell did you get the stamps?"

"Stamps are easy. But you need to study them and remember where you've been. There are no Rwanda or Uganda stamps. Those can make crossing the border into DRC difficult."

"I thought we weren't going to DRC?"

She shrugged. "It never hurts to be prepared."

"And how are we going to pay for this? I'm guessing you don't use a government credit card for covert ops."

She smiled. "The American dollar is preferred over the Congolese franc and Tanzanian and Kenyan shillings. We'll have several thousand in cash on us when we set out. Plus Mani Kalenga has a rather large bank account—with accompanying credit card—in Nairobi. We'll use that to purchase a vehicle when we get there and for hotel rooms over the first few days to conserve our cash."

He'd never really considered how undercover operators financed their missions without a trail that led right back to the Agency. Learn something new every day. "Are we going to be chipped?" he asked, referring to the subdermal tracking devices that had saved a few lives in the last two months.

She shook her head. "No. We're completely on our own for this mission. If we get in trouble, there will be no cavalry."

He'd expected that, but now, as he studied the passport and they discussed their itinerary, the isolation sank in. This was his first time going on a mission without Uncle Sam providing military flights to get him where he needed to be. Hell, he wouldn't have his M4 or his uniform. He wouldn't be a soldier at all.

This required a different mindset.

There would be no cavalry. No team. The men he trusted to watch his back wouldn't be there. Savannah James would have his six, and he would watch hers.

He hoped to hell she hadn't been exaggerating about her training and skills.

Chapter Three

It felt strangely like a bachelor party, this gathering of Cal's team at Barely North the night before departing on an op with Savvy. He was the groom, out with his buddies, and the bride was nowhere to be seen. He'd say she was off with her friends, but Morgan and Pax were the only friends she had that he knew of, and Morgan was back in the US while Pax was sitting to Cal's left.

As with any good send-off, he received ribbing over the fact that he would be spending days up close and personal with a woman who'd shot down the advances of probably half the special forces operators—Army and Navy—on the base. Not a lot of the men at Camp Citron liked her, but that didn't mean they didn't want in her pants. It didn't sit well with him that he was no better than the rest of the randy assholes.

Bastian and Pax were quiet, even as they exchanged a look. They both knew Cal was one of the many who wanted her, but unlike the others, they also knew the attraction went both ways. Cal had few secrets from Pax, his roommate on this deployment, and Bastian had questioned him after witnessing a few choice encounters between him and Savvy.

Pax genuinely liked Savannah James—but then, she'd kept him in the command center when Morgan was abducted and had enlisted his aid in tracking down the man who'd betrayed Morgan. Not to mention that Savvy had helped prevent Pax, Bastian, and Cal from facing court-martial after their AWOL rescue mission had been a success.

Pax had never been burned by Savvy's ruthless ends-justify-the-means ways. CIA couldn't be trusted; it was a basic fact of life.

What Cal didn't understand was Bastian's take on the woman. Sure, the court-martial thing counted in her favor, but aside from that, Bastian had plenty of reason to dislike Savvy.

Cal lowered his voice under the din of the conversation and asked Bastian, "Why aren't you pissed at her, Bas? She manipulated you and Brie, and then she nearly got you both killed."

Bastian shrugged and took a sip of his beer. "She was right. I needed to get Brie to open up, and we needed to go after Drugov." His eyes darkened. "The guy was plotting genocide. I'm not the kind of person who loses sleep over the ethics of killing baby Hitler. Hypotheticals of that sort are bullshit, but the gist is this: if you have foreknowledge of a mass murder, terrorist strike, or genocide, you act.

"Savvy unearths that foreknowledge. Her work gives us a chance to act. And she's got a helluva instinct for ferreting out information. None of us will receive medals for mopping up at Desta's compound, and my role in taking down Drugov will never be acknowledged, but I'm going home from this deployment knowing I helped prevent a genocide. That's more than enough for me." Bastian cocked his head. "I think the real question is why are you so bothered by her?"

Pax leaned in. "I want to know that too."

Cal frowned. He just had to open his big, stupid mouth. He sighed and gave them the truth. "She'll sacrifice anyone."

Bastian nodded. "Yes. Even herself."

And that right there might be the root of the problem. Possibly, his thoughts toward Savvy leaned more toward fear for her than anger at her. Did she ask others to do more than she would be willing to do in their place? He didn't think so.

She'd wanted him to hit her and expected him to have to do worse when they were in Dar.

They were leaving tomorrow on a mission together, and she might sacrifice him in a heartbeat. Or herself. And he wouldn't be able to stop her.

He glanced up as the door to the club opened, and there she was. She scanned the room and caught his gaze.

"Shit. Fun's over," Sergeant Stockton said in a cold voice from the far end of the table. "Cal's missus has arrived." He spoke loud enough for everyone—including Savvy—to hear.

"Shut it, Stock," Pax said. "Don't be a dick."

"Too late," Bastian said. "He was born that way."

Savvy stopped dead in the middle of the room. Her gaze bounced from Stockton to Cal.

He cast a glare at Stockton, and then nodded for Savvy to join them. "What's up, Sav?" he asked, putting warmth into his voice. It was one thing for him to have concerns about Savvy and quite another for one of his teammates to disrespect her, especially on the eve of a mission.

Savvy gave Cal an anxious look as she took the empty seat across from him at the table. "Sergeant Callahan, there's a change in our itinerary. A C-130 transport is departing tomorrow afternoon for our Forward Operating Location in Kenya. We'll take that flight instead of flying commercial."

Bypassing customs to enter Kenya was ideal, but the Manda Bay FOL was on the coast and isolated. "How are we going to get from Manda Bay to Nairobi?"

"Charter flight." She glanced at the other men at the table. "I'm sorry to disturb your evening, but I wanted to let you know we won't be leaving at the crack of dawn."

Considering he wasn't likely to sleep more than the minimum required during the coming op, a last night of decent sleep was welcome. "Thanks for the heads-up."

She stood. "Have a good night."

"Stay, Savvy," Cal said. "Have a drink. Relax."

She glanced toward Stockton. "I wouldn't want to ruin your fun."

"My fun was ruined when Stockton showed up," Cal said.

"Fuck you, Callahan," the soldier said.

Cal flipped him off without glancing in his direction, his gaze fixed on Savvy. She worked hard to conceal it, but he sensed her insecurity. She could act on an op, and inside SOCOM, she was always cold composure. But here, in a social situation that required her to be herself, she faltered. She cared about what he and his team thought of her.

Interesting.

She dropped back into the chair and took Cal's drink. "Gin and tonic?" she asked after giving the contents a sniff.

He nodded.

She took a sip.

"Hey," he said with a laugh. "I said have *a* drink. Not *my* drink."

She smiled and set the glass in front of him. "I'm not staying, and I'm not drinking. I've got a stack of reports to read and details to memorize before we get to Dar."

"You can read on the flight. Stay." He meant it. He wanted to see her relax. He wanted to spend a few minutes with the real woman, not the façade she presented. He wanted to get a fix on who she really was before they set out tomorrow.

He nodded to the waiter, who quickly came to the table. "Can I get you anything, Ms. James?"

She started to say no, but Cal shook his head, and she relented. "Vodka martini, please."

"Shaken, not stirred?" Stockton asked with a sneer.

This time, it was Savvy who flipped him off, clearly tired of the James Bond joke.

It occurred to Cal that as a SAD/SOG officer, technically, she *was* licensed to kill, or at least, she could be sent on black op assassination missions. And she'd claimed to have killed for Uncle Sam when they sparred earlier today, but she could just have been blowing smoke. Was the last name James a tongue-in-cheek nod to 007? But then, she'd said her name had been assigned. Would someone in the Operations Directorate of the CIA give a SAD operator a name that referenced the fictional MI6 spy and sometime assassin?

Behind Savvy, the big-screen TV, which played CNN when there wasn't a big sporting event going on, flashed with "Breaking News" and the official portrait of Senator Albert Jackson appeared on the screen. A little more than two weeks ago, Jackson had been in Djibouti for a ceremony on the aircraft carrier USS *Dahlgren* to honor the special forces teams that had rescued Brie Stewart—AKA Gabriella Prime—from South Sudan. According to Bastian, Jackson was Brie's creepy "Uncle" Al, an old friend of Brie's father, Jeffery Prime, and the senator had made the trip only to garner some positive PR from Brie's ordeal.

When the flight deck of *Dahlgren* appeared on the screen—footage of the ceremony—Cal called out, "Turn up the volume on the TV."

The news segment showing the nearby carrier had caught several patrons' attention and the room hushed as the volume was raised. Savvy and the others with their back to the TV turned in their seats. The chyron on the bottom of the screen said, "Senator Albert Jackson implicated in oil price fixing scandal with America's Prime Energy and Russia's Druneft."

The camera zoomed in on Brie Stewart as she delivered her speech from the flight deck. Bastian stood behind to her left with a group of sailors. The senator was behind her to the right with the carrier group's admiral and carrier's captain. Bastian's gaze was fixed on Brie, and anyone who knew him could see the man had it bad for the woman.

Fortunately, feelings between the two of them went both ways. Two days ago, Brie had departed for the US, and right about now, she was probably settling into Bastian's apartment near Fort Campbell.

A sailor seated in the middle of the room, who clearly didn't know the story of Bastian's involvement with the former oil heiress turned aid worker and definitely didn't realize the soldier was in the room, whistled at the screen and said, "I hear there are sex videos of her online from back in her Princess Prime days. Goddamn base firewalls. I want to see that rich bitch on her knees."

Bastian was out of his seat before Cal could stop him, but fortunately, Espinosa planted himself in front of Bastian and gripped his shoulders. "The fuckhead isn't worth going to the brig."

After a few incidences in which special forces—Army and Navy—had scuffled with sailors and marines, the base commander had instilled a zero-tolerance policy for fighting among troops. Circumstances didn't matter. The fact that Bastian helped stop a genocide less than a week ago didn't matter. If he threw a punch, he'd land in the brig, just like everyone else.

Bastian struggled against Espi's hold.

The seriously stupid sailor turned to see the commotion behind him, then glanced back at the TV, and must've recognized Bastian as the soldier on the screen in crisp ACU and green beret. He laughed, obviously feeling safe thanks to the skipper's policy and Espi's hold. Probably wanting to look like a hotshot in front of his friends by baiting a Green Beret, he said, "You're the guy who rescued Princess Prime? Did you tap that? I hear she's a prime piece of ass." He laughed at the obvious pun.

A moment later, the man's face slammed into the table and his feet were swept from beneath him. He dropped to the floor, and Savvy pinned him on his stomach as she wrenched his arm behind his back. "Shut up," she said to the moaning sailor. "I'm trying to watch the news." She wrenched his arm higher, then leaned down and said just loud enough for everyone in the now-silent room to hear, "I'm not in the skipper's chain of command. I can do as I please. So shut the fuck up before I do the women of this planet a favor and cut off your balls."

The sailor went silent, and Savvy faced the TV screen, completely disinterested in the man pinned under her knee. "Rewind back to the beginning," she commanded, and the bartender with the remote did just that. Damn, Cal didn't even know the big TV had a DVR. Or maybe Savvy's commanding tone conjured it.

The CNN report recounted Senator Jackson's close ties to the Prime family that had culminated in his recent trip to the carrier to thank the military for Brie's rescue. From there, it detailed his ties to recently deceased Nikolai Drugov. The news gave the public version of Drugov's death: seven days ago, while sailing off the coast of Morocco, the oligarch had been gunned down by his own crew. The ensuing investigation revealed several incidences in which Drugov had conspired with the also recently deceased Jeffery Prime—the oil tycoon had died three days ago due to complications from a stroke—to fix oil prices, and now it appeared Senator Jackson had been implicated, conspiring to control oil prices back when he was the CEO of a Texas-based oil company before he'd entered politics.

It had only been a week, and already the Drugov dominos were starting to fall. And it was the woman who'd just dropped a sailor without breaking a sweat who'd set that investigation in motion.

He owed Savvy respect. She was brilliant at her job. It wasn't even her fault that he hated her job and the organization she worked for. Plus, for the most part, she used her skills for good.

The report shifted to an evangelical televangelist whose business dealings with Drugov had been exposed in the last twenty-four hours. The news was moving fast as all of Drugov's deals were coming to light.

The Reverend Abel Fitzsimmons—a guy Cal had never heard of but who apparently had a big following in the Bible Belt—had used charitable donations to invest in Drugov's South Sudan operation. The guy wanted in on the oil business? In South Sudan?

The reverend had issued a statement that all funds paid to Drugov had been for a charitable cause involving girls and sanitation. What the hell? It sounded like Fitzsimmons had been investing in Brie's period panties. He'd ask Savvy about that at the first opportunity.

But the next part of the report really got his attention. Questions had been raised about money the evangelical minister had sent to DRC, supposedly for a school, but a reporter delving into the story was unable to confirm the Mission School had been built. This brought to Cal's mind allegations that had been made against Pat Robertson in the late 1990s and which gained attention again with the release of the 2013 documentary, *Mission Congo*. The minister had been accused of using charitable donations intended for refugees fleeing the Rwandan genocide to mine for diamonds. There'd even been talk of building a school, but the documentary presented evidence the school never educated anyone. Was Fitzsimmons attempting something similar?

Did this have anything to do with the lead they were following to Dar es Salaam? Jean Paul Lubanga, had control of Congo's mining industry, all mining claims went through him. It would be just like Savvy to tell Cal only one part of the mission, leaving out the true target of her intel gathering.

But then, Abel Fitzsimmons was American. The CIA couldn't investigate him. That was the FBI's job.

Much as he disliked the CIA and their methods, he had to admit, if investigating Fitzsimmons was the main goal, he was in. Anyone who took advantage of the desperate plight of the people of Congo deserved to burn.

His mother was from DRC. He'd visited and spent time with his aunts, uncles, and cousins who'd survived the nightmare that began with the Rwandan genocide in 1994. He had cousins who'd died in the massacre of a small village before Mobutu was ousted in the First Congo War. Others who'd been raped and later starved to death or died from disease during the Second Congo War. And two who'd been conscripted to fight while still children.

He still didn't know what happened to his aunt's sons, boys a few years younger than him.

The news report moved on to a story about police killing an unarmed black man for having a broken taillight, and his stomach twisted in a different way. He'd been that driver, and would be again when he returned to the US. The fact that he was a soldier serving his country made no difference except that his build just made officers more scared and trigger-happy. He obeyed traffic laws with a degree of precision his white friends could never understand. And it didn't matter, because he was pulled over anyway, on claims he'd been using his cell phone or other trumped-up reasons.

He couldn't wait for this deployment to end so he could visit his parents in DC, but at the same time, he'd appreciated the break from the everyday bigotry of the US mainland.

Savvy released the stupid sailor, stood, and brushed off her slacks, making a point of checking her long red nails for a chip. Finding none, she beamed at the sailor, who'd turned over to glare at her from the floor. "Don't let me hear you insulting a woman again, Rudolph. Next time, I won't be nearly as nice as I was today."

She knew the sailor's name? Cal would bet anything Rudolph's bowels had just loosened. He looked like he wanted to insult her, but he proved he had a small measure of intelligence and said nothing as he got to his feet and stalked from the club.

Savvy returned to their table and took her seat. Several of the guys—including Stockton—stared at her with jaws dropped in shock.

The waiter set her drink on the table as Bastian said, "That one's on me."

"Nah," the waiter said. "On the house."

She thanked the man and took a sip, then smiled and leaned back in her seat.

"Thanks, Sav," Bastian said. "Although I'm a little jealous you got to slam his face into the table."

"How'd you know his name?" Cal asked.

She shook her head. "I didn't. One of his buddies said it when he was telling him to shut up."

Cal had missed that exchange, but then, he'd been transfixed by the fast takedown, and hadn't really been paying attention. Based on the way Rudolph blanched, he probably hadn't heard his friend say his name either.

"So what's the deal with the senator, Sav?" Bastian asked. "Is the press going to be hounding Brie?"

"They would if they knew where she was, but given that your name has been withheld from press releases, she should be safely anonymous in Kentucky."

"You got intel on Jackson," Bastian said. "What about Brie's brother, JJ?"

"You know I can't answer that."

Behind Savvy, the door opened. Two men—one in his thirties, the other in his fifties—stopped just inside and scanned the small club. The older man's gaze landed on Savvy, and he nudged the younger man.

Shit. Was she going to get in trouble with the skipper after all? But then, these guys weren't MPs. In fact, they had a certain look about them that screamed…Agency. Cal nodded toward the door. "People here to see you, Sav."

She turned, and her spine went ramrod straight, then she bolted to her feet. "Seth! Harrison. What are you doing here?"

The older man took both of her hands in his and cradled them, a stand-in for a hug between two professionals. "We caught a flight as soon as we could arrange one. The director of the Directorate of Operations sent us personally to congratulate you on your work here."

For the first time, Savvy's head turned toward the younger of the two men, and Cal could see the tension in her body. He wished he could see her expression. Was the tension from excitement or anxiety?

The younger man studied her with a cloaked but hungry expression. Cal recognized it because he was fairly sure he looked at Savvy the same way when no one was around to notice.

"The DDO? Really? I'm honored, but it was a little excessive to send two of you. Especially when I'm set to leave tomorrow."

"But that's part of why we're here. Or at least why Harry came along. He's going with you. He's going to play the role of businessman."

Apparently, SAD had come through with an operator after all. Cal didn't even want this mission, but still, the thought of being replaced by this white, clean-cut pretty boy, rankled.

"Harry can't pass for a warlord." From her tone, he guessed Savvy wasn't thrilled with this proposal either. Maybe Cal had been her first choice after all. At the very least, this guy ranked behind Cal.

"My Russian is impeccable, Savannah." Her name didn't roll off the guy's tongue, and Cal realized that was because the bastard knew her real name. It was a petty reason to dislike a man, but it was all he had. "I'm an associate of Drugov's, not an African drug dealer."

Savvy's spine got even straighter—which he hadn't thought possible. "That won't work—"

"Let's go to your office to discuss this," Seth said.

Savvy gave a sharp nod. "Of course." She didn't so much as look back at the table or offer thanks or good-bye to Cal and his team. She walked to the door as if they didn't exist.

He reached across the table and took her barely touched martini. He didn't like martinis, but right now, he didn't care. He downed it in one gulp and set the glass on the table.

He'd been jilted by the bride at his own bachelor party.

Chapter Four

Savvy couldn't look at Cal as she left the club. She didn't want her boss to know Cal would be her partner on this op. Not yet. She knew how the man's mind worked, and she needed to build her case slowly and methodically if she had any hope of forcing Harry out of this mission.

Because of her past with Harrison Evers, Seth Olsen would dismiss her objections as emotional, unless she could back up her stance with well-reasoned logic.

She regretted telling Seth about what happened in that motel room. He'd been appalled, and he'd rightly warned her that if she chose silence, if she didn't take legal action, she would have to work with Harry. He'd also warned her that in a case of she said/he said, benefit would be given to the man with the longer track record with the Agency.

It had been five years since the incident, and two years since Harry had joined their working group within SAD, forcing her to face him on a daily basis. This assignment to Djibouti had been her escape from that nightmare. She'd figured she wouldn't have to face the threat of being sent on an op with him until she returned stateside. Now here he was, in Djibouti and apparently eager to be paired with her on a mission where she would be required to play his sex toy.

Not just no, but *hell* no.

When she'd requested SAD send an operator, she'd specifically excluded Harry from the list of potential partners. Seth knew why.

But then, her objection *was* emotional. Harry could well be the better choice over Cal, but there was no way he'd ever touch her again, even under the guise of a mission.

"It was kind of you to travel all this way, Seth."

"My pleasure, Savannah." The name was stiff on his lips, but then, it wasn't the name he usually called her. But they were in public, and Seth had always been a stickler for rules.

"I've read the reports you filed on Drugov," Harry said. "Nice work."

His praise meant nothing to her. Well, except for making her skin crawl. She ignored him and spoke to Seth. "How long will you be here?"

"I fly back Tuesday. Tomorrow, I'll meet with Agency personnel at the embassy."

"The case officer is doing a great job." She refrained from using Kaylea's name or female pronoun, because she was just as much a stickler for rules as Seth.

"Glad to hear it.

They reached the temporary structure that housed SOCOM. Savvy had a tiny office in the back. No name on the door, no title. But then, her name wasn't hers anyway. She was immensely pleased with the small, windowless room because she'd earned both it and her undefined role with SOCOM through years of hard work. She made sure she was always the most informed person in the room. She spent her evenings memorizing maps and political alliances, studying up on warlords and their goals. Chasing down intel leads on relatively unknown men who aspired to great power.

Men like Lubanga, who'd been in her sights from the moment she stepped on African soil.

She spent her mornings listening to detailed daily news podcasts during her five-mile run. She was the first person at the table for SOCOM's morning meeting and the last to leave the building each night if they were operating on a normal business-hours schedule. When teams were deployed, as they had been to South Sudan a few weeks ago, she barely saw her cot in her Containerized Living Unit. She might as well give up the private wet CLU and move into her office.

She led her boss and her nemesis to her place of pride and took her seat behind her desk. She'd give up the power seat without issue if Seth were her only visitor.

On the wall opposite her desk was a picture of the memorial wall at CIA headquarters in Langley, Virginia. The anonymous stars of fallen agents. She studied it, visible just over Harry's shoulder. Uncle James was represented by one of those stars. She'd never met James Lange, her father's brother, as he'd died within months of her birth, but she hoped her work for the organization he'd given his life to would make him proud just the same.

"I wish we could have some sort of ceremony to honor your successes, Freya, but you know Agency policy," Seth said, using her real name now that they were alone in her office.

It was weird hearing Freya again after months of being Savannah. She hated the name Savannah, but she'd understood why Seth had given it to her.

That which doesn't kill us makes us stronger.

The name was a constant reminder that she was on her own here. No one had her back. The choices she made, she'd have to live with.

But she was Freya to Seth and Harry, and her real name had its own strengths and reminders. Hearing her name from her mentor's lips brought back memories of her father. It had been fifteen years since she'd heard her father say her name. Fifteen years since she'd had a family. It hurt just as much today as it had when she was twenty-one and graduated from American University without a single relative to watch her walk.

It had been too far for her remaining aunt and uncles to travel. They hadn't been close anyway. Hadn't known how to cope with her ongoing grief.

She slapped a lid on that emotional well. This conversation was going to be difficult enough without adding the death of everyone she cared about to the emotional mix.

She focused on Seth's words, before she'd been distracted by hearing her name. The Agency wouldn't acknowledge her role in Drugov's takedown. Just like the anonymous stars for the dead, praise for the living was classified.

But SOCOM knew her role, and key leaders in the CIA knew. That was enough for her. She wasn't in this for glory or medals. She was here to make a difference. Like her uncle.

She was here to stop other teenage girls from being stripped of family as she'd been. Losing everyone who mattered in a single instant had a way of changing a person. Weeks shy of her eighteenth birthday, she'd gone from being a typical, self-centered, and well-loved senior in high school to utterly alone. Her work since then could have—and probably had—prevented attacks like the one that killed her parents and brother.

"I don't need a ceremony," she said. "What I do need is to be able to go after Gorev and Lubanga as planned, with the partner I selected. I've done my research. I've lined up the best operator for the mission, and it's not Harry."

She didn't even look at Harry as she said this. His reaction was irrelevant to her. Only Seth mattered here.

"I've got five more years in the Agency than you, Freya," Harry said. "I think I'm a little more knowledgeable than you about how to run these sorts of covert ops."

"You may have experience, but you don't know these men like I do. Can you name Jean Paul Lubanga's three wives and eleven children? Can you tell me what year he first met with Mobutu Sese Seko?"

Harry simply glared at her.

"Allow me to fill you in," she said. "When Mobutu traveled across Zaire, he appropriated the *droit de cuissage*—the right to deflower—virgins offered up to him by local chiefs. In 1995, Lubanga offered Mobutu his daughter, hoping to gain a grandchild who was son or daughter of the dictator. But the daughter was only thirteen, and she was rightfully terrified.

She refused and fled the village. To demonstrate his allegiance to Mobutu, Lubanga had her hunted down and killed. He then gave Mobutu his eleven-year-old daughter. She too was a virgin, but she hadn't started menstruating yet, so there was no hope of Mobutu offspring."

"How can you possibly know this?" Harry asked.

"I do my homework," she said. She wasn't about to say she'd interviewed the now thirty-three-year-old woman who'd been raped by her country's leader at her father's behest when she was a prepubescent child. Harry would demand to interview Zola too, and she would protect the woman—who now resided just over the border in Ethiopia—from Harry at all costs.

The CIA had sent her to Djibouti to gather intel on a number of rising powers in east and central Africa. Jean Paul Lubanga had topped that list, and she was nothing if not thorough. Savvy had tracked down and interviewed his daughter just two months after arriving in Djibouti, and she'd hidden Zola—who'd been far too easy to find—to protect her in the event Lubanga managed to seize full power in DRC.

Finding the planned gathering in the mountain of intel that had been collected from Drugov's yacht had been a gift. Now she had a chance to nab Lubanga's files. She could only hope the black bag job she had planned would give Team USA what they needed to take action against Lubanga.

The CIA wasn't political and didn't set policy. Clandestine operators like her gathered intelligence, sometimes breaking in and copying documents. Case officers developed assets for HUMINT. NSA collected and analyzed SIGINT and passed the intel to the CIA. CIA analysts used that combined intelligence data to form opinions on actions individuals and governments and terrorist organizations might take. Their analysis was passed to the Executive and Legislative branches, who used the informed opinions to shape policy decisions.

Politics was the last step, and it happened beyond Agency walls. There had been slips in that regard over the years, but for the most part, the Agency worked very hard to separate intelligence gathering from policy.

Clandestine operators and case officers were the first cog in the intelligence community machine. But the first cog was vital. Without her, no other gears would turn. Without her, there would be no IC, nothing to analyze. No way to create informed policy.

She met Seth's gaze. "I can do this, but I need a Lingala speaker. I've got one with native fluency. He's US Army Special Forces. He knows how to blend, and he's a top-notch soldier with charisma in spades. Lubanga will covet him as an ally. On the flip side, Gorev would only look at another

Russian as a rival, and he'd immediately start digging into Harry's ID."

Seth leaned back in his chair and crossed his arms. "Your argument is good, Freya, except for one point."

She cocked her head in expectation.

"We don't need Lubanga to covet your soldier as an ally, and Harry's ID wouldn't have to hold up for long. Orders for this mission have been revised. Lubanga is too big a threat to leave in place, and who knows when we'll have another opportunity like this when the man is outside Congo."

"What are you saying?"

"Lubanga is to be taken out in a way that makes it look like Gorev is behind his death. Operation Zagreus is an assassination mission."

Chapter Five

Savvy made her way back to her CLU feeling sick to her stomach. There was no way to pry Harry from the mission, and certainly no way she could drag Cal into it. One did not bring Special Forces along on black ops. There could be no ties to the CIA or US government. If things went to hell, if she was captured and imprisoned, there would be no negotiation for her release. She would be disavowed.

Cal hadn't signed up for that. He had a future with the Army and beyond.

She glanced at her watch. It was late, but maybe he was still at Barely North. She could tell him now. She changed direction and headed to the club.

She opened the door to the chill air-conditioning on the humid night. A quick scan of the room showed the tables that had been pulled together to accommodate most of Cal's A-Team were now empty. She turned to leave, when she spotted Seth approaching. Alone.

He smiled. "I was hoping to find you here. I wanted to talk, without Harry."

She nodded. She would have preferred that from the start. "We could go back to my office."

He shook his head. "I could use a drink."

Okay, so they wouldn't be talking about the mission or anything else that couldn't be discussed in public. She felt a ripple of disappointment, but she understood. She and Seth were friends and had been since she'd interned with the CIA while she was an undergrad at American University. He'd taken an interest in mentoring her, and she'd been desperate for a father figure. Having a drink together would give them a chance to renew that bond separate from the job.

Frankly, she needed it. She'd been short on friends since arriving at Camp Citron, and as much as she liked to pretend she wasn't lonely, that she didn't crave friendly human interaction, it was a lie. As often as she could, she escaped the base to hang out with Kaylea in Djibouti City, but that wasn't very often. The case officer was just as busy as Savvy was, with her full-time embassy job in addition to her covert work.

She led Seth to the table abandoned by the A-Team and took a seat. This time, she ordered a glass of white wine. Seth ordered a beer, and she could see the tired lines on his face relax as he settled into his seat.

"How is Aunt Kim?" she asked, referring to his wife. Kim Olsen had insisted on the honorific early in their relationship, and Savvy had been happy to indulge her. It wasn't like her own aunts and uncle gave her any attention.

She knew her relatives' grief had been nearly as deep as her own, and their remote nature and distant location only exacerbated the situation, but still, it hurt. Aunt Kim had filled a void as much as Seth had. She'd probably call him Uncle Seth, except he was her boss now. There had already been talk of him playing favorites with her when he gave her the plum Djibouti assignment. But she'd worked her ass off to get here, and Seth knew she'd earned it.

"She's good and told me to give you a hug and tell you how proud she is of you."

Savvy smiled. "I picked up some colorful cloth for her the last time I was at a market in the city. I was going to mail it, but you can take it home to her." Kim was a quilter whose designs were always based on the country and culture where the cloth came from.

"She'll be thrilled." Seth cleared his throat. "You know this wasn't an easy decision for me to make, Fr—Savannah." That he'd nearly slipped was a sign of exactly how hard this was for him.

She nodded. "I would hope not. Frankly, I'm feeling a little betrayed right now, Seth." Her own words surprised her. She'd never spoken this way to him before. The words had slipped out. A sign she was at the edge of her control.

The waiter arrived with her wine and his beer, forcing them to pause the conversation. She studied Seth's face, looking for anger, and not seeing it. He looked regretful. Disappointed. But not mad.

He took a sip of his beer, then leaned back in his chair, letting out a heavy sigh. "It was bound to happen at some point. You work in the same division."

"You said you wouldn't assign us to go on ops together. You promised."

"What I promised was that I'd *try* not to assign you together. And I've done my best. But for this, he's the best man for the job, and you are the best woman. Believe me, I ran through all the variables. Harrison Evers was the only option."

Except Harry made her sick. Literally. Her belly turned every time he was near. He tore at her ability to maintain calm control, destroyed her confidence in herself.

She'd had her reaction to him under control when working at Langley, but she'd lost that mental protection during her months in Djibouti. She hadn't been prepared to see him tonight, and she couldn't look at the asshole without feeling degraded. Shamed.

Her existence depended on her cool reliability, her unruffled, icy reserve as she did her part to give America an edge in the War on Terror, but she couldn't draw upon her training when she was with Harry. He shattered her focus and her calm reserve. She felt revulsion for her own inaction and worried about other women who'd suffered at his hands. Her silence had left him free to assault others.

At the crux of her self-loathing was the fact that she could have physically overpowered Harry but hadn't out of fear for her CIA career. She hadn't fought because she didn't want to lose everything she'd worked so hard for from the moment she learned her family had died because of a suicide bomber.

She also knew that she wouldn't be in Djibouti now if she'd fought Harry or reported the assault to anyone other than Seth. But still, it gnawed at her, the fact that Harry had paid no price.

"I'm sorry," Seth said softly. "I considered pulling you from the op altogether—"

"No," she said sharply.

"And that's why I didn't. So here we are."

She took a sip of her wine. "So here we are." Seth was right. Cal couldn't accompany her on this kind of op.

Black op. Assassination. Deletion. Reset. There were a bunch of names and euphemisms given this type of assignment, but what mattered was that Jean Paul Lubanga was a clear and present danger to the fragile stability of Congo. This had been decided by minds far more knowledgeable and experienced than hers, and the order had been issued from the top.

It was the perfect opportunity, with the man outside his country's borders and spending several days with criminals who could shoulder the blame. And it certainly wasn't like she flinched at the task. Lubanga's quest for power had begun decades ago, when he used his eleven-year-old daughter to buy favor with a dictator.

Seth reached across the table and took her hand and squeezed. "You can do this. By Saturday morning, you'll be flying back here, and Harry will be on his way back to the US."

She gave him a smile and nodded. She could do this. More important, she *would* do this.

She sipped her wine, and he drank his beer, and they slipped into the easy conversation of old friends who hadn't seen each other in months. He shared office gossip she'd missed, retirements, marriages, births, divorces. There were several divorces. The job was hard on relationships.

Seth had been lucky in finding Kim, who could put up with the long hours and secrecy. Savvy had never bothered to try to find someone who could handle the stress of being a covert operator's spouse.

It was nearing midnight by the time she and Seth said good night and she headed to her CLU. It was too late to knock on Cal's CLU and tell him the official verdict. He'd heard Seth's words in Barely North. The details could wait until morning. Especially considering she couldn't give him details.

Better to let him and Pax sleep. They would need to get up early for their regular job of training Djiboutians. Besides, she was too tired, too emotionally drained for one more hurdle tonight.

She did feel better after spending time with Seth. It had been comforting to chat with a person who truly knew her. And not only that, but he was the only person who knew why she'd be so upset over being partnered with Harry.

She reached her CLU and unlocked the door. She needed sleep but figured that would be elusive. Tomorrow, she would depart for Kenya on a mission to assassinate a high-powered Congolese minister, stuck in the role of sexual plaything while her rapist played her master.

Cal crossed CLUville, heading for Savvy's single unit near the end of a ground-floor row. He rounded the corner and came to a stop. The guy—Harrison—was approaching Savvy's unit from the other direction. Cal stepped behind a vehicle parked in front of the row of CLUs. If Savvy let the Agency officer into her CLU, Cal would return to his own unit and speak with her in the morning.

He was irked she hadn't seen fit to update him tonight, but that didn't mean he would wait around while she got it on with her coworker. Why else would the guy go to her CLU alone after midnight?

The base was quiet, and Cal easily heard the knock on Savvy's door. She was slow to respond, making him think she hadn't been waiting up for Harrison. So maybe this wasn't planned.

The door opened an inch, then closed in the guy's face.

Cal grinned. Okay, that was more like it. He quietly slipped between vehicles, moving closer without drawing attention.

Harrison pounded on the door. "Freya, we need to talk."

Freya?

Cal tried the name in his mind, testing the texture, rhythm, and weight of it. It wasn't close to what he'd imagined her name could be—not that he'd ever made a mental list, but if he had, Freya wouldn't have been in the top thousand choices.

But at the same time, he could see how it fit. If he remembered correctly, Freya was a powerful Norse goddess. Wife of Odin? Maybe.

Savvy's looks were more Italian than Norse, with long, straight dark hair and those big brown eyes. But then, it wasn't a surname.

Freya.

He liked it.

Savvy opened the door and stepped outside, closing the door behind her. "Jesus, Harry, are you just out of training?" she whispered. "You can't call me that here."

"It worked to get you to come outside."

"You're fucking with my ident security to score a *point?*"

The asshole shrugged. "It's not like we're in Kinshasa. We're on a military base. Everyone here is on the same team."

"That you even say that tells me you've gotten too soft for this op."

"Is that the way you're going to play this, *Savannah?*"

The way he said the name was somehow unsettling. Like it meant something entirely different to him. And the way she reacted—it was as if she'd received a painful electric charge. But she didn't do or say anything, which was completely unlike the Savvy he knew.

It was as if they guy had just declawed her. She was defenseless.

"Let's go inside and talk," he said.

"No. Say what you need to say right here."

"What I need to say is classified, and you just objected to me saying your name out here—which isn't top secret like our mission."

Our mission. It was official. Cal was out. Why the hell was he disappointed?

"Then you can tell me on the flight, because you are not entering my CLU."

"On this mission, you'll be playing my sex toy—this cover was *your* idea, by the way—and we're going to be alone together for the better part of a week. You can let me inside your damn room."

She said nothing, just stared at him. The light mounted to the side of the building was just far enough away to leave her face in shadow. Cal wished he could see her eyes, because he had a feeling she was doing nothing to cloak her feelings.

"Leave me alone, Harry. I need to sleep." She turned and grabbed the knob to open her door.

Quick as a flash, Harry grabbed her arm, swung her around, and slammed her back against the metal unit.

Savvy could fight. What shocked Cal was that she didn't. Earlier this evening, he'd watched her take down a sailor in less than a second, and before that, they'd sparred, and the blows she landed hadn't been because he *let* her.

Yet she did nothing to fight this man, didn't even raise her arms when his hand circled her throat.

"Listen, *Savannah*. You heard Seth say *I'm* in charge of this mission. You answer to me. You will do what I say, starting now. Or you can kiss your cush job in SAD good-bye. I helped get you where you are today, and I can bring you down just as easily. When I'm done with you, you'll be lucky to be offered a job with janitorial in the CIA."

Earlier today, Savvy had ordered Cal to hit her and had been concerned when he couldn't do it. Was that why this guy was brought in? Was this some sort of fucked-up test? Was that why she didn't fight back?

Her head turned, just a bit, and Savvy looked straight in Cal's direction, her face catching the oblique light. He could see the stark look of terror in her eyes.

Cal launched from his position and was upon the man in an instant. He pulled him back from Savvy and threw a punch at Harry's jaw. His head snapped back, but he kept his feet and threw his own punch, which Cal managed to block.

From there, it was a boxing match. Harry was a trained operator and furious, while Cal's protective instincts had been triggered.

Harry got in several solid blows, but he was no match for Cal. He went down and stayed down.

"That was pretty fucking stupid, soldier," Harry said through bloody lips. "I don't know who you are, but you messed with the wrong guy. I can get you court-martialed."

Too late, Cal remembered the skipper's zero-tolerance policy. This guy, like Savvy, could be exempt. But Cal was not.

"You were assaulting a woman. I was defending her."

"I wasn't assaulting her. I was prepping her for our mission, in which I'm her master and she's my slave. This was all prep work. Isn't that right, *Savannah*?"

Again, he put that odd stress on her name.

Cal turned to Savvy, who looked stricken in the stark halogen light. The doors of the surrounding CLUs had opened. They had an audience. MPs would be arriving any second. If Savvy didn't back him up, he'd just tanked his military career.

"Why do you think she wasn't fighting me? You think Savannah James can't defend herself? She can. She chose not to."

"Savvy?" Cal asked, his heart pounding as he waited for her to throw him under the bus.

Her gaze darted from Harry to Cal and back again. Finally, she said, "Harrison Evers was assaulting me. And it wasn't the first time."

Chapter Six

Savvy paced outside Captain O'Leary's office. What had she done? She'd accused Harry of assaulting her twice. In bringing up the first, unreported, assault, she'd undermined her own case. Already, she could hear the questions. *"If this is true, why didn't you report him five years ago?"*

Because he'd held control over her career.

She'd reported it to Seth, who at the time had been out of Harry's chain of command. Seth had discussed it with her at length, and in the end, left it up to her if she wanted it entered into Harry's file. Entering it into the record meant pursuing charges.

Likely the fallout would have all been on her. She said/he said. That he'd penetrated her would go uncontested. Harry would claim she'd consented. He'd told her that to pass the training, she had to prove she would have sex to maintain cover and further the mission. He'd told her she had to consent or she'd fail. He told her she had no right to say no. No right to decide who was allowed to put their dick in her body.

Even so, she'd said no. But she hadn't fought him either, fearing submitting to rape really was part of the training, really was a requirement.

After all, she was training to be a covert operator for the Special Activities Division of the CIA. They *did* expect their agents to use any means necessary. Sometimes up to and including sex.

Seth had assured her sex with her trainer wasn't a requirement to pass training. But he'd also acknowledged her "no" would be seen as ambiguous—she'd said the word but hadn't fought him—and would play against her.

She'd asked if making the allegation would end her career in the CIA. Seth said he didn't want to believe that…but he couldn't offer any reassurance either.

And now here she was, five years later, making the allegation that could take her out of the game when she was on the cusp of an important mission. Lubanga was not only in her sights: she had orders to pull the trigger.

She wasn't a fan of assassinations. She thought it was more advantageous to use ball twisting to make these bastards the USA's tool, but at the same time knew that practice had an expiration date. Despots didn't like being beholden to the US for very long. In this instance, she had no doubt Lubanga had it coming, and would perform her duty without breaking a sweat.

She'd do it for Zola, the girl who'd been raped by Mobutu on her father's orders. Zola, who'd lost her beloved sister the same day.

She stopped pacing and stared at the wall, seeing nothing but Zola's face as she shared her nightmare with Savvy. What would happen to Lubanga if Savvy was pulled from this mission?

She'd made the accusation to protect Cal. Plus it was *true*. But if Cal hadn't been at risk, she never would have said a word. If Cal hadn't stepped in, Harry might've raped her again—claiming it was preparation for the op—she'd have fought him this time, but she might not have said a word out of fear of risking the mission.

What did that make her?

She was victim-blaming herself and couldn't seem to stop.

Right now, Seth was in the base commander's office, confirming her account of the rape five years ago. Thank goodness he was here now to back her story. He was the only person who could.

Cal and Harry were both in the base's small, temporary brig. *What have I done to Cal?*

She'd been so stunned to see him in the darkness; she'd been unable to hide her terror. And when he'd attacked Harry, doing what she'd been too frozen to do, she'd been utterly grateful.

Since she was seventeen, there hadn't been anyone to defend her. She'd learned to defend herself and was fine with that until a man she couldn't fight—not without losing everything she'd been working toward since the day a suicide bomber killed everyone who mattered—assaulted her, and she'd discovered physical strength wasn't enough. Not when men like Harry had power over her.

So she'd worked her ass off to move up the ranks. Here, she'd found autonomy. If any man assaulted her here, she could fight back without fear of a crushed career. That wasn't exactly true for the female soldiers, sailors, and marines based at Camp Citron. She was aware of her privilege and the benefits of being outside military hierarchy.

She'd never expected Harry to show up at Camp Citron. She certainly hadn't expected him to take over her op and then, mere hours later, assault her outside her CLU. But then, he'd never had any reason to think or believe she'd fight back. She hadn't even called for help.

He'd counted on that.

He hadn't counted on Cal.

Her emotions were in a jumble she couldn't mask. This wasn't her. She was calm and cunning. She was the manipulator who twisted others, just like Cal said. She was never the one caught in the emotional whirl—at least, not outwardly.

Now all her defenses were gone. She was worried about Cal. Worried about her job. Worried she wouldn't be able to embark on this mission. In less than six hours, she'd gone from the top of her game to the lowest she'd been since the moment she'd decided not to pursue assault charges against Harry.

The office door opened and out walked Seth and Captain O'Leary. The base commander stared at her for a long moment before saying, "Sergeant Callahan witnessed what appeared to be an assault?"

She straightened her spine. "It didn't just *appear* to be an assault, it was one. Harrison Evers pinned me to the wall with his hand on my throat."

"I heard you got in a fight with one of my sailors this evening. Are you claiming he assaulted you too?"

"No, sir. I hit him. He said something vile about Brie Stewart, and if I didn't take him down a peg, Chief Ford would have. I didn't want to see him land in the same place where Sergeant Callahan is now because a foolish sailor was baiting him."

"You seem to think you're beyond the reach of my command, but I assure you, Ms. James, this is *my* base, and no one—not even SAD CIA operators—escape my rules."

"I know that, sir. But the sailor didn't, and I used that to my advantage."

"You've done excellent work with SOCOM over these last months, Ms. James. For that reason, you will only receive a reprimand in your file for the incident in the club. But if anything like that happens again, you'll be on the next flight home."

She wouldn't land in the brig, then. So in a sense, she *was* beyond his reach. He just wouldn't admit it. "Yes, sir," she said.

He and Seth continued toward the exit. She imagined he was eager to return to his bed—after all, it was past two in the morning.

"Captain, what about Sergeant Callahan?"

"He will be released."

Relief washed over her. "Thank you, sir."

"As will Mr. Evers. I understand the two of you have a mission to undertake."

Her gaze flew to Seth. Surely he didn't intend to send her to Dar es Salaam with Harry after what he'd just done?

"The mission is critical, Savannah," Seth said. "Earlier this evening, you convinced me you're the best suited for it, and I can't send you alone."

"Sergeant Callahan was slated to go with me on this mission. He's fluent in Lingala. I have his passport and alias set up."

"But the parameters of the mission changed," Seth said, reminding her why she'd accepted Harry as her partner hours ago.

She was going to Tanzania to kill a DRC government official. This was assassination, pure and simple. As a SAD officer, she accepted the risks. If she failed, if she was caught, she was acting alone, not at the behest of the US government. She'd likely die in a Tanzanian or Congolese prison.

Cal hadn't agreed to that.

She needed to tell him. To give him a choice.

If he said no, she'd have to go with Harry. He'd use the role of master to the hilt. He'd relish abusing her, and she wouldn't be able to fight back. Not without breaking cover. Their roles would be all too real.

"I want Sergeant Callahan for this mission," she said, even as her heart fissured over this undeniable betrayal of the one man who'd stood up for her, the one man she'd wanted from the moment she'd met his gaze across a conference table.

When Cal learned the truth, he'd hate her.

Cal studied Savvy as the C-130 sped down the runway. The plane held a half-dozen marines and supplies bound for Manda Bay. She'd chosen the seat across from him near the tail of the aircraft and donned protective headphones. Between the headphones and other passengers, there was no way for them to discuss the mission during the flight.

He'd been released from the brig at two thirty in the morning and was told he'd be departing on the transport as scheduled. Savvy hadn't stopped by his CLU to offer an explanation, and he'd decided not to go to hers. He needed to sleep. They'd have time to sort things out before departure.

But daylight brought no communication from her, and he'd been surprised to find himself alone in the vehicle that delivered him to the airstrip the US military shared with the international airport. He'd begun to wonder if the op would be canceled, when she arrived seven minutes before their scheduled takeoff.

She'd dropped into the seat across from him with little more than a nod in his direction, donned the headphones, and cracked open a file. She stared at the papers on her lap as if they held the meaning of the universe.

They reached cruising altitude. The interior was loud, but not so loud the headphones were necessary. Still, she kept them on. He'd been watching her for twenty minutes, noting that she had yet to turn a page.

He'd been looking forward to seeing her. He'd wanted to check the bruises on her neck, make sure she was okay. Find out what had happened to Harrison Evers. But the concern had evaporated in the wake of her avoidance. Her utter lack of acknowledgment of what had transpired last night.

He reminded himself she'd been assaulted. It was wrong of him to expect her to be rational, cool, and calm today. She'd said the man had assaulted her before, and Evers had indicated the same with his words and actions. She had the right to be messed up.

If this were a normal situation.

But nothing about this was normal. They were heading into a covert op, and he knew next to nothing of their plan. Worse, he needed to know if she was on her game. He needed Savannah James—or Freya Unknown-Last-Name—Paramilitary Operations Officer for the Special Operations Group within SAD. He needed the covert operator who could do everything he could do, backward and in high heels.

But he didn't know if that woman had boarded this turboprop.

Flights always took longer on C-130s, and he estimated they'd be in the air about three and a half hours. Too long to wait to find out what was going on in that complex brain of hers.

He unbuckled his harness and moved to the empty seat next to her. Her fingers tightened on the files in her lap. He reached over and extracted the papers from her grip and set them aside. He slid a hand down her arm and took her hand, interlocking his fingers with hers. Her hand was tight, stiff, then all at once, she relaxed and squeezed his hand.

After a moment, she pulled off the protective headphones and leaned her head on his shoulder.

Something in his chest shifted.

He was holding hands with Savvy as she leaned on him, and it felt…right. Good. Like something he'd needed forever but hadn't known.

Several marines sat too close for them to attempt conversation, and a guy sitting across the empty fuselage watched with unabashed curiosity. Cal didn't care.

He liked the way she leaned on him. The way she was willing to accept comfort. The way her hand felt in his.

And he was thankful he hadn't been cut from this mission, no matter how much he hadn't wanted it at first. The idea of her in the role of sexual plaything to anyone but him made his blood pressure spike.

It was messed up, but he couldn't deny it. The fact that he didn't like the idea of any other man touching her—even if it was only an act—was a problem to deal with when they returned to Camp Citron.

Right now, he was a soldier embarking on a mission, and as he would on any mission, he'd protect his teammate at all costs.

Chartering a flight from Manda Bay to Nairobi took longer than Savvy had hoped because the pilot was gone on another flight. It was early evening when he returned, and ten minutes later, they were back in the air for the short flight to Kenya's capital.

Savvy had never been in Kenya before, but Cal had when he'd traveled with his mother through the region for an extended visit several years ago. It was too late to buy a truck by the time they arrived in the city, so they got a hotel room not far from the airport, then found a nearby restaurant for dinner.

The public setting meant they still couldn't talk, so Cal maintained a lively chatter about his previous visit while Savvy listened, enjoying being on the receiving end of Cal's congenial side.

He was a charming man, which was what had drawn her to him from the start. He'd just never been inclined to be that way with her. Now either he was acting with greater skill than she'd expected, or he'd genuinely softened toward her after the events of last night.

It broke her heart to know that while she might have deserved this kindness before, she didn't now. She'd betrayed him by dragging him on this mission, and her betrayal was straight-up self-serving self-preservation.

The thought made her lose her appetite, but she forced herself to eat. She was an operator. She needed fuel to get through this mission. Fuel and sleep.

The hotel room had two beds. They could put off the charade of being lovers for a night and get the sleep they both needed. Cal did a good job of using her alias during dinner, proving he could handle this sort of op with ease. Not that she'd doubted him, but still, she'd tried to make it easy in selecting names that would be familiar for him.

Back in the hotel, alone in their room, a distance settled between them. Alone, they were operators on a mission. Professionals with boundaries. They only had to act like they were intimate when in public.

She took a shower, then crawled into bed as Cal took his turn showering. As instructed, he hadn't trimmed his beard, but he still was more kempt than she wanted. Two days of travel would help, but he'd still be closer to the movie-star-handsome end of the spectrum when they met with Lubanga.

She dozed as she tried to figure out when would be the best time to assassinate the minister. She could—and should—copy his laptop files first. That had been the original goal, and that order hadn't been rescinded.

She'd checked.

The data she gained from Lubanga's computer would be valuable to the

US as DRC filled the vacuum created by his death. Maybe they'd get proof for the DRC president showing Lubanga's attempts to gain the military's allegiance.

The bed shifted, bringing her fully awake. "Mani?" she said, using his alias even now. It was never good to slip into real names, even when alone. That was how mistakes were made.

"We need to talk, Jamie."

She liked how he understood that rule and followed her lead. He had a future in covert ops, if he wanted one. She glanced around the room. She'd swept it for bugs. No one had any reason to know they'd be here. But still, they'd booked the room and then gotten dinner. That had provided an opportunity. They should have ordered takeout, then gone to the hotel. A mistake on her part.

"The room is clean. You checked. And I just checked again while you were sleeping."

She nodded. He was right. They needed to talk. They needed to plan this mission. She needed to tell him the truth.

"Tell me about Harrison Evers," he said.

"I can't."

"I know you can't talk about CIA stuff. Hell, you probably can't even confirm he's SAD. I get that. That's not what I'm asking. I'm asking about you and him. What he did. To you."

She was silent for a long time. Too long, she knew.

Finally, Cal said, "I spent two hours in the brig last night because I defended you. I had every reason to believe I did the right thing, and every reason to think I might have thrown away my Special Forces tab at the same time."

She rolled over on the bed to face him. He was on top of the covers, while she was underneath. Another thing to like about him. He respected her boundaries and didn't assume an invitation, even though in the past, she'd hinted he was welcome in her bed. He didn't operate in the past. He lived in the now. She stroked his cheek. "You're the most handsome man I've ever met," she said without thinking.

He grinned, but then said, "Don't change the subject."

"But it's such a good subject."

He laughed. "I can't disagree, but I don't want to talk about me."

"He raped me," she blurted. "Five years ago. Said it was part of my training. He claimed the only way I could pass is if I proved I'd fuck to protect my cover. I believed him enough not to fight him. I didn't resist, but I said no. Over and over. I didn't want to have sex with him. I chanted 'this is rape' as he shoved his dick inside me. He laughed and told me to relax and enjoy it."

His jaw clenched, and he said, "Oh, Freya. I'm so sorry."

Her eyes teared at that, that he would offer his sympathy to her true self, the woman who had been raped by her trainer. "You heard him call me that last night. I should have guessed."

"It's a beautiful name. A shame you can't use it."

"I don't really know who Freya is anymore. I used to think she had a few things in common with the powerful Norse goddess, but now I'm not so sure. Freya made choices I'm not proud of."

"Freya was operating in a fucked-up world and did what she had to, to survive."

"Thank you. For understanding."

"I wish I'd beat him more instead of stopping when he hit the ground."

She shrugged. "It was nice seeing him hurt, but if you'd seriously injured him, you'd still be in the brig."

He brushed her hair from her forehead. "It would be worth it."

"You're a good man." She lowered her voice to a whisper and said, "Cassius," invoking his real name for the first time, just as he had hers.

His lips pressed against her forehead. "Sleep. We can sort out the rest tomorrow."

She closed her achingly tired eyes and rolled to the side and fell asleep.

Chapter Seven

Morning in Nairobi. Cal was in one bed, while Savannah James was sound asleep in the other. Not only did he not hate it, he was glad to be here. Glad to be with her.

But then, deep down, hadn't he always wanted this? Well, maybe this but with one fewer bed. That wish would be fulfilled soon enough. He rose and pulled aside the curtain. Dawn was breaking over skyscrapers. He loved this city. Loved visiting this part of the world with his parents, who'd traveled here when they were first dating, before they'd settled in the US.

His mother had been the ultimate travel guide, and he could see how much she'd missed her homeland when they'd visited. It had been her first time returning after the horrors of the nineties that eventually led to the overthrow of Mobutu. The years of conflict following Mobutu's ouster had caused millions of deaths, including an aunt and cousins Cal had never met, yet grieved for just the same.

He hadn't considered what it would mean to return here on a mission. As a soldier.

Except he wasn't a soldier. He was a mercenary, and a traitorous one at that. He was a dealer in drugs and wannabe diamond broker. Or at least, that was what he needed everyone to see.

He could inhabit that skin for a few days. For the greater good. They'd return to Djibouti, and his world would be centered again, then a week or so after that, this deployment would end, and he'd leave Savvy and Camp Citron and go home. He'd spend his leave with his parents and two younger brothers in DC, then report back to Fort Campbell, Kentucky, for stateside rotation.

He glanced back at the sleeping woman. How long would she be at Camp Citron? How long were SAD officers deployed before they were called back to Langley? Where would she go from Camp Citron? Back to the US, or another base?

And why the hell was he worrying about where she'd end up?

Because he wanted her and had for months. And he liked her, far more than he wanted to admit to Pax or Bastian or himself. And maybe, just maybe, he wanted more than the fling they almost certainly would have on this mission.

Was that what he'd feared about her all along? That the chemistry between them was a little too hot to walk away from?

Pax and Morgan had been like that. He'd seen it firsthand. He'd known within an hour of meeting Morgan that Pax was a goner. It wasn't like anything he'd ever witnessed before, but still, he knew without a doubt those two would combust if they didn't get together. It had been a relief when Morgan finally made a move Pax couldn't resist. Cal had thought he was a fool for holding back in the first place, orders or no orders. Captain Oswald talked tough, but there was no way he'd have taken action if Pax had been caught in Morgan's bed. Pax was too good a soldier to waste that way, and the captain knew it.

Cal had no such orders barring him from relations with Savvy, and damn if that wasn't the problem. He could use a barrier between them right now, but he had nothing. Not even righteous anger over the fact she was CIA. He might dislike the organization, but he knew damn well she stood at the front line of the War on Terror and was the unsung hero they needed. A woman willing to risk everything to gather human intelligence—or, as the CIA rather unimaginatively called it, HUMINT.

In a few days, they'd walk into a viper's nest lightly armed but ready to take on a cabal that was destroying this part of the world that he loved. These countries were his heritage. He felt a belonging on this part of the continent, an ownership he couldn't really claim. But still, Congo was part of him.

And Savvy would risk everything by entering a guarded stateroom while he hung out with the men and talked business as they drank and gambled and bragged about the size of their dicks.

Her beautiful eyes fluttered open, and as happened yesterday, when he'd held her hand on the transport, something shifted in his chest.

Fuck. He had it bad. For Savannah James.

"Morning," she said in a sleepy voice.

He smiled, liking the husky tone. God, what would she sound like when she woke in his arms? What if he pulled her close and started the day by making love to her?

No. Not making love.

Sex. Just sex. There would be no lovemaking with Savannah James. Or Freya. Hell, he didn't even know her real last name. He couldn't possibly make love to a woman whose last name he didn't know.

But he could, and—let's face it—probably would, fuck her.

He cleared his throat. "Morning. You want coffee? I was going to head down to the coffee shop." He needed to get out of this room before he did something stupid.

"That would be great. Thanks."

Ten minutes later, he was back in the room with two steaming cups of coffee. She was dressed and ready to face the day. They sat with legs crossed, facing each other on her bed, and rehearsed their cover story, adding insignificant details that gave the story realism.

She flirted and teased, as if they really were strangers meeting in a hotel restaurant as her octogenarian lover rested in his suite upstairs.

"I need you to put a hand on me whenever I'm near. Show ownership. I'm your new favorite toy."

"Where do you want me to touch you? What are you comfortable with?" After her story last night, he wasn't taking chances. He wanted her to know she was safe with him. Always.

"Anywhere. Everywhere. Honestly, the more outrageous the better. You need to *own* me, Mani. My feelings don't matter. And when I say my feelings, I mean Jamie's. I will only be Jamie Savage once we step in that world, just like I'll expect you to be Mani Kalenga."

"You want me to grope you."

"Yes."

"Even after what Harrison Evers did?"

She nodded. "You aren't Harry. You aren't even Mani. I chose *you* for this mission because I trust you. I'm okay with you touching me because I know you won't hurt me. Not really. I know you won't take advantage of the situation."

"I will never willingly hurt you. But I'm not so sure about the last part. I'm a man, Sav—Jamie. You're a beautiful woman. Touching you will turn me on. Turn us both on. What happens then?"

"You'll use it to inform your character. You'll kiss me and grope me and rub against me. These men will expect that. I fully expect there will be a sex show as part of the entertainment. This is how Gorev gathers his kompromat, after all. The more they see us getting it on, the more distracted they'll be. They'll never guess why we're really there." She lifted his hand from his lap and placed it over her breast. "You need to get used to touching me. Casually. Unconsciously. Like it's a reflex."

He cupped her, gently squeezing, then rubbed his thumb over her erect nipple. She lifted his free hand and brought it to her other breast. He gave it similar attention. God, she had perfect breasts, and he longed to lick and suck on them.

"If—if this goes further than we intend," she said, "I want you to know I'm two years into the five-year shot. I won't get pregnant. I don't even have a period anymore. I get tested for everything on a regular basis—even when I'm not having sex, which hasn't happened since I arrived at Camp Citron. I'm clean. Are you?"

He nodded.

It was strange to be having this conversation as he groped her, when he'd never even kissed her. And now his gaze fixed on her lips, and he had a pressing urge to do just that.

"Don't worry," she said, "I won't get caught up in fantasies that it means something. I know this isn't real. I know how you feel about me. What happens on the op…it's covert work. Mani and Jamie, getting it on."

And like that, the urge to kiss her evaporated. The words he'd flung at her in the gym came back to him and deflated his erection and inflated his shame. He'd been such an ass to say that to her, but it wasn't the kind of thing he could simply take back, not without forcing a conversation he didn't want. Not now.

He dropped his hold on her breasts and scooted back on the bed, giving her a sharp nod. A glance at the clock showed it was ten thirty. "Let's hit the car dealerships and get a truck. With luck, we'll be on the road in a few hours."

The wildlife park was stunningly beautiful, and Savvy found herself gawking at giraffes, elephants, and other megafauna like any tourist. They drove through this area instead of flying to Dar because they had time, but also so Savvy could describe it should her travels with the octogenarian be questioned.

They'd gone shopping in Nairobi before hitting the road and had gotten several burner cell phones. While Cal drove, she activated one and, on a whim, downloaded several songs to entertain them on the drive.

With timing she couldn't have planned, the song "Africa" by Toto came on as they neared the park and a herd of elephants loitered in the savannah below. Mt. Kilimanjaro could be seen in the distance, a stunning backdrop to the herd.

Cal laughed and turned up the volume on the music. He reached across the console and took her hand, giving her a slight squeeze.

She laughed with him, holding his hand, her gaze focused out the window at the majestic mountain and a baby elephant that rolled in the dirt. The moment was surreal. And strangely perfect. They weren't here for fun and safari. But that didn't mean she wouldn't enjoy this small moment of bliss.

"I don't know if I even realized I like this song before now," she said.

Sure, she'd downloaded it, but she'd also gotten *The Lion King* soundtrack, a few songs from the *Graceland* album by Paul Simon, and some Congolese Rumba tracks by an artist she'd never heard of.

"I love this song," Cal said.

"It's not hokey? To your mom?"

He shrugged. "I don't know. I never asked. It's a good beat. Satisfying, if that makes sense."

Sitting in the car, listening to the explosive chorus while just out the window she gazed upon one of the most beautiful sights she'd ever seen, the word satisfying made perfect sense.

They found a motel in a tourist area between Amboseli National Park and the border with Tanzania. They had a view of Kilimanjaro to the south, as awe-inspiring as the wildlife.

The motel was run-down and inexpensive, but it had a family-owned-business charm that was irresistible. The man at the reception desk was from Kinshasa, and he and Cal chattered away in Lingala, ensuring the man would remember them. It was doubtful anyone would track their itinerary, but it never hurt to be methodical. For this reason, they booked a room with only one bed. It was time to start living their cover.

The day had been strangely fun, a break from the stress of the job. It almost felt…real. Not like they were playing roles. They'd gone to a mall in Nairobi to get the phones and clothes and other odds and ends before buying the used SUV.

The mall had been the site of a devastating terrorist attack in 2013. Al-Shabaab had claimed credit for the attack. Savvy viewed the place where at least sixty-seven people had died—more than any mass shooting in the US to date—and another hundred and seventy-five had been wounded, with the same solemnity of looking at the memorial wall at CIA headquarters. It was attacks like the one in the mall that drove her. Her work could help end al-Shabaab.

Lubanga likely had ties to al-Shabaab. Taking him out would be a gift to the world. In the days after Drugov was killed, she'd found definitive connections between Drugov and Boko Haram. Her work got results. She planned to remind Cal of that when she explained the real mission to him.

Cal had been entertaining on the drive, sharing anecdotes about his A-Team's missions. He'd asked her questions about her life stateside, nearly none of which she could answer. He wasn't technically even supposed to know her real name.

But they were on a mission together, and he already knew she was SAD. She could probably relax the rules but figured it would be easier in the long run if she didn't. She needed to keep emotional distance between them, given that physical distance was impossible.

They'd eaten a light meal on the drive, and it was late by the time they carried their luggage to their no-frills motel room. Savvy let Cal have the first shower, and she used the privacy to check her email. No word from Seth. When she'd left, he said he didn't know if charges would be pursued against Harry or not. She wasn't there to make statements, and it would be easier all around if he returned to the US and Langley dealt with him. Which meant nothing would happen until she returned stateside and pursued charges.

The system sucked. She'd have to give up the best assignment she'd ever had if she wanted justice and to protect other women entering the CIA's ranks. Harry would get away with it—again—but at least this time, he hadn't really hurt her, and Cal might well have loosened a few of Harry's teeth.

Small victories.

She could also take comfort in the fact that moving forward Harry's record would carry this assault. Her earlier rape allegation was now on record as well. Seth had backed her up with O'Leary.

Cal finished in the shower, and she took her turn. She'd tell him the truth tonight. Before they were in too deep. He'd have a chance to back out, and she would have time to scramble and come up with a new plan if he did.

She stepped out of the shower wearing the T-shirt and yoga pants she planned to sleep in, braced and ready to come clean. On the bed, Cal was stretched out naked but for a pair of boxer briefs, staring at his phone.

God, the man was beautiful, from his thick biceps to sculpted abs to tapered waist and muscular thighs. He looked like a Calvin Klein ad, and she wanted to get between him and his Calvins.

He smiled when he caught her blatant stare. "See anything you like?"

She pressed her lips together in an assessing smile and scanned his body as if weighing his imperfections. Except she couldn't find any. "If you were a picture and not a living, breathing man in my bed, I'd suspect you were edited."

His smile turned to a full grin. "Come closer and see for yourself."

She took a step closer as he set his phone on the nightstand. "What's your plan here, Mani?"

"Well, Jamie, I was thinking we need to get familiar with each other's touch. If every time I lay my hand on you, we both light up like fireworks, people will guess something is up—and I'm not just meaning my dick."

"Do I light up like a firework when you touch me?"

"Yes. I can feel it, and anyone paying close attention will see."

"So what do we do about it? Aside from having sex to get each other out of our systems."

"I don't think sex is the cure. In fact, I'm pretty sure it would only make it worse. I was thinking a better inoculation is massage." He stood from the bed. "Take off your shirt and lie down. I'll work on your back and shoulders. Get you used to the feel of my hands."

She smiled, liking the idea. "You know this sounds like a come-on."

He placed a hand behind her head and pulled her closer, tilting her head back with his large palm. "When I come on to you, Jamie, you won't have any doubt." He stared at her lips as if he wanted nothing more than to taste her.

She licked her lips, an unplanned, involuntary action.

He released her and stepped back, looking pointedly at the bed. "Strip."

She pulled her T-shirt over her head, exposing her bare breasts to his gaze. This too was something they had to get used to. There was no doubt they'd see each other's bodies a lot in the coming days. The gathering would be an orgy of sorts. They needed to be prepared for anything.

He blatantly stared at her display. Her nipples tightened as she thought about this morning, when he'd cupped her breasts in the Nairobi hotel room.

"You sure you don't want to just have sex?" she asked. Her eyes fluttered closed as she imagined him sliding deep inside her.

"Get belly down on the mattress." His voice was deep and held a note of hunger.

She did as he commanded, tucking a pillow beneath her chest and shoulders and resting her forehead on another, creating a makeshift air well. He straddled her ass but didn't rest his weight there. A cool liquid hit her back, and she jolted. "You've got massage oil?"

He leaned down, bringing his low, deep voice next to her ear. "I picked it up at the Beauty World spa when you were trying on lingerie. It was the spa that gave me this idea."

His warm hands spread the oil up her back and over her shoulders. She let out a soft groan at his firm touch as his thumbs found the knots in her shoulders. "God, that feels good."

"Shhh," he said softly. "Just relax and get used to my touch."

How could she ever get used to this? His hands were the best thing she'd ever felt. But she had to admit, there was nothing sensual about the massage except for the fact that she felt his knees at her hips as he straddled her.

She tried to imagine he was a faceless massage therapist. She'd had plenty of massages over the years, given by men and women, and their touch didn't affect her in this way. But then, she wasn't on a massage table; they were on a bed. One they would share tonight. His cock was just inches from her ass. But most important, this was Cal, who would never be faceless to her.

He worked her shoulders, and she purred with the pleasure of it. She wanted more, though, and couldn't help herself. She raised her hips from the bed, bringing her ass in contact with his penis, delighted to discover he was as hard as she'd hoped he'd be.

He pushed her hips down as he rose higher on his knees. "Bad Sav."

They'd agreed he could call her Sav just as she could call him Kal. Otherwise, it always had to be Mani and Jamie.

Freya was out. Much as she'd liked hearing that name from his lips, it would be a bad habit to start. She was Jamie Savage now.

"I think you like it when I'm bad."

He laughed. "I do. But this isn't supposed to be sexual."

"You're sporting impressive wood for something that's not sexual."

"I'm not made of stone. Of course I'm aroused. Jesus, my cock is inches from your round ass, and you're groaning like you're about to come. But the massage itself isn't supposed to lead to sex. The massage isn't sexual."

She rolled to her back. He lifted his hands from her and sat up straight but remained straddling her. "Touch my breasts, Kal."

"That's not what this is about."

"I'm changing what this is about. Touch me."

He held her gaze, all humor gone from his eyes, as he did what she asked. Or rather, commanded. This was a touch they needed to get used to too. He would almost certainly have to grope her in front of the others. A way of staking his claim.

Her nipples hardened, and he played with them like they were a fascinating toy. So, Cassius Callahan was a breast man. She'd suspected, but now she was certain. "Lick them," she said softly. That too was an order, but really more of a plea.

He leaned down, bringing his erection into full contact with her pelvis, and ran his tongue over the tip of one nipple. Then he sucked it into his mouth, and she nearly came off the bed with the joyful ache it triggered.

He moved to her other breast as she ground her hips up, bringing his erection to her clit.

Lord, how she wanted this. Him. She had for months.

He sucked on her breasts, then blew across the tips, watching the nipples tighten. She cupped his face and pulled his mouth upward. They'd yet to kiss, and she was desperate for their mouths to meet at last.

He froze all at once, his body hard and stiff against her. "That's not what this is about, Sav." He sat up and scooted back, his body leaving hers. "I don't want to have sex with you."

Her body went from hot to cold in a flash. It was a burning sort of cold, like walking in snow barefoot. Her gaze fixed on his erection as she tried to find her composure. Her pride. "I think you're lying about that." The words came out husky, which was better than hurt or angry, she supposed, even though both feelings surged.

"I mean not like this. Not as an exercise in espionage. Not because of proximity. Sure, my body wants to fuck you. My dick is pretty pissed right now that I'm talking and not taking what you're offering. But when this is all over, I don't want us going back to Camp Citron confused about where we stand because we gave in and fucked in the heat of the moment. This mission is business. We need to keep it that way."

His words were logical and made sense, but she couldn't shake off the rejection in them. The excuse of it all.

"That's why I wanted us to try massage. A way to get used to each other's touch. To condition ourselves to get accustomed and *not* to react sexually. My proposal *really* wasn't a come-on."

"No, it was a test. You were testing yourself. Your willpower." Anger was building now. It was fine for him to have these boundaries and rules, especially when he got to break them at will—he could touch her and suck on her tits and put on the brakes when it got too intimate for his liking. But there was no room for him to adapt when she wanted more.

Was she getting mad because he wouldn't put out? What was happening to her?

"No! I didn't plan that part. I honestly thought massage would…help." He cleared his throat. "I need you to massage me now. I need to get used to the feel of your hands on my skin."

She glared at him. "Below or above the belt?"

"I'm serious, Savvy."

"Jamie," she corrected.

"Jamie," he repeated. "I'm serious. You touch me, and I want to pin you down and fuck you till we're both blind. I want you so bad, my jaw aches with the pain of holding back, and I'm pretty sure there's ringing in my ears. But there's no room for that sort of reaction when we're at the meeting. Not when I need to look at you as a disposable toy, and you're supposed to be on the hunt for a richer sugar daddy than Mani Kalenga. We can't appear *that* into each other. So I need to learn how to take your touch without fucking you. Without it going where we were just headed."

His words were fair. And reasonable. And still, part of her ached. Probably the vaginal part, because damn, she wanted sex right *now*. Come to think of it, her ears were ringing too.

He took her spot on the bed, similarly using the pillow to support his shoulders so he could breathe facedown. She grabbed the body oil from the nightstand and squirted a large amount on his back.

His smooth ebony skin stretched over a muscular back. His body was a work of art. She paused before straddling his butt, just taking in the beauty of him. If this were a sexual massage, she'd explore that skin with her tongue.

She placed her hands in the puddle of oil and spread outward. Her thighs relaxed, and she settled in for a long, professional massage. Well, except for the fact that she was topless and straddling him. That part wasn't very professional at all.

Cal let out a soft sigh as she set to work, zeroing in on knots and gently massaging them away. She fell into a rhythm, enjoying being able to stroke his body, touch that beautiful skin, and, strangely enough, the sexual tension faded even as the intimacy increased.

He'd been right. Damn him. They did need to condition themselves to make touching less sensual. Less electric.

It was clear she'd achieved his goal when his muscles relaxed in sleep.

She couldn't help but laugh. So now her touch had a soporific effect. Not exactly what she'd been aiming for, and definitely not a great ego boost, but it would serve their needs.

She climbed from the bed and turned out the bedside light. She returned to the shower to rinse the oil from her back, then crawled into the bed beside him. She was dressed again in T-shirt and sweats and he was sound asleep above the covers in his boxer briefs.

This was their first night sleeping together. And he still hadn't kissed her.

Chapter Eight

They drove straight through and arrived in Dar es Salaam late the following night, where they checked into a luxury hotel on the water. Several of Gorev's associates were staying at the same hotel. From here on out, they would be "on" every minute.

Savvy barely slept that night, again with Cal nearly naked by her side. She was too wound up, anxious about the coming meeting she hoped would gain them invites to the party on the Russian oligarch's megayacht.

Radimir Gorev was just as nasty as Nikolai Drugov had been, but he was even more ambitious. And if Jean Paul Lubanga's Russian-backed coup was a success, then Gorev would rise in Russian ranks, and Congo's future would be even more bleak.

Unlike most of his colleagues, Lubanga was technically adroit. His daughter said he'd taken a job in Kinshasa not long after the visit by Mobutu. His job had been in corporate management of mining operations. There he'd learned computers, recognizing that technology would give him an edge.

He rose in the ranks by learning coding and data management, which he applied to his illegal enterprises in addition to his official job. He was now as high as he could go, senior minister in charge of mining rights in a vast and mineral-rich country. On the surface, he was the president's crony. But on the side, people like Gorev were financing his imminent coup.

In the hours before she left Djibouti, she'd had a briefing with Seth in which he elaborated on an arrangement Lubanga had with a televangelist, the Reverend Abel Fitzsimmons, who wanted to be the spiritual leader of the mostly Christian DRC under a Lubanga administration. Savvy's cynical side said the reverend wouldn't care so much about the spiritual lives of Congolese people if they weren't sitting on trillions in mineral wealth, and Seth had agreed. He wanted her to report back if the reverend attended the party.

Details on Lubanga's business dealings were scant because the mining minister was as skilled with computers as any technical intelligence officer in the CIA. The best hackers in the world had been unable to crack Lubanga's system. For starters, he himself didn't go online, ever, at least, not with the computer that handled his finances. He had a government computer that went online, but it was loaded with disinformation. Like leaders of terrorist groups, he worked with a network of couriers and USB drives, and somewhere in his home country, there was someone at a computer terminal moving his money around, but they'd yet to locate the computer or the accounts. The transactions were so far removed from the man, they were impossible to connect.

But like any busy businessman, Lubanga never traveled without his laptop. He needed to plug in and read the documents that were delivered to him on those drives, and his stay on Gorev's yacht was certain to be a smorgasbord of information exchange, with information delivered from several sources.

Her original plan for their mission was simple: during the party, find his stateroom, and copy the hard drive of his laptop while Cal cornered him and made his pitch for a mining concession. But the first step was to get invited to the party.

The day dawned sunny and bright. They were nearly seven degrees below the equator, and the temperature was expected to hit eighty degrees. They spent the morning in their room, rehearsing. Memorizing. She quizzed Cal mercilessly on his cover, and he did the same to her.

In the late afternoon, she showered and dressed carefully for Mani Kalenga's meeting with Gorev's associates. She needed to look her part: sexy clothing, heavy makeup. Pretty, but not too pretty. Sexy, but not too sexy.

Cheap, but…no, cheap was fine.

Like a failed courtesan. A woman with enough sex appeal to entice Mani Kalenga, but not smart enough to have secured the octogenarian without screwing it up.

She was a desperate gold digger who'd just lost her meal ticket. Mani Kalenga would do for now, but she was looking to trade up. That was why she couldn't react to Cal's every touch with a frisson of excitement. He was just a stop on the road for her, not nearly rich enough to suit her needs.

Plus he was too young. And healthy.

And utterly perfect.

Jamie Savage was really dumb to think she could trade up from Cassius Callahan. He was a pinnacle unto himself.

She turned to face the man who'd agreed to play her master, and in so doing would be protecting her on what was likely to be the most dangerous mission she'd ever attempted. "How do I look?"

He smiled and said, "Fucking hot. Too hot for my liking given the men we're meeting. So basically, perfect."

She smoothed down his Armani shirt as she rose on her toes and kissed his cheek. "You look pretty damn perfect too."

They'd decided Mani was a mercenary who knew how to dress the part of one who wanted into the big leagues. His beard was fuller but not unkempt, and his clothes were far more expensive than hers.

Luckily, she'd set up a rather large bank account for this op, courtesy of Nikolai Drugov. Diverting a chunk of his money into accounts in Mani's name had been easy and far faster than waiting for the CIA's budget office to agree to the expense. Seth had signed off and filed the paperwork so it wouldn't come back and bite her in the ass later.

They'd made good use of the money at the mall in Nairobi, buying him high-end clothes to fit his character. The end result was Cal looked hot as hell in his new suit.

She'd spent the last two days arguing with herself over telling him the truth about the mission and had come to a conclusion. She couldn't tell him before this meeting, because if they didn't wrangle an invite to the party, the point was moot. If they failed tonight, she'd put him on a plane back to Djibouti and go after Lubanga on her own.

Zero risk to Sergeant First Class Cassius Callahan, because he'd be nowhere nearby when she took out the Congolese minister. Plus Cal's focus on this meeting wouldn't be fractured with concerns beyond their control.

She'd felt strangely free once she made the decision. She wasn't risking Cal, and she wouldn't fail the CIA. Seth had agreed to her choice of Cal for this op, but he'd never said they both had to see it through to the bitter end.

Only she had received the kill order, and only she would take that risk.

"You ready?" Cal asked.

She nodded. "Let's roll."

They stepped into the hotel's large bar and restaurant and were led to a private room in the back, where two Congolese men sat with a Russian. There was only one other place setting at the table—a fact Savvy had been counting on. She pouted for her fake lover. "Mani, you didn't tell them about me?"

His gaze showed a hint of exasperation, with an edge of restrained authority. "I set this up before we met." He gave the men an apologetic look and spoke in Lingala, giving, she presumed, the planned story about being stuck with her after hooking up with her at the park and causing her to be dumped from her tour. He didn't trust her alone in his hotel room, so he'd brought her to the meeting. He wasn't ready to put her on a flight home yet; after all, she gave a masterful blowjob.

One of the Congolese men grinned broadly as he stared at her mouth. She puckered her lips and said, "Mani, what are you telling them?"

"Only how happy I am to have you as my companion."

One of the men asked a question in Lingala, and he answered with the negative. There was enough of a French influence on the language that she could pick out basic words, but that was all.

One of the men gestured for her to sit, and he waved to the waiter and asked in French for another place setting. Probably the Congolese man had asked if she could understand them. He must have been satisfied she couldn't, since she was allowed to join their meeting. After all, there was always a chance Mani would share, and these weren't the sort of men to turn down a free blowjob.

She sat and listened with a blank face. The Russian didn't speak Lingala, but he did speak French, as did everyone, including Cal. Savvy pretended not to understand that part of the conversation and dropped the occasional heavy sigh as if this was the most boring meeting of her life. She sipped a drink and nibbled on bread.

It didn't take long for the men to ask Cal to produce an artifact, which was ostensibly the reason for this meeting—to determine if he had goods worth bringing to Gorev. Cal opened his briefcase and removed the false bottom.

Savvy squealed as if she'd never seen such a thing. "Mani! What have you got there? Oh. My. God. That's beautiful! Is it...*real?*"

"Sweetheart," his voice showed irritation at the interruption, "none of these men speak English." His words were a blatant lie, but they'd agreed he would drop it if he could, because she expected it would entertain the men. "It's rude to speak when they don't understand."

She furrowed her brow. "But you've all been speaking in languages I don't understand. So doesn't that mean you've been rude?" Then she smiled and let her gaze travel over the Russian. Anton was high up in Gorev's organization. He was the one they needed to win over. "Think he'd be up for a threesome?"

Cal's gaze narrowed. "I don't share."

She licked her lips. "But it could be fun."

Anton's face remained blank, but from the shift in his posture, she knew she'd caught his attention.

"Zip it. This is a business meeting. You're lucky I didn't leave you at Amboseli."

She lowered her voice to a husky register, as if eager to convince him she was worth his while. "That's not what you said last night."

He fixed her with a gaze that was somehow hot and sexy and angry. Mani Kalenga had an edge to him. He wasn't the least intimidated by hardened warlords and had no problem putting his flighty toy in her place.

Even better, Savvy could see the subtle signs Anton was on edge because of Mani's alpha demeanor. Anton wanted to show he was more than an underling to Radimir Gorev. And he might just use Jamie Savage to do it.

Cal played the part to perfection. He handed the artifact to the Russian and said, "Egyptian. Fifth dynasty, or so I'm told."

For the demo piece, they'd opted to go with an Egyptian artifact that had been found in a marine's CLU at Camp Citron. He'd gone to Cairo on leave and had somehow smuggled the item back to the base. There'd been suspicion he'd been dealing drugs as well, and a toss of his quarters revealed a cache of artifacts. The piece was a gold pendant encrusted with gemstones, so good it had to be fake—Savvy had been shocked to learn it was all too real, and likely something ISIS had snatched and slipped into the black market to fund their terrorist organization.

Well, now it would be used to fight them.

Anton's eyes widened as the heavy gold hit his palm. "It is beautiful," he said in French, his focus shifting from wanting to put Mani in his place to the piece in his hand. The Russian pulled out a loupe—as she'd expected he would; antiquities were his specialty—and studied it. He set it on the table and asked, "You have more? Like this?"

"Five pieces," Cal said. "All gold. All from the same dynasty."

The Russian smiled. "Gorev will be pleased. You may join us tomorrow. Bring the antiquities." He glanced toward Savvy. "And the girl. She'll fit right in with the night's entertainment."

She'd have gone even without an invitation, but this was even better. Oh yes. Anton definitely wanted to use Jamie to put Mani in his place.

Cal grinned and picked up his drink. He downed it in one gulp and set it on the table. He tucked the artifact away in the case and said in French, "Excellent. Now if you'll excuse me, I need to make good use of my companion's mouth."

The men laughed. One of the Congolese men slapped his back.

Savvy gave her best vacant look and said, "What did you say, Mani? Did you tell them we're going to fuck? Because no way am I screwing you unless you let me wear that pendant. Oh my God. I can't believe you've had that this whole time and didn't show me."

"You can wear it while you suck me off. Let's go. I want to celebrate."

He pulled her from her seat and dragged her from the private room in the back of the restaurant.

Savvy's blood was pumping high with their victory. They were *in*. The cover story had worked. The men would look at her as nothing but a vacant plaything. She'd have access to Gorev's boat.

Tomorrow, she'd get Lubanga's hard drive.

Inside the elevator, she pushed Cal into the corner, not thinking, just relishing the moment. He gave her his full, knee-weakening smile as his hand slid over her ass. "God, you're fun to watch in action. You somehow manage to make your eyes look vacant. I mean, I *know* how brilliant you are, and even I was buying the dumb-bimbo routine. And I could've sworn you don't speak a lick of French."

The thrill of success combined with the heat of his compliments and his hands on her ass had her at a fever pitch. But she wouldn't kiss him. It was up to Cal to take that step. She just pressed close and said, "You were perfect. The hint of hard-edged violence that simmered under Mani's calm exterior. It was a perfect don't-fuck-with-me vibe you managed to convey in three languages. You triggered all of Anton's inferiority complexes. He's going to trip over himself trying to steal me from you."

He stroked her cheek. "If he touches you, I might have to kill him."

She would have pointed out that the goal was for Anton to touch her—but Cal's mouth covered hers, cutting off her ability to speak or even think.

His tongue was hot and urgent. Staking his claim.

Victory felt so good, and it tasted even better. She kissed him with all the passion she'd been harboring for months. He scooped her up, turned to put her in the corner as his tongue slid against hers. Her short dress hiked up as she wrapped her legs around his hips, and he ground into her, setting her on fire with the feel of his erection against her now thoroughly wet panties.

This was how she knew it would be with Cal. All heat and fire and, oh God, his thick erection would make her blind if her eyes were open. The doors opened on their floor, but he still kissed her, and she wasn't about to tell him to stop. Not when she finally had what she wanted from him.

Cassius Callahan, in all his passionate glory.

The doors closed again, and he lifted his head. "We missed our floor."

"We could stop the elevator, and I could go down on you." Even as she said the words, she was shocked to realize she meant it. The security camera would capture them, but if anything, it would only be good for their cover.

But this wasn't her. She wasn't an exhibitionist.

Was she?

Maybe she didn't care as long as she finally got to taste Cal. Every inch of him.

He rocked his hips and that thick, wonderful cock set her aflame. Even as he did that, he whispered in her ear, "Not here. Not like this."

Then he released her and turned to hit the button for their floor again. They descended to the lobby first, and she adjusted her dress while he adjusted his erection, which would be all too visible to anyone entering the elevator. The doors opened on the lobby, and there was the Russian and one of the Congolese men.

Cal made it look like he was just zipping his fly, and Savvy wiped her bottom lip, as if she'd just finished. The men laughed and stepped inside. The Russian said, "*Ménage à trois?*"

This was French her character would understand. Savvy's skin was flushed from their kiss, perfect for this moment. "Mani! You said they didn't understand English!"

In French, Cal said, "I don't share. But you can have her when I'm done."

"I will look forward to that. I hope you finish with her soon."

Cal cocked his head. "I might finish sooner if I get a good deal from Gorev."

"Then I shall put in a good word for you." Anton nodded as the doors opened.

It was their floor. Savvy gripped Cal's hand, preventing him from exiting. The last thing they needed was for the Russian to know where their room was.

"This is not you?" Anton asked.

"No. Must've hit the wrong button. I was a little distracted." He gestured to Savvy's mouth.

"I'd like to have your problems," the Congolese man said in French as the doors shut again. Cal hit the button for an upper floor that was above the ones the other men had selected. The Russian got off first. Then the Congolese. They reached the upper floor that wasn't theirs and exited.

From there, they took the stairs the eight flights down to their floor. Inside their room, Savvy swept for bugs.

For a moment, she'd allowed herself to forget the stakes. Her attraction to Cal was dangerous.

She wouldn't be so sloppy again.

Chapter Nine

Cal adjusted his bow tie, still not quite believing that he was attending a black-tie party on a megayacht as a spy. Who knew this James Bond kind of shit was real? Cabals of evil villains really did meet to hatch their schemes at black-tie affairs. Or at least, this was how Russians got their kompromat.

Unlike in the Bond movies, there wouldn't be a casino. The women would all be paid companions, but he couldn't remember if that was in the movies. He'd never read the books. Savvy had said to brace himself for a sex show and possibly guests joining in on the staged action—and things could get rough from there.

That was what kompromat was all about, after all. Push the mark to do something violent or embarrassing and get it on tape. Gorev had a simple approach: invite everyone to his boat, give them drugs and women, and let the cameras roll.

According to Savvy, that was how Drugov initially snared Brie Stewart's brother. Once he knew Jeffery Prime, Jr. was willing to play, JJ had skated down a slippery slope into some horrific shit that was likely to land him in prison for the rest of his life—if he could be located. He'd disappeared the day after Drugov died. He was a threat to Brie, which meant Bastian had called in favors from Special Forces operators who were stationed at Fort Campbell to watch over her until he returned home in a few weeks.

Brie had assured Bastian that JJ was too much of a chickenshit to come after her, but that didn't mean her half brother wouldn't hire help. Bastian would worry until he was home by her side, and Cal couldn't blame him.

But Brie also had Morgan Adler looking after her, and Cal would never bet against the spitfire archaeologist who'd proven to be more badass than some soldiers he knew. With Morgan guarding the door, JJ didn't stand a chance.

He turned to Savvy and grabbed the knot of the bow tie. "You know how to tie these so it comes out even?"

She smiled and undid the tie. She slowly retied it, while he took her scent deep into his body. Sleep had been a long time coming last night. He never should have kissed her in the elevator. And he certainly shouldn't have pinned her in the corner and ground himself against her.

But God, she'd felt so good. And her mouth had been heat and wine and sex and everything he needed.

He wanted to possess every inch of her, with every inch of him. He wanted to feel her mouth on him. To fuck her fast and hard against the wall and to make love to her slowly in a bed. To go down on her until she came apart, and then to screw her so thoroughly, she'd feel his cock was a part of her.

That shit was twisted.

But that right there was the problem. His feelings for her were twisted. Inexplicable. He wanted to own her, possess her, in a way that was primal. Intense.

And utterly wrong.

He'd never reacted to a woman this way before, and he didn't understand it now. Certainly not with Savvy. But he suspected the primal want was at the core of his intentional dislike of her. She brought out desires he didn't want to feel. Not for a spook. So he lashed out at her, when what he really wanted was to possess her.

He needed to sign up for sessions with the base therapist at Fort Campbell. There was a good guy there who worked with Special Forces. He understood them. He'd make an appointment as soon as he was stateside.

But before he could do that, he had to get through tonight. And tomorrow. And the next few days.

Prep for tonight had filled their day, giving him little time to think about what would happen next. They'd bought another car so they'd have an anonymous vehicle to escape in should things go to shit with Gorev and Lubanga. They'd packed up and loaded everything—including Savvy's spy gadgets, computer, and the two handguns they'd managed to smuggle into the country—in the new sedan. Savvy was leaving nothing to chance. They wouldn't check out, and they wouldn't return to this hotel.

Savvy finished tying his bow tie, then ran her hands down his lapels. "You look perfect. I wish this were a dress uniform. But you look hot no matter what."

She stepped back and twirled before him. Her gown was gold sequins from top to bottom and flashed in the light, literally blinding him. "How do I look?"

"Like a lighting bolt. Energy. Power. Beauty."

She smiled at him in a way that made his heart twist. Maybe there was more here than attraction, but he didn't want to delve into that. Not when they were about to walk into the lion's den and she was going to risk everything by sneaking into Lubanga's quarters.

She could get killed tonight. She could become a star at Langley, and no one outside the Agency but him would know her name or sacrifice.

It was different for him. If he paid the ultimate price, his name would be published in newspapers across the country. Odds were, his parents would receive a call from the president. Not that he wanted any of those things, but it was a stark difference between how his death would be honored and hers would be buried.

He draped a light shawl over her shoulders from behind and couldn't help but drop a kiss on her neck. "Game time," he said.

She took a deep breath. "Cal?"

"Yeah?" he asked, curious. She sounded like she had something heavy to say.

She held his gaze for a long time, then finally shook her head and said, "Thank you. For coming with me on this mission. I never would have gotten this far without you."

"I'm glad to be a part of it. I want to bring these motherfuckers down."

"Let's do it, then."

The urge to tell Cal had almost overwhelmed her, but she'd stopped herself just in time. Telling him now would only mess with his focus when she'd made a decision that rendered telling him unnecessary.

She had no intention of killing Lubanga tonight. It was likely to be impossible anyway, given the security on the boat, and she wouldn't risk Cal that way. There was no reason for him to take part in the assassination. That was her job, not his, and she would protect him.

He was doing his part. He was taking her to the party, where she'd copy Lubanga's files per her original mission. Then she'd send him back to Camp Citron before she fulfilled her orders from the CIA.

Cal didn't have a role in the assassination. Instead, he'd be on base with a hundred alibis. And if Savvy failed, she'd take the fall alone.

It was the right call to make. She hadn't cleared it with Seth or anyone within the CIA, but she was on her own with this, so she could make her own decisions on how to best handle the job.

She smiled and leaned over and kissed his cheek as he drove to the marina where the megayacht was moored.

"What's that for?" he asked.

"I just like you. That's all."

He smiled. He looked like he wanted to say something, but in the end, he dropped a hand to her knee and squeezed.

It was enough for her.

They reached the marina, and a cool calm spread through Savvy. She'd trained for this. More important, she believed in the necessity of her work to the marrow of her bones. She was the first line of defense for a just and free world. Her work gave the abused and forgotten masses a fighting chance by exposing corrupt people who raped and pillaged for power and money.

Dead Drugov had kindly provided blueprints of gross Gorev's yacht for Savvy to study. She suspected Drugov had planned a nasty surprise for his rival oligarch tonight, but he'd been killed by Special Forces and SEALs. Too bad. Not sad.

Savvy's steps were measured and careful in the four-inch heels as she entered the main salon on Cal's arm. The salon was wide and open—more of a ballroom—and was where most of the evening's entertainment would take place.

The women who'd been hired to provide entertainment wore various forms of lingerie. Some circulated the room with trays of drinks, acting as servers, while others simply sat in seductive poses, waiting for guests to partake of their wares. She was the only gowned woman present. The dress was a signal she wasn't hired entertainment. Touch her and risk Mani's wrath.

Two women, one dark skinned, the other light, sat on a chaise lounge in the middle of the room, putting on a sex show for interested partygoers. Savvy took stock of which men watched with avid interest and which men showed indifference to the display. Lubanga and Gorev were among the indifferent—not surprising because they were the ones who'd arranged the entertainment. For them, this evening was all business.

Cal played his part and fixed his gaze on the titillating display. Savvy presented a jealous pout. "Mani!" she scolded. "I'm thirsty." She took his arm and turned him away from the show, heading toward the open bar.

His hand slid over her ass and squeezed. "Let's skip drinks and find a room."

She batted his hand away. "We just got here. I want to meet our host." She scanned the luxurious room. "I bet he's even richer than Stanley," she said, giving the name of her fictional octogenarian lover.

"Oh, honey," Cal said, "if Stanley is your baseline for wealth, you're about to have your mind blown."

"Who is the richest man here?" she asked, scanning the room.

"Probably the two dudes at the table over there," he said, nodding toward Gorev and Lubanga.

"Good to know." She turned to the bartender and ordered wine—choosing the same vintage she'd watched him pour for a male guest as she approached the bar.

He reached for a second bottle of the same type, and she shook her head and pointed. "No. That one."

The bartender winked at her. "Got it," he said.

She watched as he poured to be certain no drugs were slipped into the glass. Drinking was expected here. It would be noticed if she didn't drink at all. She and Cal would only take light sips as an extra precaution.

Anton, the Russian they'd met yesterday, approached and tried to draw Savvy away from Cal, but he slipped an arm around her waist, keeping her close. "Find your own woman, Anton," Cal said in English, giving up all pretense that the Russian didn't speak the language.

While not the official language—Tanzania didn't have one—English was the language of business and secondary and higher education, although it was being pushed out of schools in favor of Swahili, the country's national language. While at least a dozen languages could be heard throughout the room, the most prominent was English.

Anton smiled tightly. "I merely seek to keep her company while you meet our host. He is waiting to see the pendant." He waved toward Gorev, who watched as a guest interrupted the sex on the chaise to drag the black woman into one of several private rooms adjacent to the main salon.

Gorev nodded to a thin, brown-skinned woman whose eyes had the glaze of drugs masking fear. She approached the white woman, who remained on the chaise.

The white woman spread her legs and pulled the scared woman to sit between her thighs, facing the audience. The white woman stroked the darker-skinned woman's breasts, then dipped her fingers between the woman's thighs.

The scared woman stiffened and jolted. Even drugged, she resisted.

"Shhh. You will like this." The white woman spoke in a stage whisper, but she was the only one who was performing. The other woman's terror was no act, even if the drugs made her compliant.

The older woman—a madam of sorts?—met Gorev's gaze. "This one is a virgin. I've been saving her for tonight." She spread the unwilling woman's legs apart and stroked her inner thighs. "Do you want her for yourself or to give to a guest?" She spoke English with a South African accent.

Savvy's stomach churned. This must be how Bastian had felt in the slave market, seeing the children on the auction block but knowing he was there to save Brie, and only Brie. While his team of Green Berets—including Cal—

had found a way around that problem and had saved all the children, there could be no such rescue for the scared young woman on the chaise. Savvy and Cal couldn't break cover to prevent the rape.

Hell, they couldn't break cover even if they witnessed her being murdered. Anything and everything could happen on this boat tonight, and they would do nothing to stop it.

Instead, they had to watch and pretend to enjoy the spectacle.

Gorev's gaze turned to Cal. She leaned into him, presenting her vacant sex-toy front, and ran her hand down his chest. "Maybe we *should* find some privacy, Mani-baby," she said with the seductive tone of a woman afraid of losing her meal ticket.

His gaze narrowed as if irritated. "And insult our host?"

She could feel the tension in his body. They'd planned for this, but he wasn't an actor, wasn't a covert operative. He needed to keep his revulsion hidden. He was doing a good job so far. But damn, if Gorev offered him the poor girl on the chaise, he might say yes so he could help her escape untouched, and that would get them both killed.

No. Cal wasn't a fool. He knew the stakes. She had to trust him.

She *did* trust him.

Gorev nodded to a man to Cal's right. "You. Prime. You like the virgins, yes?"

Savvy pretended to sip her drink as she shifted her gaze to look over Cal's shoulder. And there she spotted the man Gorev had been speaking to.

Holy crap.

Jeffery Prime Jr., better known as JJ. Brie's brother, the one who'd been in deep with Drugov. The one who'd fled Morocco the day after Drugov was killed. The one who'd sold out his sister to cut a deal with the oligarch.

And now he was here, probably seeking asylum from a different oligarch.

JJ stepped forward, his gaze raking over the frightened woman. "For me, Gorev? I'm honored."

"Because you were so good to watch over Drugov for me. But be careful with her, Prime. Others will want a turn."

Savvy maintained her serene smile even as her stomach churned. Gorev was reminding JJ of the fourteen-year-old girl he'd strangled as he raped her in Moscow a year ago. Drugov had told Brie he had the video. Savvy hadn't found it in the materials recovered from the yacht, but she hadn't gone through every hour of video they'd managed to grab.

She wished she'd had more time to go through Drugov's files. But once she'd learned of this party, her focus had narrowed. She hadn't had time to do anything but research Gorev and Lubanga.

JJ stepped forward and grabbed the girl, pulling her into one of the private rooms—which certainly had cameras set up to record everything that went on inside. The rooms were the reason Savvy had warned Cal they might have to get intimate to maintain cover.

Better to end up in there with Cal than with someone else. If he hadn't intervened that night at Camp Citron, she'd be here with Harry.

"You. Kalenga," Lubanga said. He then said something in rapid Lingala.

Cal responded in the same language, pulling Savvy with him as he approached the power table. From his gestures, Savvy knew he was introducing her as his entertaining but also pain-in-the-ass companion. She sent Lubanga a winning smile, which he ignored. She turned it on Gorev, who was much more receptive.

Lubanga took in Gorev's reaction and said something to Cal. Cal responded by putting his hand on her ass and squeezing. She rolled her eyes and halfheartedly batted his hand away. "Not in front of people, Mani."

Cal fixed her with a look. "When and where I want it, Jamie. You know the rules."

She pouted. "You're worse than Stanley."

"I think the word you mean is better. Much, much better—which is how you ended up in this mess to begin with." He sat in an open seat at the table.

She dropped onto his lap. He slid a hand between her thighs and brushed her clit with a fingertip under the skirt of her dress. She let out a soft sound of approval. "Oh yes," she purred. "Much more pleasing than the old coot."

He gave her a smug smile, then pushed her to the edge of his lap, stopping short of dumping her. "Leave us. We have business to discuss."

"Come with me, my dear," Anton said. "I will give you a tour of the yacht."

Cal glared at him. "She's mine," he said in French.

"She can decide that," the Russian insisted, also in French.

"Not until I'm bored with her." Cal's look was hard and cold.

The Russian glared back

Savvy did her part and played dumb. "What are you arguing about, Mani?"

"Ownership of your mouth," Cal said.

She narrowed her gaze and scanned the Russian. She licked her lips and looked at Cal. "I believe my mouth is mine and mine alone."

"Not while I'm paying your bills, sweetheart."

She gave him a pout. "You promised me diamonds."

He looked to the other men at the table. "And that's why we're here."

He smiled. "You'll wear a string of them and nothing else the next time you suck me off."

She puckered, making a duck-lip pout that was never as sexy as the wearer hoped, and drew a finger down the studs on his shirt. "You know, it's polite to take turns with that."

He tilted his head back and laughed. "What makes you think I'm ever polite?"

She rose from his lap and took Anton's arm. "Lead the way, Anton. I wish to see more of this big boat." She glanced toward the private rooms. "And maybe explore one of those."

"No diamonds and no plane ticket if you enter one of those rooms without me," Cal said as she and Anton walked away.

She turned and blew him a kiss. "As you wish, my love."

When they were out of earshot, Anton said, "I think you are more in charge than Kalenga knows."

She gave him a cunning grin. "He thinks he's trained me, but I know how this game is played." She smiled at the man and winked. "And I have my sights on bigger fish."

"You are a smart woman."

She pressed her hand to her chest. "You flatter me." This guy clearly thought he'd given her the highest praise. In this world, women were objects and nothing more. Brains never factored in at all. But she knew who the idiot was here, and she wanted to ram his nuts so hard, they'd touch his brainstem, further damaging his feeble intellect. But she didn't. Not yet. He was a tool—a basic, boring crowbar. Heavy and deadly, but most effective when wielded with strategic force. She would use him to pry open the exit and enter the corridors where the guest cabins were.

"Why are most of the women here only wearing lingerie?" She wrinkled her nose. "I didn't expect that."

He cleared his throat. "It's...unusual to bring a date. We allowed Kalenga to do so because you are so charming."

"Mani...he can be sort of mean. If I don't do things just so." Strategic force, step one: make him believe she was eager to move on from Mani.

The Russian draped an arm around her as they stepped into the corridor. "Tell me about it, my dear. I am here to listen."

Step two: throw him off-balance while convincing him she was a complete twit. "Well, for starters, his cock is so big, it's hard for me to get my mouth around it. I'm sure I wouldn't have that problem with you." She widened her eyes. "I mean—I'm sure you are...just right. Not like Mani." She allowed a soft purr and said under her breath, "But he does know how to use it." Then she frowned. "He has this thing he does when he comes. I'm so sick of getting jizz in my hair."

The look the Russian gave her was pained.

She had to work not to smile. Jamie Savage was fun in a ridiculous kind of way. "Oh! You probably don't know that word. Jizz is...*spunk*." She raised her voice as if he were hard of hearing. "Um...semen? The stuff that comes out when a guy...you know. Comes. You must know one of those words."

"I assure you I do."

"Oh! Good! I'd hate for you to misunderstand."

"I hear you loud and clear, Miss...what is your last name?"

"Savage. Jamie Savage."

"You are the loveliest woman here, Miss Savage. And a delightful conversationalist."

"LOL." She couldn't help but snicker at the fact that she'd just *said* LOL instead of laughing. "Mani says there are better uses for my mouth than talking."

"I'm willing to test that theory."

She pushed him hard on the shoulder. "Oh, you! You are so funny!"

She flashed a smile as they passed a salon with a handful of men watching yet another sex show, this one featuring a man and a woman. "I've never been on such a big boat!"

He planted his hand at the small of her back as he whisked her down the corridor. "There are many rooms to see."

They raced through all the public rooms as he steered her toward the staterooms below deck. She pretended to resist, claiming she wanted to see the elegantly decorated rooms all while making suggestive comments to speed him along. Anton worked for Gorev. Important enough to have a cabin on the boat for the night, but not so important that he was allowed to stay on the yacht for the full week that Lubanga was aboard.

Anton's stateroom was on the third tier of guest quarters. Lubanga was on the second. Only Gorev was on the first tier. She needed to lose Anton and go one flight up.

Given Anton's rapid pace, it wasn't long before they reached his cabin. He pulled her inside and immediately stuck his tongue in her mouth. She kissed him back, then pulled away, as if regretful. This part of the job was the absolute worst. "I can't. Mani will get mad."

"Does he own you?"

This was a serious question. But her character would fail to see that. Jamie Savage used her body as a means of support, but it was all barter and consent. She didn't see herself as a prostitute and certainly didn't understand the realities of sexual slavery. "You are so funny! Of course he doesn't. Slavery was illegal"—she paused and pursed her lips to show concentration—"since, like, decades ago. You can't own another person, not unless you marry them." She frowned. "Mani's hot, but he's nowhere near rich enough to marry."

The Russian gave her a speculative look. "Why are you with him?"

"We got in a...kerfuffle with my...ex. He didn't like me hanging out with Mani. I was traveling with him—a safari through Kenya and Tanzania—and he dumped me at a wildlife park with nothing but my passport and suitcase. I don't have any money to get home. Mani said he'd buy me a plane ticket home once we reached Dar. But now we're here, and he still hasn't gotten me a ticket. I'm stuck with him until he does."

"Where is home?"

"Hershey, Pennsylvania. The place where they make all the chocolate bars."

"That must be why you are so sweet." He leaned down as if to kiss her, and she ducked away. At least her role gave her an excuse to avoid his cigar-breath kisses. "Mani doesn't like to share," she said, adding a nervous flutter to her voice.

"What if I get you that plane ticket?"

She gave him a considering pout. "But all my stuff is in Mani's hotel room. He won't let me have a key. He won't even let me be in the room alone. It's why he brought me to your stupid, boring meeting."

"What's your room number? I'll have one of my men get your things."

She cocked her head. "*My* things, or the artifacts?"

He ran a finger down her cheek. "If things go well, both."

She pressed her lips together and dropped her gaze as she gave a slight, seductive smile. She moistened her lips, revealing only the tip of her tongue before retracting. "You will...cut me in?"

He pressed her back to the wall, holding her wrists above her head, and jammed his erection against her belly. "Only if you let *me* in." His mouth aimed for hers.

She turned her head and fought against his hold on her wrists. She smiled as if it hadn't occurred to her she could be in danger. "You ever heard the story about giving away milk for free? I'm no dummy."

"If you don't help me, I won't help you."

She slipped from his grasp and ducked under his arm. "This isn't a good idea. Mani can be really mean." She looked over his small stateroom. "And frankly, you aren't a big enough fish for me to risk losing him."

"You bitch!" He lunged for her and shoved her back against the wall again. "If you won't give it to me, I'll take it." He grabbed her crotch.

She struck out with the side of her hand, aiming for the vagus nerve in his neck. The sharp drop in blood pressure caused his eyes to roll to the back of his head. He dropped to the ground. He would only be out for a minute or so, but when he came to, he'd be light-headed and nauseous. Most people, when hit with a sharp blow to the vagus, weren't able to walk and often wanted to vomit. The effects should last twenty minutes or so, giving her enough time to get inside Lubanga's stateroom.

Fortunately for her, Drugov had noted which room Lubanga usually stayed in. Apparently, these parties happened twice a year, and Lubanga was a regular, honored guest. His alliance with Gorev was solid. Drugov's only hope would've been to kill his rival.

She hurried up the stairs. If she ran into a servant or a guest, she'd say she was running from Anton, which he'd only confirm when he eventually came after her.

Luckily, she made it to Lubanga's quarters without crossing anyone's path. She pulled a lock pick from her hair and had it open within ten seconds. Gorev used cheap locks on all the doors except his own. But then, there were probably guards posted on Gorev's room as well. Good thing he wasn't her target.

Inside the room, she made a beeline for the laptop computer on the desk under the porthole. It was a sleek machine, exactly as she'd expected. She opened the lid. The home screen demanded a password.

She pulled a tube of lipstick from her bra—she hadn't bothered with a purse for the evening—and extracted a mini USB drive from the base. She plugged it in, blessing the CIA's tech team that had created this little wonder.

The device did its job and zipped past security. It also served as a lightning-speed modem for a laptop that didn't have an internet connection. Within seconds, the hard disk began uploading files to cloud storage she'd configured before she left Camp Citron. While the files uploaded, she scanned the list of file names. One caught her eye, and she found it hard to breathe.

Zagreus.

How many people knew Lubanga's codename? Cal and his superiors at SOCOM. Seth and Harry. A few up the chain of command in the CIA. It would have stopped there, except this was an assassination mission. Orders like that always went all the way to the top. But would the director of the Directorate of Operations know the code name?

Zagreus was a relatively unknown figure from Greek mythology. That it was the name of a file on Lubanga's computer could only mean one thing: they'd been compromised.

Chapter Ten

This place was hell on earth. Cal sat with a Russian oligarch who wanted to buy stolen antiquities as Cal was doing his best to charm a would-be Congolese despot into granting him a diamond-mining claim on a river in his mother's birth country all while watching a sex show put on by women—at least one of whom wasn't willing.

Twice, he was offered to partake of the offerings on the chaise. He refused on the grounds that he preferred Jamie's highly skilled blowjobs over virgins and hoped to hell they'd quit asking. He also hoped they wouldn't comment on the fact that Jamie had been gone too long with Anton for a jealous guy like Mani to be comfortable.

But he played his role because their lives depended on it. He wanted all these bastards to burn in a rain of hellfire. To make that happen, Savvy needed to do her job.

"Diamond mining is hard work," Gorev said in English. He'd gotten irritated with the lengthy conversation he couldn't understand, but Cal suspected Lubanga had wanted to test his fluency, to see if he was legitimately connected to Congo.

"I've got workers lined up," Cal responded.

"It's hard to keep workers motivated," Gorev said.

Cal held the Russian's gaze. "I know a hundred women and children in South Sudan who are desperate to eat. I can pay them next to nothing and they'll be grateful for it."

"You'll need guards," one of Gorev's associates said. "They'll steal your diamonds."

"I was in the US military. I know some guys. Badass. Pissed at the world. No one fucks with my men."

"I have a man who will manage your operation. Oversee your guards," Lubanga said. "He will inspect every diamond. I get half the carats pulled from the river."

"A third," Cal said, knowing Lubanga expected pushback.

"Half. Or you get nothing."

"I'm the one paying the workers. Paying the guards. Taking all the risks. Without my workers, you'd have half of nothing."

"There are a dozen men here who would like this mining claim. They will give me half," Lubanga said.

Cal scanned the room. The men here were drinking and watching the sex show or fucking in the private rooms. "These men are easily distracted. They lack motivation. I wouldn't count on them to deliver a pile of dog shit. A third."

"Sixty/forty."

"Sixty-five/thirty-five," Cal countered.

Lubanga stared at him. Eventually he leaned back and said. "Done."

Cal was surprised he'd agreed, but then, Cal didn't really give a damn about the terms. He'd just wanted to draw out the conversation. Savvy needed to get back here soon, because now that that piece of business was done, he'd need to show irritation with her long absence.

Gorev reached for the Egyptian pendant that Cal had refused to sell until after the diamond concession had been negotiated. "Where did you get this?" he asked.

Cal gave a slight shake of his head. "So you can go direct to my source? I don't think so."

"I will give you fifty thousand for it."

"It's worth five times that." He mentally apologized to Morgan, who would freak if she knew he was assigning values to artifacts.

"Sure, if it were a legal sale at Christie's," Gorev said. "You are new to the antiquities market. You'll never get that much."

Like the diamond claim, Cal didn't care about selling. He just wanted to draw out the negotiation to give Savvy time. "A hundred and fifty grand."

"A hundred," Gorev said. "But only if you throw in the girl."

Sweat broke out on Savvy's brow. The device managed to bypass Lubanga's password to upload files to her cloud, but she couldn't *read* the files, not until after they were uploaded and she was on her own computer. All she could see was the list of files being uploaded.

She had no idea what the file said. Had someone in the CIA tipped Lubanga off? Did he know Cal was a Green Beret? That she was SAD?

Precious seconds ticked by as her mind raced with possibilities. If Lubanga knew their aliases, they were dead.

Shit. She and Cal had to leave. Now.

A noise sounded in the hall. A footstep?

There was only one excuse she could use for being in this room. She pulled her dress over her head and dropped it on the floor.

Only seventy-five percent of the hard disk had uploaded to her cloud. It would have to do. She closed the laptop and yanked the gadget from the USB port and tossed it out the porthole, then climbed on top of the bed, draping herself seductively, wearing nothing but the expensive lingerie she'd purchased in Nairobi a few days ago.

The door was shoved open fifteen seconds after she'd assumed her pose.

She flashed a seductive smile, as if she expected to greet Lubanga, then pouted at seeing one of Gorev's security guards. "Where is Jean Paul? I've been waiting *forever*."

The man's eyes narrowed. "What are you doing here?"

"Waiting for Jean Paul. He told me to come here."

"Mr. Lubanga doesn't screw whores."

"I'm not a whore!" She smiled and spread her legs for him. "I'm a courtesan."

He yanked her arm and pulled her from the bed. "Mr. Lubanga can decide what to do with you." He dragged her to the door.

A shriek in the hall caught everyone's attention. Dread shot down Cal's spine. Savvy had been caught.

He glanced toward the archway, keeping his gaze coolly indifferent. Curious. A guard dragged her through the opening.

He bolted to his feet. *Shit.* She wore nothing but a triangle of sexy lace over her crotch and a matching bra filled with her perfect breasts. She had an athletic build, faintly defined abs. More *Sports Illustrated* than Victoria's Secret model. Strength and beauty. He hoped everyone was distracted enough by her round breasts and ass and failed to see her as a threat.

"What the fuck is going on?" he asked as he shoved at the guard who was manhandling her.

The guard didn't budge.

Cal elbowed him in the face, a quick jab to show he meant business. "She's mine."

The guard fell back, releasing her.

Freed, Savvy tried to crawl away. She let out a convincing sob as she cowered, not from the guard, but from Cal. "I'm sorry, Mani."

It was vital he stay in character. He narrowed his gaze and loomed over her. "What the fuck did you do, Jamie?"

Blood dripped from the guard's nose. "I found the bitch in Mr. Lubanga's cabin. In his bed."

He swung his gaze back to Savvy. "In his *bed*?" His voice came out low and angry. "In his fucking bed?" He grabbed her hair and pulled her so she was on her knees before him. "Were you trying to replace me?"

"No! I just thought…" She looked down and let out a sob. "I'm sorry…"

There was no room for softness here. The salon had gone silent. Even the sex show had ceased. Every eye was on him and Savvy. Mani Kalenga was ruthless. Nasty. And violent.

"You ungrateful whore." He raised his arm and backhanded her across the face. Full force. The big gaudy ring on his finger connected with her cheekbone.

The slap of skin to skin was horrific. A sound he was certain to relive in his nightmares for the rest of his days.

Her head snapped back, and she toppled to the floor again. She stared dazedly up at the ceiling. He wasn't sure if her reaction was real or not.

His hand stung from the blow, and he shook it out as he watched a tear spill from her eye. She cupped her cheek, then her gaze snapped into focus, and she attempted to crawl backward, on her back, like some sort of messed-up crab walk of terror.

She was trying to get away from the brute who'd hit her. From him. And Mani would never let her get away with something like that.

He grabbed her hair and jerked her to her feet. "You worthless whore." He delivered the words in a cold, low tone, the one his asshole uncle had used when he'd had too much to drink and got violent. He would stand on the front lawn and demand his children and wife stop hiding in Cal's house and get their asses home, leaving only when Cal's dad stepped on the porch with a shotgun and told his sister's husband to get the hell off his property.

Tonight, Cal had to channel his inner Uncle George.

"You think you can dump me for someone richer? You think I'll let you go that easy?" He grabbed her ass and pulled her to him. "You're mine until I'm done with you."

His arm was a vise across her back. With his other hand, he cupped the back of her head and further brutalized her, this time with an angry, forceful kiss.

She struggled against him, but he held her close, kissing her with violence so he wouldn't have to hit her again.

It was one or the other—more blows or violent kisses.

Her struggles slowed and then transformed. She gripped the lapel of his jacket and kissed him back. Her tongue was hot and insistent in his mouth.

Was she acting? It didn't feel like an act. Didn't taste fake. Her mouth was sweet and urgent on his, and to his horror, he went rock hard.

She let go of his lapels in favor of circling his neck. She rubbed her body against his, and he wanted to strip, to be skin to skin.

Jesus. They needed to get out of this ballroom. Off of this boat. He dragged her toward one of the private rooms, to the disappointed shouts of several of the men. He pushed her through the door, then slammed it closed and locked it.

Dammit, this was no refuge. It was little more than a cell. With cameras. A dead end.

Was their only choice now to have sex in front of cameras? He wanted to be inside her. Hell yeah, he wanted her. But not like this. Not for the titillation of others. Not playing a role.

Cassius wanted to have sex with Freya. Not Mani and Jamie. Not even Cassius and Savvy. He wanted Freya. And Freya wasn't in this room. Nor was Cassius.

He planted his mouth on her neck as he backed her up against the wall. He lifted her, wrapping her thighs around his hips. His erection settled between her thighs. He rocked his hips, making them both feel good with the friction.

She made a sound low in her throat.

"I want you," he whispered as he kissed her neck and nipped her earlobe. "But not like this."

"I know."

"What do we do?" He covered her mouth with his. Cameras. He couldn't forget the cameras. He couldn't make it obvious they were talking.

Her tongue stroked his as his erection pressed to her clit.

Jesus. Kissing her was intense. Touching her was even better.

"Mimic?" she whispered. "Or…I could go down on you."

He groaned. He wanted that. Had fantasized about it for months. But not like this. Never like this.

He kissed her again. He'd just have to risk dragging her out of the room and off the boat. It was the only solution he wouldn't regret. If they lived long enough to look back on this night.

She slid a hand between them and into his pants. She wrapped her fingers around his cock, and he thought his eyes might roll back in his head. He knew she was trying to make this easier for him. His body blocked the cameras. No one could see her hand on his cock.

"Let me suck you, Mani," she said loud enough for the recording devices to pick up. "Let me make it up to you."

Her hand felt so good, and this situation was utterly twisted.

Behind him, the door burst open. Flimsy fucking locks.

Before he could set Savvy down, he was yanked backward and Savvy ripped from his arms. She dropped to the floor.

Anton. *Fuck*. He'd forgotten about Anton. She must've done something to ditch him.

The guard he'd elbowed in the face was more than happy to take a swing at Cal while Anton went after Savvy.

"You fucking bitch!" Anton shouted as he backhanded her.

White-hot rage shot through Cal. Revulsion rose too. He'd done the same thing minutes ago. He lunged toward Anton, but the guard nailed him in the stomach, then pushed him back.

"I will fuck you while your American watches." Anton yanked her head back, exposing her throat. "Then I will cut you right here."

Cal elbowed the guard in the gut, then shoved his head into the wall. The guard dropped, unconscious, clearing the path to Anton.

Anton's hands were fumbling with his fly as Cal came at him. Cal yanked him away from Savvy and grabbed him by the throat. He slammed his back against the wall. "Touch her again, and I will rip your fucking throat out."

A knife appeared in Anton's hand. He slashed toward Cal's stomach. Cal turned the blade back and shoved, his hand wrapped around Anton's on the knife. The long, sharp blade pierced Anton's gut with ease.

"I told you she's mine." He jerked on the Russian's wrist, making sure the knife cut a wide swath through his belly. Blood poured over Cal's hand, soaking his sleeve and spilling onto his jacket and shirt.

Anton slumped forward, mouth open in shock. He slowly slid to the floor.

Cal took Savvy's hand. "Time to go."

She nodded. Her eyes had the glazed look of shock, even horror. He'd bet it was an act. But damn, she was good. She gave a slow, almost numb nod and followed him out the door, her hand clasped in his.

All eyes followed them across the room as he approached their host. Still holding Savvy's hand, he picked up the pendant with his other hand, smearing it with Anton's blood. "A hundred and ten. And the girl is mine."

The Russian nodded. "Done. Leave the pendant. Money will be delivered to your hotel."

"No. I want the money now." He slipped the pendant in a blood-soaked jacket pocket and turned for the door.

"Fine," Gorev said. "You will have it now."

Cal turned to see Gorev nod to a servant.

Precious minutes ticked by as they waited. He should have left the artifact and allowed the money to be delivered. He hadn't because it would have looked suspicious. Same with just walking out, leaving the artifact behind.

Savvy stood meekly at his side, leaning against him. He wrapped an arm around her waist, reminding him she was nearly naked. "She needs her gown."

Lubanga was silent for a long moment, then said, "No. If it is in my stateroom, it is mine."

He really couldn't argue that point.

A servant arrived with stacks of hundred-dollar bills in a briefcase. Gorev counted out eleven stacks. Cal flipped through them to make sure they were all hundreds and dropped them in a cloth sack the servant provided. He then set the pendant on the table. Transaction complete, they turned to leave.

"We haven't discussed the other artifacts," Gorev said.

Cal didn't bother to turn back. "I'll be in touch."

"Meet me in Kinshasa in a week, Mr. Kalenga," Lubanga said. "I will have the paperwork for your mining claim drawn up and ready to sign."

Cal gave a sharp nod. He and Savvy escaped the ballroom at last.

Chapter Eleven

Savvy didn't take a deep breath until they were in their SUV, driving away from the dock. They couldn't speak, because odds were, the truck had been bugged while they were at the party. It had been an unavoidable risk.

They couldn't waste time scanning for a bug when they needed distance from the boat. Cal was bound to be freaked out about hitting her. Not to mention he'd killed a man.

Well, Anton might not die, but no one was rushing to get him medical aid, so odds were he was dead already.

Not that Cal would freak out over the death. She knew for a fact he'd killed in combat. But this was his first kill as part of a covert op. This wasn't a battle with enemy lines drawn. It was different when there was deception involved.

She'd set Anton up. She'd used him to escape the room and had enraged him by humiliating him. It was her fault Cal had killed Anton. Her fault Anton—no matter how vile he was as a person—was dead.

Cal had been magnificent in his role as Mani, staying in character even when everything went to hell. She'd feared his acting ability would fall short, but he'd delivered a flawless performance. So good she wasn't sure if it was Mani or Cal who'd kissed her with such intensity.

It would take a while to reach the Japanese sedan they'd purchased this morning and parked near an ocean beach. They would abandon the SUV and head to a new hotel. This would buy them time to regroup and figure out their next step.

She needed to tell Cal about Zagreus.

And the fact that this had been a kill mission—except now, she wouldn't kill Lubanga. Not until she knew who in the CIA had leaked the operation to the target.

Cal drove, taking a long, slow Surveillance Detection Route through the city. If the car was bugged, they were being tracked anyway, but at least this way, they'd have a few minutes to change cars. The sedan couldn't be bugged—no one even knew it existed—and they'd take yet another long SDR before heading to their next hotel.

It was hard to believe it was only just after twenty-one hundred hours. They'd been at the party for about an hour. All that prep and days of travel for one intense, horrible hour, and they were done. At least he hoped they were.

If Savvy hadn't managed to copy Lubanga's files, he couldn't see a way to get back on the boat. The ruse of her trying to trade up sugar daddies would never work again. The CIA would have to send someone else.

Tomorrow, they'd fly to Camp Citron, and he'd be Sergeant First Class Cassius Callahan again. She'd be Savannah James. They'd part ways when he returned to the US in a week. They might cross paths again in another country, another deployment, but more likely, he'd never see her again.

That was partly why he'd turned down her offer of sex the other night. He wanted to be able to walk away from her at the end of the op with a clear conscience. But after tonight, was that even possible?

He squeezed the steering wheel. He'd backhanded her, then kissed her, brutally. Forcefully. But the worst part was he'd gotten a fucking hard-on in the process.

She shivered and turned on the heat. She still wore nothing but underwear. He'd offered her his suit jacket, but it had been damp with Anton's blood and she'd declined. Instead, she'd piled the stacks of hundred-dollar bills in the jacket and tossed the cloth bag out the window. Good thinking. It was probably bugged.

He reached out and put an arm around her, pulling her close to his side, sharing his body heat. She curled up against him as he drove through the dark streets of Dar es Salaam.

He came to a stop at a red light, and she reached up and turned his face, pulling his mouth down to hers. She kissed him, openmouthed and deep. A connection he needed in the wake of their forced silence. Her tongue slid against his, taking, giving. He responded in kind.

A car honked, and he lifted his head to see the light had changed. He pressed the accelerator, still holding her close but his focus again on the road and the SDR. They needed to be alert for followers. Any sign of a tail and they'd have to lose them before going to the sedan, or they'd have to abandon the sedan—which held all their supplies.

With a hundred and ten thousand dollars, they'd get by, but it would be better if they had access to Savvy's spy gadgets. After an hour of seemingly aimless driving, Savvy gave him the thumbs-up. It was safe to head to the sedan now. There'd been no sign they were being followed.

Twenty minutes later, they pulled into a parking lot near the ocean. The sedan was parked across the street next to an open-air market that was nothing but shuttered stalls this time of night.

He unbuttoned his shirt and handed it to her. At least the blood was dried now and wouldn't stain her skin. With the market closed, there weren't many people around, but she'd still draw attention crossing the street in nothing but a bra and underwear. This close to the water, they might look like a couple that had opted to go skinny-dipping, with her clothes being caught by a wave, so they shared his.

Not something that would be approved of in Tanzania—where public displays of affection were frowned upon—but better than the alternative, being arrested as foreign agents.

They could only hope it was too dark for anyone to notice the blood on the white shirt.

She donned the shirt and buttoned it up. He grabbed the jacket wrapped around the money, and together they crossed the street. They reached the sedan without incident and within a minute were back on the road. Savvy did a quick scan of the car with a bug detector, coming up empty as expected. She scanned the money too, just in case. It was clean.

"What will happen to it? The money?" he asked.

"It will fund more missions like this one. A small portion of Drugov's money was redirected to fund Mani Kalenga's bank accounts. It was faster than going through channels and getting all the right forms signed. Not every project requires buying cars and chartering planes, but it's nice to have the money when needed. You and I will both be signing forms in triplicate when we get back, documenting where every dollar went along with where this money came from."

She climbed into the backseat. A glance in the rearview mirror showed her changing into a T-shirt and sweatpants, which she was able to retrieve by pulling down the seat to reach her suitcase in the trunk.

"Can you grab me a tee as well?" he asked.

She did, and he pulled it over his head at the next traffic light. They settled into silence again as he drove down side streets and main thoroughfares through the city. He wasn't ready to talk to her about what had happened on the boat, not when he couldn't look into her eyes as he apologized for all he'd had to say and do.

Things he'd said about her mouth and body, the way he'd objectified her. It was the role she'd signed up for, but that didn't mean it hadn't cut them both to play it out in front of men who saw her as a possession.

After thirty minutes of driving, Savvy said, "We can't go to the hotel I chose when we were at Camp Citron."

"Why not?"

"We need to hide until I go through the data I uploaded from Lubanga's computer."

"You got in?" He'd guessed she had, or she would have found a way to signal their efforts had been a bust, but still, it was a relief.

"Yeah. I copied about seventy-five percent of his files. It should be enough."

"And we need to hide because?"

"I think we were compromised—by someone in the Agency."

She didn't elaborate, and he didn't press. There would be plenty of time to debrief when they were out of the car and safely tucked away in an anonymous hotel. He felt exposed out here—even though they'd changed cars and swept for bugs. "So where do we go?"

She pulled a cell phone from the glove box—one of the phones she'd purchased in Nairobi. She tapped the screen. After a few minutes she said. "Got us an Airbnb. One bedroom, one bath. It's a pool house on a larger gated estate in a quiet neighborhood. Owner is expecting us in thirty minutes."

"That fast this time of night?"

"Yep. I promised him a hundred-dollar bonus."

Considering hotel rooms could be pretty cheap here—some only fifteen dollars a night—this was an extravagant payout for late arrival, but considering the stacks of Benjamins in the back, it wasn't exactly a problem. He was more concerned about putting innocent people at risk, but that couldn't be helped. At least no one would know where they were.

"How did you get the Airbnb account set up so fast?"

"I did that when we were in Kenya. Just in case. I'd already checked the listings and put out feelers but opted to stay in the same hotel as Anton." She cleared her throat at that.

Anton, who was probably dead.

Not that Cal grieved for the prick. He'd been about to rape Savvy. He just wondered if his body had already been thrown overboard or if Gorev would wait until they were at sea.

The phone GPS issued directions, and he followed the voice, taking a few wrong turns on purpose, still looking for a tail. Savvy had warned him to never directly drive to their destination. The GPS could recalculate their route.

"What's our cover story?" he asked. "The landlord is going to want an explanation for a last-minute late-night arrival."

"We arrived in Dar today, checked in to our hotel, and went to the beach, then out to dinner. While we were out, our hotel room was robbed and my jewelry was taken. We were just getting ready for bed when I discovered the theft. The hotel accused me of lying about the jewelry since nothing else was missing. I don't feel safe there anymore and insisted we leave."

"Solid."

"Thank you."

"You're pretty good at this spy thing."

"Thanks. You're pretty good at the soldier thing. And you were great tonight."

"I was horrible tonight," he said

"Well, you were great at being horrible."

He tightened his fingers on the steering wheel again. "Yeah. That's what I'm afraid of."

The phone GPS issued another direction, which he ignored. They'd been only fifteen minutes from the house when Savvy made the arrangements, but it took the full thirty and a few extra to get there. While he drove, Savvy applied makeup to her face, covering her bruises.

At last they reached the gated estate, and he punched in the code that Savvy provided for the gate. Their host met them in front of the pool house, which was set apart from the main house by a separate driveway and garden. The pool nestled between the two buildings at the back of the estate. "How much is this place a night?" he asked.

"Sixty-five US dollars."

In the US, a place like this would easily be several hundred a night. He felt like they were cheating their hosts, but many factors led to the low cost of housing in Tanzania, not the least of which was the aftereffects of the Rwandan genocide and lengthy war that engulfed Zaire/DRC.

Their host was kind and efficient, quickly showing them around the house. He expressed remorse at their experience at the hotel and promised they were quite safe on his property. Each guest was given a separate gate code, which was only valid for the length of their stay. They paid cash in advance for a week. What Airbnb didn't know wouldn't hurt them.

The homeowner left them, and at last, they were alone. Safe and anonymous.

After bringing in their bags, he closed and locked the door, then leaned back against it. Savvy went straight to the freezer and pulled out an ice cube tray. She dumped a handful of ice into a towel and held it to her cheek.

The cheek he'd hit.

Fuck. They'd been driving for hours, and she'd needed ice. He hadn't given her so much as an ibuprofen. He crossed the small room to stand inches in front of her. He studied her expression but didn't touch her. "Does it hurt?"

"Not too bad."

He lifted the ice pack from her cheek to inspect the bruise in the full light of the kitchen. The makeup downplayed it, but he could see the swelling. He gently pressed his lips to the welt along the bone.

"I'm so sorry," he whispered.

She held his gaze. "I'm not. You did what you had to do." She tucked her forehead against his chest. "But I'm sorry for putting you in that position. Sorry you were forced to do that."

He cradled her head between his palms and gently nudged her face up so she would see his eyes. "I'm glad it was me, not someone else from Camp Citron. Not Harry. It means a lot to me that you trusted me with that role."

"You're the only one I trusted for this mission." She pressed the ice pack back to her cheek.

He cleared his throat. This was the part that would be hardest to say. But he had to acknowledge it. "When I...when I got hard—it—it wasn't because I'd hit you. That isn't what turned me on."

Her nostrils flared, and she blinked. "I know." She took a deep breath. "It was an intense moment. You handled it perfectly by kissing me like you did. You saved us both by turning the violence sexual."

And he could have fucked her in that room, with cameras rolling. He'd been hard and eager. It would have been so easy. And it might've happened if Anton hadn't interrupted.

She stepped back from him. "You want to take a shower? I'm going to make some tea."

He took that to mean she needed space. He could give her that. "Sure. You planning to work tonight?"

She shook her head. "The files are probably encrypted. I'm too brain-dead to deal with that tonight. I'm going to have some tea. Take a shower. Then try to sleep."

He wanted to invite her to share his shower, but it didn't feel right, not after he'd struck her and then violently kissed her.

The next move was hers.

The three-quarter bathroom had a square, tiled shower stall. Small, but he didn't need luxury. All he wanted was to wash the smell of Anton's blood from his skin. The water quickly heated, and in a matter of seconds, he was soaped from head to toe—well trained by three-minute showers at Camp Citron. Done washing in just over a minute, he stood in the hot spray, thinking of all the things he wanted to say to Savvy but didn't know how.

He was in awe of her, the way she risked every part of herself for her job. It was a kind of patriotism that was beyond his imagining. He risked his life and his health for his country on every mission. He understood that.

But she risked her body. Risked degradation. She'd allowed herself to be objectified in addition to endangering her life. She'd exposed herself to rape and torture. And if she were caught, the US government would disavow her. No rescue would be forthcoming.

No hope. No justice.

He hadn't quite appreciated the extent of the risks she took until he was sitting in the middle of a room with men who would use, abuse, and discard her without a second thought. And she'd walked into that room fearlessly presenting herself as a whore in order to get the job done.

He'd been such an ass to her in the months he'd known her. He'd never given her the respect she deserved. He'd openly denigrated her because her job required her to lie, manipulate, and risk others. But that was nothing compared to what she was willing to do. She asked nothing that she wouldn't do herself.

She took a blow to the face without complaint and had thanked him for delivering it.

He'd been in lust with her for months, but now he was in awe.

The door to the bathroom opened. He froze in the hot spray. His heart rate kicked up. He held his breath and waited for her to speak, join him, or leave.

After a long moment, she said, "I changed my mind about the tea. Decided I need to shower instead. Do you want company?"

His cock thickened even faster than he could say, "Yes."

The curtain shifted, and she stepped into the square stall, her perfect, athletic body as naked as his own. He leaned against the wall to give her room as she stood in the spray. She tilted her head back to let the water drench her hair and run down her beautiful body.

He wanted to touch her, to run his hands over her slick breasts, to cup her ass and kiss her as the steamy water rained down. The fact that she'd stepped nude into his shower was a sure sign she invited his touch, but still, he needed her permission. Direct and unequivocal.

He wanted her to want *him*. And not because she was reacting to a traumatic evening.

She ran her fingers through her long, dark hair, her eyes closed as hot water sluiced down her skin. Her arms and face were darker, freckled by the sun, while her breasts and torso were a pale, spotless peach.

Her eyes opened, and she held his gaze. She worked shampoo into lather in her hair, creating rivulets of bubbles that ran between her breasts or over the top, then down her belly and into the triangle of dark curls he wanted to explore with fingers and tongue.

She reached down to touch herself and his gaze snapped up to meet hers. She smiled and took a step closer to him in the already confined space. Her breasts brushed against his chest.

"Touch me. Please. I want—need—your hands on me."

That was as direct as it could get, and he ran a hand down her side, cupping her breast briefly before sliding lower to cup her ass and pull her snug against him.

She touched him in response, running her hands over his shoulders, down his arms, circling his waist to his back. "Your body is beautiful, Cal. A work of art."

"It's work. I don't know about art."

She laughed. "A masterpiece. I love watching you work out on base. You have this intense focus. It's the only time you'd let me look at you, because you're blind to everything but the task at hand."

Her words hit him in the gut. She hadn't intended them as a blow, but he felt it just the same. "I'm sorry. I put up barriers to you because you scare me."

Her lips twitched. "I scare a badass Special Forces soldier?" Her mouth bloomed into a full smile. "I like the sound of that."

He picked her up, the ache in his gut relaxing a fraction. "Oh, Freya, you're the scariest woman I've ever met. The first moment I met you, I wanted to possess you."

She wrapped her legs around his hips. This time, there was nothing between them. Just her wet, slick body and his ever-thickening erection.

"You could've had me then. You can have me now." She slipped her arms around his neck and kissed him. Her mouth was open and hot, her tongue taking his, offering absolution for his words and actions.

In spite of everything, she wanted him. From the way she kissed, he could believe she needed him, needed this, as much as he did.

His need was deep. Desperate. And not just for her body. Hell, he didn't know exactly what he needed, he just wanted to sink into this moment. To lose all sense of time and place and just take in the perfection that was this woman whose last name he didn't even know.

He kissed her, his mouth taking all she offered and more. Deep and carnal and so hot, his erection was on the diamond end of the Mohs' scale. He raised his head and looked into her eyes. Water drops landed on her lashes, and he swiped them away so she could see. "You sure you want this, Freya?"

Her beautiful lips spread to reveal a row of white teeth with one canine slightly out of alignment. An endearing imperfection, because he only saw it when she smiled. "Make love to me, Cassius."

His rarely used name on her lips was damn hot.

He shut off the water and stepped from the shower, not bothering with towels as he carried her to the bed.

They both needed this. Tomorrow, they'd head back to Camp Citron. Tonight, they needed to escape, this brief moment of connection when he could be Cassius, and she could be Freya.

He set her slippery, wet body on the bed and stood above her, staring, her pale skin in contrast to the colorful geometric design of the cotton blanket. For all they'd been through in the last few days, this was the first time he'd seen her fully naked. He was eager to spread her legs and see all of her.

He wanted to taste her. To touch her. To make her come hard and fast and then again slower, longer. More than anything, he wanted to connect with her—not just physically. He wanted the sharing of bodies to be the emotional connection they both needed.

She smiled, flashing that crooked tooth, and sat up, meeting him at the foot of the bed. She ran her hand down his body, pausing when she reached his erection. She licked those beautiful lips and wrapped her hands around him, stroking him from base to tip.

He watched her hands, enjoying the visual as much as the touch. Her light fingers a contrast to his dark penis. Her gaze fixed on the same place where she touched him. "So beautiful," she murmured. She leaned forward, as if she was going to take him into her mouth.

He stopped her. "Not...now."

She raised a brow. "You don't like oral sex?"

He drew her body up, so they were chest to chest. "I love it. But...all the things I had to say about your mouth—I hated treating you like that. It's one thing for me to have fantasies about a woman I've been attracted to for months, but another to say crude things about your lips as if it's my right, to diminish you by crassly boasting about your 'talents' to assholes who use and abuse."

She cupped his face. "You weren't talking about me. Mani was talking about Jamie. Neither person is real. I knew it wasn't *you*."

"I'm glad. But still...tonight...this is for you. I want to give you everything. Let me worship your body as you deserve. Let me show you that I'm not that guy. The only thing I want from your mouth is to make you scream with orgasm. And to kiss you. Because I love how you taste."

She leaned into him, her breasts meeting his chest, her arms wrapping around his neck, and her mouth on his. "I love the way you taste too." She slid her tongue inside.

He met the stroke of her tongue with his own. He caressed her body, sliding his hands down her back, cupping her ass. Being skin to skin with her was better than his fantasies.

She scooted back on the bed, and he followed, his body sliding against hers. He kissed her and touched her. He was ready to explode at the feel of her hands on him. He left her mouth to kiss her breasts. Lick her nipples, suck the tips. "What do you like, Freya?" he asked.

"You."

"But what do you want me to do? Where do you want to be touched?"

She took his hand and pulled it down to her thighs. She placed his fingers on her clit. He grinned and stroked the sensitive spot, then he followed the path of his hand with his mouth. At last, he reached the spread of her thighs. He looked his fill before dipping his head down to lick her clitoris. He took his time with it, like she was his favorite flavor of ice cream.

He felt her body release tension. She sank into the mattress, relaxing at the sensual stroke. He grazed his teeth over the bundle of nerves and she jolted as she gave a gasp of pleasure. Then he licked again as his fingers explored the rest of her, tracing her labia, spreading them and slipping a finger inside. She was wet and hot and eager for him.

He was hard and ready, but he'd only just begun exploring. His tongue moved lower, joining his fingers. He slipped inside, and she made a sound that made him even harder.

He licked her slow, long, and deep. Savoring the pleasure he gave her, enjoying the feel of her nails raking his scalp as he licked and sucked, bringing her to the edge of release. When he was certain she couldn't take it anymore, he lifted his head and moved, his skin sliding against hers as he positioned himself to finally give them both what they needed.

His hard cock settled at her vaginal opening, and he teased her with the head. He hadn't had sex without a condom in years and had never done so without being in a committed relationship, taking the intimacy of this moment to the next level. He watched as he played, slipping the head inside, feeling her clench and gasp, then retreating before he filled her. Teasing them both to the aching point.

He pulled back and went down on her again, stroking her clit with his tongue, then in one rapid move, he shifted and slid his cock deep inside her, going as far as she could take him in one deep, hard thrust. She groaned and gasped and clenched tight, and he was lost, buried inside this woman, finally as connected as two people could be.

He rolled so she straddled him, and he gazed up at her as she rocked, riding him, her breasts bouncing, her eyes closed. Another roll and she was beneath him again. He thrust in a slow, sensual rhythm, prolonging the buildup and ratcheting the intensity higher.

Her thighs wrapped around his hips, and she made low, soft sounds that threatened to push him over the edge. She was utterly beautiful as she shared her body with him. She took everything he gave her and panted for more.

He increased the rhythm, and she let out a soft, guttural noise as she clenched down on him. His body coiled for release, but he wouldn't get there before she did. He slid a hand between them and stroked her clit with his thumb. She gripped his shoulders. Her pants became a whimper, then a pleasured groan as her body quivered and quaked.

No longer holding back, he stroked hard and fast. His body pulsed as orgasm rocked through him. Intense, just like everything else when it came to her.

He collapsed and rolled to the side, still inside her. He held her against him as his heart rate slowed, then he shifted while kissing her, leaving her body but remaining skin to skin. No way was he ready for space between them. He rained kisses on her face as he stroked her back.

Wearing a dreamy smile, she opened her eyes and said, "Thanks, I needed that."

He kissed her neck. "Me too. And I'm not done. Just resting."

She laughed even as her eyes drifted closed. "That's good, because it's my turn to make you feel good."

He kissed her temple. "You already have, Freya."

After a few minutes, he rose and cleaned up in the bathroom, then walked through the small one-bedroom house, turning off lights, making sure they were locked up tight. He grabbed the bag with their handguns and brought it into the bedroom.

Sound from the bathroom told him Savvy was in the shower again. He checked the guns, then placed one on each nightstand.

Savvy returned to the bedroom, face scrubbed of makeup and hair smelling of tea tree conditioner. They settled into the bed together. He pulled her nude body to his, spooning with her in the dark room. They lay in silence for a long time before her breathing evened out into a sleep rhythm. Cal was still wide-awake. The sex had energized him. It had been deeply intimate in a way he hadn't expected. It had been years…maybe forever, since he'd had sex like that. It had in no way resembled the mindless screw he'd once imagined sharing with this woman.

He cared about her, more than he wanted to. And after seeing her in action on the job, what she did for a living terrified the hell out of him.

Chapter Twelve

Sharing a bed with Sergeant First Class Cassius Callahan—after finally getting physical—was a transformative experience. Savvy watched the big, beautiful, naked man as he slept. The power had gone off at four in the morning, and they'd kicked off the covers in the increasingly hot bedroom, leaving Cal's body exposed to her avid gaze.

Power outages were common in Tanzania, where only one-third of households had electricity at all. She and Cal had both woken at the sudden silence of the air conditioner. A quick check using her cell phone showed it was a problem with the grid and not of special concern to them. Power was expected to return to the city in eight to twelve hours. They'd gone back to sleep—after making love again in the silent darkness.

Now dawn had risen, and the bright sunrise breached the curtains and caressed his smooth chestnut skin. She'd never seen a more beautiful body. That it belonged to this soldier who was the epitome of honor and strength made her heart squeeze. She could—almost certainly would—fall in love with him. But they both knew there couldn't be a real future for them. Not when she was SAD stationed abroad and would have more missions like this, and he was Special Forces, based at Fort Campbell but spending months at a time deployed in whatever hotspot the Army chose to send him. All they could have was now.

But she'd take now, without hesitation or regret.

For the rest of her life, she'd guard her memories of this night with him. She knew the fragility of memories, how they could be tainted or lost in a swirl of emotion. But last night had meant something deeper to him too. He didn't need to say it for her to know it was true. A man didn't make love like that if he didn't care. And she would hold on to that knowledge forever, no matter what happened when this mission was behind them.

She reached out and touched him, running her hand over his chest, down his abs. His cock thickened and his mouth curved in a smile, but he didn't open his eyes. She leaned down and licked his nipple, which puckered. His smile deepened.

She followed the path of her hand with her tongue. By the time she reached his penis, he was fully erect. She watched his handsome face as she took him in both hands and stroked the shaft. "Will you let me go down on you now?" she asked.

He made a sound low in his throat and nodded.

She leaned down to take the tip in her mouth, and his eyes popped open. She held his gaze as she ran her tongue around the head, then opened wide and took him as deep as she could. She sucked as she stroked the base. He was hard and smooth and perfect, and she loved giving him this pleasure. She ran her tongue along the shaft from base to tip, then sucked on him some more, making eye contact as she did so.

Hot brown eyes stared back at her. He threaded his fingers in her hair. "So beautiful to see your mouth on me like that, Freya. So hot."

She released him, keeping a hand on his shaft and stroking as she said, "You shouldn't call me that."

He gave a slight shake of his head as he ran a thumb over her bottom lip. "In bed, I refuse to call you anything else. You aren't Jamie. I'm not having sex with Savvy. I'm making love with Freya, the person, not the covert operator."

She could argue that Freya was the covert operator. Savvy was just a fake name and didn't change who she was.

But then she remembered the real meaning behind her alias and was glad he only wanted to call her Freya as they shared their bodies. She ran her tongue over his cock again, then said, "Okay, Cassius. But only in bed."

She went down on him again, and he wrapped his fingers in her hair. His hips thrust upward, pressing as deep as she could take him. "What's your last name?" he asked, his voice husky as she pleasured him.

She used the excuse of having a full mouth to avoid answering. It hadn't been her fault he'd learned her real first name, but she wouldn't violate the oath she'd taken by revealing her last without cause.

She released him from her mouth and straddled him. He slid inside easily, sending pleasure rippling through her. She rode him, using her knees to control his thrusts. He sucked on her nipples and stroked her clit. Pleasure swirled from the points of contact, and she came hard, shuddering and groaning with the sharp, powerful orgasm.

He rolled her to her back as her body continued to pulse, and thrust into her, bringing her higher as he reached his own climax. The room was stiflingly hot with the closed windows, and they were both sweaty and smelled of sex, and she was ridiculously happy. She laughed with the joy of it.

They made a good team, in and out of bed.

He kissed her as his breathing returned to normal. "You just fulfilled a fantasy of mine."

"What's that?"

"Waking up to oral sex."

She smiled. She'd been careful to make sure he was awake before she'd made that move, but it was close enough. Knowing it was a fantasy of his, she might be even bolder tomorrow, assuming they were still here.

Shit. She needed to send him back to Camp Citron now so she could finish the mission. Except, maybe she couldn't, because they'd been compromised. It might not be safe to send him back to Djibouti.

All at once, her happy mood evaporated.

She'd hoped to protect him from the truth, to give him plausible deniability, but she had to tell him everything. Now.

Cal was feeling about as relaxed and happy as a soldier could while on a covert op in an African country where being found could mean death. But then Freya's demeanor changed. It was subtle, but pressed close to her as he was, naked and exposed, it wasn't something he could miss, even in a postorgasm haze.

"What's going on?" he asked. He heard the tension in his own voice and knew that, as much as they'd shared, he still harbored a remnant of suspicion when it came to Savannah James.

In a flash, Freya the lover was gone. She was Savvy. Had always been Savvy. Any glimpse of Freya had probably been a trick of his mind.

The thought triggered an ache. Not her fault he'd seen something that wasn't there.

She rose from the bed and turned to her suitcase. She pulled out a silk robe she'd purchased in keeping with her role of Jamie the courtesan. "I need to download Lubanga's files and see what we got."

"No electricity."

"I've got a fully charged portable satellite hotspot."

"You said last night we might be compromised. Why?"

"When I was uploading Lubanga's files, I saw a document named Zagreus."

Cal felt the blood drain from his face. He imagined he'd turned some sickly shade of gray. "What the fuck? How is that possible?"

"Either Special Forces or the CIA gave him information."

"SOCOM wouldn't—"

"You'd be surprised what they would do. But I'm with you on this one. I don't think it was SOCOM."

"How many people knew the code name?"

She shrugged. "Not many. I named him, by the way. The name is unique. Relatively unknown." She flushed. "My mom was a Greek scholar. She wrote a paper on Zagreus. I chose the name for her."

He frowned. Was this mission personal for her, in a way she hadn't told him? "Does Lubanga have anything to do with your family?"

Her eyes widened. "No. The CIA wouldn't allow that. It just…was meant to be a reminder of why I do this shitty job. Both my parents were scholars. My dad studied Vikings—hence my name. Dad named me. Mom named my brother, Apollo. But there's no connection between my parents and this mission."

She had a brother. Parents. It shouldn't surprise him, but still, it did. She seemed so very alone. As if she'd sprung to life from foamy waves, like Aphrodite. "What happened to them? Why *do* you do this shitty job?"

She shook her head. He knew she'd refuse to answer, but it had been worth a try.

"So we're compromised." He rose from the bed. "What do we do now?"

"I need to go through the files, to be certain. But you need to leave Tanzania. Head back to Kenya, or catch a flight from Dar back to Djibouti."

"We," he said. "We leave together."

"I can't leave."

"Why not?"

She held his gaze for a long moment. Finally, she said, "It depends on what I find in the files, but…for now, officially, my mission isn't complete."

"Your mission was to get the files from Lubanga. You did that."

Her jaw tightened. Her eyes flared with…remorse?

His stomach clenched. "What haven't you told me, Savvy?"

"I'm sorry, Cal. The mission changed after I first recruited you. I didn't know about the change until Seth and Harry arrived. Then Harry—"

"Skip the excuses and get to the fucking point."

"Lubanga's rise in power is a threat to the stability of DRC. The US wants him removed as a player."

"Removed how?"

"I was ordered to kill him."

Chapter Thirteen

Cal fixed Savannah James with a hard glare as his stomach churned. The mission was assassination, and she hadn't bothered to give him a heads-up at any time in the days they'd been traveling together? Anger struck him mute, but in his head, he was yelling.

He turned, looking for something to punch or kick, but this was a rental. Safe. If their hosts heard the sound of furniture breaking or him shouting at the conniving woman he'd just spent the night screwing, they'd be out on their asses.

His hands shook with the desire to punch something. He finally managed to speak, the words came out low with restrained anger. "Why. The fuck. Didn't you. Tell me?"

She took a step forward, as if she would touch him. He flinched and stepped back.

Her eyes widened with alarm, as if she thought he might hit her.

That caused his anger to ratchet up higher. He'd been gutted by the need to hit her last night, and she knew it. He would never lose control like that for real. That had been Mani, a character she created and he had to inhabit. He breathed deeply through his nose, containing the anger. Releasing it in slow, even breaths.

"I'm sorry," she whispered. "I…I didn't tell you because if you'd refused the mission, Harry would've been sent in your place."

He understood why she couldn't work with Harry, but that didn't excuse not telling him. Not giving him a choice in this. "If we're caught, the US will disavow us. My years of military service would mean nothing. My family would be told I was a traitor. They'd tell my mother I was here to cut a deal to traffic in Congolese diamonds. Do you know how many family members she lost in the wars? It would gut her to think one of her sons had joined the men who are raping her homeland."

"My plan was to send you back to Camp Citron before I killed him. You can still go. This is my mission. Not yours."

"Did you plan to kill Lubanga last night?"

"No. My orders were to kill him, but I wanted to get his hard drive first."

He took a step back. "Copying the hard drive wasn't your mission? We risked ourselves for...*nothing*?"

"Not nothing! My original mission was to copy the drive. When Seth changed the mission, I decided to do both. I mean, how could we pass up the opportunity for this kind of intel? And the original order wasn't rescinded. Once he's taken out, someone else is bound to step in to run his operation. We need to know all the players. How they operate. So I made the call. Data first. Then I planned to send you back to Camp Citron and do what the CIA ordered me to do."

"Lying comes so easy to you, doesn't it?"

She blanched. "I lie for my job, but I'm not lying now." Her eyes teared. "I was trying to protect you. If you didn't know about the kill order, you'd have no problem denying it."

He doubted her tears were real. Was anything that had passed between them these last few days real?

Had last night been real?

"So you didn't tell me because Harry would rape you. Fine I can accept that. But you continued not telling me to *protect* me? I'm calling bullshit. You were protecting yourself and no one else."

"At first, I was protecting myself, yes. And it made sense not to tell you until we got the invite to the party, because if we didn't get in, your role would've been moot. But then we were in, and I...couldn't risk you in that way. If the power wasn't out, if we hadn't been compromised by someone in the CIA, I'd be driving you to the airport already."

For some reason, the idea that she'd expected him to just abandon her while she returned to the lion's den made him even angrier. She hadn't trusted him with any aspect of this mission. "But now we're compromised, and flying out of here under the name Mani Kalenga or Cassius Callahan could be dangerous. We don't know what they know about me."

"Yes."

"So I'm stuck here. With you. And if we're found—which is more and more likely because we've been fucking *compromised*—I will be disavowed right along with you. You took me on a black op mission without informing me it's a black op."

She nodded. "You deserved a choice in this. I'm sorry. I hate myself for not seeing this coming and not warning you."

"That makes two of us."

She flinched, and a tear fell. "I was afraid to be here with Harry. He would have raped me. Again. And I never would have been able to report it, because it *would* be part of the mission. No one at Langley would do a damn thing about it."

"Did it ever occur to you that *you* could refuse the mission? Send Harry to do the hit and stay at Camp Citron?"

"I couldn't. He'd fuck it up. He doesn't know what Lubanga's capable of. Plus, I wanted to do it for Zola."

"Who is Zola?"

"She's Lubanga's daughter. A refugee who settled in Ethiopia." Savvy went on to tell a horrific story of rape and murder of young sisters, making their impossible situation even uglier.

Dammit. Savvy had a point. He wanted Lubanga taken down, but that didn't excuse her failure to share the nature of their mission. "I always knew you were willing to burn anyone at anytime, if it got you what you were after. I feared you'd do it to me. I just didn't expect it to happen before the op even started."

He ran his hand over his face. His beard was fuller than he liked—per her specifications. He wasn't even comfortable in his own facial hair. "How can I even believe you had no plans to kill Lubanga last night?"

"I wasn't going to do it until after you were gone. I swear."

"One thing about being a professional liar, Savvy, is that when you say things like 'I swear,' no one believes you."

"I lie for the mission. I lie to people like Anton and Jean Paul Lubanga. But I don't, and haven't, lied to you."

He raised a brow. "Really? So you told me this was a black op days ago, and I didn't notice?"

"That wasn't a lie. It was an omission."

"From where I'm standing—compromised and stuck in Tanzania—that feels like the same damn thing." The anger that filled him was dangerously close to bubbling over. Jesus. He'd made love to her, repeatedly. He'd begun to think maybe he wanted more with her.

He'd believed he'd been wrong about her for all those months, but his suspicion had been spot-on. "How do you plan to kill him?"

"I don't know. I'd hoped he'd take me on as a mistress, but he never looked at me twice. The guard who found me in Lubanga's quarters said Lubanga doesn't sleep with whores. Given his lack of interest in the sex show, I'm inclined to agree. Maybe I'll show up on the boat and offer myself to Gorev. Say I ditched you because you were too rough with me. I'll figure something out that leaves you out of it."

His stomach clenched at the idea of her showing up on that boat again as a sacrifice to Gorev. "You'd have to fuck him if you wanted to stay around long enough to off Lubanga."

She shrugged. "Not my favorite plan, but I'm prepared to follow through."

"Is that what last night was about? Were you hoping to soften me up for when the truth came out? Was fucking me part of the job too?"

She flinched as if he'd struck her. "You're an asshole."

He couldn't deny that. And God, the way she'd flinched. Last night, she'd tried to crawl away from him after he'd backhanded her, and he'd picked her up by her hair. In the middle of the night, he'd held her close and breathed in the scent of that same freshly washed hair.

"So what happens now? I won't help you kill him. I'm not a murderer."

"I'm not a murderer either. And you've killed far more men than I have for Uncle Sam."

"In battle. With rules of engagement."

"You've raided compounds and killed. How is sneaking up on mercs in the middle of the night and slitting their throats any different? Lubanga deals in children and drugs. His legal business—managing mining claims—pays him millions each year in kickbacks and who knows what else. He's earned what's coming to him."

"And you're his judge and jury?"

"No. I'm his executioner. The judge and jury are the US government. Kill orders are never given lightly, and they always come from the top. It's not my job to question the order, any more than you question yours from SOCOM."

"Have you ever assassinated someone before?"

He didn't expect an answer. She would say it was classified and leave it at that. But she surprised him and said, "No. I've killed in self-defense. Once. I've never been given a black op assignment like this before."

"How did you receive this order? What's the protocol?"

She rubbed her arms. "It was verbal. From Seth. It's why he flew out to Djibouti. He had a good excuse with the need to pat me on the back for the work with Drugov. Perfect cover for delivering the order—and bringing a covert partner."

"Seth gave you the order. And you didn't confirm it with anyone else?"

She glared at him. "I exchanged a coded communication with Langley before we left Camp Citron. I'm not a fool."

"But it was coded. So it didn't say, 'kill Lubanga' outright."

"What's your point?" she said. Her tears were now gone as she argued with him.

"My point is that dear old Seth set you up to go on your first assassination mission with a man who raped you. He's CIA, so he sure as hell could have set it up for you to get confirmation of the kill order that he conveniently delivered himself. I'm saying that you saw Lubanga's code name on the asshole's computer. This op was compromised by the CIA, and a smart operator should be looking at her boss and wondering why he set her up."

Savvy wasted no time and ran straight for the toilet, where she lost the contents of her stomach. But she hadn't eaten since before the party last night, so there wasn't much to lose.

She slumped against the wall, wiping the sweat from her forehead.

She wanted to deny Cal's suspicion, but she couldn't. There'd been something off about Seth's sudden arrival. And the fact that he'd brought Harry with him...that had turned her cold. When Harry had been transferred to Seth's unit, she'd thought he'd finally do something about the rape she'd reported years before. But instead, he'd promised she'd never have to work with Harry on a covert op. Then he broke that promise by bringing the man to Djibouti.

She'd be here with Harry right now if not for Cal. She owed him so much, and he hated her now. Again.

Stomach empty, all she had left were tears. She gave herself over to them, crying more for Cal's loathing than for Seth's betrayal. Grief over Seth's betrayal would hit her later, she knew. But right now, she was falling in love with Cassius, and she'd duped him. She'd risked his life and reputation to save herself. He'd never forgive her. Why should he? She'd done nothing to deserve forgiveness.

She rose from the bathroom floor after mopping her face and wiping her nose with toilet paper. She needed to get her shit together and figure out what was going on. She and Cal were in a lot of trouble. It didn't matter how he felt about her, they had to work together so they could go back to Camp Citron. Once there, he could go home and she...she could figure out if she was still working for the CIA.

They'd never see each other again.

She stuffed the pain down. Later. She could fall apart in Djibouti, after Cal departed.

She exited the bathroom to find the cottage empty. A note on the counter said Cal had gone to the store to stock up on groceries. Good plan. This house was safe and anonymous; they could—probably should—stay here for a few days.

With Cal gone, she took a quick shower. The water was lukewarm after hours without power, but it was sweltering hot in the closed-up cottage, so the temperature was welcome.

They could probably open the windows, but she opted for security over comfort. Bad enough that she and Cal were apart while he foraged for food. She dressed in yoga pants and a T-shirt, the first time she'd been able to dress comfortably in days, grateful she didn't have to leave the cottage today.

She pulled out her laptop, intending to start going through the files, and ground her teeth together when she realized the battery was dead. Fine. If she couldn't go through Lubanga's files, she would use a notepad and write down everything she knew about Seth Olsen and Harrison Evers.

Cal sat in the sedan, holding the small satellite phone SOCOM had given him with instructions to keep it hidden from Savvy. After all, he was spying on her for SOCOM. They'd wanted to know why she had so much power—or autonomy—within the Directorate of Operations. Would SOCOM have wanted him to accept this mission if they'd known it was intended to be a hit?

Maybe.

Would he have done it?

Maybe.

Did it change how he felt about her omission?

Not even a little bit.

But right now, his real question remained: had the kill order really been issued from the top? This might not be a hit mission at all. At least, not a hit on Lubanga. What if Seth Olsen had sent Savvy here to be killed? Had that been why he'd chosen Harry as her partner? There was no doubt Harrison Evers rattled Savvy, throwing her off her game.

And Lubanga knew his own code name. Damn, they needed to read that document. He should probably wait before making this call, but he doubted he'd be away from Savvy long enough to make a call after this, and he wasn't ready to fess up and tell her he had a satellite phone. Especially not now.

He decided to call Pax. Keep his questions off the record. Find out what his team knew about this little field trip with Savannah James.

The image of her beneath him last night flashed in his mind. Her body wrapped around his as he thrust inside her. *Shit.*

He shook his head against the memory. Hours ago, he'd been questioning if he wanted more than a fling. Stupid, stupid fool.

He understood her reason for not telling him at first. Hell, he hadn't even seen her until after he'd boarded the plane. There'd been no time to talk from the moment he'd punched Evers. But she could have told him in the hotel that first night. Had she really planned to send him back to Camp Citron to protect him?

He didn't know what to believe, which just made anger coil inside him. Jesus, his feelings for her had gone deeper than he wanted, triggering hostility that took his breath away. It was a blow to the nuts every time he thought about holding her close and sliding deep inside her body.

He punched in Pax's cell phone number. They would be with the trainees this morning, so it was unlikely he would answer, but he could leave a message, and they could talk after Cal got groceries.

But luck was with him, and Pax answered. "Been waiting for your call," he said without preamble.

"How did you know it was me?" he asked. This was a new sat phone, and he hadn't shared the number with anyone.

"Captain Oswald figured you'd call me first. Said to keep my phone with me at all times."

Dread settled in his gut. "Why? What happened?"

"Word came down this morning that Savvy funneled Drugov's money into a private account."

"So? She said that was how the mission had been funded."

"We're talking half a billion dollars."

"What the fuck?

"Yeah. A half billion of Russian Mafia money—and then she bolted for Tanzania, with you."

Chapter Fourteen

Savvy began by writing the date, June third, at the top of the page. She stared at the number as the meaning sank in. Another year had gone by. She'd been so focused on the job, she'd put it out of her mind, hadn't realized another June third was upon her.

She took a deep breath. The date was irrelevant. Her hand shook at first, but as she wrote about the first time she met Harrison Evers, the trembles eased. It was long past time she did this.

She'd written several pages in chronological order by the time she got to the rape. She'd never been a big drinker, but in that moment, she wished she had a shot of something to soften her brittle emotions. Mentally reliving that experience now, on June third of all days, when she was full of self-loathing for sabotaging any chance at a relationship with Cal, might be too much for her.

But she had to face it. That she'd never documented it until now was her own damn fault. So relive it she did, describing the motel room in Savannah, Georgia, right down to the putrid scent of Harry's sweat and the sadistic thrill he'd shown at her powerlessness.

Tears dripped from her cheeks onto the notepad. A car drove up to the cottage. She recognized the sedan with Cal at the wheel, so she kept writing. He entered as she finished her description of the rape. Next, she needed to write up reporting it to Seth, but that could wait.

She wiped her face as she met Cal's gaze. "I was just writing my account of the rape," she said, so he wouldn't think the tears were about him. Her tears over him had dried an hour ago.

She rose from her seat to help him unload the car. He said nothing, for which she was glad. She was too raw. She helped him put the food away as she nibbled on a loaf of French bread. Her stomach was a mess, but she needed to eat. The white bread was pasty in her mouth, but she dutifully chewed and swallowed.

The kitchen was tiny, but Cal made sure there was space between them as they worked in tandem. She didn't touch him, but she could smell him.

Smell sex on his skin.

Memories of last night overtook the chore she'd just completed. Better to think of Cal than Harry.

For a few brief, sweet hours, Cassius had been hers. "I'm sorry," she whispered, knowing the words were inadequate.

He stared at her, his face blank. Finally, he said, "What have you done, Savvy?"

The way he said it made her step back. "What do you mean?"

"What are you apologizing for? Is it because you didn't tell me about your bullshit kill order, or is there something else you haven't told me?"

What did he want her to say? All she had was the truth. "I'm apologizing for pulling you into the mission without telling you about the kill order. For remaining silent instead of telling you the truth and how I planned to keep you out of it."

His jaw was hard. He held her gaze for a long moment, then said. "Fine." After a long pause, he added, "I could maybe accept it if you said the order was classified, but you haven't used that excuse."

She shrugged. "Classified or not, if I planned to have you by my side when I took him out, I would have told you. I wouldn't have put you at that kind of risk without warning."

"And yet, here we are. Compromised. Stranded. And you didn't warn me."

She nodded and put the carton of eggs in the fridge. They finished unloading the groceries, her stomach still uneven. That chore done, she returned to the notepad.

"Why aren't you on the computer?"

"Battery's drained. The outlet I plugged into at the hotel must've been off." Power was sketchy in Tanzania—the current blackout a perfect example.

She stared at the notepad, not seeing it or anything else in the cottage. What had Cal meant when he asked what she was apologizing for? Had he called SOCOM while he was out? Had he compromised their location?

He wouldn't do that. His ass was on the line as much as hers.

It took her a moment to realize she heard the whirr of the refrigerator, then she noticed the air conditioner was on. Sweet electricity. It would take a few minutes to power everything up, but at least she could get online and find out what was in Lubanga's files.

Cal didn't know what to believe. Was she nothing more than a—highly successful—thief? Or had Seth set her up? Why drag Cal along if this was merely a brilliant heist? Sure, she'd known he was attracted to her before they ever left Camp Citron, but she'd be insane to think he'd blithely accept her thievery and they'd disappear into the sunset.

Special Forces was his life. His team was his second family. He would never give up his country, his career, everything he was, for sex and money. And she knew him well enough to figure that out.

It didn't add up.

Now he was in a situation. Pax had warned that if he didn't report to SOCOM, he'd be considered AWOL. If SOCOM was tracking his phone, they'd know he called Pax. Pax had said he'd answer questions if asked, but he wouldn't offer the information that Cal had called. It was a shitty thing to put his best friend through, but Cal needed more information before he called in. This could be an attempt by the CIA to use SOCOM to trap Savvy.

After hanging up, he'd pulled the battery. He'd been miles from the Airbnb. Their location was safe.

The irony of asking Pax to omit information from SOCOM, when that was exactly why he was angry with Savvy, wasn't lost on him. But he and Savvy needed to read Lubanga's files, many of which were likely to be in Lingala, to figure out what was going on.

She needed him, and the CIA was working awfully hard to make sure she wasn't successful. How big a wrench had she thrown in Seth's scheme when she ditched Harry in favor of him?

She set up her computer and portable hotspot at the small dining table that separated the kitchen and living room.

He watched her as she typed in the password to her secret cloud storage, a reminder that at this point, he was just as implicated as she was and equally screwed without her help in clearing *his* name.

"I want all your passwords," he said.

She turned and gave him a curious look. "You know I can't do that. I'm CIA. I can't just give you intelligence gathered by the CIA."

"I helped gather it."

"So? SEALs took data from bin Laden's compound. Does that mean they had a right to access the data?"

He reminded himself she didn't know she—and by extension he—had been accused of stealing half a billion from a dead oligarch. But he wasn't ready to tell her. Not yet. They needed to read the files first. He needed to be certain she wasn't part of something bigger. A honey trap ready to bring him down.

His father worked for the State Department and had a bad history with the CIA. What if Cal had been chosen not because he spoke Lingala or because Savvy wanted to escape with him and a bunch of cash, but because of his dad?

"You need me to read the documents in Lingala."

She nodded. "But you don't need my passwords for that."

He sighed. "If you find proof Seth Olsen betrayed you, you will share *everything*. Including passwords. I have the right to that information, considering my ass is on the line right along with yours."

She gave him a sharp nod, her full lips diminished to a hard, thin line. "That's fair." She turned back to the computer. "It will take some time to download Lubanga's files. My satellite hotspot is over the counter, not CIA tech, and slow."

Cal was anxious to get into the files, but he knew it was better to go slow than use a modem provided by the CIA. "I'll make lunch." He'd noticed all Savvy had managed to choke down was the torn-off end of a loaf of French bread. They both needed to eat.

It had been months since Cal had cooked for himself, a task he usually looked forward to after a long deployment. This morning, he'd woken up to Savvy's mouth on his body, and he'd been eager to lay in supplies so he could make her a big, postsex breakfast, like he did when stateside and a woman he was dating spent the night.

A big breakfast after sex was his favorite way to spend a weekend morning.

But fantasies of bacon and French toast in bed and playing with syrup until they were both sticky and sweet had been crushed by reality. Now he watched her in profile as he made tuna sandwiches. She sat before the computer, her spine ramrod straight.

Could he forgive her?

He understood why she hadn't told him. Jesus, she'd been raped by Harrison Evers. Cal would have to be a heartless asshole not to understand the awful position she'd been in. And he had to admit, her plan to send him off once he got her the access she needed, while something of a kick in the gut, would have protected him from fallout over her mission.

He couldn't help but wonder if she'd been sent here to fail. To be killed by Lubanga. The fact that she'd managed to ditch Evers and partner with Cal could be the only reason she was alive right now, sitting at that computer.

The thought made his stomach churn. He didn't want to live in a world without Freya no-last-name. And that answered any questions he had over whether or not he trusted her. Like a dumbfuck, he wanted to go to her, to pull her into his arms, and kiss her.

Hell, he wanted to do more than kiss her. But she'd betrayed his trust. How could desire and anger exist inside him at the same time? But then, Savvy had always triggered his strongest emotions.

He locked down his sympathy. They had work to do.

Sandwiches and salad made, he dropped into a chair beside her. "What have you got?"

"Nothing yet." Her focus was on the screen, but he could see a reaction to his nearness ripple through her.

They'd never quite figured out how to contain their physical reaction to each other. At least it hadn't given them away last night. If anything, it worked in their favor, giving Mani extra reason to be enraged at her attempted betrayal.

"The first packet downloaded," she said, "but I couldn't find the Zagreus file. I hope it's in the next batch." She fixed him with a stare. "Did you call anyone while you were out? Does SOCOM know where we are?"

He was glad for the second question, that one he could answer. "SOCOM doesn't know where we're staying."

The computer chimed. The second bundle of files had finished downloading. She clicked on the file tree.

He scanned the names. Some were in Lingala. He translated the names, and she flagged the ones that looked interesting. She scrolled to the bottom, and there it was, Zagreus.

She opened the file, revealing a list in two sections.

Zagreus / Jean Paul Lubanga – Dar es Salaam
Reverend Abel Fitzsimmons – Lynchburg, Virginia
Senator Albert Jackson – Washington, DC
Jeffery Prime, Jr. – Dar es Salaam
Mikhail Petrykin / Harrison Evers – Dar es Salaam

Jamie Savage / Savannah James / Freya Lange – Dar es Salaam
Sergeant First Class Cassius Callahan, US Army Special Forces – Dar es Salaam
US Attorney General Curt Dominick – Washington, DC
Senator Alec Ravissant – Gaithersburg, Maryland
Chief Warrant Officer Sebastian Ford, US Army Special Forces – Camp Citron
Gabriella Prime / Brie Stewart – Fort Campbell

Cal shoved his sandwich aside. He couldn't eat now. "Your last name is Lange?"

She met his gaze, her face leached of all color. "Yes."

"What does this mean?"

"I don't know. Why are our names in a document with Reverend Fitzsimmons? What is Harry doing in Dar?"

"Is Mikhail Petrykin his alias?"

"Yes. He was going to pose as a Russian associate of Drugov's, but he never used that alias—not even for his flight to Djibouti—which means two, maybe three people would know the name that was set up for him."

"SOCOM wouldn't know. This document had to come from the CIA."

She stared at the screen. "I wonder...the name of the file. It's the first word in the document—the default name when saving a file in Word."

Seeing the name had tipped Savvy off last night. Was it possible a lazy file save might've prevented them from walking into a trap last night at their new hotel or this morning at the airport? The airport where, according to Pax, it was highly probable Russian Bratva were searching for them both.

"Why isn't my alias listed?"

She rubbed a hand over her face. "I never told Seth the names I'd set up for you." She touched the screen. "Why are Bastian and Brie on this list?"

"It could mean Brie is in danger." The fact that they knew she was in Kentucky was alarming. "We need to call Bastian. Give him a heads-up."

She nodded. At least she didn't argue with him on this point. "What does the US Attorney General have to do with us? Or Senator Ravissant, for that matter?"

"Ravissant is the new senator from Maryland. My parents voted for him." Cal would have voted for him too, but he'd changed his registration to Kentucky a few years ago.

With thirty-plus years in the State Department, Cal's dad had met most of the major players in DC at one point or another, plus he'd had front-row seats when the sitting Secretary of State had been involved in a scandal that had nearly led to the murder of Curt Dominick before he became US AG.

His father had deeply informed political views, and visits home always included long discussions about politics, local and national, giving Cal more than casual background knowledge of the attorney general. "Dominick is friends with Ravissant. There were photos of the senator and his girlfriend dining with the AG and his wife right before the election last November, after the scandal with Ravissant's military training compound in Alaska. It was the AG's way of showing he trusted the candidate without endorsing him."

"I remember that. A public endorsement could be seen as a Hatch Act violation."

"Exactly. According to my dad, Dominick is a straight arrow. The guy lives the law."

Savvy stood from her chair and paced the room. "What the hell does this list mean? Why is each person's location listed? Do you think your dad is wrong about the AG?"

Cal shrugged. He didn't have any more answers than she did.

She leaned over and tapped the screen. "We should start at the top, with the televangelist. What's his association with Lubanga and Gorev? He had a deal in the works with Drugov—I think he was donating to Brie Stewart's menstrual panty project."

"Is it possible he knew what Drugov's plan was there?" Cal grimaced, thinking of the genocide that didn't happen. "It could've been an honest charitable donation."

Savvy sighed. "The fact that he's associated with two oligarchs doesn't look innocent or charitable to me. Before I left Camp Citron, Seth said Fitzsimmons was angling to become a spiritual leader in Congo if Lubanga seized power. Now we see his name listed in the same group as JJ Prime—who we know was connected to Drugov and is now hanging with Gorev."

"The attorney general and Senator Ravissant don't fit, unless my dad is wrong—which is possible."

She frowned. "But they're in the bottom group. With us. I know Drugov had it out for the AG because the Justice Department was investigating potential price fixing between Druneft and Prime Energy. Albert Jackson has been caught up in that as well. You said the senator and AG are friends. Maybe whoever sent this list sees Alec Ravissant as a way to go after the attorney general? Ravissant could be vulnerable thanks to that Alaska scandal. Buzz in the intelligence community is that there was a whole lot more to what happened in the wilderness. It might've involved DIA—and Russia."

"So that could explain their names on the list. So the bottom part a hit list?"

She bit her lip. "Maybe. Someone could be trying to clean up loose ends. We need to look at all the files. We're missing something. All we've got is wild speculation."

He nodded. "But first I need to call Bastian and tell him that he and Brie are on this list."

"Fine. But not from here. If the call were to be traced..."

"I know." He wasn't ready to tell her he had a satellite phone, so instead, he said, "I'll use one of the burner phones and drive to the business district to make the call."

She nodded. "I'll go through Lubanga's files while you're gone."

He picked up the keys from the table next to the door.

"Be careful, Cal. Drive a full SDR. Don't take any chances, and protect yourself at all costs."

Instinct said he should kiss her goodbye. Every time they separated, there was risk. This could be the last time he saw her. A kiss now would be the most natural thing in the world for him to do.

Except he couldn't.

"Will do." He stepped outside without looking back.

Chapter Fifteen

The tiny house was achingly silent when Cal left, and part of Savvy wondered if he'd return. This was his chance to escape. He could drive to the airport and catch a flight back to Djibouti, free and clear.

She couldn't really blame him if he did. She hadn't earned his loyalty. He had no reason to believe she'd really planned to send him back to protect him from fallout should her mission fail. But still, the idea of him leaving her—no matter how deserved—triggered an ache.

Sergeant First Class Cassius Callahan was everything she wanted in a man and partner, but he was also the one she'd known she would never have for more than a passing fling. Until he'd made love to her in a way that made her think he might want more.

Then her deception killed his feelings faster than a supersonic bullet.

She shook her head to clear it. She needed to comb through Lubanga's files. Whether Cal returned or not, she needed to do her job and figure out who was friend and who was foe.

Files that were written in Lingala she dropped into a folder for Cal to read. She could translate the French ones herself but was most interested in the English ones, as that was the common language between Gorev, Lubanga, and Fitzsimmons.

An antique clock on the sideboard ticked away the minutes in the otherwise silent room as she searched the files for references to the evangelical televangelist. But she couldn't simply search on terms because, as she soon learned, many of the documents had been converted to JPEG files. They were images, not searchable text. An extra layer of security for a very cautious man. But then, his laptop didn't even have a Wi-Fi connection or LAN port.

Finally, she got lucky and opened an image file that mentioned Fitzsimmons. And herself.

Versailles métro – 5 Juin
<u>revenu</u>
A Fitzsimmons

N Drugov

<u>*dépense*</u>
militaire
R Gorev
F Lange
C Dominick
A Ravissant

Revenu and *dépense* were easy: income and expenses. The names were obvious. This had to be instructions for someone who moved his money around. June fifth was two days away. Versailles subway was a lot more confusing. Was something happening in France on the fifth? As far as she knew, the city of Versailles didn't have a subway.

She stared at her name. Times New Roman font. So very familiar and yet utterly baffling. Why was she an expense? Was he paying someone to get rid of her?

A sound at the door startled her. She hadn't heard Cal drive up and expected him to be gone much longer, given the time it would take to drive the necessary SDR. She glanced toward the door. Her body jolted with the force of a lightning strike at seeing Harry in the doorway.

Twenty minutes into the SDR, with no sign of a tail, a point that nagged at Cal came to the forefront of his mind.

Harrison Evers was in Dar es Salaam.

Savvy had been told Harry would fly back to the US with Seth. But the agent hadn't. Instead, he'd gone to Tanzania. To complete his mission of taking out the minister, or was he operating on other orders?

That Seth had lied to Savvy about Harry returning to the US was just another clue as to who the leaker was within the CIA. Also worth noting: Seth's name wasn't on the list at all. But then, Cal was certain he was the author. He had access to every person's location, including Brie Stewart's. The Agency had needed it for follow-up interviews.

Cal pulled onto a side street and parked. He had a bad feeling about leaving Savvy alone for too long. He didn't have time for a lengthy Surveillance Detection Route. He needed to get back to her, fast.

But he also owed Bastian a call.

He dialed Bastian, but his call went to voice mail. "Bas, I just saw your name and Brie's name on a list found on Jean Paul Lubanga's computer. It had your location and listed Brie as being in Kentucky. It might be a good idea for her to go off the grid for a bit, until we know what's going on. Maybe she can get her brother Rafe to pony up for a security detail. She could hire retired Special Forces operators. I think Martinez is working for an outfit in Cincinnati. I gotta go. Sorry to drop this on you without more info, but that's really all I've got. I'll call again when I can."

He hit the End button and dropped the phone on the seat. His soldier's instinct told him he needed to get back to their rental house right away.

S avvy bolted to her feet, knocking over her chair. She moved fast, but Harry had the element of surprise. Plus he was the one man on the planet who rattled her, which slowed her reaction time. She stumbled on the legs of the chair as he came at her fullbore.

Before she knew it, she was pinned to the floor next to the sofa. She managed to raise her knee and launched him off her, then charged, following him into the wall.

A lamp on the side table toppled over and shattered on the floor. She reached for a shard of glass and held it to Harry's throat.

His eyes widened with fear. Probably because he knew she wouldn't hesitate to slice him open. She had a million questions, but only one was important in this moment in time. "How did you find me?"

When he didn't answer, she ran the razor-sharp edge along his jaw, opening a deep cut, then returned the blade to his carotid. "How did you find me?" she repeated.

"Your computer," he said, barely moving his mouth so as not to bump the shard. "I installed a program back at Camp Citron."

Oh hell. She'd thought the computer was safe because it was clean—a new one she'd picked up just days before the op. It hadn't even been on her desk when Harry and Seth had been there. He must've spotted it in her bag in her office.

And he must've installed the program while Seth shared a drink with her at Barely North. Pain at that betrayal made her dizzy. She tried to hide her reaction.

"I thought you'd figured it out when it stopped pinging yesterday morning. I was surprised when it suddenly went off an hour ago."

But of course, the reason it hadn't pinged was that the battery was dead. Otherwise, he would've found them while she and Cal slept. They'd been saved by a dead battery.

Harry struck with the speed of a snake, clamping her hand on the shard, cutting her. Blood seeped between her fingers before he released her hand and extracted the sharp fragment, then tossed it across the room.

She'd lost her advantage, so she aimed for Harry's eyes with her long nails. He shoved her backward. They rolled on the floor, through the broken lamp, which sliced into her back. She slammed into the table, toppling the computer that had given her away.

"Was the Green Beret better in bed than me, *Savannah*?" One of Harry's hands closed around her wrists, pinning them above her head.

She kneed him in the groin, but he blocked it. "Why are you here? What is your mission?"

Blood dripped from his chin onto her face. "To kill you, of course. And make it look like your pet Green Beret did it."

"Who are you working for?" No way was Harry the mastermind of this shitshow.

"Sweetheart, I'm the boss here."

"Right. You're nothing but a toady."

He backhanded her hard, connecting with the bruise she'd gotten from Cal last night and making her head swim as pain pulsed through her skull.

He stared down at her, his glee evident in the light in his eyes. He enjoyed inflicting pain, liked having her trapped and afraid. "It's a shame I don't have more time to do this slowly."

She managed to catch her breath as the pain settled to a dull roar in her brain. "Why do you hate me so much?"

"It was never about you, sweetheart. I don't give two shits about Freya Lange or your mission to avenge your family."

"I don't want to avenge—"

He twisted her nipple, causing pain to pulse outward from her chest. "Whatever. I don't give a fuck about any of that. You were going to fail the spec ops training. You knew it all was a test. Fake. You couldn't stay in character because you knew your life didn't really depend on it. So I took your training to the next level. It was no longer a game without real risk. You had to submit or lose everything. I created Savannah. I showed you your weakness. Gave you your strength. You would be nothing without me."

She bucked against his hold. "You don't get to claim one ounce of who I am today."

"Oh, but I do." With his free hand, he stroked her cheek. "One of my specialties is taking female operators to the next level. Seth always assigned me the tough cases."

The pain in her head was lost to the bile rising up her esophagus. The worst part—worse than the ceramic shard digging into her back, worse than the man who loomed above her, holding her wrists in a viselike grip—was the fear that there was a kernel of truth to his words.

Had she been on the path to failing the training? Had being raped somehow made her a *better* operator?

Fuck that.

Even as she wanted to scream, her brain served up memories of Seth implying as much over the years. She'd brushed his subtle words off as the view of an older man who couldn't possibly relate or understand. She'd given him a pass on the misogynistic take because he was her mentor.

Pain surged, making her whole body go tight with rage. Seth had been behind the assault and had used his mental leverage to get her to accept the rape, to remain quiet about it. His underlying message, the one she'd kept her eyes and ears closed to for five long years: rape had been her due for wanting to join the man's world of elite special operators.

"You were one of my best success stories," Harry said. "It's a shame I have to end you."

She struggled against him, but he held her down. "Why? Why kill me?"

"You side-stepped your chain of command and convinced SOCOM to go after Drugov."

She tried to control her breathing. She needed to calm down. She could fight Harry as long as her emotions were in control. She needed to be able to think. It was no wonder Harry had been sent after her. Seth knew what being around him did to her mind.

"You're no good if you can't be controlled." He yanked at her waistband, pulling down the yoga pants. "So now I will end you as I fuck you." He wedged her legs apart and rammed a knee between her thighs, keeping her legs spread with his own even though the waistband of the stretchy pants was caught on her knees.

His grip on her wrists tightened. Instead of fighting, she forced her body to relax even as she felt him opening his fly.

She waited. Pliant. Trapped by clothes, his weight, and his hand on her wrists. He shifted to insert his hips between her thighs. His grip on her wrists loosened, almost imperceptibly, but she'd been waiting for it. She surged upward with her whole body, breaking her hands free. She slammed her wrists into the cut on his face.

The blow connected, throwing him off-balance and giving her fist an open shot at his balls. His body curled inward even as his weight fell full force on top of her, trapping one of her hands between their bodies. With her free hand she grabbed the flap of skin that hung off his jaw, digging in with her nails so the slick, bloody skin wouldn't slip through her fingers, and yanked.

He howled with pain and rose up, freeing her trapped hand. She groped along the floor for something to hit him with and came up with another shard from the lamp. She plunged it into his throat.

Shock replaced the pain on his face as blood spurted from the open artery onto her face and neck. She shoved him aside, crawling out from under him as he tried to stanch the flow with his fingers.

But it was too late. By the time she was free of his weight, he was slumped on the floor, blood loss too rapid for him to do anything but stare up at her, his dick limp and face showing agony until his eyes glazed over.

Chapter Sixteen

Cal stood in the doorway, his heart in his throat as he took in the scene. Savvy sat in the middle of the room, next to the dead body of CIA SAD operator Harrison Evers. Blood drenched her T-shirt. Her yoga pants were caught on her thighs. Evers's pants were around his knees, his flaccid prick making it clear what he'd been doing when Savvy overpowered him and opened an artery.

Cal crossed the room and pulled her into his arms. Jesus, if he'd just been a few minutes faster. "I'm so sorry." He murmured the words in an endless loop of soft apology.

She said nothing, just wrapped her arms around his waist and held on. At least he could give her this. There'd been no one to comfort her after the first time she was raped, and he hadn't been able to hold her after Harry attacked her on base.

Except, they had to leave, before someone showed up looking for Harry. Reluctantly, he released her. "I'm sorry, Savvy, but we need to get out of here."

She nodded, her eyes still glazed.

"Get changed," he said, "while I load the car."

She shook her head.

"You've got his blood all over you. You should probably take a shower. But make it fast."

She shook her head again.

"I'll take care of everything while you get cleaned up. I'll put Harry in the trunk."

She pulled up the yoga pants, her eyes still dazed, but finally, she spoke. "No."

"We can't leave him here."

She shook her head, and this time met his gaze. He could see reason in her eyes, behind the haze of shock at the assault. "We need to find his car. Put him in the trunk. He probably parked somewhere in the neighborhood."

She'd gone from shocked to full operator mode, and Cal couldn't be more grateful. "Sounds like a plan."

She patted down the pockets of Evers's pants and held up keys and a USB drive. "When we have time, I'll plug this into my computer, see what was so important he carried it on him." In a flash, her faint smile of triumph disappeared. "Shit! My computer." She grabbed it from where it lay on the floor, stepped into the kitchen, then, to his complete shock, smashed it against the marble countertop.

"What—"

"He tracked us through a program he loaded in the computer. He must've done it after the meeting in my office. I went to Barely North—to find you—and Seth followed me, convinced me to join him for a drink. Gave plenty of time for Harry to screw with my laptop." The computer had cracked but not broken. She pressed the open hinge to her knee, snapping the screen from the keyboard. "Someone might have access to the hard disk even now. Can't remove the battery, so destroying the hard drive is best. I should shoot it. And burn it. It's the only way to make sure the CIA can't retrieve the data."

"You can't fire a gun in this neighborhood."

She nodded, but still, she ran to the bedroom and returned with her pistol.

"Savvy!"

She released the magazine so it dropped on the floor, then checked the chamber and dumped the bullet before slamming the butt of the empty gun into the keyboard. She repeated the blows on the keyboard until she was able to pry out the hard drive.

She held up the disk, triumphant, sweating, and covered in blood. "We need to buy a new computer. I can download Lubanga's files from the cloud again."

"Does the CIA have access to Lubanga's files? You used a CIA device to upload to the cloud."

"The upload device is just the tool—a conduit—connecting computer to cloud storage. I configured where the files would go before we left Camp Citron. I didn't use any official CIA online storage because authentication protocols to log…well, it's CIA. It can't be done in a hurry like I was to copy Lubanga's files. I set up a temporary storage account, only I know how to access."

He nodded. If the CIA didn't know where Lubanga's files were, then they couldn't use her subsequent downloads to track their location. Good. "You need to shower, and we need to dispose of this body. Then we need to get the hell out of Dar and figure out how we're going to get back to Camp Citron."

"I can't go back to Camp Citron. He's… I'm pretty sure he's working for Seth." She ran a hand over her face. "Fuck. I killed a fellow CIA SAD operator. No one will believe it was self-defense. Not without proof that Harry came here to kill me, that he's the traitor."

"You have me. I'll back you."

"You weren't here."

She was right. He actually had no idea what had gone on in this room. All he knew was he'd found her kneeling over a dead body. The room indicated she and Harry had fought. Her pants were down, Harry's genitals exposed. Cal could make a reasonable guess, but there was nothing to stop the CIA from saying she'd staged it. "Let's deal with the body, then decide our next move."

"Use the key remote to find the car. Drive it through the gate. We'll put him in the trunk. We can drive out to the savannah and leave it. Him."

"You shower. I'll find his car."

She nodded, and he grabbed the key.

He paused by the door, then turned and pulled her against him again. This time, he kissed her, then pressed his face to her neck. He could feel her pulse against his cheek. She smelled of blood and sweat and soap from her earlier shower. Her chest brushed his each time she inhaled.

Freya Lange was alive and breathing with a rapidly beating heart, no thanks to him. "You won't take the fall for this. I won't let that happen."

"Harry said he was going to make it look like you'd killed me."

He lifted his head and nodded in resignation. He'd expected that. He ran a finger over the bright welt on her cheek. It was worse than it had been earlier. Evers must've hit her in the same spot. Rage and protectiveness surged. He looked at the dead body on the carpet. "Is there any chance he was working alone?"

"No. Harrison Evers is a follower, not a leader. I think Seth is the one calling the shots."

He brushed his lips over hers. "Then Seth Olsen is going to be very sorry. Nobody messes with what's mine."

The words were more than a little bit caveman, and ridiculous given that Savvy had saved herself without Cal lifting a finger, but they'd surged from that possessive place where, apparently, Savannah James had been residing for some months, even if he hadn't wanted to admit it.

But even better, his cheap, juvenile words made her smile. He'd revert to one hundred percent caveman if it made her smile after the trauma she'd just suffered.

She kissed his cheek. "Thank you."

"Lock the door behind me, and keep your phone and gun within hand's reach of the shower. I'll call before I enter the cottage."

She nodded. Her lips brushed his. He kissed her back, the moment lasting longer than he intended. Outside, he took a deep breath of the muggy air. Shock, rage, fear, and protectiveness all vied for top emotion.

Had Evers raped her today? Not that the distinction mattered. Sure as hell she'd been violated even if the man hadn't penetrated her.

He wished he'd beat the shit out of the asshole at Camp Citron when he had the chance. Hospitalized, Evers wouldn't have been able to come after Savvy.

He walked through the gate and scanned the residential street, hitting the alarm button on the key chain. Silence. He figured Evers would park on the main road, where other cars were parked on the street, and headed in that direction. He got lucky and found Evers's blue sedan parked between two other cars on the busier street. He drove it through the gate on the rental property, noting that the homeowner's car wasn't in the garage.

He hoped to hell everyone in the main house was out for the day and heard nothing that had gone on inside their small cottage. He called Savvy and warned her he was returning.

"'Kay. In the shower. Left a present for you in the living room."

Inside, he found Evers's body wrapped in the throw rug he'd died on. Savvy had bundled him up and cleaned the mess from the lamp and laptop destruction. All that was missing was a ribbon. He scooped up the rug and stowed the body in the trunk, grateful their landlord didn't drive up while he was hiding a body and stealing their very nice rug. He'd leave a lot of money on the counter to pay for the loss of rug, lamp, and other damage.

Back inside the cottage, Savvy was out of the shower and getting dressed. She stepped into the main room as she pulled a clean shirt over her head. "I've been thinking. We can't go to the airport here or take a train. People are probably scouting both already. Our best bet is to drive to the airport in Kigoma, on Lake Tanganyika. It's a long drive, but no one will be looking for us there. You can charter a flight to Nairobi, and from there, you can fly back to Djibouti."

He stiffened at that. "And where will you go?"

"Congo. Right before Harry showed up, I found a document that referenced Versailles, a subway, and June fifth. I'm wondering if it meant Versailles in the Jungle."

"Mobutu's palace," Cal said. "The legendary ruins."

"Yeah. Aren't there tunnels under the palace? Maybe that's what the word subway referred to."

"I think so. I don't know much about Mobutu's Versailles."

"I'm going to need a new computer, to download the files and see if I can find more info. But it's a starting point. June fifth is just two days away."

"You aren't going into Congo alone," Cal said. He opened his suitcase and grabbed a clean shirt. He'd gotten blood on him when he'd held her. This was the second shirt in two days he was abandoning due to being blood soaked. "We'll get a computer, supplies for Congo, and hit the road."

"After we dump Harry's car somewhere."

He nodded and grabbed the most easily portable food he'd purchased earlier. Bread, peanut butter, fruit. Protein bars. He loaded those and a few other items along with their suitcases into the back of their sedan.

Less than forty-five minutes after he found Savvy sitting beside Harry's dead body, they were back on the road, Savvy driving their car, Cal driving Harry's. It took another thirty minutes to reach the outskirts of the city. He drove the vehicle off the road, down a winding track that cut through savannah, and tucked it between trees so it would be hidden from the main road. This wasn't a full-on wilderness area. There was plenty of traffic and human activity. The car and body could be found in a day or a month. Sooner if Harry had a tracker on his vehicle.

But they would be long gone even if it was found tonight.

Back in the sedan with Savvy, she moved to the passenger seat, and he took the wheel. "Use your phone to find us a sporting goods store," he said.

"We're going to play baseball?"

"Not that kind. If we're going into Congo, we need to be prepared for anything. Outside of the bigger cities, there aren't hotels or anything. We need a tent, sleeping pads. Basic survival gear."

They found a shopping mall with both an electronics store and a store with outdoor gear. They loaded up on everything imaginable, paying cash with Gorev's money. From there, they hit the road. Cal had looked up the route on his GPS. They had at least a twenty-one-hour drive ahead of them, which they'd do in shifts without stopping for more than short rest breaks.

An hour passed before they were far enough from the city that the tightness in Cal's chest eased. He reached across the console and took Savvy's hand in his. She glanced sideways and squeezed his fingers.

"I'm not sorry I killed him," she said softly.

"I'm not either. But I am sorry I wasn't there to help you."

"I think he waited until you left. He wasn't dumb enough to confront us both." She squeezed his fingers again. "He didn't rape me this time. He was about to, but I stopped him."

"I'm glad. But I'm so damn sorry he ever got near you again. I shouldn't have left. The fact that the document said he was in Dar should have tipped me off. It did actually—it's why I came back early—but too late to help you."

"The CIA is going to call it murder."

"The fact that we didn't call in and report what happened won't look good."

"But if I call—" She took a deep breath. "Seth sent Harry to kill me." She released his hand. She made a low sound in her throat and murmured, "I wonder if Aunt Kim knows what he is."

"Aunt Kim?"

"Seth's wife."

Shit. If she was "Aunt Kim" to Savvy... Seth's betrayal would hurt her no matter what, but this cut even deeper than he'd imagined.

"I want you to go back to Camp Citron," she said. "Harry wasn't there for you. You aren't in danger if you return."

Her offer wasn't much different from her plan to send him away while she killed the minister, but she needed his help. And he didn't walk away from a teammate in need. Hell, how long would she have remained frozen in that living room if he hadn't been there? And who knew what she'd face in DRC?

"You don't speak Lingala," he said.

She shrugged. "I'll find someone who can. I've got money. Lots of it."

He again remembered Drugov's half billion. No. She hadn't taken the money. He didn't believe it. Would never believe it. Savvy had been set up.

But for some reason, her desire to send him packing made his anger spike. "Sweetheart, you think you can replace me that easily?"

"Of course not. But if anything happens to you—I—I wouldn't be able to live with myself. This is my fault. My problem. It has nothing to do with you. I roped you in because I needed a Lingala speaker. But this isn't about you. Go back to Camp Citron. Rejoin your team. Finish your deployment and have a good life. I'm releasing you from this mission."

"You can't do that."

"Actually, I can. This is my op."

"Sure. But you aren't the reason I'm here."

She frowned at him, then said, "Eyes on the road, Callahan."

He turned back to the roadway, seeing a curve up ahead. He should pull over for this conversation because he wanted to see her face, but they had too many miles to cover to waste time with arguing by the side of the road. "I didn't take this mission because you asked for me."

She crossed her arms. "Oh, really?"

"Really. My XO ordered me to accept it. SOCOM wants to know how you appeared to have so much autonomy and power. They wanted me to find out where some of your intel is coming from. You said the Yemen op a year ago was a success when it was a failure for my team. Hell, it caused a rift between Pax and Bastian that took a crisis for them to get past."

"Yemen happened before I was sent to Camp Citron. I had nothing to do with it."

He shrugged. "Your predecessor also had unusual autonomy. I think SOCOM is as interested in you as in your chain of command." He cleared his throat and added a suspicion his commanders hadn't suggested, but which was now very much on the radar. "SOCOM also wants to know if you've been pocketing the petty cash used to pay informants. They ordered me to accept this mission so I could spy on you and report back."

"Did they order you to fuck me to get me to spill my secrets?"

"No!"

She let out a soft laugh. "It would only be fair if they did, considering I asked Bastian to do just that with Brie."

"I didn't sleep with you because of orders from SOCOM."

"Then why did you sleep with me?"

He tightened his hands on the steering wheel. "Because I wanted to." Lord, how he'd wanted to. And he wanted to again. He'd been right all along about sex with Savvy only making the heat between them worse. Far from getting her out of his system, now that he'd had a taste, he just wanted more. Which was twice as shitty, considering what she'd gone through today.

"And now?"

"What I want now is irrelevant."

"You know," she said, "I could call you a hypocrite for being pissed at me for not being forthcoming about the change in the mission, when the only reason you're here is because you were spying on me."

He nodded. That was fair.

"Why are you still with me? You can leave. Go back to Camp Citron."

"I just told you, I have orders. Lubanga might be your mission, but you are mine."

"And any modicum of power I held within the CIA is gone now. I just killed a coworker, and my mentor—a man who was a father figure to me—is almost certainly the one who set me up and betrayed me. My career is over. There is no reason for SOCOM to want anything from me now. Leaving won't violate your orders."

"I'm not leaving you, Freya."

"Don't call me that."

"Why not? You've been compromised. Your real name is on the list. Maybe if you tried being Freya, we can figure out a way out of this mess."

"There is no 'we' in this mess. It's all me." She tucked herself into the door, moving as far away from him as she could. "You want to know why my alias is Savannah?"

"A name you obviously don't like? Yeah."

"Because Harry raped me in a hotel room in Savannah, Georgia. And Seth said I needed to use the experience to make me stronger. A little slice of 'that which doesn't kill you' bullshit, but the real shit of it is, I *believed* him. He told me I was going to be Savannah James—Savannah because the name would remind me that I was on my own and no one has my back, and James for my Uncle James, a case officer who died in the line of duty, to remind me of honor, sacrifice, and the danger of the job. And I believed his bull crap about needing the name Savannah to make me stronger. When really, it was a nasty move to keep me in my place. To make me remember every damn day that the CIA owned everything about me, even my ability to say 'no.' Want to know what Harry's last words were?"

Cal was afraid to ask, but she needed to tell this story, so he had to listen. "Tell me."

"He said, 'You're no good if you can't be controlled. So now I will end you as I fuck you.' He and Seth were in on the emotional torment together. Every time he called me Savannah, he gave it a nasty edge to make sure I knew he was aware of what the name meant. It was a mind fuck from the man who raped me and the man who was the only 'family' that came to my college graduation."

"You've known Seth Olsen that long?"

"I interned with the CIA as an undergrad. Seth basically recruited me when I was nineteen." She rested her forehead on her closed hands. "So I'm well aware of exactly how alone I am in the world, and how screwed I am, and I want you to go back to Camp Citron and resume your happy life with your buddies who all hate me for no other reason than I'm dedicated to my job. Let me handle this my way."

Cal pulled over to the side of the road. They were way past the point of him being able to drive and listen, let alone talk to her. "Pax and Bastian don't hate you."

She shrugged. "Two men out of twelve don't hate me. Lucky me."

"*I* don't hate you."

"Right. You said you hate me this morning."

"I did not."

"I said I hated myself for not warning you, and you said, 'That makes two of us.'"

"I was angry. Jesus, I'd just found out you'd withheld a vital piece of information about our mission from me."

"*My* mission. This is my mission. Not yours."

"Why are you working so hard to drive me away?"

"Because I don't want you to get burned too. I'm *destroyed*, Cal. There is no way out of this where I come out exonerated. I killed a fellow agent."

"He assaulted you. Twice. Three times."

"Yeah, and the only person who can corroborate my account of the rape five years ago is Seth. He can change the story he gave Captain O'Leary, claiming I must've lied to him. You know how it will be twisted. They'll claim I set Harry up. And you…you won't come out of this well either. You back me, and they'll gut you. You'll be off your Special Forces team. Who knows what they'll implicate you with? You don't need to burn with me."

He could tell her he was already implicated, but that would only bolster her argument. If she knew about the stolen Russian money, she'd push him away for sure.

He took her hand and pulled it to his chest. "I'm not going anywhere, Freya, not without you. We're in this together, to the bitter end. But I need a promise from you."

She looked at him as if to say he wasn't in a position to be cutting deals, but he was. Because she didn't want him to leave. Hell, she *needed* him.

And not just because he spoke Lingala.

She needed a partner. Someone who would have her back. Nothing quite like helping hide a body to hit home the danger she'd been in. If she'd left Camp Citron with Harrison Evers, she'd probably have been dead before they reached Dar es Salaam. He'd come full circle and was now grateful she'd lied so he'd accept the mission.

"What's the promise?" she asked.

"Promise you'll look for a way out of this that doesn't sacrifice you. Promise you won't give up. That you'll fight for this."

"Of course," she said, her brow furrowed in confusion. "Why do you think I won't do everything I can to survive?"

"Because you're trying to get rid of your best asset—a fluent Lingala speaker who knows the players and the lay of the land. I've been to Congo. I'm Special Forces. Munitions expert. Better than average sniper." He smiled, unable to stop himself from making a joke. "Brilliant in the sack."

She rewarded him with a laugh.

Emotion hit him in the gut. He could still make her laugh, after the shit she'd just gone through. That meant something. He cleared his throat and got serious. "Pushing me away is a surefire way to sabotage your mission. So why do you want to get rid of me?"

She dropped her gaze to her feet in the well under the dash. "Because if you leave now—because I told you to go—it will hurt a lot less than being abandoned later."

He placed a finger under her chin and lifted her face to meet his gaze. "I will never abandon you." He leaned in and kissed her. He wouldn't shy away from the change in their partnership. He didn't know if they'd continue as lovers, but he wouldn't pretend it didn't happen.

He pulled back and looked into her eyes. He saw a vulnerability that she usually masked, but then, it would be worse if she slipped into her role of Savannah James after all that had happened in the last twenty-four hours.

The bruise on her cheek had already reached the purple stage. They'd gotten looks at both the electronics and sporting goods store. He ran his fingertips lightly over the ridge of the welt, careful not to press on the swollen, purple skin. She had cuts on her back too. Before leaving the cottage, he'd put antibiotic ointment on and bandaged three shallow cuts. And then there was the slash across her palm that bisected her life line. He'd glued it closed and wrapped it in gauze.

Her full lips twitched as he catalogued her injuries. "You should see the other guy."

His eyes widened as her meaning sank in, and he couldn't help it, he laughed. He shook his head and leaned in and kissed her again, quick, lips only, then leaned his forehead to hers. "Note to self: don't mess with Freya Lange."

"I'm scared, Cassius." Her voice was soft. Low. A tone he'd never heard from the confident and wildly skilled SAD operator.

"So am I," he admitted. He wasn't afraid of Lubanga, Gorev, or even Seth Olsen. He was scared Freya—the woman inside the operator—would somehow be lost forever in the coming struggle. "We can do this. We're going to win this battle. Win this war. Together."

She kissed his cheek and leaned back. "Thank you."

His heart squeezed at the look she gave him. It was unlike any expression Savannah James wore.

Cassius Callahan, meet Freya Lange.

The name Freya hadn't fit her in his mind when he first heard it, but now it was becoming how he thought of her. He could see the persona and discern the edges where Savannah ended and Freya began.

And now that he knew what the name meant? He never wanted to call her Savannah again. No wonder she preferred being called Savvy or James. He remembered what she'd said about James. "Your uncle was CIA?"

"Yes. My father's brother."

"Were you close?"

"He died a few months after I was born. He's one of the stars on the wall at Langley."

He remembered the photo in her office. The wall was important to everyone who worked for the CIA, and it didn't surprise him she had a photo of it, but now he knew it went even deeper than Agency pride for her.

Jesus. Would Harrison Evers get a star?

He silently vowed to do everything he could to prevent that from happening.

Chapter Seventeen

"This is interesting," Freya said as she read a document on the new computer. "Fitzsimmons questioned Lubanga on the prevalence of artisanal miners in Congo and protection for mining claims."

They'd been on the road for several hours, and she'd used her satellite hotspot to download Lubanga's files to the new machine. Now she combed through the files while Cal drove, looking for references to Fitzsimmons.

Artisanal mining was unregulated mining—in some cases, looting by an individual or small group—and it often involved child labor and extremely unsafe conditions. Artisanal and Small Scale Mining—commonly referred to as ASM—usually involved subsistence miners who used hand tools. Because it was illegal, they often worked in protected areas, endangering wildlife and themselves. In DRC, ASMs mined diamonds, cobalt, coltan, and even uranium.

"What kind of artisanal mining is he worried about?" Cal asked. "Diamonds? Coltan?"

"Doesn't say." She reread the document. There wasn't much to it. No dates except the JPEG creation date: three months ago. No locations. Nothing concrete that could be pinned on the ministry. "Doesn't even mention the school he's supposedly funding." She'd been searching the files for the location of the school, but so far, between encrypted files in English and French that would take time to crack, unsearchable JPEG files, and documents in Lingala, she'd come up empty.

"It's weird," she said. "As an American, I can't help but think, how is it possible to hide a school? But in DRC…"

"Yeah. You need to let go of your notions of infrastructure. The gaps between organized towns and cities are vast. You can hide a lot in the in-between spaces, even if that isn't the goal. Put some effort behind it, and you can be invisible."

"I'll keep looking, but so far, our best lead is 'Versailles subway.' It's a starting point." Even better, there were known tunnels under Mobutu's African Versailles. No mention of a subway, but maybe the reference was more about underground passages. She'd looked up the location of the jungle palace—now a ruin—and had been relieved to see the main town, Gbadolite, had an airport. They could charter a flight and might even be able to skip—or bribe their way through—customs. She had several items she didn't want anyone looking at too closely. Even satellite phones could be seen as suspect when entering DRC. Her satellite hotspot would be very suspicious. And it would be nice if they could keep their handguns and a few other goodies she'd brought.

A road sign indicated they neared Morogoro, a large city with plenty of options for food and fuel. "We should refuel the car and fill the jerry cans. As far as I can tell, gas stations get farther apart after Morogoro, and they might not be open twenty-four hours." She closed the laptop and set it on the floor. "I'll drive, and you can read the documents in Lingala. Maybe we can find something more about Fitz or whatever is supposed to happen in Versailles on the fifth."

Cal nodded and took the exit. They spotted a dirt path that paralleled the main highway and agreed to stretch their legs for a bit after fueling up. They had a long night of driving ahead of them. As eager as she was to get the hell out of Tanzania, a walk with fresh air would do her good.

After getting gas, they grabbed a snack from their food supplies and set out on the path. This far inland was much muggier without Indian Ocean breezes, and the warm air was like an embrace. Pedestrians and bicycles filled the path on the sultry evening. A few people sharing the path were white, so Freya didn't stand out as much as she might elsewhere in the more rural parts of Tanzania.

Cal touched her hand, but then released it. "Handholding and other public displays of affection aren't really acceptable here, but handholding is okay in Congo. Definitely no kissing in public there or here."

She nodded. Being around Gorev's associates was not the same as being among Tanzanians.

"We need a new cover story," he said quietly. "There's no need for you to play whore or courtesan in Congo."

"What do you have in mind?"

"Married couple. I'm taking you to see my mother's country for the first time." Except for the married part, it was true, which would make it an easy cover to maintain.

"Works for me. Where are we from?"

"May as well stick to the truth as much as possible. I grew up in the DC area. You know DC from your time at Langley. So DC, Maryland, or Virginia. Your pick."

"DC. We're wealthy enough to charter flights for this trip and travel in as much style as possible in Congo, so I guess we're both attorneys?"

"You're an attorney. I couldn't fake my way through legal terms. I'm a defense contractor. My company provides private security for diplomats." And with a father in the State Department, he also knew a bit about that world.

"Perfect. How long have we been married?"

"I think only a year," he said. "Your mom is starting to nag us for grandkids, so we decided to take this trip because it's something we wouldn't do with children, at least, not until they're much older."

She wanted to close her eyes and slip into this fantasy of a quiet life with Cal. She'd never wanted kids, but the idea of raising a child with him triggered an ache that was new. She had a feeling he'd be an amazing dad.

The fantasy is just escape. It's not Cal and kids that you want. It's to be out of this nightmare. To be safe. To be less alone.

But then she looked up at the man by her side and knew it was also Cassius Callahan. She was drawn to him like a magnet and had been since the first time she sat in a SOCOM meeting and met his gaze. She remembered the exact moment, the frisson that had spread through her. His look had been curious, interested. He'd changed later, when he'd learned she was CIA.

The change in him had led her to look up his service file—she had access to all the special ops teams information—and learned his mom was from DRC, which at least gave her a hint as to his disdain.

She realized now she could finally ask the question that had nagged at her then. "The CIA helped Belgium assassinate Lumumba, paving the way for Mobutu to seize power in Congo. Is that why you dislike the CIA so much?"

"It's part of it."

And now, she'd gotten him roped into another CIA assassination mission—of another Congolese man. Or, at least, she'd believed that was her mission. Now she wasn't so sure.

Regardless, she was too raw to delve into all the reasons he didn't like her, and regretted bringing the subject up. "I have more passports in different names. We'll have no problem entering the country."

"Who are we now?"

"The names don't matter so much. We won't use them anywhere but at checkpoints. I kept your initials, so you're Charlie Carson. I'm Sandy Jones."

"So you didn't take my name when we married."

"I could point out that you didn't take mine."

He smiled. Oh, how she loved that grin. "True. Cassius Lange sounds pretty good, actually. But then people would wonder why everyone calls me Cal."

She knew he was just being silly, but for some reason, she felt a flutter at his use of their real names, casually combining them in matrimony. "Well, it could be your initials. What's your middle name?" She found herself mentally hoping it was Andrew or something else that would fit the A in CAL.

"Rishi. Named for my mother's father."

"That's right. I forgot. Guess you should probably keep your name, then."

He smiled again. "You ready to head back?"

She nodded, and they turned to walk to their car, discussing their new cover, deciding on the necessary details to prepare for their journey into the Democratic Republic of the Congo.

Freya was asleep as they neared the lakeside town of Kigoma just over twenty-four hours after leaving Dar es Salaam. Cal nudged her awake. "We're almost there, sweetheart." They'd decided to use endearments instead of names as much as they could, given that he'd have a hard time adjusting to calling her Sandy after rehearsing Jamie for so long.

It didn't hurt that the endearment came naturally. Something he found both alarming and pleasant.

Her eyes fluttered open, and she took in their surroundings. She woke up like a soldier, he'd noticed. Ready to fight. But then, she'd been trained in much the same way as he had. She was an elite operator in her own right. The only difference was that his physical training continued on a daily basis as his work involved training others, while her work had been largely a desk job as she consulted with SOCOM and shared her expertise in intel gathering and analysis.

She could go toe to toe with him in the gym, and, he now knew, had a libido that kept pace with his in the bedroom. She could be his ideal woman, and for the first time since meeting her, the idea didn't terrify him.

But it should. Given their situation? It definitely should.

They drove straight to the airport. It was early afternoon, and they hoped to find a pilot to fly them to Gbadolite, the ancestral home of Mobutu Sese Seko. His Versailles in the Jungle.

The first pilot they spoke to had another run to make and wasn't available until the following day. The second pilot's plane was grounded for a mechanical problem. The third ended up being the charm—for the right price, which was steep. Thank goodness money wasn't an issue on this op.

They grabbed their belongings from the car, including a new backpack that was the same size as the pack he wore on ops, but in neon orange and green that proclaimed camping enthusiast, not military. The eastern part of DRC was overloaded with different militia groups trying to take over the country. Any hint of military affiliation, and no amount of bribery could get them into the country.

Freya had a special backpack for hiding her spy gear and should be able to pass inspection no problem. Cal's pack was loaded with their camping supplies and the basic, over-the-counter electronics, including binoculars with night vision he'd picked up at the sporting goods store. They were far from military grade, but they'd do in a pinch and could pass border inspection. Freya had night-vision glasses for both of them in her spy gear, but they didn't have magnification. The only item in his pack that was military grade was his GPS, but in Congo, over-the-counter GPS wouldn't do. Given that all their gear—including the GPS—was shiny and new, they'd look like tourists who'd loaded up on all the best gadgets for their adventure.

Thankfully, the customs inspection was cursory, due in part to the cash Cal dropped to speed it along, but they had the perfect excuse—they needed to depart right away if they wanted to beat a storm that was predicted to roll into Gbadolite later that evening. As long as they didn't hit any weather, the flight would take just under two hours.

An hour after reaching Kigoma, they settled in their seats in the back of the small plane. Cal reached across the armrest to take Freya's hand and threaded his fingers through hers as they sped down the runway.

They circled around and gained altitude as they crossed the lake border between Tanzania and Congo. It wasn't long before he was looking out the window as his mother's country passed beneath them.

Congo. He was going back to Congo.

He'd grown up on his mother's stories of the mining village she lived in until she was thirteen. Her stories of the jungle, the river, they'd been wildly magical. Even her stories of the Kinshasa of her teen years had a special quality.

She'd left willingly, but that didn't mean she didn't cherish her homeland. She'd just fallen in love and saw a different opportunity for her children.

He'd seen her cry many times as her country was brutalized by war. When her sister and nieces were raped, her nephews conscripted. His mother had survivor's guilt for escaping.

When finally it was safe to visit, she'd brought Cal and his brothers, and they'd seen the magic and the horror that was Congo, and he'd been captivated. His heart raced now, excitement and dread coursing through him.

Congo wasn't home. Would never be home, yet it held a piece of his heart, and he carried pride in his Congolese heritage. That pride had spurred him and his brothers to learn to read and write in Lingala, when it was primarily a verbal language.

He'd not just claimed his Congolese side, he'd owned it. Honored it.

And now he was returning, hoping to find information on a corrupt government official who planned a coup, so they could stop it. If that didn't honor his heritage, he didn't know what would.

Freya squeezed his fingers. "The mountains are so beautiful."

He ran his thumb over their entwined hands, reminded of their flight from Djibouti to Nairobi. He brought her knuckles to his lips, something he hadn't done on that first flight. She smiled and leaned into him. He couldn't help himself and draped an arm across her shoulders. It worked for their cover—not that the pilot could see them from his closed cockpit—but more important, it felt right.

In the same way entering Congo felt right.

This thing with Freya, it had a flow like water in a mountain stream. It was natural, shaped by the landscape. It could be wild, with shallow, rough rapids, but it also could slow to a deep pool, calm and serene.

This was the calm between rapids, he knew, but he'd take it.

The plane was small and loud, and they settled into the silence as they crossed mountains and rainforest. After so many long hours in the car, by comparison, the flight passed quickly. As they descended to the runway at Gbadolite, Cal brushed his lips across Freya's temple even as he girded himself for the roles they had to play when they landed.

For tonight, they'd head to the formerly grand Motel Nzekele, which was now run-down, with an emptied swimming pool and dilapidated theater, but which they'd been assured still accepted guests who dared to make the trek to the once-luxurious palace. They'd talk to the locals, get a feel for the area—Cal's language skills would pave the rutted roads, making it easy for them to gather intel—but after they secured a room, he planned nothing more taxing than sleep. They'd only slept in two-hour shifts during the drive from Dar to Kigoma. They were both due a solid night's rest.

Tomorrow, which would be the fifth of June, they'd begin the real work of tracking down what was happening in Versailles that day.

On the tarmac of the old airport with the single, long runway that had been built to accommodate Mobutu's chartered Concorde flights, Cal tipped the pilot and thanked him for a smooth, easy flight. Raindrops splattered the cracked pavement; they'd beaten the predicted storm by a handful of minutes.

Gbadolite was the rare city in DRC that had electricity, thanks to a hydroelectric dam on a nearby river constructed for Mobutu to power his

Versailles. Most of DRC lacked infrastructure, but here, there were roads and ruins. Sure, the jungle was consuming the roads, and the ruins were a sad reminder of a horrific kleptocrat, but the area was unique for having lights and appliances. The sorts of things he took for granted on a daily basis, even in Djibouti.

Because of this affluence, locals were inclined to hold fond memories of Mobutu. This oasis in the jungle was the one place where Mobutu had created jobs and prosperity. His palace had employed hundreds, and for many years, this had been a thriving paradise.

Then Mobutu was ousted, Laurent Kabila was in, and the palace was looted of all its glory. Now, twenty years and a few weeks after Mobutu fled the country, his ancestral home was a shell of its former glory as the jungle reclaimed Versailles.

Visitors were rare, and most flights to Gbadolite came from Kinshasa, not Tanzania, so their arrival was met with anticipation from locals, three of whom lined up to offer them a ride from the airport to wherever they wished to go. They were whisked to Motel Nzekele in short order, and the skeleton staff of the decrepit, formerly five-star hotel were similarly eager to rent them a room.

At last they were alone in a private room, after a grueling two days. Forty-eight hours ago, they'd been on Gorev's yacht. Twenty-four hours ago, they'd been on the road, fleeing Dar es Salaam.

Now they were somewhere that was more of a nowhere, a strange, remote roadside attraction, and they could let their guard down for a few hours and get some sleep.

Customs had been cursory on this side—a perk of the airport not having an international terminal, or even daily scheduled flights. No one in the world knew where they were. For anyone from Lubanga's circle to guess this destination, they'd have to know which files Freya had downloaded and read and then make the mental leap to Gbadolite with that information. It was more likely they'd opt for Kinshasa, or back to Nairobi.

In short, they were safe, and all Cal wanted was sleep. Well, he wanted Freya too, but all he'd get was sleep. They had too much to sort out between them to blithely pick up where they'd left off yesterday morning. But still, they slept in the same bed, the heat of their bodies further heating the musty, muggy room.

He didn't mind the heat, and her scent filled his senses, making him want to pull her close, in spite of the humid air. It came as no surprise when he woke in the darkest hours of the night to find Freya at his side, curled against him.

He imagined waking her with his mouth, as she had done for him. Just the thought made him hard. He wished he could stroke one out, but the bathroom attached to their room had no plumbing and no door. He'd have to get up and walk down the hall to the only intact bathroom on this floor of the hotel, just to jack off in private.

He might as well be back at Camp Citron, where he shared a CLU with Pax and had only the shared latrine and shower that served all enlisted with dry CLUs.

He listened to her steady breathing in the dark, quiet room. He'd forgiven her in his mind some time after she'd plunged that shard in Evers's neck. But even before that, he'd understood she'd been in an impossible situation. Cal had been her best hope and the right choice.

She'd be dead if Cal hadn't come with her. If she'd been partnered with Evers, he would have killed her at some point when she slept, like she was now with her warm body soft against Cal's side.

He pulled her tighter against him, and his lips found her neck. Jesus. She'd be gone. He didn't want to live in a world without Freya Lange, a woman he had yet to really get to know.

He drifted back to sleep, waking when sunlight hit his skin about an hour after dawn. Freya was still in his arms, but she was awake this time, and his morning erection was more than evident. He came fully awake and slowly pulled back from her. Much as he wanted to bury himself inside her right now, this wasn't a good idea.

She rolled to her side and held his gaze. Her hands rested on the mattress between them. One moved, as if she intended to run a hand along his bare pecs. He loved having her hands on him. He wanted her touch. He wanted her to explore his body. He wanted to watch as she took his hard prick into the circle of her palm and fingers and stroked him. He wanted her mouth on him. He wanted the wet heat of her slick vagina. He wanted to possess her, to make her come.

And her eyes said she wanted all that too.

But that would seriously mess with his ability to walk away from her when this mission was over. And he didn't want Freya Lange in his life. They'd never work as a couple.

It had nothing to do with race—hell, he was biracial, with a white father and black mother. His parents, his community, would welcome her with open arms. Except for the CIA thing. His parents weren't fans of the Agency after they'd screwed with his mom all those years ago. Not to mention the way the CIA had fucked up Congo. But his parents probably wouldn't hold her employer against her as much as Cal had.

There was no way to know where Congo would be now if the CIA hadn't conspired with Belgium to assassinate Lumumba, but there was a good chance the country wouldn't have had thirty-two years of Mobutu.

Of course, none of this was Freya's fault. It had all happened before she was born. But her dedication to the Agency and her methods had always alarmed him. She mirrored the CIA's attitude of "I know what's best for everyone" added with the willingness to sacrifice others upon the altar of her smug infallibility to shape the world in the way she believed it should be.

At least, that was what he'd believed back at Camp Citron. And then…she'd been right about Drugov.

The CIA did vital work; he wasn't blind to that. Hell, they'd found bin Laden. And Freya had proven to be one of the good ones, the sort of operator they needed. The kind who copied the computer files *before* the assassination.

But still, that didn't make her girlfriend material. He wanted someone who didn't risk everything for the job. Someone who didn't lie and manipulate. Someone who wouldn't sacrifice him.

Someone who wouldn't sacrifice herself.

He scooted back, putting even more space between them. Honor was everything to him. He wouldn't lie to her about where this was going. "I want to have sex with you, but there is no future for us when this is over, and I don't want to hurt you."

Her eyes dimmed, showing the hurt he didn't want to inflict. But what did he expect? He was rejecting her. Pain was inevitable.

She cleared her throat. "I know you won't ever be able to forgive me, and I understand that. I was terrible for not telling you. I just thought, maybe now that you know what Harry was, you'd at least understand."

"I do understand. And I do forgive you."

Her eyes widened. "Really?" Tears pooled. This was the real Freya, because there was no way Savannah James would show him tears.

"Yeah. Really. I one hundred percent forgive you. But that doesn't mean we can resume being lovers." He was in full retreat. They both knew what they'd shared in Dar had been more than sex. That was the problem. "There is so much between us—we're past the point of *just* being lovers. But that's all I want from you. A screw and nothing more."

She rose from the bed and walked to the window, staring out across their view of grass and ruins.

The pane was cracked but clean, and the light shone through. Everything about this place was run-down, disheveled. But clean. The caretakers of the hotel took pride in their work, maintaining a few rooms for the rare guest.

Morning sun brought out pale streaks in her dark hair. Her skin glowed, but the bruise on her cheek remained in shadow, invisible as he took in her silhouette. "I think I'm falling in love with you," she said, her gaze fixed outside.

He would always remember this moment, how achingly beautiful she was, standing in the window, giving him words he didn't deserve. He wanted to launch himself from the bed and take her in his arms, make love to her against the wall. But instead, he curled his hand into a fist and did the right thing. "That's why I won't have sex with you. Not when you want more than I'm willing to give."

She nodded. "Thank you."

He rose from the bed and headed for the door. "I'm going to take a shower." He needed to give her space and to get rid of his damned erection before he did something stupid.

Chapter Eighteen

They started as any tourist would and hired a driver to take them to the ruins of Mobutu's palace. Freya packed the most important of their belongings—computer, backup batteries, mobile hotspot, burner cell, and satellite phone—into a backpack that was designed to carry and conceal the precious electronics.

Cal packed their cash and other goodies into his own pack, leaving the camping gear behind. They planned to return to this hotel, and it would be odd if they set out with everything they owned on their backs. From here on out, they would keep the most important of their supplies with them at all times, within reason.

Their driver offered to be their guide through the city. They accepted his offer to drive them around for the day, but passed on his offer of accompanying them into the various attractions they would visit to act as translator. Cal gave this response in Lingala, and the driver lit up, surprised and happy to have found a long-lost son of Congo, as he put it.

The two men spoke in Lingala for the fifteen-minute drive to the ruins in Kawele, their voices cheerful, as if they were old friends. Watching Cal and the driver interact was utterly charming. He smiled and laughed, and she knew that even though he had a fake name and fake career, this was the real man. This was congenial, easygoing Sergeant First Class Cassius Callahan. At Camp Citron, he was everyone's best friend.

Even when Pax and Bastian were at odds, Cal remained close to both without prejudice. That was the man she'd been attracted to upon their first meeting, and the man he'd never been with her, much to her disappointment.

Everyone viewed her as cold and remote, while Cal was the exact opposite. She'd been warm and outgoing before her parents died. After that, it was her drive that got her through day after day. Freya, the girl who'd had dreams of being a wildlife biologist, had faded as a new, harder, colder woman emerged.

Somehow, Cal managed to be the driven soldier and hard, cool operator without losing his warm nature. After hours, he could laugh and joke with his team, but in the field, he was the quiet professional who got shit done.

Cal might be who she wished she could be, but she knew it was too late for her. She didn't know how to drop her guard.

Well, except with him.

She felt no shame or regret in admitting she was falling in love with him. It was the first time in her life she'd ever used those words, and she was glad she'd had the courage to say them, even though it just gave him another reason to push her away. They could die on this mission. She wouldn't die regretting the things she hadn't said.

She also knew he cared about her. It might not be love, but he cared enough to be honest about the fact that sex between them was more than he could handle, an emotional bond he didn't want. That eased the sting of rejection. A little. He didn't push her away because he didn't care; it was the opposite.

She respected his honesty even as she ached with the loneliness of being with him, but not having him.

They reached the palace, and the driver said in English, "It is a shame you can't see the larger palace, but the military is using it to house soldiers. We don't get many tourists in Kawele and Gbadolite. I think we would get more if people could see both of the palaces."

Freya figured it wasn't the lack of sightseeing that was the problem so much as access, but the man did have a point. She viewed the overgrown driveway, hardly able to believe it had only been twenty years since Mobutu's fall. These weren't ancient ruins. This was lavish excess, enjoyed at the expense of the masses, dwindling into decay.

She might be here on a covert mission, but she was just as eager as the next tourist to see the jungle reclaiming this monument to greed and kleptocracy.

She opened the door to the ancient, battered car and studied the decaying brown-and-gold gate with a diamond motif both in the metal and the framing structure. Beyond the gate was a long, overgrown driveway. Their driver introduced a man waiting by the gate as the head of the village of Kawele.

The village head smiled. "Admission is twenty dollars," he said in English.

As tempting as it was to pay more—these people had so little—it was unwise to draw attention as big spenders. She and Cal had discussed this before setting out, and he agreed to only pay the basic rate. Exchange complete, Cal then paid their driver to wait with the car for their return.

The village head unlocked the gate and pushed it open. The hinges creaked, lending ambiance to the crumbling walls. They passed through the opening and entered the grounds. They weren't alone as they walked down the long driveway. Children and adults dotted the ruins. Some, Freya presumed, were caretakers, while others were there to offer their service as guides.

They reached a tunnel lined with rough red bricks, and on the other side could see the once-grand fountain that had greeted visitors in Mobutu's heyday. The tiered fountain, styled after Versailles, had once played music. Now the giant basin was bone dry and home to a garden of weeds.

An archway beckoned beyond the fountain, and it was there they were greeted by what must've been another fountain. Two lion statues stood sentry, but it was obvious two other lions were missing from their posts. The stonework and marble was cracked and chipped, with green shoots growing in the crevices.

"Is it weird that I love this?" she said softly. She'd read enough articles about the place during their long drive to know most of the residents of Gbadolite and Kawele were upset with the decay. In this small pocket of Congo, they had lived well under Mobutu.

But Mobutu had been a blight on this country, on his people. The list of his sins against the people of Congo was vast, and during it all, he lived in luxury in his Versailles, paid for with money that should have gone into education, health care, roads, telephones—even the most basic infrastructure would have saved and changed lives.

"Not at all," Cal said. "He gutted and robbed this country so he could build this monument to himself, and it didn't survive him even a month after he was gone. This is his legacy, this decrepit waste. Not the grandeur." He also spoke in low tones to avoid offending the locals.

They walked down the corridor that led to what had once been Mobutu's bedroom. Freya had read that he would show off his room by flicking a switch that triggered panels to slide apart and reveal his bed, which rose from the floor.

While his people starved and children labored.

They found the alcove where his bed had been, and she smiled to see nothing but green slime. Fitting.

The palace was roofless. Gone were the paintings, chandeliers, stained glass, and Louis XIV furniture. The marble had been shattered or taken. There was now graffiti on the walls. Words in Lingala and French, which Cal translated. Drawings of people and animals. Symbols she didn't understand.

They explored the roofless rooms even as the sky opened up and rain began to fall. They left the interior to explore the no longer lavish pool that was built into many terraces. It must've been stunning once upon a time.

As they explored the ground, she searched for a door or cellar entrance.

Anything that could be an entrance to the tunnels beneath. Information online had been scant as to the extent of the tunnels, but Mobutu had bragged about his nuclear bunker and there was speculation that one tunnel crossed under the border into the Central African Republic, which was only about ten miles north.

They'd agreed they wouldn't ask about the tunnels right away—they'd wait to see if a tour was offered—but it appeared the bunker wasn't part of the regular tour package.

There were fewer people on the grounds now that the rain was picking up. If they wanted to question locals, they might need to come back later after the rain stopped.

But there was one local who'd been shadowing them from the beginning who wasn't deterred by rain: a young girl—she couldn't be more than seven or eight—with big, beautiful eyes and gorgeous, springy curls.

Freya offered her a smile and asked in English if she knew of a place they could get out of the rain.

The girl frowned. "Lingala? *Français?*"

Before Freya could repeat the question in French, Cal knelt down and spoke to her in Lingala. The girl lit up and nodded, then said something in response. She then looked around and smiled again, and spoke again.

To Freya, Cal said, "I decided to be direct and asked if she knows how to get to the tunnels. You want to get out of the rain, and I heard there was a cool bunker. She said tourists aren't really supposed to go underground, but since no one's around, she'll take us for ten dollars.

Freya smiled. She'd forgotten they could be direct with a child—they weren't likely to be suspicious at the question in the way adults would. She was so used to playing roles, she was overcomplicating something that was really quite simple.

Cal paid the girl, who lit up at the ten-dollar bill. She led the way to a staircase to a lower terrace, and from there, they followed her down a path to a door that looked like it led into a lower level of the house that was cut into the hillside. If they'd circled this far, they'd have seen it for themselves. But it was better to have a guide. Especially when they learned the door was locked. The girl gave rapid instructions and then zipped around the side of the house, out of sight.

"She said to wait here. There's a small window she can crawl through, and she'll unlock the door from the inside."

A moment later, the door opened, and there was the girl, all grins. They followed her into the dim vestibule. A long dark tunnel extended in one direction. On the opposite side was a short hall. Daylight filtered through, indicating it probably led to the window the girl had used. The girl led them into the hallway.

The tourist in Freya wanted to explore for the fun of it. The operator was on full alert. They were in the basement that had to lead to the tunnels, thanks to this adorable little girl.

The girl said something that made Cal smile.

"What did she say?" Freya asked.

"Your hair got flat in the rain."

Freya smiled. Her hair had gone from frizzy in the humidity to drowned rat when the skies opened up. She should have braided it this morning to keep it out of her face. She pulled back the damp strands as she knelt down to speak to the girl at eye level. "We can't all be so lucky as to have curls that hold up in the rain."

The girl's hair was absolutely beautiful. She wore it longer than many of the children Freya had seen in in the last few days, she'd noticed many trimmed closer to the scalp. This girl's dark curls stood in vibrant clusters.

"What is your name?" Freya asked in French.

"Amelie."

Freya offered her hand. "It's nice to meet you, Amelie, I'm Sandy. Thank you for getting us out of the rain, even if it was too late to save my hair."

Amelie shook Freya's hand and responded in French. "Would you like to see more of the tunnels?"

"Very much," Freya said. She nodded to Cal.

He pulled out a twenty and offered it to Amelie. "In case you get in trouble for taking us down here," he said in French for Freya's benefit.

The girl smiled and started to reach for the bill then stopped. "We don't have light. The tunnels are very dark."

Freya pulled out her cell phone as Cal tucked the bill in Amelie's hand and pulled out another phone. "Lead the way."

They followed the girl down the passage, the ground gently sloping downward as they went deeper into the earth. When they came to intersections, Freya noticed graffiti symbols above or next to different passages marked the way. Amelie led them down the corridors that were marked with a spiral and what looked like a number or hash sign, maybe. Tic-tac-toe? But the grid was a bit taller on the vertical. As they went deeper, a diamond shape with a cross through it—like a kite without a tail—appeared next to a few passages.

Freya asked Amelie what the symbols meant.

"Those are new," she said, pointing to the kitelike symbol. "Mama says not to explore those passages without an adult." She smiled. "But today I am with adults." They walked farther down the corridor and came to another archway, where she pointed to a circular spiral and the hash sign. "Those are our friends. You never get lost if you follow the friendly circle."

"And this one?" Freya asked, pointing to the hash sign. "What does it mean?"

"That is an old sign. Here forever. I don't know who made it or if they are here anymore."

Did the symbols represent different factions? DRC had plenty of factions, some aligned, some not. Fighting these days happened mostly near the border, close to Uganda and Rwanda, and there were dozens of factions. The map of what territory belonged to whom changed weekly.

It wasn't too surprising that this area—which was pretty much the only region in DRC that held fond memories of Mobutu—could be a hive of hidden antigovernment groups.

Which faction supported Lubanga's bid for power? Spiral or diamond cross?

Did the people of Kawele and Gbadolite support Lubanga, or did they only see the façade he presented, that of the president's puppet? Lubanga had fooled the president into believing he was loyal. Did that mantle extend to the unstable region to the east?

The passages under the palace were a vast network of tunnels broken up by rooms—some must have been storage chambers that were now devoid of anything valuable. She and Cal would come back and explore tonight, without Amelie as their guide. The hash symbol became more prominent, the vertical bars consistently longer than the horizontal ones.

Freya was curious where Amelie was taking them, as she had a definite goal in mind as she led them down the mazelike passages. Freya memorized the route. The symbols made it easy.

As they turned into a new passageway, Freya noticed the hash sign had a third horizontal bar. She paused to look at it and in a flash it hit her. Not hash signs...tracks.

Could "subway" have been literal? "Amelie, are there trains down here? Could this symbol mean train tracks?"

The girl frowned. "Mama has never told me about trains. My brother and I have explored everywhere, and we've never seen a train."

So maybe it wasn't literal. Or maybe the train tracks had been removed when the palace was looted.

"Come. This way," Amelie said. "We're almost there."

Was "there" the nuclear bunker? Was that what excited the girl? But in the end, Amelie led them to a locked steel door. "I don't know what is behind this door. My big brother and I have tried for months to pick the lock. He thinks there is a throne made of diamonds behind the door. I think it is made of gold. Who would want to sit on diamonds? He said I'm stupid and the diamonds would be embedded in metal. I said that proves I'm right. Gold is metal. Mama says there are no riches left, and it just leads to the bunker. Mama doesn't understand this door."

Freya smiled, flooded with joy to know that the magic of childhood and secret doors survived deep in the heart of the jungle. Of course, this little girl lived next to an overgrown palace, the kind of place that was ripe to fuel a child's imagination. Elsewhere in Congo, children didn't have this luxury. Children in the east were conscripted to fight, or they battled famine and disease as they fled from the various factions.

But here, even in the midst of an underground maze that might have been claimed by two different factions, this little girl got to be a child.

She wanted to hug her and tell her to stay gold. But she didn't because she also didn't want to scare her with an unwelcome touch from a stranger.

"Perhaps there is a menagerie beyond the door?" Freya said. "Maybe this leads to a zoo above ground, hidden by the jungle. Lost to humans once they lost the key."

"You understand the door," Amelie said solemnly. She pursed her lips. "The lions and elephants would have to learn to get along if they're in a jungle enclosure, or they'd have eaten or stomped on each other years ago."

"Maybe the chimpanzees brokered a peace agreement. They are natural diplomats. I wouldn't be surprised to learn one of them was named king."

"President," Cal said. "It's a democracy, after all."

Amelie smiled. "I like this idea." She glanced back down the passageway. "We should go back. Mama will be looking for me."

They followed the little sprite down the corridors, retracing their path. Like Amelie, Freya too wondered what was beyond the metal door. Odds were Amelie's mother was right and it merely led to the nuclear bunker that Mobutu had been so proud of, but she'd noticed three things as they stood by the door: the brass of the hinges and lock didn't match the rest of the hardware, indicating they were relatively new; wiring mounted to the ceiling suggested that whatever was behind the door had electricity; and a very small kite symbol had been etched into the upper left corner of the door right next to a hash—or train track—symbol.

Chapter Nineteen

Gbadolite didn't exactly have rental car companies, but similar to the way Motel Nzekele still rented rooms to the determined traveler, they were able to rent a car from a hotel employee. The vehicle was necessary because they could hardly pay a driver to take them back to the palace at midnight. Way too many questions would be asked.

They spent the afternoon prepping for their nighttime raid. Freya searched for anything and everything she could find on the diamond-cross symbol, drawing Cal's attention when she crowed with excitement, having found the symbol drawn in dirt that coated a vehicle parked behind the Reverend Abel Fitzsimmons in a televised interview. He was in Kinshasa at the time, raising money for his Mission School.

Official or unofficial, this was the link they'd been looking for. They were on the right track.

Cal left Freya to her searching and hung out in the lobby to work the locals. His cover story was the local cuisine hadn't agreed with Freya—or rather Sandy—and he was letting her sleep in peace while her stomach settled.

He returned to their room after two hours with news that a flight from Dar es Salaam had just landed. Today was the date in the document. Did the incoming flight have something to do with that? Coming from Dar es Salaam, it almost had to. Was Lubanga here?

Without any answers, all they could do was move forward with their plan to explore the tunnel under the palace in the dead of night.

They prepped carefully for the night op, with their backpacks fully loaded. They planned to return to Motel Nzekele if they could, but they were going on a midnight reconnaissance mission without a clue as to what they'd find. Returning to the shabby, former five-star hotel might not be possible.

They set out just an hour after nightfall with a basket laden with food they'd purchased in town. Cal had spoken to the concierge in Lingala, telling him of their intention to visit the hydroelectric dam on the Ubangi River and enjoy a picnic with stargazing.

The concierge had warned of the insects being attracted to light and food, which might make the meal less romantic and more malaria inducing, but Cal waved off his concerns. He heard the man say something under his breath about stupid Americans, and Cal held back his smile as he took Freya's hand and exited the hotel.

They drove to the dam as stated and climbed out of the car to view the river and scout out a spot where they could picnic. They strolled hand in hand, which felt more natural than it probably should.

He was reminded of the hotel room in Kenya, where they'd practiced touching each other. How far they'd come since then. She was falling in love with him and he...he cared about her. More than he wanted to.

She triggered his protective nature. He'd rage at witnessing any woman being assaulted, but at Gorev's party, when Anton had gone after her, his fury had been deep and primal.

He hadn't even felt the blows he'd taken from the security guard. His focus had been on Freya and protecting her from Anton. A similar dark rage and protectiveness had risen up when he'd found her sitting beside Harrison Evers's body. He'd been too late to help her, and his body was still wound with the tension of ramping up for a battle that never happened.

They chose a spot as far from the lights of the dam as possible and laid out their blanket and picnic dinner. Insects found them, but it wasn't as bad as if they were in the direct light. They both took daily antimalarial drugs along with a host of other pills to stave off illness while on an op.

With time to kill, Cal shared stories of his mother's childhood. She'd grown up in a small village, moving to Kinshasa at thirteen with her mother and siblings when the hard rock diamond mine her father had worked in suffered a collapse that killed him and twenty other miners. He'd visited his mother's village a few years ago, meeting for the first time aunts and uncles who had returned to the village when the mining operation resumed after the Second Congo War ended. An uncle—his aunt's husband—was the overseer for what was now a small open-pit diamond mining operation. It was one of the few regulated and official diamond mines in Congo, established before Lubanga got his hooks into the mining sector.

Finished eating, they packed up their meal and lay down on the blanket, gazing up at the sky, Freya using Cal as a pillow. Clouds were rolling in, which was perfect for their night op, as the moon was waxing gibbous—more than fifty percent illuminated. They could use every cloud to darken their path. Even though they appeared relaxed, Cal could feel the tension in her body, the coiled energy, as she lay beside him.

He knew she was running scenarios in her mind, planning how they would enter the palace grounds. Freya was a planner, right down to the last detail. Just like she lined up extra cars and bank accounts. Embarking on this journey without safety nets set up had to be terrifying for her, and yet she faced each task with unwavering determination. But then, their lives depended on it.

He still hadn't told her about the money she'd been accused of stealing. His original reason for not telling her was moot now. He believed in her innocence like he believed the Earth was a sphere. He would tell her now, except he needed her focus on the task at hand. He'd tell her later, when they were safely back at the hotel, when she could process it without further shattering her faith in the organization she'd devoted her life to.

He gazed up at the stars that peeked between clouds. This mission was unlike anything he'd done before. He'd always preferred training locals over combat, enjoyed honing the skills of young men eager to protect their communities. But he'd never shied away from the necessary violence of ops. His team had been sent to Djibouti to train Djiboutian soldiers, but they'd been pulled in to several ops during his months in-country—ops that saved women and children from being sold into slavery, and he was damn proud of the work he'd done for Uncle Sam these last few months.

But this, going after intel on a man who'd pillaged his mother's country, who'd made victims of the people of Congo, felt like the mission he'd been born for. If he could save boys from being conscripted like his lost cousins, or girls like Amelie from being raped or starved or forced to work in mines, then he could face his mother with pride.

He hadn't realized how he would feel, being in Congo on a covert mission. How satisfying it would be. Maybe he should have considered Delta Force instead of Special Forces, but he'd disdained covert operations before now.

Just like he'd disdained Freya.

"You haven't told me what happened to your parents," he said softly.

She was silent for a moment. Finally, she said, "They were in Greece for an academic conference. My mother was presenting a paper on"—she paused and took a deep breath—"Zagreus."

He took her hand in his and squeezed.

"I never should have made this mission personal that way. That'll teach me." Her fingers curled around his, holding on. "My older brother was an undergrad in Paris at the time. He went to Athens to see them. I was a senior in high school, a month away from taking AP tests. I wanted to go to Greece but opted to stay home and study. I was in the running to be salutatorian of my class and didn't want to mess it up.

"It was a sunny spring day. They were in a market, playing hooky from the conference, enjoying being tourists. A suicide bomber stood just two feet from my brother when he detonated the bomb. My brother died instantly, my father a few hours later. My mother lived in a coma for several weeks. She was likely brain-dead, but I couldn't... I didn't know what to do. I turned eighteen on my graduation day. We'd planned a big graduation and birthday party, but instead, I was in Greece at my mom's bedside. It was going to be my decision if and when life support would be stopped, but she died at five twenty-two a.m. on my birthday, saving me from having to make that decision."

He slipped an arm around her and pulled her snug against his side. "I'm so sorry." He'd heard the hitch in her voice. The cool, always-in-control operator couldn't tell this story without tears, and he was glad she hadn't learned to cut off or hide those emotions. He'd judged her harshly for her line of work, and now he felt like an ass. "You got into intelligence work because of how they died."

He felt her nod against his chest. "The bomber...he was a known threat. The Greek intelligence agency had him on a watch list, but they weren't actually watching him. There's probably nothing more that could have been done, but still. I have to try. To prevent others from losing their family like I did."

He pressed his lips to her forehead. "Your birthday is in June? What date?"

"I hate my birthday."

"Understandable. But when is it?" If they were back at Camp Citron for her birthday, he'd take her to dinner. Do something, anything, to show her she wasn't so alone.

"It's June third," she said softly.

He closed his eyes against the wave of horror. Two days ago. "Harry tried to rape you again on your birthday."

"Yes. And I killed him." She was silent for a moment, then added. "I *really* hate my birthday."

He'd made love to her on her birthday. He could take solace knowing they'd shared something special that day. But they'd also fought, and he'd left her crying in the bathroom. Not that it hadn't been justified. But Jesus.

"When we get back to Camp Citron, I'm going to take you out. We'll celebrate properly." As if a night at Barely North could ease the horror, but it was all he had to offer.

"I probably won't be going back to Camp Citron, but thanks anyway."

"You made me a promise. You're going to try to clear your name. We'll prove Harry showed up in Dar to kill you. I can vouch for you."

"But you weren't there. You didn't see. And the fact that we've become lovers changes things."

"You promised me you'd fight."

"I will. I'm going to bring these bastards down. But I'm also a realist. I've learned something in my thirty-four years."

He lifted her chin, bringing her mouth level with his. "And I've learned something in my thirty-one years."

"What's that?"

"That Freya Lange has a spine of steel. And while she wants everyone to believe her heart is made of ice, it's really blue fire. It burns bright and hot and sparkles like a diamond."

She shook her head. "It's just an organ."

"We're all only human."

"I don't want to be. I don't want to hurt. I don't want to love. I don't want to care."

He ran his thumb over that full bottom lip. A physical feature that had caught his eye the first time they'd met. He'd seen the mouth but not the person. Then he'd learned the person was a spook, and he'd resisted the attraction, stopped trying to see her. He never gave her a chance.

There was no holding back his emotions now. Hadn't been since before he'd made love to her. "But I'm glad you care. I'm glad for your human heart of fire. You matter. To me." He wanted to kiss her. Hell, he wanted to make love to her. But that would open a door he'd just spent the last two days barricading closed.

"Thank you," she said. The pain was gone from her eyes, replaced with a warmth she used to hide. The blue glow of lightning.

How did he ever think she was cold personified?

Light flashed in the distance, followed by the rumble of thunder. The storm would be upon them soon. She let out a sigh. "It's dark enough now. We should head to the palace before the storm hits."

He nodded, appreciating how quickly she could change gears. She was an operator through and through. They had a mission to complete, then he could sort out his conflicting feelings.

Chapter Twenty

They hid the car off the road about a mile from the palace gate. They both changed into skintight, solid-black clothes. Freya admired Cal in his catsuit. The fabric clung to his muscles in a way that made him look like a superhero. Black Panther in the flesh, and every bit as hot as the actor who played him.

"You got paint for your face?" he asked.

She nodded. She'd wear a mask, but it would be too hot in the tunnels, which were already humid with rank air. She pulled a hood over her head to hide her brown hair. She quickly put on the black grease, making sure it covered all exposed skin. Cal touched up a spot she'd missed, then leaned down and kissed her, his lips lingering on hers a heartbeat longer than a casual kiss.

"I know this is dangerous, but this is way better than preparing for Gorev's party. I hated watching you use your body as currency with those fuckers."

She gave him a wry smile. "And I'm more comfortable with that kind of op than this one. I might've been unarmed, but I knew what we were walking into. This…" She let her voice trail off, then cleared her throat. She didn't need to prove herself and her training to Cal anymore. She could be honest with him. "This unknown terrifies the hell out of me."

"And I'm more comfortable with this than the suits and negotiation bullshit."

She pulled a small pistol from her pack and slid it into a pocket in her waistband made just for that purpose. Cal did the same with his gun. "You're great at both," she said. "If you want to do more covert work, Delta could probably use you on some missions. Especially down here, with your language skills."

He looked across the dark landscape. They were parked in a thicket of trees, which protected them from the light rain. "I could see working here. Helping these people. But there are so many factions. It's hard to know which one will actually do some good. The US has a shitty track record for picking indigenous leaders. Mobutu is exhibit A."

True. And Mobutu had arrived on the scene after the Congo Free State had already been brutalized by Belgium. King Leopold's greed had fueled the first genocide of the twentieth century. Things improved marginally during the colonial period as the Belgian Congo, but it was after independence when the Republic of the Congo had had a chance, but then the rightful leader was taken out with help from the CIA and Belgian intelligence, opening the door for Mobutu.

"Still, you should consider it. The plan for DRC isn't to choose a new leader so much as remove men vying for the job who would be as bad or worse than Mobutu. Lubanga is exhibit B."

"Do you really think the kill order was legit? Do you believe you were supposed to take out Jean Paul Lubanga?"

She shrugged. "I don't know. Does Lubanga own Seth? Was I sent in to botch the kill? Or did Seth make up the order so I'd take out his puppet master? Either way, I would've screwed up. Dead and/or disavowed."

She handed Cal a small pair of night-vision goggles. These weren't the NVGs he was used to wearing on Special Forces ops. These were spy grade and could fit in a sunglasses case. They weren't as powerful as the military-grade version, but they did have an infrared illuminator for navigating tunnels with zero ambient light, which they'd need tonight.

In addition to NVGs and pistols, they had knockout gas disks, tranquilizer darts, and blowguns. This was a recon mission, and until they knew if people they encountered were friend or foe, they wouldn't harm them. She tucked the small blowgun with seated dart into a specially designed quick access pocket above the breast of her catsuit and handed Cal his to do the same. The gas disks were tucked in an outer pocket of each of their packs for easy access. They would only be effective in small spaces and could be useless in the network of tunnels beneath the palace.

She'd carefully packed her backpack with their electronics. Her new computer was thin and compact and stored in a specially designed pocket that would protect it from water and other hazards, important when it was impossible to know what they'd find in the tunnels. What she hoped to find could well be a unicorn: intel to feed CIA analysts.

Her redemption wouldn't come from killing the men who'd set her up, it would come from finding the intel that would expose their treason. She'd had plenty of time to think since facing Harry in Dar es Salaam, and one conclusion she'd drawn: her deep dive into Drugov's business was the key. If she'd had time to keep digging instead of embarking on this mission, would she have found a connection between Seth and Drugov?

Seth had set her up and sent Harry to take her out. He was in her crosshairs now, and she hoped to hell he was freaking out back at Langley, wondering if she'd return from Congo with enough to destroy him. Seth hadn't counted on her having a Green Beret fluent in Lingala by her side. He'd underestimated her, as had Harry.

She might not come out of this operation with her reputation intact, but she looked forward to facing down Seth just the same. And if she had her way, Cal would be long gone by then, and she'd be on her own, deep in the heart of darkness.

She ran her hand over the pack to ensure everything was tucked away and invisible to the casual search. Their various passports were hidden within the padding of her backpack—it would survive all exterior inspections and X-ray, but a determined searcher would find them with a knife. The remainder of the money they'd gotten from Gorev was split between the two packs, unhidden. If they had to give up the money, so be it.

She cinched the shoulder straps on the pack. "Ready?" she asked.

"Let's roll."

Skirting the main road, it took ten minutes to hike from the car to the palace perimeter. The townspeople didn't expend much energy guarding the grounds, but that didn't mean they wouldn't have guards on the ruins. And anyone could be in place in the tunnels.

It took another ten minutes to cross the grounds and reach the door Amelie had taken them to earlier. Freya had plugged the latch when they left; now all she had to do was push open the door and step inside.

She and Cal paused and listened. Silence answered. A minute later, she heard small scurrying sounds. Rodents, most likely. She'd seen droppings earlier in the day. The heat in the narrow chamber was oppressive. Not surprising given that they were a mere three hundred miles north of the equator.

What other critters inhabited this underground network? Given the jungle setting, it wasn't farfetched to think they could run into exotic animals. They were on the northern edge of the northeastern Congolian lowland forest ecoregion, and the list of animals that thrived in the tropical broadleaf forest was vast. The jungle surrounding Gbadolite was home to okapi, various bat species, owl-faced monkeys, swamp rats, and dozens of other rat species. Eastern lowland gorillas lived in the biome as well, although those apes lived more to the southeast.

Before her parents died, she'd planned to study wildlife biology. She'd dreamed of being the next Birutė Galdikas, Dian Fossey, or Jane Goodall. Now here she was in Congo, and it wasn't until this moment that she realized she was finally fulfilling a childhood dream of visiting great ape habitat. Sort of.

They set out down the long corridor, footsteps silent with soft-soled shoes and careful placement as they navigated debris that had accumulated over the years since Mobutu's ouster. They didn't waste time exploring corridors they'd passed earlier in the day. That would come later. For now, they went straight to the locked metal door. It was as good a starting place as any, and it had those intriguing electrical conduits. Electricity was everything here.

The gutted palace didn't have power, but the tunnels did? That meant something. And she and Cal would find out what.

At last they reached the door, a slower journey than earlier in the day with the need for silent footsteps. While the lack of guards made the journey easy, it also filled her with disappointment. Surely if there was something here, guards would be posted.

Were these tunnels no longer used? That made no sense given that Kawele and Gbadolite had infrastructure that most of Congo did not. One of the failings of the various warring factions to the east was that they had no infrastructure or technology with which to wage their war. If one wanted to truly take over—or liberate, as the rebels would argue—DRC, this would be the ideal place to set up shop. The locals were sympathetic, they had reliable electricity, a decent runway, and even underground bunkers and an escape route into the Central African Republic, all courtesy of Mobutu.

The roads were passable, making it possible to drive from Gbadolite to the port city of Businga just a hundred and thirty kilometers away. From Businga, one could travel on the Mongala River to the Congo River or simply pass through and continue another two hundred kilometers by road to Lisala and the Congo River.

Basically, if one wanted to stage a coup, Gbadolite was the perfect staging point. With a rapidly beating heart, she pulled out her set of lockpicks and made quick work of the mechanism, a soft click telling her they were in.

Cal leaned down and whispered directly in her ear. "Nice work."

His breath on her ear sent a small frisson through her. Even now, as her heart raced as they stepped into the unknown, he affected her.

This attraction was insane. And dangerous.

She stepped back and waved toward the knob. They'd agreed he'd enter first. He'd done this sort of blind entry far more often than she had. Right about now, she was wishing she hadn't insisted they leave body armor in Djibouti. She'd figured if they got this far, it would be a situation where they'd have gone through customs and items like that would be confiscated and raise unwelcome questions. She could pass off the small NVGs as sunglasses, but body armor and M4s were a lot trickier. As it was, they'd been lucky to smuggle in handguns.

Cal silently pushed the door inward. Well-oiled hinges gave not a hint of sound. Good. But it also meant someone was very careful of this door.

Cal slipped through the narrow opening, and Freya followed, silently closing the door behind them after seeing a dark, empty corridor ahead.

They were in unmapped territory. She crouched low and followed Cal. She hadn't done an op like this in a long time and was dangerously rusty, unlike that door hinge. She didn't squeak, but she feared the sound of her heart was just as audible.

Special forces were smart to continually train, even when deployed. Any day they weren't fulfilling their assignment of training locals or off on an op, they were practicing. Day in, day out, she saw SEALs, Special Forces, and Delta operators running drills to hone their already razor-sharp skills.

Cal was on his game as he led the way through the dark. She hadn't exaggerated her abilities when she'd first discussed this mission with him, but she had to acknowledge that her work at Camp Citron didn't keep her as mission-ready as she should be. Not for this anyway. She'd taken on the acting required on Gorev's yacht without a hitch. This was different.

The paved floor gave way to dirt, and before long, it was clear they were descending. The air was oppressively hot, and sweat dripped down her neck and pooled between her breasts.

PVC pipe ran along the ceiling. Conduit for electrical wires. The PVC was the Yellow Brick Road leading them to the Emerald City.

She and Cal both suspected the door led to Mobutu's renowned nuclear bunker or the tunnel to the Central African Republic—or possibly both—but neither of them had been ready to put money on finding a train down here. The descending corridor only confirmed this pessimism. It felt like they were descending into a mine.

As far as she knew, this part of Congo didn't have the range of mineral deposits found farther east and south. But then, Congo's vast wealth of resources underground made it easy to believe that when this palace was constructed, the workers could have come across valuable veins of ore.

It was even possible that they hadn't reported the find, preferring to tap the resource themselves. After all, artisanal mining was common in DRC, and few minerals were sold legally through the government. Much of the country's coltan supply was sold through Rwanda or Burundi, while diamonds were sold through CAR and the Republic of the Congo.

Had the locals mined under the palace without Mobutu's knowledge, or was this a private operation by Mobutu?

It was possible these tunnels had been dug even while Mobutu entertained Pope John Paul II and televangelist Pat Robertson in the palace above. But were the diggers working for the dictator or against him? Given the local attitude toward the despot, she would guess they worked for him. But everything had changed since the palace's heyday.

They reached an intersection marked with an assortment of symbols and words. Cal studied them. He spoke softly, breaking their operational silence. "One of the tunnels collapsed ahead. Proceed with caution."

"I want to keep going." She pointed up to the PVC pipes. "Follow the electricity."

She braced for an argument, but Cal nodded.

They followed the path where the PVC led, forced to crouch due to the low ceiling. Their packs made it hard to fit through the narrow spaces. Were they risking everything for nothing?

After a set of serpentine curves, the space widened and the ceiling rose. The corridor spilled into another tunnel, this one wider, taller, and extending far into the darkness in two directions. And in the center lay narrow-gauge train tracks.

Operational silence was the rule, but in her mind she was whooping and maybe reeling with surprise.

An old mine cart lacking the front axle sat next to the track, but the rails themselves were clear. The room had a faint exhaust smell, as if an engine had run earlier in the day.

Amelie didn't know about the train because it was deep down, far past the locked door that fed her fantasies. Freya hoped the girl never made it past that door, because her mother was right, she shouldn't follow the kite symbol without an adult.

The tunnel disappeared in two directions. A glance at a compass showed it ran north-south at least for this small stretch of rail.

Looking to the south her NVGs presented a crisper image. A light source was ahead, about thirty feet. They headed toward the light, walking on the tracks to avoid the debris that lined the tunnel wall.

The source of the light became clear. In a shallow alcove, was a door with an inset window. Light shone through the window, and the whirr of air-conditioning emitted from behind the door.

They crouched low, out of sight of the window. Cal extended a mirror from a telescoping rod to see into the room. She removed her NVGs so she could see the reflection. A bank of computers—ancient ones, that took up the entire wall—in a climate-controlled room. But more important, a man wearing headphones sat in front of a modern desktop computer, tapping buttons as he stared at a large screen.

Cal pulled out a knockout-gas disk. He hoped the room was small so the gas wouldn't disperse too much—the window was narrow and didn't offer a good view of the room.

The disk was too thick to slide under the door, but the floor was dirt, so he cut a gap with his knife, making a silent prayer that the headphones the man wore were noise cancelling, the air-conditioning would cover the sound, or that it could be mistaken for rodent activity. Any excuse would do.

He activated the gas and shoved the disk through the gap with his knife. He peeled off a glove and used it to plug the hole, then stood to look through the window. White gas clouded the room but cleared quickly, revealing the man slumped forward at his desk.

"Nice," Freya whispered.

They waited the required ninety seconds for the gas to disperse before he turned the knob. If the room was big and there were others in the space, they might meet someone conscious—and very angry—on the other side.

He pulled his gun and entered the room, Freya crossed behind him in a practiced law enforcement maneuver that covered his back while he covered the unknown room.

He knew she was trained, but moments like this, where it showed without the need to communicate, made him acknowledge just how much he'd underestimated her.

The room was both small and empty except for the lone unconscious man. Cal approached the computer monitor from the side, making certain he wasn't in view of the built-in camera. He pulled the headphones off the man and placed them over his own ears, relieved to hear Congolese rumba music. The man hadn't been chatting online with another person.

Freya put a piece of tape over the camera and muted the microphone as Cal moved the man from the seat and bound and gagged him. He should remain unconscious for at least forty-five minutes, but they didn't want to take any chances should he wake early.

While Freya worked the computer, Cal returned to the outer tunnel. The tunnel and tracks extended deep into the darkness to the north and south. He stood guard in front of the open door to the computer room. No one would sneak up on them like they had the bound man sleeping in the corner.

A slight sound from Freya caught his attention, and he entered the room, stepping up behind her but keeping his gaze moving, alert for movement on the tracks even as he glanced at the screen. As far as he could tell, she was uploading files to the cloud, just as she had with Lubanga's computer. "Everything working?" he asked in a whisper.

She said nothing, her gaze fixed on the screen, so he read the text, glancing up frequently, keeping his attention divided between computer and tunnel. It took him a moment to realize what he was reading with each quick glance.

The file open on the desktop was a document with instructions for moving money around. Similar to the file Freya had found with income and expenses, this was a list of instructions, but with much more detail. The other file had probably been an early draft, before Lubanga had dollar amounts to plug in. Here was a list of money transfers from Russian and German banks. A large payment—income—from an account called "Mission School Fund" was to be turned into bitcoin.

The school was a fraud, then—that wasn't a surprise, except for the fact that it was so blatant. If these were charitable donations from Fitzsimmons's ministry to fund a school, was it possible the reverend didn't know the school didn't exist?

But the fake charity probably wasn't what had Freya so upset. She'd suspected the school was a fraud all along. He read on and came to the important part.

Millions of dollars were to be funneled through several accounts. The money needed to be dispersed quickly to obfuscate the trail. Dozens of transactions were required to shift the money. Cal guessed it was so Russian Bratva wouldn't find it, because this had to be Drugov's missing money.

The entire half billion had been moved to one account and was being dispersed from there. Freya had explained how Lubanga moved his money around. The most secure method of transfer was to load the money onto a USB drive. The money couldn't be accessed without the physical drive and a password, and sometimes even biometric security like a thumbprint. Odds were, the flight that arrived this evening had carried a USB drive containing a half-billion dollars, ready to be transferred into Lubanga's accounts, and from there be dispersed to dozens of other accounts.

According to the instructions on the screen, ten million of that money was to be deposited into a holding account in Kinshasa. The name on the account: Freya Lange.

Freya stared at the screen. She'd heard Cal's question, but her brain was buzzing, her skin flushed. She could spare exactly five seconds for a freak-out, then she had to get to work. She checked the open internet portal. It was a bank. The man at the computer had been moving money into different accounts, as instructed.

He'd dropped the entire bundle into a dozen accounts and now was dispersing those funds. It looked like...three hundred and fifty million remained of what had been about a half billion.

That meant a hundred and fifty million had already been dispersed, laundered, or exchanged for bitcoin. This guy had been busy while she and Cal stargazed and traversed the tunnels.

But where had the money come from? She looked over the document with instructions—thankfully written in French—and found the source, the same as she'd seen in the document she'd found two days ago that led them here: *A Fitzsimmons* and *N Drugov*. Drugov's accounts had held more than five hundred million at the time of his death. This was Bratva—Russian organized crime—money.

She felt queasy as the pieces came together. She'd found his money when combing through his data and had filed a report with Seth. He'd authorized her to move a hundred grand to finance the op and support Mani Kalenga's cover as a successful mercenary looking to move up. It wasn't standard procedure, but not unheard of either. And it was a quick way to fund an op with little lead time. She'd filled out at least a dozen forms explaining where the money had come from, where it was going, and how it would be used.

In the meantime, she'd moved the rest of Drugov's money into a holding account—before Drugov's Bratva friends could find and reclaim it. She'd bet anything that if she looked up the transactions of that account, every penny would be gone, and her fingerprints would be all over it.

She took a deep breath. It was too late to recapture all of Drugov's cash assets, but at least she could stop the hemorrhage and try to save her name.

She looked at the list of those who were to receive large deposits. Among them were JJ Prime, Senator Jackson, Senator Ravissant, the US Attorney General, and DRC soldiers stationed in Gbadolite and elsewhere. That was where the bulk of the money was going—to undermine Congo's military.

Lubanga was using Drugov's money—which he must've gotten from Seth Olsen—to fund his coup. Worse, Gorev had Lubanga in his pocket. If Lubanga managed to seize Congo, Russia would control DRC's mineral wealth. They'd have diamonds, cobalt, coltan, and lots of untapped uranium. Yellowcake would find its way into Syria and Iran.

And it would be too late for the US government to do anything about it.

What the hell was Seth doing? Most traitors did it for the money. Benedict Arnold. Aldrich Ames.

But this... If Russia controlled Congo, the power shift would be massive. The Congo wars had already embroiled much of Africa and claimed millions of lives. Bring Syria and Iran into the mix, and it would quickly escalate. This cash infusion to back Lubanga's coup could quite literally be the first step toward World War III.

Chapter Twenty-One

Freya closed her eyes and took a deep breath. It wasn't too late. World War III wasn't inevitable. Because no one had predicted Freya wouldn't blindly follow orders. No, she'd enlisted a badass Green Beret to help her, and together, they could put a stop to this.

She cracked her knuckles. It was go time. "Guard the tunnel," she said to Cal, her focus on the screen.

"What are you doing?"

"Investing in bitcoin." She'd moved some of Drugov's money into bitcoin before the op, so the accounts were set up and the USB key to access her wallet was in her pack.

She grabbed the key and plugged it in. She would scatter the money into dozens of transactions, all for different amounts, so no one could find the money by searching for a single matching transaction.

Multiple transactions as she was doing would drive up the price and value of existing coin. No one already invested would complain about that. She was making everyone richer. In spite of the air-conditioning, sweat dripped down her neck. She pulled off the hood that covered her hair and kept working.

Dozens of bitcoin addresses were generated and stored in her wallet. The wallet lived on the key. Once the transactions entered the blockchain, the only way the money could be accessed was with the USB drive. A three-hundred-and-fifty-million-dollar memory stick.

It would take time for the transactions to process—ideally, she'd do this over the course of days—but she wasn't about to be picky. At least the files could upload to the cloud as the transactions processed. This computer was likely the financial heart of Lubanga's operation. This was where he moved his money around. She could have the mother lode of financial data for Lubanga's entire organization. Even better than what she'd gotten from his laptop in Dar.

Lubanga's extreme caution with online communication and financial transactions explained this remote outpost. For the center of his operations, he needed a computer with reliable and unlimited power, a very good satellite connection—Mobutu provided those with his dam and satellite dish array—and people with the technical skills to maneuver in the financial world, the dark web, cryptocurrency, and cryptosecurity.

CIA monitored this region for SIGINT but the area was something of a black hole for radio and satellite signals. Given this set up, there had to be some highly effective signal blockers in place—provided by Russia, if she were to guess.

A courier with the USB drive containing the money and these instructions must've been on that afternoon flight today. This wasn't the sort of thing one trusted to email.

She searched the desk for a portable storage device, finding several in a drawer. She slipped all the drives into the pocket that concealed her passport, then took a screen shot of the instructions and included the image in the file upload. She'd do everything she could to avoid taking the fall for this bullshit thievery. The US Attorney General would be interested to see his name on the list of payouts. That right there could be her saving grace—or her downfall if he was corrupt and wanted to bury this.

Next, she searched the unconscious man's pockets, finding another USB drive. His private drive? Maybe, but it was fair game. This guy was in league with a man who could further destabilize Africa and the Middle East. Lubanga was no rebel leader, no liberator. He was greed, avarice, and rotten to the core.

Goddamn Seth. What the hell could possibly be his motive? She had no doubt he'd destroyed the paper trail that showed she'd reported the money and turned it over to the CIA. She was recovering the money, but would anyone believe she hadn't taken it in the first place?

The data on this computer could be crucial to proving her innocence. Seth could be the owner of one of the numbered accounts on the distribution list. What was the payout for treason? What made a man who'd devoted his life to the CIA turn to the dark side?

As these thoughts buzzed through her brain, she set up the final transfers. She took money earmarked for soldiers and a coup and turned the dollars into bitcoin. She watched the progress bar as it slowly processed the movement of money from one cyber home to another, recording it all on her bitcoin key.

Cal stepped back into the room. "We need to hurry. I heard something in the tunnel to the north. Could be someone coming."

She nodded. "Almost done here."

He returned to the tunnel.

The upload progress indicator was at eighty-five percent. The speed at which the files transferred proved the internet connection was faster than anything they had at Camp Citron.

The progress bar reached a hundred percent, and she pocketed the USB upload device. They had what they'd come here for as far as intel, but now she could strike a blow. She plugged in another of her USB drives and initiated the program that would find this computer's online backup and corrupt the files.

While the virus attacked Lubanga's cloud storage, she quickly calculated the amounts for the last bitcoin purchases and launched the transactions. They were still processing, but they could complete without her being logged in. Same for the virus, now that it was activated it would destroy the files even after the computer was shut down. She had the bitcoin addresses in her wallet, which was all she needed. She pulled the virus from the first USB port and her key from the second and tucked both into her backpack with the other drives. It was a shame the bitcoin key was too big to swallow.

Cal stepped back into the doorway. "Someone's definitely coming."

She stood and paused, staring at the CPU. A hacker as good as the unconscious guy must be could trace what she'd done. He might even have a keystroke recorder running on this computer.

She needed to destroy it. This would make noise, but people were coming anyway, and this was the only way to ensure no one could immediately trace what she'd done.

She pulled a knife from her pack and stabbed through the case, ripping off the front. She yanked out the hard disk, then pulled her pistol and shot into the disk six times, evenly spaced.

"Are you fucking crazy?" Cal's words were shouted, but then, there was no need for quiet after the sound of gunshots.

This wasn't good enough. The CIA could still retrieve data from a shot-up drive. Lubanga might have his own team who were just as skilled. It would take time—days, maybe weeks—but still, it could be done. She needed to burn it. "I need aerosol. And a lighter."

He grabbed her arm. "We've got to go."

She scooped up the drive and crammed it into her pack. She'd burn it later.

She stumbled as she followed Cal down the tracks heading south, into the darkness of the tunnel, blind without her NVGs.

He cursed as he pulled her deeper into the darkness. He wasn't wearing his goggles either. She heard him fumble with his pack in the dark, then he grabbed her hand, his steps becoming surer.

Shouts sounded behind them. It was hard to guess how many men, given the echoing of the tunnel.

"Of all the stupid bullshit." His whisper was concealed by the shouting behind them. "Jesus. I knew you'd sacrifice anyone, but I didn't think you'd do it like that. Motherfucker. What were you thinking?"

"Without the drive, Lubanga is crippled. Gorev is crippled. It might contain all their financial data. I toasted the computer's backup with a virus. They might be able to recover some of the data, but it will take time. It's possible we just wiped them out financially." She managed to dig her NVGs from the side pocket as she ran.

"Couldn't you have waited to shoot it?"

Able to see now, she quickened her pace, and they sprinted along the tracks. There had to be an out up the line somewhere. She didn't want to believe this was a dead end, but it was that fear that forced her to take action and shoot the hard disk. "No. Not if they catch us. If the drive were intact, they'd get it back and be up and running in a matter of hours." Plus they'd have her bitcoin key.

"They're more likely to catch us thanks to the shots." His words were low and punctuated by panting breaths as they ran.

"If they do catch us"—she took a shallow breath, the need for speed making it hard to talk—"the disk is damaged. It would take time to restore the data—and that's only if they have the required skills."

They ran past alcoves and piles of debris, and she wondered if they should tuck down and hide or keep moving. But stopping could mean capture; only moving offered hope of escape.

The sound of a motorbike behind them triggered alarm. *Shit*. She'd sort of counted on their pursuers being stuck on foot as they were. She hadn't seen a bike in the tunnel, but there was a lot of mining debris lining the walls. The bike—or bikes, from the sound of it—could have been in the piles by the broken mine cart and she wouldn't have noticed.

Cal swore and ducked into a deep alcove. He pulled her back against the wall, tucking her into the darkness just as light reached the opening to the tunnel. The bike's headlight would have caught them had they remained on the tracks.

The engine sound roared near, and Cal launched himself into the tunnel. Her NVGs glowed with the added light from the bike as he clotheslined the rider. The bike toppled and slid while Cal fought the man. Another bike skidded to a stop just short of running over both men. The rider from the second bike leapt from the vehicle and charged her, pulling his gun as he did so.

She had two bullets left in the magazine. Better make them count. She squeezed off one shot. The man dropped. Center mass.

She stepped into the main tunnel to see Cal had the first rider in a chokehold, the man's gun-filled hand pinned to the ground under Cal's knee. She turned to the second bike and used her last bullet to fire at the tank, causing gas to leak. The old bike seat was torn, revealing ancient foam rubber inside. With her knife, she cut out a thick chunk of foam and slit the side. She plucked the hard disk from her pack and placed it under the flowing stream of fuel, soaking it, making sure gas showered the bullet holes and saturated the disk inside, then she tucked the drive in the slit in the foam and placed the bundle under the leaking tank.

She really should have matches. Why didn't she have matches? Cal had them in his pack, but he was busy.

She turned to the body of the man she'd shot and checked his pockets. The computer room had smelled of cigarette smoke, giving her hope these men were smokers.

Cal released the man he'd been fighting. The man slumped over, unconscious or dead.

As she laid fingers on a lighter, Cal righted the first bike and climbed on. "Let's go," he said.

"One second." She grabbed a cigarette from the man's pocket and lit it, coughing and feeling slightly dizzy as she inhaled. She hated cigarettes, but it would burn longer and ensure the gas caught, thoroughly destroying the disk.

She climbed on the motorbike behind Cal, then tossed the cigarette. It landed in the pool of liquid. A heartbeat later, the stream lit and the vapor ignited with a satisfying *foomp*.

Cal twisted the throttle, and they shot down the corridor, heat from the blaze caressing her cheek as she looked over her shoulder to ensure the disk burned. Her NVGs flared bright, and she lifted them, settling the goggles along her hairline as she watched the flame.

The flash disappeared, but the foam remained, engulfed in orange-and-blue flame.

She tightened her grip on Cal as they sped down the dark tunnel. A gradual curve and there was only darkness behind them. She faced forward. Cal had turned off the headlight, navigating with his NVGs. With her goggles seated above her eyes, there was nothing for her to see in the unrelenting darkness. She'd put them back on in a moment, but for now, she rested her forehead against Cal's pack and closed her eyes. She took a deep breath.

The first salvo in the battle to prevent Lubanga from seizing power had been fired. Now they were off, racing down a dark tunnel that might not have an exit.

Chapter Twenty-Two

Cal gunned the engine and hoped the tank was full. The gauge was broken, not a surprise given how hammered the bike was. Transportation in Congo was never pristine or pretty.

Second to having gas, he hoped there was an exit ahead that the bike could maneuver. Well, he'd take any exit, but given that they couldn't return to Gbadolite, having a vehicle would be nice. His final hope was that if there were only one exit, it would be at the end of this tunnel and not behind them.

This op had gone from having a spy-movie feel to more of an Indiana Jones-and-horror vibe. Would they find an underground chamber filled with child slaves and a villain who ripped out hearts?

One thing was certain, Freya was no damsel in distress. She'd taken a brief pause to catch her breath after seeing her name attached to massive theft, and then she'd dived in and fixed it.

Shooting the hard disk had been a shock, but he had to admit, the idea that she might've destroyed all Lubanga's financial records—maybe even access to his money—had Cal grinning from ear to ear. And she'd left the charred remains of the disk behind for Lubanga's men to find, so they'd know exactly how screwed they were.

It had been brilliant of her to turn dollars into bitcoin. He didn't know much about the cryptocurrency except that it required a key—usually in the form of a USB drive. He'd seen her take all the drives from the computer room. Each one could hold bitcoin or another cryptocurrency. In taking the drives, had she just bankrupted Lubanga?

Cal had stared in Jean Paul Lubanga's eyes and negotiated paying kickbacks for a mining claim in which starving women and children would do the work, all while sex-trafficking victims put on a show in the background. Lubanga was soulless. He ran on greed and a thirst for power and could reignite the Congo Wars.

That Freya might've destroyed his finances made everything that had transpired to bring them here worth it.

Destroying Lubanga's finances would be crippling in a way that was more devastating than assassination. Assassination assumed there wasn't someone worse waiting to step in. But would-be dictators needed to pay their armies. They needed to pay the guards who beat the slaves. If Lubanga had been cleaned out, Team Democracy had just won a major battle—with only eight shots being fired.

Any lingering doubts he might have harbored about Freya had been wiped away. The woman was a crazy, all-in soldier, willing to risk anything.

They'd gone at least five miles when he noticed a subtle shift in the pitch of the tracks. They were ascending. He'd guess they'd been at least three or four stories deep at the nadir, they had a ways to go to get to ground level, but this was a good sign.

He glanced at his compass. As expected, they were going south. Was there an escape route into the Central African Republic behind them, at the opposite end of the tracks? Before the gunshots, he'd heard the men on the tracks. They'd been coming from the north, the direction of the CAR.

Given the infrastructure and tunnel, Gbadolite was the best staging ground for a coup. None of the factions fighting in the east had been able to take Gbadolite with its garrison of soldiers stationed in the other palace, so Lubanga had opted to buy the soldiers' allegiance.

But Freya had nixed that.

The tunnel narrowed as the grade increased. Freya's grip on his hips tightened. Ahead of them, there was nothing but black, no definition to the path. Were they nearing a dead end?

He slowed the bike. "Going to turn on the headlight. NVGs aren't cutting it for distance." He flipped up the goggles as he flicked on the light, able to see now the long, deep curve ahead.

He braced himself for the unknown. They could turn into a battalion of Lubanga's men here. Or no one.

If the entrance under the palace wasn't guarded, what did that mean for this end, well over eight miles south? But the men who'd come after them had been on the tracks, not in the palace tunnels.

"Grab my gun," he said to Freya, knowing she hadn't had a chance to reload her weapon. He'd keep his hands on the throttle and brake and let her do the shooting.

She pulled his weapon. Her knees tightened on his hips as she adjusted to a one-handed hold on his hip.

He leaned into the turn, hoping the headlight would blind anyone in wait around the bend, but it was possible no one at this end of the tunnel knew they were coming. He'd snapped the guy's neck when they fought in the tunnel, and Freya's shot had been deadly, leaving, as far as they knew, only the unconscious bound man in the computer room alive to warn others.

Maybe they were home free.

The report of a bullet killed that fantasy. It was impossible to gauge where it came from given the echo down the chamber, but Freya must still be wearing her NVGs with heat sensor, because she fired into the darkness just as the headlight illuminated a man crouched in an alcove.

The man's head snapped back, and he dropped as they zipped past. Cal took the next curve at speed and swerved to miss several heavy mine carts lined up on the track, blocking their way.

Freya rolled from the back of the bike as it fishtailed. He turned a hundred and eighty degrees to see her fire off two shots, taking out two men with AKs who'd likely been blinded by the headlight. They'd fired, one bullet zipping past Cal's head alarmingly close.

A third man was in the path of the bike, beside the tracks. Cal did his own roll, pulling his knife as he pitched the bike into him. A moment later, he had the man pinned under the bike, his blade to his throat.

"Who do you work for?" he asked in French.

The man spat in his face and dislodged the knife.

Shit. He was gonna make Cal kill him.

Fine.

Cal punched the man in the face with his other hand. They rolled. They guy was thick and muscular, and he knew how to fight. Cal took a blow to the face as he kicked upward, dislodging his opponent.

Cal rolled to his feet at the same time the other guy did. He charged Cal, and it was over with the man's next heartbeat. Cal's blade sank deep into his chest.

Cal turned to Freya, breathing heavy, adrenaline pumping. She stood in profile to him, running her flashlight over an alcove.

"Anyone there?" Cal asked.

"No. But I found tools and…gas cans." She lifted a jerry can and shook it. "Five of them. And they're full."

Thank you, God.

He lifted the bike and threw the kickstand. While he topped off the tank, she grabbed machetes, a hammer, a wrench, and a few screwdrivers from the tool cache and collected the AKs from all three men she'd shot.

"Look at this," she said, holding up the Kalashnikovs.

They weren't 47s. They were AKS74Us—short assault rifles. The short barrel and folding stock made them easier to conceal, while the distinctive open triangle stock made them lighter than other assault rifles. AKS74Us were rare, especially in Africa.

"They might've been gifts from Gorev," he said. Terrorist groups had coveted the Russian rifles ever since Osama bin Laden was photographed with one.

"I was thinking the same thing."

"When this is over, we'll send Gorev a thank-you note." Things were looking up. They had a bike, fuel, concealable AKs, and a hell of a lot of money.

He strapped two full jerry cans to the back of the bike, which had a platform just for that purpose. In a land where roads were narrow and unpaved or nonexistent, motorbikes were the most reliable, best transportation to be found, and this bike was tricked out for just this sort of journey.

They had enough fuel to reach Lisala or Gemena and could figure out their next steps from there. He strapped his pack to the back along with the fuel cans, so it would be easier for Freya to ride without the bulk between them.

He climbed on as she secured the machetes and folded AKs to their gear, then straddled the seat behind him, her thighs against his hips. They set off down the tracks again and rounded the curve to see a flatbed cart loaded with fifty-five-gallon steel drums blocking their path and what appeared to be a large metal bay door with train tracks running underneath.

Over the engine noise, he could hear rain pounding against the metal door. They'd reached the exit.

He skirted the cart and halted the bike by the crank that would roll up the door—no electricity required. Freya hopped off, but she didn't go for the crank; instead, she headed for the cart they'd passed.

He shut off the engine at her hand signal and dismounted.

"I need the hammer," she said, her gaze fixed on the drums.

He plucked it from their gear and approached. "You want to see what's inside?"

"Yes. My guess is the men were delivering something when they heard the engine—or got a call from someone at the other end—and left this to take up positions in the tunnel to ambush us."

The trolley was motorized—which explained the stockpile of gas cans—and held three drums painted dark green. He used the claw end of the hammer to pry open the latch on the ring clamp of a barrel. She removed the ring and lifted the lid. He shone the light into the container, revealing a yellow powder.

He recognized the contents as Freya said the name.

"Uranium oxide concentrate. Also known as yellowcake."

Chapter Twenty-Three

Freya stared into the drum, mind racing with the implications. Yellowcake. Goddamned uranium, ready for enrichment. "How would uranium get this far north? The Shinkolobwe mine is at the other end of the country. Uranium smuggling goes through Zambia."

Shinkolobwe was the country's most notable uranium mine, having provided the fuel for the Manhattan Project, and to the best of her knowledge, all of Congo's uranium deposits were in the south.

"It's at least a thousand miles from here," Cal said.

And these were Congo miles, which were like dog years. It was a long, difficult way to smuggle goods.

"Maybe security into Zambia has improved. It appears this is Lubanga's operational center. And it has an unregulated airport along with a tunnel into the Central African Republic. With a cargo plane, it would be a snap."

Had a second plane arrived while they were in the tunnel? The earlier plane had come from Dar es Salaam, not southern DRC.

Freya replaced the lid. By some accounts, yellowcake wasn't yet significantly radioactive—that happened later, with enrichment. But breathing it in could be deadly.

Sweat dripped down her cheek. The thick, warm air of the tunnel became overbearing when not riding on the back of a moving bike. They needed to get out of here. They had no idea if reinforcements would be found in the road ahead or come at them from the tunnel behind.

"No one moves yellowcake like this for a legit nuclear power plant," Cal said. "If they were doing that, they'd sell it in Zambia along with the other artisanal miners."

She nodded. The uranium was destined for a terrorist group or enemy state. ISIS. Syria. Al Qaeda. Boko Haram. Al-Shabaab. There were too many options, all of them terrifying. They couldn't take it with them, and they couldn't leave it here.

"Let's reseal the barrel, roll the cart out of here, and toss them into the jungle. They'll be recovered, but at least we'll make them work for it."

She nodded. It was also the only thing they had time for, given that men could be coming after them down the tunnel even now.

He placed the clamp ring around the rim.

"Wait!" she said, as an idea popped into her head. "I have trackers."

Cal lifted the ring. "The kind you can plant on objects and they transmit the location via GPS?"

"Yes. They're small and transmit location information via satellite. They're monitored with a URL."

"How long does the battery last?"

"If I set it to only transmit every twelve hours, about ten days."

"You want to drop one in this barrel, so the CIA can track it?"

"Yes." She pulled off her pack and dug in the concealed pocket, then pulled out a tracker the size and shape of a thick American nickel. It was covered in a pale, reflective plastic that would blend with the yellow powder. She set it to transmit twice a day and activated it.

"Give it to me," Cal said. She looked up to see he'd tied a T-shirt around his mouth and nose. In one hand, he held a long metal rod he must've grabbed from the tunnel debris.

She was strangely touched by this protective gesture, even as she wanted to argue this was her risk to take. But they didn't have time for arguing, so she handed him the disk.

He lifted the lid, keeping his face averted from the open drum, and dropped the disk inside. He used the metal rod to push it deeper into the barrel, then slowly extracted the rod so as not to stir the powder and cause it to form a cloud of toxic dust.

Once the rod was clear, he dropped the lid back in place. Freya secured the clamp ring while he set the rod by the wall and doffed the shirt that covered his face, leaving it with the rod.

He returned to her side. "I'll get the cart running. You open the bay door."

The crank was well oiled, but the door was heavy, and she was sweating by the time she got it high enough for the cart and bike to pass through.

Outside, it wasn't just a rainstorm, it was a deluge. Cal drove the cart and she moved the bike outside and closed the door again. The jungle hugged the tracks, but the rails were clear for the seeable distance, making her wonder how far the line went.

"Let's keep going. Look for a place where we can roll these down a slope. May as well make it hard for them," Cal shouted over the pounding rain.

She nodded. They'd be less likely to suspect a tracker had been planted if they had to work to find the drums.

She followed him on the bike while he operated the cart. About a mile down the tracks the ground to the right began to slope, even as the jungle seemed to grow thicker. Finally Cal brought the flatbed cart to a stop.

She climbed off the bike as he pitched the first barrel off the cart. It rolled and was quickly swallowed by the thick vegetation. Freya pitched the next one, which followed the first into the bush. Cal dumped the third, then restarted the cart, and sent it on autopilot down the rails.

Freya climbed onto the hillside, collecting broadleaves to cover the flattened trail the drums had left. Between the thick vegetation and the heavy rain, hiding three fifty-five-gallon barrels of uranium oxide concentrate was surprisingly easy.

She turned her face to the sky. She was certain she hadn't gotten any of the toxic powder on her, but still, she was glad for the cleansing rain.

Morgan had complained about dealing with venomous snakes when she did fieldwork. Freya looked forward to one-upping her with this story.

Cal pulled out his military-grade GPS unit. "I'm saving the coordinates." She stepped up beside him as he studied the map, then tucked the unit away. "We'll follow the tracks for another mile or two—if they're passable. Then we'll cut through the jungle and enter the rainforest. It's the best way to lose any pursuers."

She nodded and climbed on the back of the bike. He paused before her, slipped a hand behind her head, and kissed her hard. Full, openmouthed, carnal.

Rain poured over them. Thunder roared in the distance. Lightning flashed, and she kissed him back. The kiss wasted a precious five seconds, but it was worth it.

He released her, flashed a grin, and, without a word, mounted the bike in front of her. She gripped his hips as they set off into the darkness, following train tracks in a narrow channel that cut through the broadleaf forest.

They quickly caught up to and passed the flatbed cart. Gradually the jungle thickened, encroaching right up to the tracks. They were under full canopy, hiding the tracks from satellites. The need for machetes even when following the tracks was readily apparent. The bike could maneuver, but the unmanned cart would eventually get tangled.

Freya looked up to the canopy. Rain filtered through the leaves, splattering her skin. It couldn't wipe away the dark greasepaint that coated her face, but in her mind, the deluge cleansed her. Nature's baptismal, washing away uranium and blood, smoke and gasoline.

They'd struck a blow against Lubanga. They might be able to track the yellowcake. And tucked away in her pack, she carried three hundred and fifty million dollars of Bratva money.

Not bad for one night's reconnaissance mission.

She tightened her grip on Cal's hips and placed her cheek on his back, closing her eyes, thankful that he had the hard job of navigating the bike down the overgrown path. She was eternally grateful he was with her, helping her fight for this vast, strange, wild, and wonderful country.

They left the rail line as soon as Cal spotted an opening in the thick vegetation. It was slow going, and several times, they had to backtrack when their route proved impassable, but finally, they broke through and reached mature tropical broadleaf forest, where the canopy was so thick, the forest floor was clear of undergrowth.

Cal had visited equatorial rainforests with his mother when she took him to her childhood village east of Kinshasa. This forest was much the same, with tall, broadleaf evergreens supported by triangular buttresses—aboveground roots that were broad and flat, which were necessary for trees to thrive in this environment. Thick, woody vines draped from the trees, connecting one to the other. These lianas started from small shrubs on the floor and sent out tendrils to nearby saplings. Both grew upward together, forming the rainforest canopy that protected Freya and him from the heavy rainstorm above.

A vast array of fauna inhabited these woods, and he wouldn't be surprised to come across a poisonous snake or an okapi—a strangely beautiful beast also known as a zebra giraffe. In the understory—the layer between floor and canopy—they might find leopards along with hundreds of species of birds, insects, and reptiles.

Here, all beasts had free rein, but were likely warded off by the noise of the bike as he and Freya rode south, making good time in the dark now that the floor was clear of undergrowth.

The quality of the light changed, telling him that above the canopy, dawn had broken. Only two percent of sunlight reached the floor in rainforests such as this, which explained why villages were found outside the forest with only rare indigenous people—in this area known as the Twa—having permanent settlements.

Twa people spoke Bantu languages, of which Lingala was one. If they found themselves stuck and needing help, he might be able to communicate with them.

Midmorning, he stopped the bike; he needed a break and assumed she did too. They'd been riding for hours and had hacked their way through a jungle to get here. They'd put so many rough, twisted miles between themselves and the tunnel, it would take a miracle for anyone to track them this far, this quickly. They could take thirty minutes without fear.

He relieved his bladder, then changed into clothes that would look more normal for extremely foolish tourists exploring the rainforest without a guide. He tucked the AKs into a spare bag he'd carried in his pack to conceal them, and strapped the bag to the back with the jerry cans.

When they reached a city or town, he didn't want to raise questions by arriving in ninja suits with assault rifles flapping in the wind.

Freya did the same, donning lightweight hiking pants and a button-down shirt of the same moisture-wicking fabric. Not that it would help in the sultry rainforest. It was hard to tell if the moisture in the air was from rain or if it was just normal humidity. The canopy blocked rainfall as much as it did sunlight.

After changing, Freya used facial wipes to remove the dark greasepaint from her face. He helped by checking for streaks that wouldn't pass for dirt smudges. He took the wipe from her hand and cleaned the edges, then leaned down and dropped a lingering kiss on her lips. He lifted his head and could just see her smile in the dim light.

He couldn't help himself and slipped a hand behind her neck and kissed her again, this time going deeper, possessing her mouth. Taking what she gave and demanding more.

She replied with mouth and tongue, offering him everything. All of her. Which was exactly what he wanted. He acted without thought, letting his primal instincts run free. He was hopped up on adrenaline and the smell of her skin, the feel of her body against his.

He scooped her up and pressed her back against a flat buttress root that was more wall than tree. He felt her ankles come together as she encircled his hips and ass with her legs. His erection rubbed against her center, and they both groaned as their tongues met and stroked with equal urgency.

He should put on the brakes. They needed to talk and plan. But right now, he just wanted to possess her. To take the fiery energy of escaping death more than once the previous night and screw her against a tree in the sultry rainforest.

Her hands at his fly said she was game. He pulled back, giving her access, and she freed his cock. She stroked him from base to tip, and he shut his eyes.

Holy shit, that felt good.

The moment was extra vibrant. Turned up to eleven. The air was thick, fragrant with earth and the sweet scent of a flowering vine in bloom. And

Freya was hot and sultry, stroking him to insanity.

He released her, setting her on the ground just long enough to whisk her underwear and pants down her legs and over her lightweight athletic shoes. He tossed the items over a draping vine, then lifted her again. He hesitated for the barest fraction of a second, his eyes on hers in the dim forest light, then he penetrated her, sliding deep with one stroke as her legs again closed around his hips.

This no-condom thing was pretty damn awesome. *She* was pretty damn awesome.

She kissed him, her tongue doing to his mouth what he was doing to her with his cock. She was slick and hot, and their joining was urgent and un-fucking-believably perfect. He was drenched in sweat thanks to the thick moisture in the air and the press and exertion of urgent sex.

They'd escaped death and now were claiming their reward. She was his. Now. Yesterday. Tomorrow. Always.

Her body tightened, and her breathing changed. She released his mouth and tilted her head back to rest against the trunk of the tree, exposing her neck for his mouth. He kissed her throat as he thrust into her, then lifted his head to watch her in the gray light as pleasure lit her expression. He was doing that to her. She was giving the same to him. She cried out, the raspy sound a cousin to the calls of wildcats of the rainforest.

The sexy noise, the sensual expression, the wild feel as her inner muscles tightened on his cock, pushed him over the brink. A powerful orgasm rocked him, the feeling so intense, his knees turned weak. He leaned into the tree, sandwiching her between hard wood and his depleted body as waves of pleasure continued to pulse from where their bodies joined.

They'd barely said a word since he'd shut off the engine of the bike, and now he felt a rumble of laughter rising in his chest. No words, just laughter at being buried deep in her while on the run in a Congolese equatorial rainforest.

Joining the Army had led to some interesting experiences, and this was one he'd carry with him until his dying day. When he was ninety-five, he would close his eyes and think about this moment. How she felt. How she smelled. The look on her beautiful face as she came.

His laughter escaped, and she joined in. Her body quaking, her inner muscles contracting on his penis. He kissed her as he laughed and slid from her body. He stopped laughing long enough to say, "You're amazing," then kissed her nose and released her, still chuckling.

"So are you." She grabbed her pants from where they lay, draped over a vine, then bent to search for her panties, which must have fallen from their perch.

He tucked himself away, watching her ass and loving the view. "We've gone far enough that we could try to find a village. Maybe we can rent a bed for a few hours and do that again but conventionally."

She stood, underwear in hand, and shook them out, likely to rid the panties of forest creatures. He'd tried to prevent that by hanging them on the vine, but he'd been too eager get inside her to pay attention and do it right.

"Unconventional was pretty great." She stepped into the panties. "And I don't think we should linger too long. I was thinking on the ride that we should head to Lisala and try to get a flight out of town. Fitzsimmons is paying Lubanga for a school. I want to try to find it."

"It's probably a diamond or other mining operation. The payment could be a bribe for the mining claim."

"Yeah. And I'm worried. What if children are involved? What if children are doing the mining?"

The idea had crossed his mind more than once too. "It makes the school the perfect cover then, a great way to round up kids as workers."

"Exactly."

"Most diamond mines are in the south, but there are some—like my mom's childhood village—that are closer to Kinshasa." He considered their options. Before they could try to find a nonexistent school, they needed to get out of this area. In Congo, travel was rarely easy. "Like you, I've been thinking. The airport in Lisala is tiny. If anyone is looking for us, that's where they'll be. But we could hop on a cargo barge. Tourists travel on them occasionally, so while we'll be noticed, it won't be that strange. My Lingala and your French will help us to blend. We could head upriver to Kisangani or downriver to Mbandaka. Those airports are bigger. From there, we could fly to Kinshasa, or out of Congo."

"The barge—in either direction—would take what, five days?"

He nodded. "Probably longer."

She cocked her head. He loved the way she looked when she did that. He'd bet she was running a dozen different scenarios in her mind, like a chess player, working the odds of failure or success. Finally, she said, "Do they check ID on the barges?"

"I think they do at some of the ports along the way. Our fake passports will be fine. As far as I know, it's just cursory. A way to collect tolls—bribes. No one reports the names of passengers up or down the line unless there's an issue."

She frowned. "Can we afford five days or more of travel time?"

"I don't think we have a choice. I can't call in a ride from SOCOM. Even if I did, they'd fly into the Republic of Congo—probably Brazzaville—

and expect us to meet them on the river."

Brazzaville, the capital of the Republic of Congo, was right across the river from Kinshasa, so unless they could get to where the river split the two Congos, calling for help was useless.

"A flight would save us days, though."

Freya was operating on US time, where it was so easy to jump a thousand miles. This was Congo, where it took weeks—sometimes more than a month—to get from Kisangani to Kinshasa.

"The airport is too big a risk." He stepped forward and pulled her into his arms. "I don't want you doing anything suicidal like when you shot the hard drive." He kissed her to let her know he wasn't angry—at least, not anymore. "And running headfirst into a trap is suicide, no matter how much you think you can beat it."

She nodded. "I'm sorry—about shooting the disk without warning you first. It was a split-second decision. I should have warned you, but it was also the right call."

He knew that. As a former analyst and current operator, she knew how important the data was. Her training revolved around protecting the data and protecting herself, but he didn't doubt she considered protecting herself secondary.

As a soldier, for him, people came first. *She* came first.

In that moment, everything was crystal clear. She would always come first for him.

He imagined being ninety-five, remembering wild sex against a tree in an equatorial rainforest in Congo, and looking to his right, seeing Freya by his side, and sharing the memory with a naughty grin.

And damn, now he wanted that.

Chapter Twenty-Four

After eating protein bars and topping off the gas tank, they set out again. Freya clung to Cassius's back, her cheek pressed to his spine as they passed through the forest. This was a rainforest of fantasy and fairy tale. Sultry, wild, and achingly beautiful.

It was a shame they couldn't hear the natural sounds of forest over the bike engine, but they weren't tourists hoping to hear the call of exotic birds and big cats. Lowland gorillas were unlikely to be found in this forest—they were in the rainforests farther east—but still, this fulfilled a long-forgotten dream. That she was with Cassius Callahan only made the experience sweeter.

It didn't matter that they were on the run or that the Russian Mafia was likely after her for stealing half a billion dollars. In this moment, she allowed herself to forget Seth had betrayed her. She'd dwell on that nightmare later.

Right now, she held on to Cassius and breathed in his scent. If she pressed her face just so, she didn't notice the exhaust smell from the bike, and it was just the two of them in a vast, wild rainforest.

Indigenous people lived in these woods, she knew. Hunter-gatherers who'd been here for thousands of years. They were short of stature, dark skinned, and sometimes offered their services as guides through the forest. It was unlikely they'd meet any Twa on this rapid trek, but she wondered if any were nearby, alerted by the loud motorbike, watching their passage.

If so, they likely thought them a couple of fools, crossing the rainforest without guides. And they'd be right, except that Cal was a Green Beret and trained not just to survive but to fight in this heat, darkness, and terrain. And she'd had similar training. If they lost the bike and had to cross on foot, they could do it, but it wouldn't be easy. She wasn't about to get cocky and disrespect the hazards of the forest.

They reached the edge of the mature forest; the ground cover became thick and impenetrable in places. Rainforest transforming into overgrown jungle. They agreed to press on, searching for a passable route through the woods, forced to walk the bike and cut a path with machetes.

The forest lightened with increased sunlight that fed the growing plants. Insects swarmed, attacking all exposed, sweaty skin. They fought their way through for hours with little conversation beyond deciding on when to cut through and when to turn back and find an easier path.

Welts covered Freya's arms and face from both insects and the whipping of branches. She ignored the pain as she sipped from a water bottle and passed it to Cal. They were running low on water and would refill at the next stream. It was tempting to fill the canteen with rainwater collected on broadleaves, but those small, static pools were likely to contain mosquito and other insect larvae. If they got desperate, they wouldn't be picky. They had purification tablets. After last night's rain, there was no shortage of water.

Hours later, they broke free of the jungle. Freya had a new appreciation for the ease with which they had entered the rainforest, but then, the path of the old railway had cut through the thickest part of the jungle, and they'd had a relatively thin swath to breach to reach mature forest.

This had been straight-up bushwhacking. Her arms ached, her skin itched, and her throat was dry. But damn if she didn't feel exhilarated upon stepping out of the jungle into a clearing and seeing a road in the distance.

The sky was cloudy as another storm threatened, but warm, thick air embraced her. She felt a surge of energy.

They hadn't exactly conquered the jungle, but they'd survived it. Plus, they'd escaped Gbadolite, recovered millions of dollars, found and hidden yellowcake, and struck what could be a devastating blow to Lubanga's finances.

She'd take it as a win.

She reached for Cal, who was as sweaty, sticky, and welty as she was, and slid her arms around his neck, being careful not to irritate either of their wounds. She grinned up at him. "I feel like we should get a jungle bushwhacking scout badge or something."

He laughed and dropped a soft kiss on her lips. "My mom sews. She can make us badges when we get back to the States."

She laughed, liking the idea of meeting his mom. "Deal. Now, let's get to that road and head to Lisala."

They'd chosen their route out of the jungle using Cal's GPS and came out more or less where they'd expected. Lisala, with a large port on the Congo River, was just sixty-five kilometers—about forty miles—to the south. Traveling by road, they would arrive in town in just over an hour.

Her butt was sore from the endless riding over bumpy ground, but her arms were grateful for the break from bushwhacking, and the road felt smooth as silk after the forest floor. In no time at all, they were on the outskirts of town and heading toward the river.

Lisala had suffered with the loss of infrastructure over the last twenty years. The town was a mix of traditional thatched-roof buildings and concrete construction with sheet-metal roofs. Everything was worn and battered and many of the once-paved roads were being reclaimed by nature.

Cal parked the bike near the river, where buildings clustered and an informal market neared closing time at the end of another sweltering day. The rain had stopped, but the air was thick with moisture. They both climbed from the bike to stretch their legs. He rolled his shoulders, which had to be tight from controlling the bike on the slippery, muddy road, going faster than conditions allowed.

The smell of grilling fish had Freya's stomach clenching with hunger. She made a beeline for the vendor, a woman who looked to be in her twenties who had two children—identical twins—playing in the dirt next to her grill.

With the first bite of fresh, hot food, Freya let out a groan of pleasure. She couldn't remember the last time she'd been this hungry. "This is the best fish I've ever had," she said with a mouth full of food.

Cal laughed at her garbled speech, then bought more fish from the woman, emptying her grill so she could pack up. "From the river, straight to the grill. Fish doesn't get any fresher than this."

Freya finished her first piece, then moved on to the second. After her initial hunger was down to a manageable level, she said, "We should ask about barges." She nodded to a vessel visible downriver. "Is that one leaving tonight or tomorrow?" she asked the woman in French.

"That barge should leave tomorrow," the woman said. "It arrived yesterday and has been unloading and loading new cargo all day."

"Which way is she headed?" Cal asked.

"Kinshasa. If you want to go to Kisangani, another barge is due tomorrow or the next day."

Cal gave the woman a tip for the information, and they quickly finished eating, then hopped back on the bike to hurry down to where the barge was moored.

Less than an hour later, Cal paid the skipper to secure their spot on the barge and paid for their bike to be stored with the cargo. Their place on the deck was only a few square feet, but it would be theirs for the next five days until they disembarked at Mbandaka, the next major port.

"A lot of couples traveling together sleep on shore at night, when they can," Cal said. "Camp out by the river. We've got the tent and sleeping pads we picked up in Dar. It'll be a lot more comfortable than the deck of the barge, and we'll be protected from insects and rain in the tent."

"Sounds good to me." If they had to sleep on the barge, they'd only have a tarp as protection from the rain, there wasn't enough room to set up even the small two-person tent.

From a store near the dock, they purchased food and other supplies—a bowl and fork for each of them. A bucket for drawing river water for bathing and drinking. Rope, because rope was always needed. A better pack for storing and disguising the AKs. As they shopped, weariness settled into Freya's bones. It had been more than thirty-six hours since she'd slept, and the time in between had been…active, to say the least.

Adrenaline had faded. She could see Cal drooping too. They both could rally if they had to—they'd been trained for it—but there was no need. She'd planned to boot up the computer and work tonight, but she'd have plenty of time to comb through the computer on the barge. Now, more than anything, she needed sleep.

It was full dark by the time they were setting up the tent. The flashlight, necessary for reading the directions, drew biting insects, so Cal tossed the laminated card aside. "We can wing it."

"You have to stake it down first," she said when he started sliding the poles through the loops.

They continued to bicker; Cal was doing it all wrong and needed correcting. He let out a frustrated growl when the rain picked up. Lightning flashed in the distance.

One of their fellow travelers chuckled and asked in French, "How long have you been married?"

"Too long," Cal said.

Freya laughed and tossed the rainfly over the top of the tent. "Eternity," she added.

Cal snapped the rainfly straps in to the corner posts on his side while she did the same on hers, and the tent was built.

They said good night to their amused neighbor and crawled inside, dragging their packs and the bag with the AKs inside with them. More lightning flashed as Cal gathered her against him and his mouth covered hers. She squealed as she bumped the side of the tent, and it tipped, rolling to the side.

"Huh. Guess we should have staked it down," he muttered as he pinned her on her back—rolling the tent upright again. He grabbed her hands, pulling them above her head and holding them there with one hand as he lifted her shirt with the other. He pulled down her bra, and his mouth found her nipple.

She'd thought she was too exhausted, but his mouth on her body woke all the important parts. Lightning flashed, followed by a rumble of thunder.

The image of him sucking on her breast was burned in her mind in the pitch-black darkness of the tent. She tried to free her hands—she wanted to touch him—but he held her tight. He moved up until his lips were pressed to her ear. "Do you want this, Freya?" he whispered.

Rain pummeled the tent. They were hidden in a dark cocoon. Sheltered from the rain. One couple in a sea of tents. She hadn't felt this safe since before Harry arrived at Camp Citron.

No one in the world knew where they were.

There was a lot to be settled between them, but one truth was he wanted her. He cared for her. This might be a fling, but it didn't feel like one. She'd thought the sex in the rainforest had been an impulse, not necessarily the start of something.

"I always want you, Cal," she whispered back. "But…can we get out the sleeping pads first?"

He laughed. "Still directing tent construction."

"Hey, I was right about the stakes, and water is soaking through the floor. For a Green Beret, you don't seem to know how to camp."

She felt his body shake with laughter. "Sure I do. But it's hella fun to play with you."

And she liked the way he played. This was the man she'd watched him be with everyone at Camp Citron but her. Playful. Congenial. Warm. Fun. And oh so very sexy.

He released her hands and pulled out the thin sleeping pads from his pack. He inflated one while she blew into the other. It wasn't much padding, but it would keep them off the wet ground and offered insulation.

Bed made, he made love to her silently, so as not to disturb the neighbors. She couldn't hold back her pleasured gasp as he penetrated her, thick, smooth perfection. The rain covered the sound of his body slapping against hers as he thrust, hard and fast.

She wrapped her legs around him, loving the feel of his skin against hers. She got lost in the feel of him, the stroke and slide.

So good. So perfect.

He was everything she'd ever wanted. This moment was every fantasy come true. He was her Cassius. Her soldier. Her partner.

She let out a cry as she came. His mouth covered hers, silencing her as she felt his body quake with his own orgasm.

Afterward, she pulled on her clothes—they needed to sleep dressed and ready to run—and he pulled her back to his chest, spooning with her as they both dropped quickly into exhausted slumber.

An hour after dawn, the barge set off downriver, heading toward Kinshasa. The vessel was overloaded with people—at least two hundred—most of whom had been on the boat from the outset in Kisangani. Near the back was a space for several goats and a few monkeys. Goods were crated and covered in tarps across the center of the deck. Items being shipped downriver included palm oil, grain, used clothing, and it looked like…two SUVs. Their own motorbike was among the cargo tucked under colorful tarps.

The full voyage from Kisangani to Kinshasa often took three weeks or more. From where they'd joined, it could take ten to fourteen days to reach Kinshasa. Their plan, unless they learned something new on their days en route, was to disembark in Mbandaka. From there they would fly to Kinshasa or Brazzaville. The captain estimated they'd reach Mbandaka in five days.

While it was a relief to be setting out from Lisala, that didn't mean they were out of danger of being found. They'd be in constant contact with people from villages that dotted the river. Any pirogue that paddled up alongside the boat could be filled with Lubanga's men, looking for a white American woman and her black American companion.

But still, in spite of the concern, her heart beat with a sense of…*adventure*. A feeling far different from the adrenaline and fear that came from covert ops.

This was the Congo of lore, the very heart of darkness written about nearly a hundred and twenty years ago by Joseph Conrad. *Heart of Darkness* had shown the wild river and the exploitation and cruelty inflicted upon the Congolese by Europeans wanting rubber and copper, at the time Congo's most valuable resources. The river was largely unchanged in spite of all the technology that had come in the intervening years, and the exploitation and cruelty continued as well. Some was perpetrated by DRC's own leaders, but behind it all lurked foreign businesses, having moved on from rubber to diamonds, cobalt, coltan, and so many other commodities.

Yet the river remained unchanged. Untamed. The Inga dams were found between Kinshasa and the Atlantic. This part of the river flowed as freely as it had in Conrad's day. As it had a hundred years before that, before Europeans invaded, colonized, took, and killed.

A buzz of excitement coursed through her—similar to the buzz she felt being near Cal. But this was a different sort of attraction. This buzz was about being alive in this moment on an overloaded, noisy, crowded, smelly barge that was being pushed by a tugboat down the vast river of dreams.

This was romance and adventure, in all its tarnished, dirty glory. There was one toilet on the barge—essentially a wooden box with a hole that dumped right into the river—and no beds or berths or anything resembling comfort. And yet she felt this vessel was the most magnificent thing she'd ever encountered.

Burdened with cargo and teeming with people, the barge somehow managed to stay afloat. Some passengers made their home in the stacked goods, while the rest took up every square inch of open deck. She and Cal had been lucky to squeeze in. In Lingala, he'd sweet-talked a few passengers into scooting over to make room—although the money he slipped them probably won them over more than his words.

They didn't need to worry about food for the journey, as other passengers set up grills to cook fish and sell during the voyage, in addition to locals who would paddle up in pirogues to sell their wares.

Painted in weathered letters on the side of the boat were the words "No Passengers" in French, but an entire economy had built up around this river journey, and the barge captains made much of their living from hauling people in addition to moving cargo.

This was Congo. The real deal. Not the faded glory of Gbadolite. This was how the majority of Congolese lived, lives entwined with the river that gave them food, transportation, and commerce. Congo had mountains, a volcano, rainforests, jungles, and a small stretch of Atlantic coast, but arguably the most defining feature was the vast river that ran through it all. Nearly three thousand miles long, stretching almost all the way across the thousand-mile expanse of the country.

The Congo River was a story of twos and second place. The river crossed the equator twice. It was the second-longest river in Africa—the Nile was the longest—and had the second-highest water flow of any river in the world, edged out by the Amazon in South America. Two national capitals were situated on the river—Kinshasa and Brazzaville. It had two names: the Congo River and the Zaire River. And it flowed through the Congo rainforest, the second largest rainforest area in the world—the largest being the Amazon rainforest.

She'd read all these facts back at Camp Citron in preparation for the journey. But she'd never really expected to catch a ride on the river. She hadn't even expected they'd enter DRC.

"You like this," Cal said with a grin.

"I freaking love it," she said, grinning back.

"Me too. My mom told me so many stories about the river when I was growing up, and still, the first time I saw the rapids—the crazy ones near Kinshasa—I was stunned. And out here, the way the river has a gazillion tributaries and islands... From above, it looks like a tangled mass of yarn—

it's beautiful. Powerful. Wild." His mouth curved. "Like you."

His fingers entwined with hers, the only public display of affection they could share on this very public barge. "Although I have a feeling the novelty will wear off when we're trying to sleep tonight if we can't camp on shore. Or waiting in line to use the toilet when someone has dysentery."

"True." She leaned her head against his shoulder, wishing she could kiss him. "But right now, this is the only place in the world I want to be."

He leaned against the stacked bags of grain that would be their backrests for the next several days. "Me too," he repeated.

Later, she'd get on the computer and continue combing through the files she'd gotten from Lubanga and the new ones she'd grabbed during their raid in Gbadolite, but for now, she wanted to take in this experience. The conversations of their fellow passengers, the smell of fish being grilled on braziers, the gentle flow of the river and the various channels that were divided up by dozens of islands.

Loud, stinky, crammed, dilapidated, and sweltering in the morning sun, the barge was utterly glorious. Cal struck up a conversation with a fellow passenger in French, learning the man was heading to Kinshasa in hopes of finding work. Other travelers were hauling grain or other goods to Mbandaka to sell. They'd catch another barge going upriver to Kisangani.

Some would sell their wares to the pirogues that rode up to the boat each day, traveling for only a short period before returning home. Selling from barges was their job. They weren't going to a destination; they were on a floating market.

Cal purchased fish for breakfast. They ate while walking down the barge, meeting other travelers, looking at the various items for sale. A diamond with a cross through it—the kite symbol they'd seen in the tunnels in Gbadolite—caught Freya's eye. She nudged Cal and indicated the crate marked with the symbol.

He lifted the tarp to reveal more of the crate, but there were no other markings. He turned to a passenger and asked about the symbol in French. "I've seen that before. Do you know what it is?"

A young man of about twenty shrugged, but a woman who traveled with a small child answered. "It's the symbol for the Mission School. It's probably supplies for the students."

The symbol they'd seen in the tunnels were for Fitzsimmons's school? He was more involved with Lubanga than they'd realized. "The Mission School?" Freya asked.

"It's a boarding school near Mbandaka," the woman said. "Funded by some big American preacher. They have electricity. Computers for every child."

Cal studied the woman's toddler. "You want your daughter to go there?"

She beamed, touching the little girl's pretty, kinky hair. "Yes. She will be a doctor. Or she can be a teacher and come back to our village and teach us all. I will read. Taught by my own daughter."

Freya's eyes teared at the fierceness in the woman's voice. So few had a chance at an education here. And Abel Fitzsimmons was exploiting that need, probably to mine fucking diamonds.

"I haven't heard of this school. How long has it been operating?"

"A year. Maybe more? We just learned of it in our village about six months ago, when missionaries came through to recruit children. Two kids were the right age and passed the tests, so they were chosen."

"How old were they?"

"Nine and ten."

Freya felt bile rise. Nine years old. Was that the prime age for placer mining? Old enough to work, too young to fight? Fitzsimmons was preying upon people's dreams for their children.

They returned to their spot on the barge, and she pulled out her computer. Her excitement over the voyage was gone as the reality of why she was here had settled in. Break time was over. It was time to take these motherfuckers down.

Chapter Twenty-Five

If it was near Mbandaka, Cal's best guess was the school was southeast, maybe near the Ruki River, which flowed into the Congo at Mbandaka. It was still a large area to cover, but they had a starting point. Cal stared at the map Freya showed him on the computer. Situated on the equator, there weren't a lot of roads in the area. Just a lot of jungle and swamp forests.

They might not be able to find it, because sure as hell if what they suspected was true, no one was going to offer up tours to visit the "school."

"Is there anyone at the CIA you can reach out to?" he asked. "Get your side of the story out? You need to tell someone about the money."

"I've been thinking about that too. There are a few analysts who might listen. And maybe the case officer in Djibouti, but they might be too removed from Langley to be able to help."

"You mean Kaylea Halpert," Cal said. He knew he was right about Kaylea.

Freya laughed. "I really can't say."

"It's totally Kaylea. I saw her with you at Barely North that one time. You're comfortable with her in a way you aren't with most people. I'm guessing some of those nights you aren't on base, you're hanging with her in Djibouti City."

She smiled. "I like Kaylea. She doesn't take crap from anyone."

"Probably because she's CIA."

Freya rolled her eyes.

"Email your contacts and Kaylea," Cal said. "Tell them about the drums. Give them the URL for the tracker. Tell them about the money. Harry. Everything."

She nodded. "I need to write up a report first. Organize my thoughts. We'll only have one shot at this. It could compromise our location."

"It's a risk we have to take."

"They could just as well think I've gone off the deep end. Seth will probably say the money I recovered is to cover my tracks. A hundred and fifty million remains lost."

"But the"—he glanced up, again ensuring none of the other passengers were paying attention to them—"cake we found should count for something."

"Only if Lubanga's men recover it, and it moves, giving them something to track."

"I need to call SOCOM." They hadn't discussed this, but it was long past time he checked in. He braced for argument.

She surprised him by nodding. "Pax or Bastian, though. Not Major Haverfeld or Captain Oswald."

"I can't ask Pax or Bastian to withhold information from command. It would be a shitty thing to do to them."

"I know. They won't withhold anything, you just won't make direct contact until we know your status with SOCOM."

That was fair. Cal needed to know if he was a wanted man. He also needed to inform them Freya had recovered most of the money she'd been accused of stealing.

He grabbed the satellite phone from his pack. She eyed the phone, and he handed it to her. She inspected it, then popped open the back, finding the empty battery slot. She grinned and said, "God, I love how in tune we are."

His heart had kicked up a beat, but then settled in as she finished her sentence. Had he hoped she'd say something else?

He couldn't deny he had feelings for her. He just didn't know what they were and really didn't want to analyze them. This was a wild adventure in Congo. A separate reality.

He cared about Freya Lange. Probably more than he wanted to admit. But he didn't exactly see a future for them. He had to ask himself, would he feel this way about her in the real world, when the adrenaline faded? Or was this all about the rush and energy of the mission?

Were either of them even capable of stability when confronted with mundane home life? He reached into his pack for the battery. It was a problem for another day. "I figured they planned to track us with the phone."

"I'm sure they did." She frowned. "You might want to ask if Seth suggested it."

He nodded, handing her the battery. "It's possible. I was issued the phone just an hour before we departed. I think Olsen met with my XO that morning."

"He did." She ran a hand over her face, wincing. "He insisted I give him your service file." She wrinkled her nose. She really had a perfect nose, even red from the sun. And the scrapes on her face from their bushwhacking yesterday didn't diminish her appeal any either. "Seth knows everything about you."

This wasn't news—he'd suspected as much—but the full meaning sank in, kicking away flowery thoughts of noses and lips and other tangents best ignored. Freya wasn't the only target here. He was in just as deep.

"I'm sorry," she said softly.

He shrugged. This was exactly where he wanted—and needed—to be. He might not like every step of the journey, but he was still grateful to be here. "We'll fix this."

"It's not that simple."

"Sure it is. Seth Olsen might've fucked with my reputation, but sure as shit I'm going to *destroy* him."

"God, you're hot when you talk that way."

He smiled, wishing they weren't on a barge surrounded by a couple hundred people. "And you're hot when you breathe." This morning, she'd washed with powdered soap and a bucket of rainwater. Her skin smelled of soap and rain and river and sultry heat.

He'd always preferred the seasons in Northern Virginia over the thick, seasonless air of central Africa. But the way the heat embraced everything, the way she looked with a fine sheen of sweat on her flushed skin, he was revising his opinion.

His gaze landed on the phone again. "Camp Citron will get our location when I call. Are you prepared for that? They could tell the CIA."

Cal got along well with the brass, which could help them both here. He was a good soldier who did his job well and without complaint. When Pax and Bastian had been at each other's throats, he'd been the buffer that kept the team running smoothly, and his XO knew it.

But it was still a chain of command, and higher-ups didn't know him as well, nor were they likely to give a shit if there was even a whisper that Cal was on the take. And this was damn well more than a whisper.

"Write your report for the CIA," he said. "Let me read it, then I'll figure out exactly what I'm going to say to Pax. We want to make sure the truth is out there before we reveal our location, in case SOCOM doesn't believe me and they contact Olsen."

"Good plan."

Rain started to fall, and they set up a tarp to shade the computer from the drops while she worked. The patter on the tarp reminded him of the week he'd spent in South Sudan last month, when a deluge had destroyed the roads in a matter of hours. Savannah James had never been far from his mind during the South Sudan mission—partly because he'd sought her help in rescuing a few kids, but there'd been more to it even then.

Now he'd had a taste of her, and the last thing he wanted was to eject her from his mind. But the underlying fear of just who and what she was remained. Freya Lange would risk anything—and anyone—for the mission. He used to fear that meant she'd sacrifice him, but now that was the least of his concerns. The person who needed the most protection from Freya was Freya herself.

The barge hit a sandbar six hours after leaving Lisala. Some passengers groaned and griped, but most simply shrugged it off. Delay when traveling was part of life here. After two hours of the tugboat attempting to work the barge free, the captain announced they would stay for the night. Another tugboat was on its way downriver and would help free them the following day.

Freya was low on battery power, and the captain agreed to let her recharge. Fortunately, she had a separate charger and battery and didn't need to leave her computer in the wheelhouse.

They decided to sleep on the shore and paid a local to take them ashore in her pirogue. The dugout canoe was narrow and long, and in the heat of the day, the splash of the water over the sides was welcome.

A third of the passengers opted to sleep on land, and a mini-village sprang up in the tall grasses that lined the river. The rain had stopped, and Freya and Cal chose where to pitch their tent, picking a place that was close enough to the others to feel safe, but far enough to offer privacy.

It didn't take long before braziers were set up on the bank and fresh-caught fish was sizzling over coals. Food wasn't a problem, and Freya had already found a favorite donut maker, having enjoyed one for lunch earlier in the day.

She let Cal set up the tent on his own as she walked through the makeshift village. Several goats were grazing in the grass, but the monkeys remained caged on the barge.

She scanned the bags, tents, and tarps for the kite symbol, wondering if anyone traveling with them was headed for what they believed to be a school, or if any travelers worked for the ministry.

She didn't see the symbol on anyone's belongings. She bought grilled fish and more donuts and returned to Cal and their tent.

He'd stripped off his shirt in the heat, and she paused to look at his muscular back, her belly doing that fluttery thing it had done from the first time she'd seen him shirtless in the gym. She knew plenty of buff guys in the military and CIA. Cal was more muscular than some, less than others. She'd reacted to the other men too, but Cal was the only one who continued to trigger the flutter months after their first meeting.

With most men, the attraction went away as she got to know them. Not that she didn't like them. Pax, Bastian, and Lieutenant Randall Fallon—a particularly handsome Navy SEAL—were all fine men inside and out. But Fallon didn't make her belly twist. And she'd lost interest in Pax and Bastian long before Morgan and Brie came along. There were a few Delta Force operators she'd worked with who she'd been initially attracted to, and at least one who'd been interested in her, but she'd built a working relationship with them based on respect. The attraction couldn't be acted upon and had quickly faded.

Not so with Cal. Never with Cal. It had always been front and center, no matter how inconvenient. No matter how much he disliked her.

But then, that might be why it hadn't faded. He'd been a challenge. Except that didn't make sense, because there were plenty who didn't like her on Camp Citron, including handsome SEALs and Delta Force operators.

"Your husband is a handsome man," a woman said in French-accented English.

Freya turned to her with a smile. "I am very lucky."

The woman frowned. "He is not…" She lowered her voice to a whisper. "FDLR?"

The woman referred to one of the last factions of Rwandan *génocidaires* still active in the Congo, *Forces démocratiques de libération du Rwanda*, or the Democratic Forces for the Liberation of Rwanda, in English. While she'd known Cal's military bearing could raise questions, this one was alarming. "Oh no. He's not a rebel. He's American. We're here on vacation."

"But he is a soldier. Yes?"

She nodded. "Former military. Again, American, not Rwandan. We've never been to Rwanda."

"Some Americans have joined the fighting. Especially men like him, who have family from here."

"His family is from Congo. Not Rwanda. He's not a militant. He's showing me his mother's country. That's all." Knowing people would see how much she worked on the computer and they'd note they had satellite phones and other expensive technology, yet traveled on a barge, she added, "I'm a travel writer, writing about Congo for an American magazine. We've always wanted to take this trip, so I pitched it to my boss. And here we are." She cocked her head at the woman, who looked to be in her midthirties. "Would you be willing to be interviewed for the article?"

The woman took a step back, giving her a suspicious, but not hostile, look. "What do you want to know?"

Freya didn't quite recognize her accent, but given the woman's concerns, she took a guess. "Are you from Rwanda? Were you a refugee?"

The woman's eyes darkened, and she nodded. "Yes. When I was a child."

So this woman had survived the Rwandan genocide only to find herself in Congo for the First and Second Congo Wars. No wonder she feared Cal was part of a group intent on continuing a war that had officially ended in 2003.

Freya knew the stats. Nine African countries had fought in the Second Congo War. The war and its aftermath caused over five million deaths—most due to famine and disease—making it the deadliest conflict worldwide since World War II.

Some considered the Second Congo War to be the Third World War, given the scale and loss of life.

"I promise you, my husband isn't with FDLR. He loves this country." She glanced toward the woman's family, who had set up camp nearby. "Are your children missing school while you're traveling?"

"That's why we're on the river. We're going to Kinshasa, so the children can go to school. Our village has no school."

"I heard there's a Mission School near Mbandaka. They have computers for all the students." She hated saying this. The last thing in the world she wanted was for anyone to send their children to this "school," but she needed information.

The woman made a face. "Rubbish. Kids go to that school, but they don't come back."

It was a relief to know word of mouth was protecting some children, at least. And by the time she left Congo, the school would be shut down for all time, preventing more children from being sent into slavery by hopeful families who wanted nothing more than an education for their children.

Freya thanked the woman and asked if she could interview her the following day. The woman nodded with another suspicious look in Cal's direction, but she seemed to have accepted he wasn't a *génocidaire*.

Freya approached Cal, holding out the fresh grilled fish and donuts she'd purchased. "I got us dinner," she said.

He took the fish, and she dropped down on a square of tarp he'd set out to protect them from the wet ground. He joined her on the mat. "What were you talking about?" he asked quietly.

"She's concerned you might be FDLR." She relayed everything she'd learned between bites of fish. She had a feeling by the time this journey was over, she'd be less enthused about eating fish. But she'd never get tired of donuts.

"I wonder how many kids have been sent to the school," Cal said.

"I doubt we'll ever know. It's not like families will be able to step forward and be counted when there is no news, no radio, no decent flow of information into some villages."

"One of my mother's sisters moved to Kisangani in the nineties. Two of my cousins were conscripted during the Second Congo War," Cal said. "My aunt doesn't know what happened to them. They were boys. Close to my age." He looked down at the ground. "My aunt and her daughters were raped when the men came and took her boys. Gang raped. One solder after another."

The eastern part of Congo had been named the rape capital of the world. Stories like this were why.

"My cousins," Cal continued, "could still be alive. They could be part of the same rebel group that took them. They could have committed similar atrocities on other families. My aunt doesn't know what she would prefer—that her beautiful boys are still alive but have become monsters, or that they died in battle before their minds were warped." He lifted his head and met Freya's gaze. "What a horrible choice—to wish your children were dead so they aren't living monsters."

"I can't even imagine," she said. And she couldn't. It was too much. A turmoil that went so far beyond the losses she'd faced. And what they were doing here, it had nothing to do with Cal's aunt or the Second Congo War. But they were looking to stop a dictator who was trafficking in yellowcake that could well start the Third Congo or Third World War.

There was that.

They finished eating and then retreated into the tent. They needed to go over her write-up for the CIA analysts, and he needed to plan his call to Pax. The tent gave them a thin layer of privacy, but it was hot inside. Hotter than being on the barge in the midday sun.

Cal was shirtless, and Freya considered going topless as well, but that would feel weird. She didn't sit around and do work half-naked, unless it was an op like on Gorev's boat, and then she was too focused on her role to give a crap how dressed or undressed she was.

But still, she appreciated Cal's bare chest. "I keep thinking I must've imagined how sculpted you are, but then I see you again, and I practically swallow my tongue. You have an amazing body, Cassius."

His eyes flared with heat. They'd been professional all day, keeping their distance as required by custom in Congo, but now they had walls, even if they were paper-thin.

He leaned over and dropped a kiss on her neck. "I love it when you use my real name. No one outside of my family calls me Cassius anymore." He spoke softly. His deep voice sounded like her favorite dark chocolate tasted, smooth, sweet, with a hint of tang. "It feels intimate. Different."

It surprised her that he wasn't steering the conversation away from intimacy, but rather toward it. "Why did your parents name you Cassius?"

"Not long after my mom moved to Kinshasa, Muhammad Ali and George Foreman fought the Rumble in the Jungle there. It was a pivotal event in her life, coming right after losing her dad in a mining accident, and it was pivotal for Kinshasa and Zaire." Cal looked down. "She was thirteen and grieving, and largely responsible for her eight younger siblings while her mother worked. She says she idolized Ali, even before he won the fight—both men trained in Kinshasa for months in preparation, and Ali's bluster played well with the locals." He smiled. "She doesn't even like boxing. But she loved Muhammad Ali. Anyway, when I was born, she wanted to name me after him for his triumph over adversity. For the activist and pacifist who'd refused the draft and had to literally fight his way back to the top.

"But she was raised a Christian, so naming me Muhammad wouldn't work. My father suggested Cassius, his original name. Ali called Cassius Clay his slave name, but they both figured that was more the surname Clay than his given name, Cassius, so it wouldn't be disrespectful to honor him that way." He shrugged. "Plus they both liked the name."

"Do you like the name Cassius?"

"I do. As a kid, teachers called me Cassius and friends called me Cash. But the military only uses last names, and Cal was a natural, easy shortening, so Cassius and Cash faded away. I don't mind being called Cal, but I like hearing my real name from you, because then there's no mistaking that we're playing roles. It's not part of the op. It's Freya and Cassius." He ran a finger over her lips. "When I'm inside you, I'm Cassius, not Mani or Charlie or whatever name I'm supposed to be using. And you're Freya. Only Freya."

Her heart pounded at his touch. Was he saying this was more than a fling for him? Had they entered relationship territory?

She hadn't attempted a relationship since being hired by the CIA when she graduated college. Relationships were near impossible in her line of work. Not to mention the security clearance needed for the men she dated to pass muster. Of course, Cal already had that clearance, and he knew exactly what she was. There would be no hurdles but the job—a job she probably wouldn't have once this op was over.

That brought up another question: who would she be without the CIA?

She had scant few friends and only distant relatives for family.

She tended to hold back from people, to maintain a protective reserve. It saved heartache when she had to manipulate them, like she had Brie Stewart.

Brie was a good person. An aid worker devoted to helping people in dire need. But Brie would never have talked to Savannah James about her family like she would to Bastian. And the CIA had no other way of gathering intelligence on JJ Prime because he was an American citizen. So Savvy had used Bastian to get to Brie, and then she'd sent the woman on a mission that could well have gotten the aid worker killed. Brie wasn't trained—not even in the way Morgan Adler had been. Sending Brie to Morocco had been a huge risk, and Savvy knew it.

Deep down, she'd been sick about it. But she'd never dared show her feelings to anyone in SOCOM.

And then there was Morgan. Savvy genuinely liked Morgan. She was brains, beauty, energy, and fire. She was fun and bold and genuine in a way Savannah James couldn't be. It had been damn fascinating to watch the woman bring Master Sergeant Pax Blanchard to his knees. Freya had howled with laughter when she realized the tracker going off in the middle of the night meant Morgan had finally gotten Pax into her bed. Hell, she'd wanted to ask the woman how she did it, because the only attention Cal would give her was negative.

Of course, she knew there hadn't been any feminine sorcery on Morgan's part in reeling Pax in—it had been a simple case of two people who were meant to be together. Pure chemistry.

She'd held back from Morgan, not engaging in the girl talk she'd always longed for, but not because Morgan couldn't help her with Cal. No, her reason was much more basic. Morgan was in danger, and Savvy couldn't bear the thought of losing a friend.

She'd walled off her heart on her eighteenth birthday because she didn't know of any other way to cope. Her relatives had been relieved she was a legal adult with an inheritance large enough to afford college and a place to live. No one *had* to take her in. So no one did.

She'd told herself she wanted it that way, and eventually, she came to believe it.

Now here she was, sharing a tent and a mission with the man she feared she was falling in love with, and he was saying this crazy thing between them meant something to him too. But she was afraid to hope. Afraid to open up that last closed-off corner of her heart.

Because if Cassius left her—by choice or by accident—she doubted she'd ever recover.

She grabbed her computer from her pack. "We need to go over my write-up for the CIA."

He gave her a look. "What just happened there? Your face went through a whole series of expressions. Did I upset you?"

She shook her head. "No." She wanted to say more but couldn't really find the words. He hadn't said he wanted a relationship. He just said he liked being inside her. But she'd known that already. She'd gone off on a tangent in her mind that they didn't have time for.

Cal stared at her for a long moment, then reached for the computer. "Let me read your report."

"The money section is a little tricky. I was honest about everything, but damn, even *I* think I look guilty when I read it." She rubbed her arms, feeling a chill in the sweltering tent. Just the memory of the shock she'd felt in the tunnel set her heart racing.

Her mentor had pinned a mind-bogglingly massive theft on her, ensuring not only that Russian Mafia would be after her, but that no one in the CIA would ever trust her. Shoot to kill. And she was sending this information right back to the CIA. Reaching out could be her death warrant.

"If only I'd known about the theft before we entered Congo. The fact that we ran after dumping Harry's body… It only makes it all worse. Maybe if I'd contacted Langley then—"

"How would that have changed anything?" There was an edge to his voice.

She shrugged. "I don't know. But maybe, if I didn't immediately flee, they'd believe me about the money." She met his gaze. Her belly rolled, this time not in a good way, not the fluttering of a few moments ago.

Her superpower was reading people. She knew when the intel she was getting was solid and when it was bullshit. She knew how to connect dots.

For all the wrong reasons, she'd been trying to read Cassius Callahan since the moment they met. Because of those wrong reasons, she hadn't been able to decipher his body language. But over the course of this op, she'd finally cracked his code. Or so she'd thought. But now she realized in her haze after their fight in Dar, she'd missed something. She'd had a hint back at the Airbnb, after he returned with groceries, when he'd asked her what she'd done, but that tidbit had been buried in her mind after she'd killed Harry.

But now she could read him like a bulleted list and froze as the truth washed through her. "You sonofabitch." The words were a low whisper. She covered her mouth, holding in a moan of betrayal.

His eyes widened. Guilt clouded his features. It might as well be a sign announcing his confession.

"You knew. This whole time you knew about the theft of Drugov's money." Hurt kicked her in the gut, followed by rage. *He'd known.*

"Not the whole time—"

"Since Dar. Since the Airbnb. You fucking knew. And you didn't say a goddamn word."

"I didn't know if it was true at first—"

"Convenient. And what is your excuse *now?*"

"You were fragile, and we had a mission—"

"Fragile? I'm fucking *fragile?*" She kept her voice quiet, even though she wanted to shriek. She was the goddamned queen of control. "Since when? Since I infiltrated an oligarch's cabal? Successfully fought off a rapist and would-be murderer? Since I hacked a system and stole back over *three hundred million* dollars?"

She fixed her gaze on him, letting him see the fire in her eyes. "I have strength you can't even begin to understand. Fighting Harry was horrible, but it didn't break me. If anything, I'm stronger."

She gave a bitter laugh. "In one way, at least, Seth was right about making Savannah my name. Reliving the nightmare every time it was invoked *did* make me stronger. I've been forged from steel and honed by fire. As I said before, I can do everything you can do, backward and in high heels. So don't give me your condescending bullshit to justify leaving me in the dark."

The grass-colored tent gave Cal's dark skin a greenish cast. It was too bad it was just a trick of the light. She wanted him to feel as sick as she did.

He'd known.

"Was it revenge? Because I held back information from you, you had to do the same to me? What else haven't you told me?"

Something like guilt washed over his features. "Please, Freya. I'm not that petty or that much of an ass. I was honestly worried. About you. About what it would do to you to know that Seth's betrayal went even further. I was going to tell you after our reconnaissance of the tunnels. But then you found out on your own."

"You've had plenty of opportunity to confess since we left the tunnel, but you didn't have enough respect for me to speak up."

She'd thought it would hurt when he left her. She'd had no idea it could hurt even more to have him by her side and know he didn't trust her.

Had all his pretty words been a lie to keep her close? Maybe she didn't know him at all.

She wanted to flee their tent and set off on her own, but regardless of how he felt about her, at this point, there was no escape. They were stuck together.

Chapter Twenty-Six

Freya sat in the tiny tent, head high, spine ramrod straight. She was strength and beauty, and every word she'd said was true. Looking at her now, Cal had to wonder how he'd convinced himself she would break with the news of Seth's never-ending betrayal.

She glared at the flimsy tent entryway, and Cal could guess at her thoughts. But he also knew she was too professional to flee. She would never abandon her mission, and Cal was a major piece of it. No matter how much she wanted to leave him to rot, she wouldn't do it. So she directed her anger at the tent flap she wouldn't use. She was trapped by circumstance and duty.

Thunder rolled in the distance. The storm was back. Further trapping her.

Days ago, she'd admitted she was falling in love with him. Last night they'd made love in this tent, and yesterday he'd had her against a tree. In the rainforest, he'd started imagining a future that included her.

Now she wanted nothing to do with him. Were her feelings for him dead, killed in an instant? Or in a coma, able to be awakened, revived?

Regardless, he deserved it. And it gutted him to know he'd hurt her.

Not telling her about the money hadn't been payback. It had been…stupid ego. Casting himself as her protector, shielding her from knowledge he'd thought would weaken her.

Freya Lange didn't need a protector; she needed a partner. He reached out to her, but she jerked away. "Don't touch me!"

The expected rejection still triggered an ache. "I'm sorry." They were the only words he had. And they were true and deeply felt.

"In Dar, I told you the truth about my mission," she said softly. "From that moment forward, I've told you the truth about everything, even classified details I could have withheld. It would have been nice if you'd treated me with the same respect."

"I should have told you. I didn't at first because I didn't know what to believe." He kept his voice low. "As I told you before, I took the mission because SOCOM wanted me to spy on you. They wanted to know why you had so much autonomy within your organization. So when Pax told me you were suspected of stealing half a billion dollars, I couldn't just blow it off. I had to be certain you were innocent, and frankly, I wasn't. Not then. But I protected you by keeping our location secret."

He risked touching her again and planted his hands on her shoulders when she didn't pull away. "Pax warned me they were going to declare me AWOL if I didn't check in. I've thrown away my place on the team. I face jail right along with you. I'm risking everything for this mission. For you."

She shrugged. "Your superiors will protect you. They ordered you to work with me. Your ass is covered."

That could be true, but SOCOM also could have fried him. He'd disobeyed an order. Even if delivered by Pax, it was an order.

"Regardless of how you feel about me," Cal said, "we're in this together. We still have to work together if we're going to get out of this alive."

"I tried to leave you in Dar. You could be back at Camp Citron with your team right now."

"But I'm not. I chose to stay with you. You need me."

"No. What I need is a partner who tells me everything. Who doesn't think I'm fragile. Because right now, the only thing that's broken me is knowing how little you respect me."

"Don't respect you? Sweetheart, I think you're amazing. I'm in awe—and a little terrified—of what you're willing to risk. I'm the chickenshit here because I'm afraid of how I feel about you. Afraid to care. Afraid to love. Because, damn, you go all in. Mission first. Mission last. Mission only. And I will lose my shit if something happens to you."

"Please. Don't start lying now. We both know you don't like me because—and I'm quoting here—I 'lie, manipulate, and bend people.' Sure, you wanted to screw me, but you also said that if we fucked during the mission, it would mean nothing to you."

He'd known those words would come back to bite him in the ass from the moment he'd uttered them. "I was lying then—to you and myself. I'm not lying now."

"So, what, you're saying you love me? Please. I'm not that gullible."

"I'm not bullshitting. I don't know what I feel for you, but it's more than lust. More than friends with benefits." It was the truth. He was as confused about his feelings for her as he was about quantum physics. He found the concept of quantum theory fascinating, but couldn't explain it to save his life, no matter how many times his brother broke it down for him. Unlike his brother, his brain wasn't wired that way. His brother might be able to write a mathematical proof that explained why when he was with Freya, the world felt more vivid, intense, and real, but that geometry was beyond him.

But he didn't need a mathematical proof to know what he felt for her was significant. "My chest hurts, knowing I've fucked this up. Knowing I've hurt you. And when this feeling doesn't hurt—in my chest, my mind—it soars. I think of you, and I'm flying high. I'm with you and my body buzzes in a way I can't explain, especially given the situation we're in. How the hell can I be feeling this way when we're fleeing through a rainforest, on the run from mercs and rebel groups and Russian Mafia and who knows who else?

"How could I have felt satisfied when we left Gorev's yacht? But I had you by my side, so I was. You were safe and strong and clever and amazing." He placed his open palm behind her head, pulling her closer so she'd look up to meet his gaze. "I just know that when I'm with you, I get a charge of energy, pleasure. A zing that's missing without you. And when I'm inside you, I feel a connection. More than sex. Deeper. More intense. More than I expected. More than I want. You're addictive in a way that scares me. You're like a drug I'll never get enough of. I want that zing. That intensity. The thrill of being with you. In you. And that scares the hell out of me given the risks you take."

A tear spilled down her cheek.

He wiped it away with his thumb, still cradling her head, then leaned in. "I'm not bullshitting. I want to go to Langley and castrate Seth Olsen for everything he's done to you. I wish I'd arrived in time to spare you from having to kill Harry."

"Dammit, Cassius. I want to be angry so I can keep my heart out of this. That way it won't hurt so much later."

"It's too late. For both of us. There was no going back from the moment we kissed in that damn elevator. No going back when we practiced touching in Kenya. No going back after we sparred in the gym and I couldn't hit you because I couldn't *not* see you as the woman I've wanted since we first locked gazes at a meeting in SOCOM headquarters." His lips brushed over hers. "There's no going back for me, Freya. I know because I fought this every step of the way. But here we are, and I'm all in now."

Her arms slipped around his neck, and she tucked her head against his chest, looking down so he couldn't see her face. His heart pounded as he waited for her response, but she didn't owe him an answer just because he'd accepted his feelings.

If they were out of sync, it was his own damn fault for not acting in Gbadolite, when she'd said she was falling for him.

"I feel like I could shatter right now," she said at last. "I guess this means you're right and I am fragile."

He tightened his arms around her, closing his eyes, loving the feel of her in his arms, against his body. "Sweetheart, you are harder than a diamond and a thousand times more precious. You're the strongest person I know. Fierce. Determined. But if you do shatter, I will hold you until you're back together."

She lifted her head to face him. "Make love to me, Cassius. Make me come apart in a good way."

He wanted to. Lord, how he wanted to. But they'd both regret losing sight of the mission. Their responsibilities. "Later, I will give you everything you want. But right now, we need to contact the CIA and SOCOM."

Her face flushed, and she dropped her forehead to his shoulder. "Shit. You're right. Jesus. I've never been this incompetent before." She pushed away from him. "What the hell am I doing? We found yellowcake, and I'm—"

He cut off her self-recriminations with a hard kiss on her lips. "Stop. This isn't exactly a normal mission. It's personal in a way neither of us anticipated. You've become a victim of Jean Paul Lubanga and Seth Olsen. You were attacked by a fellow agent. It skews everything. We haven't been in a safe place to contact superiors before, but now we can."

She nodded. She handed him the computer with the write-up she'd completed as the barge was pushed down the river. "Let me know what you think."

The two-person tent was a narrow half dome, leaving scant few inches between them as he sat with the computer on his lap on his side of the pallet, and she lay beside him.

He got to the section where she outlined how she'd found and recovered the money. The number of zeros hit him once again. A hundred and fifty million had gotten away.

With that kind of money in his accounts, Lubanga didn't need a coup. He could buy a bunch of real estate anywhere and start fresh. But Congo had so much more. He couldn't remember the estimates of how much wealth was in the ground in Congo, but it had to be in the trillions.

He glanced at Freya. She tracked those sorts of stats. "How much mineral wealth remains in the ground in Congo?"

"The most often quoted figure is twenty-four trillion dollars, but that estimate was years ago. Most minerals have only gotten more valuable since then."

Yeah, that was motivation for Lubanga to stay in the game even with this payout. Cal studied the numbers on the screen. "I've never understood the lure of extreme wealth—I mean, if I can be happy in a tent in one of the poorest places on earth, why would I need several hundred million dollars?"

"You're happy right now?"

"I know everything is stacked against us. We're stranded for who knows how long. But we're safe. We're together. We've got food and shelter. Yeah, I'm happy." He met her gaze. "I'd be even happier if this was a real vacation. Some time off to explore Congo. Make love to you under a waterfall in a rainforest." He smiled, his gaze raking her body. Later. Later he could have all of her.

She ran a hand down his thigh. "A shame we can't keep a few million and just disappear. After we're done exploring rainforests and waterfalls, we could escape to a private tropical island."

"It would be great for a vacation, but we'd both get bored in two weeks."

"True. You're such a people person, you'd miss training locals, miss your team. I'd miss being part of the intelligence community. Miss solving puzzles." She sat up and leaned against him. "When I first joined the operations division, I missed being an analyst. I thought I'd like being out there, gathering intel, but it was the puzzle afterward I enjoyed more. Looking at the pieces and trying to figure out what it meant. Joining SAD and working with SOCOM helped. The missions were intelligence based, acting on intel that had been gathered, and some, like sending Bastian and Brie to Morocco, required me to do a quick analysis—no time to wait for Langley to spend months pondering the situation—to determine the action. I know my role with the CIA is over. I'll be lucky to escape prison. But a part of me has this dream that when all is said and done, I'll be able to stay on as an analyst. I'm good at it. I never should have left that role."

"You're good at this too," he said. "Look at how far you've gotten us, on a mission that was originally just intended to copy a computer hard drive in Dar es Salaam."

"But look at what I missed. I didn't see Seth's betrayal. For all my vaunted skills at reading people, I didn't see that coming."

"Seth used Harry as a shield to blind you. You were so focused on what Harry might do, you couldn't see Seth. He knew how to play you because he's been in this business far longer than you. Plus, he's the one who trained you."

She nodded. "I suppose you're right." She sighed. "So what do you think of the write-up? Should I send it?"

He read the final paragraphs, the speculation that Fitzsimmons was using the school as a cover for diamond mining. He frowned. "Is there a connection between Olsen and Fitzsimmons?"

"I don't know. But the CIA will. Their background checks are unlike anything else, and they're ongoing. If Seth has business with Fitzsimmons, someone will find it."

"If they believe you enough to start looking."

"Yeah. I think they will, if they find the yellowcake. If they don't, I'm screwed."

"We're screwed."

She shook her head. "I won't let you take a fall with me, Cal. I'll confess and say I took the money if I have to, just to convince them you're innocent."

Fear shot through him. "You will not."

"You don't have a choice in this."

"Hell, yes I do. And you aren't going to lie to protect me. Ever."

"I'm not going to let Seth destroy you too."

He could see in her eyes she meant it. His greatest fear was that he couldn't save her from herself.

Freya took a deep breath and hit Send. She'd set up a Virtual Private Network—VPN—to hide their location, but she had no doubt the CIA would crack it and find them. She just hoped it would hold up for a few days. Regardless, it was done. She'd told the CIA she'd killed Harry and left his body on an African savannah.

Savannah. Sort of fitting, when she thought about it. She'd cut herself off from the horror of that day, the look in his eyes as he expressed his intent to rape her again and kill her. She set the computer aside and pulled her knees to her chest, determined to hold back the sob. She wouldn't break down now.

Cal's arm came around her, pulling her to his side. "It's okay to cry. I was wrong in calling you fragile, and crying wouldn't make it so."

She leaned into him, even as she gripped her legs even tighter, hugging herself while closing her body to him. "I'm afraid to dive into the horror right now. Like I might not be able to pull out. I have to function. Later, when we're home, then I can fall apart."

"I'd like to be there, to hold you when it happens."

She lifted her forehead from her knees and faced him. "No. I...don't want you—or anyone—to witness that."

He was silent for a long time, and she guessed he was coming up with an argument for why she shouldn't shut him out, and her heart sank a little at the idea that even her mental breakdown had to be on his terms.

She was so not cut out for relationships.

"Okay," he said softly. "All I care about is that you take care of you. I hope you'll let me in—so I can be there for you—but if you need space, it's cool."

And just like that, his understanding broke her. Like a dam pummeled by floodwater, she couldn't maintain the wall she'd built around her heart. It shattered, leaving the pounding organ exposed to abuse.

Cassius Callahan was inside her barriers. She had no defenses left.

She planted a hand around his neck and pulled him to her, kissing him with a raw passion she'd tried to hold back. His tongue slid into her mouth and claimed her as if he'd been waiting for this moment his entire life.

Noise outside the tent was slow to get her attention, but it dawned on her that the tone of the words being spoken by their neighbors was alarming. They broke apart, both looking toward the zipped door of the tent.

She pressed her lips to his ear and whispered, "What's going on?"

"Soldiers. Looking for someone."

Darkness had fallen, but they could see the glow of a light through the thin tent fabric. The soldiers were downslope, closer to the river.

She reached into her pack and pulled out the passports they were using for this leg of the journey. They wouldn't help much if they were looking for a white female. Freya was the only white woman on the barge.

Cal listened to the shouts outside and frowned. "They're looking for an FDLR spy."

Shit. Had the woman she'd spoken with earlier reported Cal to authorities? Or did others on the barge suspect him of being a Hutu nationalist?

Or that could be an excuse, and it was really Lubanga's men, searching for both of them.

She tucked the computer back in her bag. Her heart pounded in the sweltering enclosure. The soldiers drew closer to their tent, shouting orders. One by one, people responded, giving their names and destinations—words she could understand no matter the language spoken.

They would reach their tent soon. They'd have to step out, submit to inspection. She reached out and took Cal's hand, lacing her fingers between his. They'd come too far to give up now. She looked at her pack, where her pistol was tucked in a hidden pocket. When the soldiers unzipped the flap, she could shoot. Striking first could be the only thing that saved them.

But if they were looking for Cal on a tip from one of their fellow travelers, then they were just soldiers doing their job, protecting the citizens of DRC from an organization that was responsible for multiple terrorist attacks in the eastern part of the country.

They couldn't shoot soldiers in cold blood. They weren't the enemy.

How far away were they? How many campers remained to inspect? They were on the edge of the camp. The last tent before the tall grasses gave way to the jungle. She grabbed a knife, ready to slice open the back of the tent. They could slip out into the thick vines. Hide in the shrubs. They would have their packs at least.

But no tent. No food. No motorbike. Escape from here was a last resort.

A man said something in a language she didn't recognize. More shouting was followed by a grunt of pain and a woman's shriek.

Cal stiffened beside her. It went against his nature to hide inside while a woman was being hurt. Beaten?

But just as they'd had to do in Dar es Salaam when the poor young woman was about to be raped, they could do nothing. She reminded herself of the barrels of yellowcake. The planned coup. This was bigger than one woman's suffering, and if they stepped in to help now, much more could be lost.

The soldiers barked more orders, but their voices faded as they moved away. The woman's shrieks turned into quiet sobbing.

"What happened?" Freya whispered.

"They found their guy. The woman is screaming that her husband is not a Hutu. At least, I think that's what she's saying. It's a Bantu language, probably a Ruanda-Rundi dialect."

The camp settled down. The block party atmosphere that had filled the impromptu village was lost, those who had been chatting by the river quieted, likely going to sleep.

"It's too quiet for me to call Pax now," Cal said. "In a few hours, when everyone's deep asleep, I'll hike down the riverbank and call him."

It was a solid plan. Pax would be sleeping too—they were two hours behind Djibouti—but that could work in their favor, as he'd be alone in the CLU he usually shared with Cal.

Freya was as scared about reaching out to SOCOM as she was about the CIA. But not for herself. Right now, Cal's career was Schrödinger's cat. Until they called SOCOM, they could believe everything was okay. But once they learned the truth, he might never be able to forgive her for roping him into this nightmare of a mission.

Chapter Twenty-Seven

Pax Blanchard jolted awake the moment his cell phone buzzed. Morgan knew not to call in the middle of the night—not when he was waiting to hear from Cal. So the call was either SOCOM or his missing CLUmate.

Caller ID showed him what he'd been hoping to see, and he jabbed at the Answer button. "Wassup?" he said, in case the caller wasn't Cal. If someone had nabbed Cal's phone and dialed a previously called number, he wouldn't give anything away.

"Pax." Cal's voice. Strong. Firm.

Relief flooded through him. He hadn't been this worried about a teammate since Bastian had gotten lost on the way to the rendezvous in South Sudan a month ago. And Cal was in an even more volatile situation—something that shouldn't be possible, but here they were.

Most of his teammates were like brothers, but Cal was Pax's best friend. He'd helped Pax hold it together when Morgan went missing and he didn't judge when Pax nearly broke. "Jesus, man, I've been worried."

"Yeah. Uh…sorry about that. It hasn't really been possible to check in. Things really went to shit after the last time we talked."

"Yeah. I know. That CIA agent you punched went missing in Dar es Salaam."

"Shit. I was hoping that was quiet still."

"It's all over the news."

"Motherfucker. Any mention of F—Savvy or me in the stories?"

"No. The official story is an American businessman went missing in Dar. Suspected Russian Bratva action related to Drugov. We know it was the CIA guy because the BBC and CNN posted his picture. We all saw him in Barely North. Definitely your guy."

"The CIA probably tipped off the media to put pressure on Savvy."

"What's going on, Cal? What happened to the CIA prick?"

"He's dead. Freya killed him when he tried to rape and kill her."

"Jesus."

"Yeah."

"How is…Freya?" Freya must be Savvy's real name. What did it mean that Cal was defaulting to her real name now?

"Shit. Forget I called her that. Savvy is fine. She had some bruises, and she's going to need a shit ton of therapy when this is all over, but she's holding up like a champ. Really amazing, actually."

And that answered Pax's unasked question: Cal and Savvy were involved. He'd be happy for them—hell, they'd been circling each other for months—but right now, Savvy was wanted for treason, theft, and probably two dozen more serious crimes.

Christ, she'd killed a fellow CIA agent. How could this possibly end well for her?

"Be careful there, man." Shitty advice, but it was all he had.

"Too late," was Cal's reply.

Pax wanted to be supportive. Really, he did. But fuck, what if Savvy was guilty? His gut said no, but she was CIA; she was highly trained to present a false image. He cleared his throat. "She's wanted for the missing money. Major Haverfeld is going to bat for you, but you're being pulled in."

"I figured as much." Cal went on to tell him about the night raid and Savvy recovering a large chunk of the cash and converting it to bitcoin.

Pax let out a low whistle. "So now you've got mercs on your ass?"

"There's been no sign of a tail, but probably."

Pax didn't say what he was thinking, that Cal could save himself—and possibly Savvy—if he returned to Camp Citron without her. "Where are you now?"

"Can't say. We're trying to track down the location of the Mission School. I was kinda hoping you could do some research for us there. We need more info on Fitzsimmons and his alliance with Lubanga. And there's this, uh...other thing. We found three barrels of yellowcake in the tunnel under Gbadolite."

"The fuck?"

"Yeah. We hid the drums in the jungle—but they'll probably be found soon. Savvy tagged one with a GPS tracker. I'm going to give you the URL to download the data and see if it's being moved. She checked this afternoon, and it hasn't moved yet."

"You've had a busy week."

Cal let out a grunt that was probably supposed to be a laugh. "Is SOCOM going to track this call?"

"Probably."

"Tell them Savvy isn't the enemy."

"I will. I don't know if they're buying it, though. Seth Olsen is crucifying her, and knowing she killed a fellow agent..."

"We're running down all the leads we can to figure out the connection between Olsen and Congo," Cal said. "They'll have to believe her if we can expose Olsen."

"You think Olsen has something to do with the school and diamond mining?"

"Either that or he's connected to Gorev and Lubanga. Olsen told Savvy to assassinate Lubanga. That's a fact. We believe he gave Lubanga the mission code name along with Drugov's half billion. Someone sent Harry to take her out—and Olsen is the only logical choice. My guess is she was getting too close to finding proof Olsen is dirty as she combed through Drugov's files, and Olsen had to sabotage her."

"Has she sent any of this info to the CIA?"

"Yeah, to a few analysts she trusts and the case officer in Djibouti City. We don't know if it will do any good, but she needed to get her version of the story out somehow. Obviously, I'm telling you shit that's classified. Stuff she can't say to anyone except fellow Agency people."

Pax understood what Cal meant. Savvy was keeping her oath of secrecy to the CIA, even as Seth Olsen was systematically destroying her. He was glad Cal wasn't too scrupulous to remain quiet—but then, Cal's oath was to the Army and his team, not CIA. He could talk, especially when he was under suspicion right along with Savvy.

"'Kay. I'll talk to SOCOM. See if we can buy you a few more days. For what it's worth. Captain Oswald is on your side."

"See if you can keep him there."

"Will do." Pax hung up and stared at the phone. He needed to report this call to SOCOM. He'd landed in shit when he didn't report right away that Cal had contacted him before. But he was worried. Seth Olsen was more powerful than any of them had guessed. SOCOM had wondered why Savvy operated with autonomy, and the answer was her direct supervisor.

But now the man had turned on her, and he was using all his power and influence to destroy her. It was clear Cal wouldn't abandon her, which meant he'd go down too. Unless his A-Team could find a way to save them both.

Cal returned to the tent where Freya waited. He'd hated even the small distance that had been between them—they needed to watch each other's backs—but they'd agreed someone should stay behind in the tent. The scare with the soldiers searching for a rebel had also underscored that they needed to remain alert at all times, especially now that Freya had emailed people within the CIA.

She'd used a VPN to hide their location when sending her email, but knowing the Agency would use all their considerable resources to break the VPN, they couldn't count on their location remaining secret. Once the Agency realized they were on the river, they'd start searching for the barge. With so many islands and channels and barges, it wouldn't be easy, but the risk remained.

He updated her on what Pax had said and encouraged her to go back to sleep. His sleep shift would start in two hours. One thing he liked about working with a professional, she didn't argue. She just rolled over and dropped into sleep.

Two hours later, he woke her and took his turn, grabbing five hours before it was time to pack up and return to the barge. Fortunately, the second tugboat arrived an hour after dawn, and they were free of the sandbar by nine in the morning.

They settled into their spot on deck and noted the mood of the other passengers was muted after the previous night's raid. No one appeared angry that a man had been removed from the group; the anger was focused on the man himself and the idea he might've been FDLR.

The *génocidaires* of Rwanda had destroyed so many lives; even the whisper of affiliation was enough to presume guilt. This central part of DRC didn't see as much of the fighting and terrorism that plagued the eastern portion of the country, and locals would do anything to keep it that way.

Had the woman Freya spoke with yesterday been searching the camp for potential *génocidaires*? Had she reported the man who'd been taken away? Or had he been a genuine threat?

It was one problem Cal didn't have time to worry about, yet he did. The future of DRC remained bleak until the people could get a grip on the government and end once and for all the conflict that had begun with the Rwandan genocide in 1994.

Much easier said than done.

These thoughts swirled in his mind as they were pushed down the river at a speed of about ten miles per hour. The deck of the barge roasted in the June heat. They were getting ever closer to the equator. The day was hot, around eighty-five degrees, but the sweltering air and flat metal deck made it feel much hotter.

The captain announced they would sail through the nights to make up for lost time after being stuck. Apparently, they were several days behind before that disaster. But then, what was behind when the supposedly ten-day journey from Kisangani to Kinshasa regularly took a month?

Not that Cal would complain that they wouldn't camp on shore that night. They needed to get to Mbandaka as soon as possible. He and Freya were sleeping in shifts anyway, so he could give her both their spots to stretch out on, while he found a seat in the cargo and watched over the sleeping passengers.

She returned after a trip to the barge's one toilet, her eyes lit with excitement.

"What's going on?" he asked.

She leaned close and spoke in a whisper that would be hard to hear over the general noise of the crowded vessel. "I found more crates marked with the kite symbol. They're clustered with other goods destined for Mbandaka. If we put a tracker on one of the crates, we can follow it."

His excitement matched hers, but they were still at least three days out from the city on the equator. "Best to wait to tag the crates until an hour before we reach port, keep the battery fresh and us hidden in case the CIA hacks the URL."

Freya had explained to him that she'd set up the URLs for all the trackers back at Camp Citron, but none had been activated until she planted the tracker in the yellowcake. Once she'd sent her contacts in the Agency the URL for the yellowcake tracker, they could potentially figure out the URLs for the other trackers in her possession. It wasn't a certainty, but it was a risk. Which meant it was best not to activate a tracker they would remain close to any earlier than necessary.

She nodded. "Then all we have to do is follow the breadcrumbs to get the proof we need that whatever Fitzsimmons is funding, it's not a school."

At last they had a plan.

Now, if they could just avoid getting captured before reaching Mbandaka, they'd be home free.

Three days after being freed from the sandbar, Freya was officially tired of eating fish. She was also tired of both sun and rain, but not tired of the river itself. She loved the rocky islands and multiple channels, the jungle that hugged the bank. The small villages they passed and the pirogues that rode up alongside. The glimpse into the way of life remained fascinating, even if the travel itself was wearying.

This journey would forever stand out in her mind as one of the most amazing things she'd ever done—yet this was everyday life for many of her fellow travelers. Their strength in hardship had her in awe, and she wished to hell they hadn't been forced by necessity to develop that strength.

Colonialism had been devastating to all of Africa, but Congo, having been claimed as the personal property of Belgium's King Leopold, had suffered more than most—if one were to put a scale on atrocities. The world these people lived in was fully shaped by Leopold's nightmarish reign, followed by a century of corrupt leaders. Twenty-first-century DRC wasn't much better off than the twentieth-century version, but they were trying, and if foreign governments and businesses would stop interfering and do more to help, the country had the resources to grow and become a world power.

Twenty-four trillion dollars could buy a lot of infrastructure.

She leaned back against the cargo that was her backrest and watched life on the barge. A man played guitar while another drummed, and together, they played a lively Congolese rumba. A few children danced. Several passengers washed clothing, wringing the items out over the side of the vessel and laying them to dry on the tarps that covered cargo.

Because they'd been going nearly nonstop since being freed from the sandbar, the barge was scheduled to make port in Mbandaka some time in the coming night. They would disembark in the morning with the other passengers. She would plant a tracker on a crate an hour before dawn.

It was possible that tomorrow night, they would locate the "school" and get the evidence they needed to show that the televangelist was no Christian. Even if she never cleared her name, she would take comfort in knowing her work had freed enslaved children and brought down a false prophet.

Cal dropped into the open seat beside her and handed her a canteen. The water had been filtered with charcoal, boiled, and purified with tablets. It still might not be enough, but at least they had their antimalarials and antibiotics if an infection took hold. Sickness was an issue for several travelers, and Cal and Freya were more susceptible than most given that their immune systems hadn't been in regular contact with river parasites over the years.

She took a long drink from the canteen. She'd been sweating so much in the heat, she needed to replace the water, even if it was risky. "Thanks," she said.

His fingers entwined with hers, the only type of physical contact they'd had since they'd kissed in the tent. She was reminded of when he'd taken her hand on the flight from Camp Citron. A simple touch that had conveyed so much.

She'd lost track of the days since that flight. The miles traveled. The horrors witnessed. But she could remember every moment of that touch. Of the unfolding it had triggered in her heart. Of the hope it signified. And now his hand entwined with hers meant even more. He was with her for the long haul. He'd risked everything for her, to be by her side now.

He hadn't known what he was risking when he first signed on for the mission, but he'd certainly known by the time they entered Congo. But still, he was here. And that meant everything.

She wouldn't let this job destroy him. If only one of them could escape the trap of this mission, it would be Sergeant First Class Cassius Callahan.

Chapter Twenty-Eight

The jungle around Mbandaka was exactly like the other jungles they'd explored, except this time, they had a beacon to follow. And an actual plan. Not to mention that for once, they had a good idea of what they'd find when they got there.

After disembarking with their packs and motorbike, they purchased breakfast from a street vendor and sat on the riverbank, eating as they watched crates being unloaded from the barge. Upstream, rusted riverboats—remnants of the colonial era—sat on the bank, a dead fleet.

If Freya were here as a tourist, she'd take photos, and so she did, but then she returned her attention to the barge and continued snapping photos of the lone man who claimed the crates with the kite symbol. He loaded them into the back of a pickup truck, which also entered her photo library.

She checked the signal for the tracker on her computer. It was transmitting perfectly. To save battery power on the tiny device, it was set to update the location every thirty minutes. With the frequent transmission rate, the battery would last a few days at most.

The one she'd planted in the yellowcake had been set to transmit once every twelve hours, extending battery life to ten days or more. Half of those days had been used up now, but yesterday, there'd been movement. The drum had traveled a mile north before the signal was lost—likely because it was now inside the tunnel, where the transmitter couldn't connect with satellites.

Cal left her by the river to fill the tank of the bike and the empty jerry cans, while Freya watched the truck with the crates. When the driver left the parked truck to visit a small grocery store, she followed him. She and Cal would need food, and she had no idea how long their next journey would take.

She purchased smoked fish, beef jerky, and a precious block of cheese. She added bread to the basket, and canned beans and vegetables. They had enough to last a few days, at least.

It was noon by the time the truck left town. As much as she feared letting the vehicle out of sight, she had to trust that technology wouldn't let it disappear. Waiting for the next transmission had her sweating even more in the equatorial sun.

Relief settled in when the data came and included the full route the tracker had followed. It recorded everything. In the minutes since the truck had left the riverfront, it had traveled south two and a half miles and was now exactly on the equator. They would wait another thirty minutes for the next transmission before setting out. The bike could go much faster than the laden truck on the pitted dirt roads. They had to give the truck a solid head start so they wouldn't be spotted following it.

Thirty minutes later, they had their direction. The truck was still moving south. They followed, moving slowly and taking breaks to make sure they remained thirty minutes behind. It was late afternoon by the time the tagged crate stopped moving. After two reports of no movement, they moved in on it, hiding their bike in the jungle two klicks away from the final coordinates.

They moved on foot. When they were a klick from their destination, they hid in the thickness of the jungle and waited. Night fell. Insects grew louder as the birds went quiet. A large cat or other creature made a sound in the distance.

They each donned their skintight night-op suits, and Cal helped Freya apply the dark greasepaint to her skin. His lips brushed over hers, and he leaned in to whisper in her ear. "When we get back to Camp Citron, I want you to put this suit back on just so I can peel it off you and fuck you blind."

She smiled and kissed him but said nothing. What could she say? She doubted she'd return to Camp Citron as anything but a prisoner.

Cal's adrenaline pumped as they waited for the midnight hour to roll in and they could inspect the so-called school.

He and Freya agreed it was time to call Captain Oswald and let his XO know exactly what was going on. He outlined the situation and gave the GPS coordinates of the crate. SOCOM could dive into that information and send a team to liberate the children if what they suspected was true.

They might send someone to arrest Freya and him, but that was a risk they had to take.

Before hanging up, Cal asked, "What are you hearing from CIA?"

"Not a word. I went around Seth Olsen, but no one on the food chain will talk to me."

"Shit."

"You're sure she's telling the truth? About the money? About the dead agent?"

Cal looked at Freya. Or at least, he looked in the direction where he knew Freya was. They had no light and weren't wearing their NVGs—they needed to save the charge for the night's recon mission. In the nearly absolute darkness, he couldn't see her expression. She couldn't hear his XO's side of the conversation, but she could guess.

He knew Captain Oswald had to ask the question, but that didn't mean he liked it. "Yes. She's innocent. I'm innocent. We're busting our asses out here trying to stop a coup and save some kids."

"I hope you're right, Sergeant."

"I am, sir."

"Report in after you locate the school. We need pictures. Preferably video. If the asshole is using children, we'll bring him down."

"Yes, sir."

It was hard to approach a place in silence in the jungle. Freya knew that special forces from all branches of the military practiced that sort of thing often. She'd learned the skills herself when she trained for SAD, but she was out of practice. Djibouti didn't have much in the way of jungles, and prior to this deployment, she hadn't been in any jungle but the urban kind.

Ingrained lessons came back to her as she attempted to move with the stealth of a panther. At last they arrived at the perimeter of an encampment. Three long canvas tents—old military squad tents that probably dated back to the Korean War—were lined up side by side. There was another structure farther back, hidden in the trees. Was that the "school"?

The camp was quiet, but they remained on the lookout for guards. They separated to circle the squad tents, blow darts at the ready should they come across a patrol. They were both fast and silent, and reached the truck that had delivered the crates at the opposite end of the camp at the same time.

A whiff of cigarette smoke told her why they hadn't spotted a sentry. With a hand signal, Cal indicated he'd caught the scent too and would take care of it.

Only one guard on duty and he was taking a break? But then, this place was so remote, they probably didn't think they had much to fear except children escaping.

Cal was back by her side a moment later. "Did you tranq him?" she whispered.

He nodded and showed her the used dart before tucking it away. "I propped him against the bumper. He'll think he dozed off while taking his break."

"Perfect." They didn't want anyone to know they'd been here. Best not to spook the guards and have them do something drastic to the children before a team could arrive to liberate the kids.

If this was what they thought it was.

If they were way off base and this was really a school? Well, then they still didn't want anyone to know they'd been here.

The guard would be out for at least a half hour. First, they scouted the squad tents, each entering from opposite ends. An adult male slept on a cot in front of the door. A tranq dart to the neck ensured the man wouldn't wake while they searched. She retrieved the dart and glanced across the tent to see Cal also bending over a cot in front of that opening.

She walked silently down the center aisle between rows of cots stacked like bunk beds. Each cot was filled with a sleeping boy or girl. She guessed they ranged in age from eight or nine to fourteen.

This could actually be a school. They needed to check out the building on the other side of the trees, where there would probably be more guards. Cal snapped photos of the sleeping children with an infrared camera. They would delete them if they were wrong and this really was a school.

They peeked in the other squad tents, seeing a similar setup to the first. These were barracks, nothing more. She signaled for Cal to lead the way through the trees to the structure on the other side. There were no guards around the building, which turned out to be a mill.

Even though it didn't surprise her, it still made her stomach twist. The children weren't just mining, they were operating a mill. Before entering the structure, they needed to scout the area. Another clearing not far from the trees drew their attention.

They carefully approached the opening. It appeared that what had started out as an open pit mine had led to tunneling. Cal led the way down into the pit while she watched his six. In the pit, they found several mine shafts cut into the earth. The ceiling was low, the opening narrow—child height and width.

He snapped photos with an infrared camera, just as he had the children. Then he changed the setting to video and whispered a narration of what they were viewing as he recorded the shaft, kneeling to record the first few feet of the tunnel.

Freya wondered if they could make it back here tomorrow and get footage of the children entering and leaving the mines. It didn't get much more damaging than that.

They returned to the mill and slipped inside, startling a guard who'd been sleeping on the job. Another blow dart from Cal, and the man was dispatched. Hopefully he wouldn't remember the encounter, or if he did, he'd think it was just a dream.

Inside, she spotted crushing stations followed by large vats. It was at the far end of the room that everything became clear.

Fine powder was spread out on trays to dry.

Horror filtered through her as she realized what she was seeing.

These kids weren't mining diamonds. The powder was yellow—like mustard. The children were mining uranium.

Chapter Twenty-Nine

Hours later, they were far away from the awful school, and Cal was feeling sick to his stomach about leaving the children there. This was the third fucking time in as many months he'd been slapped in the face with child slavery, but the other two times, he'd been able to *do* something about it. The children had been liberated. And he'd helped with that.

Tonight, he'd been forced to leave them. Tomorrow would be another day in the uranium mines. Literally.

Motherfucker.

They could have taken out all the adults holding the children there. They could have freed the kids.

But then there'd be no evidence implicating Fitzsimmons. No proof of what the asshole was up to. A team could show up in a few days, free the kids, round up the leaders, and take out the whole operation.

As Freya had said to him after the op in South Sudan, they might've saved fifty kids, but there was nothing to stop the market from forming again. Without removing the men behind the market, there could be fifty more kids enslaved a few weeks later.

Freya believed in saving *all* the children—not just the ones who were enslaved now, but the ones who would be enslaved tomorrow. Sometimes that meant sacrificing. Not saving the kids in the moment, but returning with a plan.

Cal got it now, in a way he hadn't been willing to see before. Sure, he'd understood in his mind, but he hadn't been able to wrap his heart around it. And he'd thought Freya heartless for her stance.

Now, much as his heart hurt, he knew they'd done the right thing in leaving those kids. And he knew Freya was suffering for it just as much as he was.

It was the most horrible thing he'd probably ever done. The children worked in mines that weren't ventilated, mining fucking *uranium*. They'd been breathing it in.

He took a deep breath. The air was thick with moisture. Jungle air. It smelled of earth and vines and leaves and rain. But it was *air*. Not uranium dust.

He knew they had to leave the kids, but he fucking hated it.

Freya sat next to him in the darkness. They'd finished setting up their tent in the remote, wild jungle, but they'd yet to climb inside.

They both wore their NVGs, giving off no light to reveal their location, and he could read her body language, knew she was struggling with the same demons.

A month ago, he hadn't been able to read her. Or maybe he just hadn't wanted to. But now he could, and he knew she paid the same mental price he did. He pulled off both their goggles and kissed her, then he tucked his face into her neck. "I misjudged you when we argued about the slave market. I get it now. I'm sorry."

"Thank you," she whispered.

"I thought you were cold, calculating. I convinced myself you couldn't have a heart to make the decisions you were willing to make. I grouped you in with the agents who'd messed with my mom. They'd tried to sacrifice her for some kind of greater good that wasn't good for anyone."

"What are you talking about? The CIA messed with your mom?"

"I thought you knew about that. That it was in my file."

"The CIA doesn't have a file on you. We don't monitor American citizens. We can't. The only file on you I've seen is your service file provided by SOCOM."

"The CIA has a file on my mom from when she dated my dad, before she moved to the US. They continued to monitor her long after I was born."

"If such a file exists, no one shared it with me. She's an American citizen now. The CIA can't touch her."

"Doesn't mean they didn't try." He needed to go back to the beginning, tell her the whole story. "I assumed you knew my dad was CIA. His work for the US embassy in Kinshasa was his cover."

He felt her body go rigid, then she relaxed against him. "I feel so stupid for not guessing that. It never even crossed my mind that your dad was CIA. His background isn't mentioned in your service file."

"He parted ways with the Agency before I was born. He ended up working for the State Department in a job that aligned with his cover from when he'd been CIA, so he never put CIA on his résumé. He wasn't exactly happy with the Agency when he left. People in State knew his experience. He didn't need to advertise." Insects were chirping, and a mosquito buzzed around his face. "Let's move into the tent," he said. "And I'll explain the rest."

She crawled inside, and he followed her, zipping their little hidey-hole tightly closed. They rolled out their sleeping pads and inflated them, then lay down. It was her turn to sleep for a few hours, but he would tell her his story first. It was long past time he told her why he'd reacted so badly to learning she was CIA all those months ago.

"My dad met my mom at an event at the hotel she worked at in Kinshasa. It was a political thing, but this was Mobutu pretty much at the height of his power, so basically, it was a gathering of kleptocrats and their ilk. Dad was shopping for informants. Mom was trying to keep the staff—she was an assistant manager—from poisoning someone and causing an international incident. Dad witnessed some guy pinching her ass, and then the guy followed her when she left the party to check on the staff in a service area. Dad was concerned, so he tailed the guy and decked him when he got too handsy with Mom, and a few days later, she showed up at the embassy with a peanut butter mousse she'd made for him as a thank-you. They started dating, fell in love, and about a year later, the CIA decided to bring him back home to put an end to the relationship.

"But Dad had his own ideas and had asked my mom to marry him and move to the States. She was reluctant. She had a good job in Zaire—she was fluent in English, French, Lingala, and could speak enough other Bantu languages that she started off as a translator for a hotel, and when she showed aptitude for managerial tasks, she moved up the ranks. It was hard for women to get jobs like she had in Zaire, and even harder for someone with only a high school education. She knew she'd have a tough time getting a job at all in the US, let alone in management. But she loved my dad and knew he couldn't stay. She didn't know he was CIA. Hell, he wasn't supposed to get seriously involved with a foreigner. And he certainly wasn't supposed to bring her back as his wife.

"Mom finally says yes, and Dad submits all the paperwork required for her to get a green card and things. He'd already reported his relationship up the line at work, but everyone ignored it until he let his boss know he planned to marry her. That's when they called him home."

Cal closed his eyes, thinking of how his parents told this story. The way his mother laughed and his father's anger spiked. Mom had grown up in a dictatorship and expected the government to be shit, while Dad had been idealistic—pretty crazy when Cal thought about it, considering he'd been in the CIA—but somehow, that idealism had remained intact until the CIA tried to destroy the love of his life.

"Basically, they yanked him back to the US and tried to convince him that Mom was a honey trap. They did everything they could to keep him from bringing her to DC, but he'd done something they didn't expect—he married her before leaving Kinshasa. And, wouldn't you know it, he'd also gotten her pregnant. With me."

Freya leaned on his shoulder in the dark. Her lips brushed his neck, and he wondered if the way he felt right now was anything similar to what his father had felt all those years ago, when he'd been yanked away from his pregnant bride and his employers began a campaign to convince him she was a spy for Mobutu, looking to land a prime spot in DC so she could report back on CIA operations.

"Now, I know the CIA's concerns weren't unfounded in a general sense. Yes, there were honey traps out there, looking to land green agents. But my dad wasn't green, and my mom wasn't honey. She had zero connections within government. My parents were quite simply crazy in love. My dad ended up quitting his job. As I said, he got a job with the State Department. Coworkers there helped him with the legal wrangling that finally got my mom to the United States just three weeks before I was born. My dad later found out that one of the reasons the CIA objected to his marrying my mom—aside from the fact that she was black and he was white, which was an issue raised a number of times—was the fact that they'd wanted to use *him* as a honey trap for some East German woman. They'd planned to send him to Berlin when he finished his assignment in Zaire.

"Dad spent the last thirty-plus years griping about how the CIA doesn't give a damn how they use people. I was fed a steady diet of 'individuals don't matter' and 'they'll sacrifice anyone without a second thought.' Between his anger and the shit the CIA has done in places like this, I grew up with a...somewhat skewed view of the Agency."

He'd never really put it into words before, had never actually faced his bias until the day he met Savannah James and felt an instant charge. Then he'd learned she was CIA, and he'd felt a crushing disappointment. Which he'd proceeded to take out on her, as if it were her fault. "I really am an ass. I'm sorry."

She'd been silent as he spoke, only her touch in the pitch-dark tent gave him a hint as to her reaction—small kisses and the teasing of fingernails on skin. Now her hand stroked his chest. "You know, I enjoyed the zing of sparring with you. You couldn't hide the attraction any more than I could. You weren't as bad as you think you were. And I wasn't exactly sweet to you either. It went both ways."

He smiled. "Probably because every time I saw you, I wanted to pin you to the wall and kiss you. And then you'd say something provocative, and I just wanted to possess you more."

"And I wanted to be pinned and possessed."

He was rock hard and ready to go. But the last time they'd kissed, they'd been so caught up in each other, they'd been slow to react when soldiers invaded the camp. As far as they knew, they were safe here. But it was a risk they couldn't take. "When we get back to Camp Citron, I'm going to spend at least forty-eight hours in your CLU pinning and possessing you."

She laughed. He loved her laugh. It was warm and joyful. How had he ever convinced himself she was cold and unfeeling when she had that laugh?

He slid a hand under her top and cupped a breast. He could stop there. He wasn't an addict. He stroked the nipple into a point, and her breathing changed. Jesus, and this was just touching her breast. If he slipped a hand in her pants…

He pulled back and took a deep breath. "You should go to sleep. I'm going to report in to my XO. Tell him what we found tonight."

"Tell him tomorrow we'll go back to Mbandaka and charge the modem. Then I'll be able to upload the video and photos."

She'd attempted to do that the moment they'd stopped to set up camp, only to find the satellite modem was dead. She'd managed to load the images and video to her computer and a USB drive. They had backups.

Tomorrow, the world would see what Fitzsimmons's ministry was doing to children in the Democratic Republic of the Congo.

Tomorrow, they'd be one step closer to wrapping up this mission and getting their lives back. Starting a new future.

Dad had always said he'd fallen in love in a Congolese jungle. Now Cal couldn't help but wonder how closely he was following in his dad's footsteps.

With a population of over three hundred thousand, Mbandaka, the capital of Équateur Province, was the largest city Freya had visited in Congo. The town had more infrastructure than most, and in addition to an airport and a university, there were even a few hotels and other services for travelers.

There were enough hotels that they decided to risk renting a room using one of Cal's fake passports. Freya was desperate for a real shower, and some of the hotels offered private bathrooms. That alone was reason enough to risk breaking out a bonus passport.

She waited in a café as Cal arranged for a room in one of the larger hotels that overlooked the river. Later, he entered through the lobby, then let her into the hotel through a side door. A white woman was more likely to be remembered by the staff, while a Lingala-speaking black man would hardly be noticed at all.

The first thing she did upon arriving in the room was plug in every device she had. All the batteries were now dead or in the red zone. She'd recharge the electronics while she recharged her body with a glorious hot shower.

She wished Cal would join her in the spray, but caution was the rule. One person had to remain vigilant at all times. Refreshed and revitalized, she stepped out of the bathroom and let Cal have his turn.

While he showered, she packaged up the video and photos and sent a download link to Cal's XO. She debated reaching out to the CIA analysts again and decided against it. They hadn't responded to her earlier report. If they'd cracked the VPN, they might believe she was still on the river. No point in letting them know she was in Mbandaka.

At this point, it was clear redemption wouldn't be found in CIA channels. She and Cal were pinning their hopes on SOCOM.

SOCOM would help her take Fitzsimmons and Lubanga down.

But still, there was one person in the Agency she could contact. In spite of Cal's urging, she hadn't reached out to Kaylea Halpert. At the time, there hadn't been much Kaylea could do to help her with the CIA from her position in Djibouti. But now they weren't looking to Langley for support, they were looking to Camp Citron, and Kaylea was in the perfect place for that.

Months ago, she and Kaylea had set up a Gmail account to communicate outside government channels. They never sent email using the account; they posted draft messages that the other person would see when they logged in and delete when read. It was a simple technique that covert operators used the world over, and sometimes Kaylea and Freya shared information on informants that they didn't want part of any official record. Plus they could set up their occasional night out in Djibouti City without people in the embassy discovering they were more than casual acquaintances.

She'd checked the Gmail account daily, finding nothing. Either Kaylea knew nothing of what was going on—entirely possible as she wasn't in SAD and probably wouldn't recognize Harry's photo on the news—or she'd opted to wait to hear from Freya. The third option, of course, was she thought Freya was guilty and was distancing herself, and if that was the case, Freya couldn't really blame her. They weren't *that* close.

She logged in to the Gmail account and felt a ripple of surprise flavored with apprehension at seeing "1" next to the drafts folder.

Time to find out if Kaylea was still on her side. When she saw the message, relief and gratitude flooded her.

Holy shit! I just heard. What the hell is going on? DO NOT email my work address, I'm being monitored—have been for at least a week but didn't know why until today. Posting this from a burner. I don't know if I can help, but I'll try.

Freya deleted the draft and posted her own: the message she'd sent to the analysts days ago and the updates shared with SOCOM, including links to view the uploaded videos and the URL for the yellowcake tracker. She also sent Kaylea the link to her cloud drive, where all of Lubanga's files were stored. Freya hadn't dared to give them to the analysts, in case the files disappeared, but during the long days on the barge, she'd had a chance to set up a second cloud, and she'd copied the files. She had a backup. She hit Save and logged out of Gmail.

It was possible the message from Kaylea was bait, and she'd fallen for it, but deep down, she didn't believe it. Couldn't believe it. There were good people in the CIA, and Kaylea was one of them.

Cal stepped out of the bathroom and dropped onto the couch beside her. She told him about Kaylea's message.

"I *knew* she was CIA." He grinned.

She smiled. "Yes, you're very smart."

He laughed and kissed her. "Damn straight." He looked at the computer. "What are we doing now? Researching Fitzsimmons?"

She nodded. She'd gone over the USB drives she'd taken from the tunnel back when they were on the barge. It would take a forensic accountant to fully understand the finances and reach of Lubanga's organization, but she had what the US needed to connect the most important dots, and now Kaylea had that information too.

One thing was clear: Lubanga was working for Gorev—which meant if Lubanga took control of DRC, Russia would have the riches of Congo in their pocket. Freya had already suspected that, but the money confirmed it.

Fitzsimmons's connection was a little less clear. She'd assumed the school was a front for diamond mining and the man operated on pure and simple greed, but they'd seen with their own eyes what the "students" were mining.

How did that fit in? Obviously, there was still a profit motive, but illicit yellowcake was more likely to fuel nuclear bombs than to supply nuclear power, and one didn't arm people with nukes without a bigger agenda. What good was money when the world was decimated by nuclear holocaust?

The thing about black-market yellowcake was that buyers were the type who actually planned to use it. It wouldn't be used to create a standoff designed to result in a stalemate that supported a fragile peace. No. Whoever purchased uranium oxide concentrate was after the big bang, either to cause devastation or so they could seize the world stage as a nuclear power.

There were any number of rogue states that were after yellowcake, but those were unlikely allies to an evangelical minister. So why would Fitzsimmons sell nuclear material to a group that was ostensibly his enemy?

Sure, there was a big payday, but a diamond concession from Lubanga could—and probably would—pay more with less risk of discovery and ruin. What was Fitzsimmons's long game? Drugov's files had had precious little information on the televangelist. She'd spent her time before embarking on this mission memorizing everything she could about Gorev and Lubanga. It was time to find out what made the Reverend Abel Fitzsimmons tick.

She opened the browser and started with a basic search. Beside her, Cal smelled of Irish Spring. She wanted to breathe him in while running her hands over his scalp, neck, back, and ass.

But dammit, they had a job to do.

She opened the televangelist's website and clicked through the profile he wanted the world to see. From there, she moved to news coverage that was less flattering and included his investment in Drugov's South Sudan operations, along with his claim that it hadn't been an investment, it had been a charitable donation towards sanitation products for girls.

She clicked on a link to watch his daily cable program, surprised to see he didn't stand within a megachurch, with a mega-audience, behind a gilded pulpit. His sermon was delivered from a shockingly simple wooden podium.

"He must be hiding his money," she said as she dove further on the web, searching for information on his ministry's finances.

The CIA wasn't allowed to monitor American citizens. That was the FBI's job. Freya didn't doubt the FBI had a file a foot thick on this man and his ministry, but even if she were in good standing with her employers, no one from the FBI could or would share, and she didn't have the time or resources to do the sort of digging she needed. She checked the public records of the charity arm of the organization.

On the surface, it appeared the ministry had a hefty bank account. A large portion of the outflow was earmarked for ministry work in Africa—with the bulk going to DRC. No surprises there.

She returned to the videos. Fitzsimmons was all fire and brimstone when he stood behind his plain pulpit. She didn't spend a lot of time watching evangelical preachers, so she didn't know how he compared. He had a certain zeal when he spoke of the coming end of days. Fervor with a tinge of longing.

"Do you think he's the real deal?" Cal asked. "The finances of the organization look clean. Every article about the charity, every link that details where the money goes, everything except for the school appears legit. He doesn't drive a fancy car. Doesn't live in a mansion. Maybe he really wants to be the spiritual leader of Congo. It's possible he doesn't know what's going on with the school."

"That would mean he's never been to the camp and hasn't seen what the donations are financing." She frowned at the image on the screen, considering the idea. "It might fit the reverend, but it doesn't mesh with what we know about Lubanga. He doesn't give a damn about the religious leadership in Congo, which means there's something in it for him if he's letting Fitzsimmons become the voice of Christianity in DRC."

"True," Cal said. "I just think if money were his goal, it would show. He'd mess up somewhere and there'd be a paper trail to a yacht or a hidden vacation home. Something that shows why he siphoned off money in the first place. Why the hell would a guy this devout, who is so damn careful to present a frugal façade, want to arm terrorists with nukes?"

She returned her gaze to the screen and upped the volume. From what she'd read about the reverend, this recorded sermon followed his favorite theme.

"*And as we learned from Luke 17,*" Fitzsimmons said with televangelist fervor. "'*On the day when Lot went out from Sodom, fire and sulfur rained from heaven and destroyed them all—so will it be on the day when the Son of Man is revealed.*' *Yes, my children, we will have fire from the heavens! When Jesus returns, humanity will be divided into two groups: those who live only for themselves, who live without regard for God, who haven't submitted to His kingdom; and those who are true to the teachings of the Lord.*

"*The selfish, godless souls will fall under His judgment. They will be struck down in a firestorm! A rain of fire and sulfur, as when Lot went out from Sodom! Vultures will feast. The second group, the faithful, you, my children. You. You who have submitted your life to the kingdom of Jesus, you will escape His judgment. You, who don't live for this life only—accumulating objects to flaunt wealth and avarice. Fancy homes. Expensive cars. Diamond jewelry. These are the property of the godless. The trappings of the devil. The faithful who have remained true, who have shunned worldly goods for the sake of earning a place in Jesus's kingdom, you are the ones who will escape His judgment. At the end of days, we, the faithful, will be received into the kingdom of the Lord!*"

On the surface, the sermon explained why the man was so careful with his public image. His wife could hardly be seen wearing diamonds when this was his main selling point. He then continued on to ask parishioners to give their excess to the church, as Jesus wanted.

And many thousands did just that.

She backed up to the middle of the sermon and watched his face with the volume low, trying to read him.

"They will be struck down in a firestorm! A rain of fire and sulfur, as when Lot went out from Sodom!"

She paused on his face, his words echoing in her mind.

Text she'd seen on the ministry's website came to mind, and she clicked to bring up the window. A banner filled the top of the page with a quote from the New Testament.

> *Then he said to them, "Nation will rise against nation, and kingdom against kingdom; there will be great earthquakes, and in various places famines and plagues; and there will be dreadful portents and great signs from heaven." – Luke 21:10-11*

After several seconds, the words changed to a different New Testament quote.

> *When you see Jerusalem surrounded by armies, then know that its desolation has come near. – Luke 21:20*

"Those are both references to the end of days, aren't they?" Cal asked. "My knowledge is a little vague when it comes to Bible quotes."

"My parents were both scholars in the humanities and schooled my brother and me in the basics of all the major religious texts. We didn't delve deep into Luke, but I think that's the part where Luke shares what Jesus said about the Second Coming. Some religious sects believe it's a road map. Directions to bring about judgment day. Jesus won't return until Jerusalem is surrounded by armies. There must be war and famine and plagues..." Her voice trailed off as the truth sank in.

Fitzsimmons *was* the real deal. She hadn't researched him enough to write up a professional analyst's report, but her gut—which had been trained by the best analysts the CIA had to offer—was flipping over the idea that Fitzsimmons was a true believer.

War and famine and plagues. Famine and war were a problem in South Sudan, Congo, Yemen, and so many other areas in Africa and the Middle East. Drugov had tried to trigger a massive Ebola outbreak in South Sudan—which surely would count as a plague. That must be Fitzsimmons's connection to Drugov, the spreading of a plague.

But that wasn't all. Fitzsimmons believed that for Christ to return, Jerusalem had to be surrounded by armies.

She stared at the screen, hearing his words from the sermon echoing in her mind. *"They will be struck down in a firestorm!"*

Her body went cold as his motive crystalized. "He's not after money or power. Fitzsimmons wants uranium so he can bring about the end of days."

Chapter Thirty

Three hours later, after exhaustive online research, Cal was on the phone with his XO, relaying Freya's theory as she wrote up an analysis for SOCOM. It felt like a leap of logic, but at the same time, she'd once been an analyst, and this was exactly the type of opinion she'd been trained to form. Presented with evidence, what were the likely motives, actions, and outcomes?

His gut said she was on the money. She'd been on the money with Drugov, and her instinct had helped stop a genocide. Now they were looking at World War III.

The end of days. He knew there were evangelicals who were eager to bring it about, but he'd never suspected any would be willing to go so far as to invest in a uranium mine to make it happen.

He finished his conversation with Major Haverfeld and Captain Oswald. Both men would attempt to convince SOCOM to send in a special forces team to close the mine and liberate the kids, but the situation was tricky with Freya's role. The CIA wouldn't sign off on anything she'd touched—so they couldn't mention her.

He didn't want to know the contortions they were going through to get the pertinent information up the right channels without identifying either Cal or Freya as the source. Hell, he'd bet the information hadn't been shared beyond the fence of Camp Citron. Until Seth Olsen was unmasked, the CIA couldn't be trusted.

The intelligence community had been compromised by several attacks within and without in the last year. What did it mean that Seth Olsen, who wielded a good deal of power in the Directorate of Operations, was a traitor?

And then there was Fitzsimmons. Where had his plan for Armageddon originated? Had they found the uranium ore first and then come up with the plan for a phony school? Or did Fitzsimmons just send the money and let Lubanga do the rest?

It made sense that the uranium was being moved through the tunnel under Mobutu's palace. It hadn't been mined at the southern tip of DRC and transported overland or by plane. It had probably gone upriver on a barge.

Even more alarming, a new source of uranium had been located, and once they managed to rescue the kids, artisanal miners would step in. That was what happened at Shinkolobwe. The mine had been closed for years, but locals were desperate, so they mined anyway.

Freya pushed back from the computer and stood. She rolled her shoulders. "I've never written an analysis with such scant information, but it's all I've got for now. I've also never written an analysis where I could include video of a slave camp I witnessed with my own eyes. So. There's that."

He moved to stand before her. He placed a hand behind her neck and leaned down to kiss her forehead. "Did you send it to SOCOM?"

She nodded. "What did Captain Oswald say?"

"He and Haverfeld are going to try to find a way to send a team without buyoff on the mission. Misfiled paperwork, a transport to a forward operating base in the Republic of Congo. There are ways to make it happen. But it'll probably take several days. CIA is ramping up the search for you. That's probably why Kaylea heard the news. Haverfeld thinks you'll be publicly burned soon."

That was the ever-looming threat. Freya's name and photo released to the world. Identified as a covert CIA operator. And not just any kind of operator. Special Activities Division. The one that may or may not commit assassinations…and orchestrate coups. Black ops.

"Fuck," she said softly.

"Yeah."

"What about you? Is the CIA going to go after you next?"

He shrugged. "They can try. My XO won't have it."

She smiled up at him. "Lucky."

He kissed her nose as he cupped her ass. "You know it." Behind her, the computer pinged. "Email?" he asked.

She nodded and turned to the computer. "This could be from my contact at CIA. Finally." She clicked a few buttons. "I'm running the incoming message through a scan to make sure it's not a Trojan horse or any other kind of trap. Checks out." She opened the message.

After a moment, she gasped.

She stepped back from the screen and slapped a hand over her mouth. Her face had gone pale. Her eyes were wide with shock. "I'm so sorry, Cal. So sorry."

He frowned and moved closer to the computer. "What's going on?"

"So fucking sorry."

He took another step toward the computer, dread prickling up his spine. He tilted the screen back to read from above. "Oh my God."

"I'm sorry. Seth, he insisted on reading your service file. He must've seen your dad's name, and it rang a bell. My guess is...the CIA had files on your mom from before she moved to the US. In the eighties, they must've visited the village where she grew up and tracked her siblings."

Cal stumbled backward as horror settled in. After everything his aunts and uncles had been through during the Second Congo War, now they had to face this.

He read the text on the screen again. It was, essentially, a ransom demand. Presumably from Lubanga.

At noon, two days from now, Freya Lange and Sergeant Cassius Callahan were to deliver the USB drive containing three hundred and fifty million dollars to Cal's mother's childhood village. If they didn't show up, FDLR rebels would kill every man, woman, and child in the village. Starting with Cal's Aunt Patrice and her ten-year-old son, Samuel.

Chapter Thirty-One

"How the fuck did Lubanga get this email address?" Cal's question was more of a shout.

Freya paced the small hotel room, her mind racing. "My confession that I killed Harry was a wild card. Seth must've been brought into the loop. He saw the email, got the address, and gave it to Lubanga."

It had to be Lubanga who'd sent the email. The man wanted his money back, and he'd found the perfect set of hostages in CIA files. Cal's *family*.

It was all her fault. She'd brought him into this.

They couldn't give a would-be dictator three hundred and fifty million dollars so he could fund his army and seize Congo, but she also couldn't let an entire village of men, women, and children die.

She didn't doubt for a minute that Lubanga would follow through. He threatened to use *génocidaires*. Terrorists. Killing children was in the name.

"I'm so sorry, Cal." She whispered the words this time. They didn't help. She knew that. But they were how she felt.

"It's not your fault, Freya."

"But it is. I'm the one who dragged you into this mission. None of this would have happened if I'd just gone with Harry like Seth wanted."

"You'd probably be dead in that scenario."

She shrugged. "Your cousins would be safe."

"Yeah, but no one would have found the yellowcake. Or the kids and the mine. Those kids will be saved. Thanks to us. Because we came here together."

He was trying to absolve her, but it wouldn't work. A tear rolled down her cheek. She swiped it away. "How many people live in the village?"

"What are we doing, ranking to decide who it's better to save? The kids or the village?"

"How many?" she repeated.

"I don't know. Two hundred? Maybe more. We *can* save them."

"We can't! We're only two people. For all we know, Lubanga has an entire army."

"Yeah, but he can't pay them," he said.

"They won't know that until after they slaughter everyone in the town. This is a no-win situation. We can't save the village, we can't give Lubanga the money."

"It's a trap. We know it's a trap. Lubanga knows it's a trap. We will step into it anyway."

"You said to me in Lisala, 'Running headfirst into a trap is suicide, no matter how much you think you can beat it.' You feel differently now?"

"We won't run headfirst. We'll plan carefully and escape before the jaws snap shut." He pulled her into her arms. "Listen, I'm going to call my XO and give him this latest development. You're going to start tracing that email and see if you can prove it originated with Lubanga."

She nodded, because what else could she do? One foot in front of the other, even when you were walking toward a trap. She pulled Cal's head down and kissed him, sliding her tongue inside. She needed this intimacy with him.

After all, in two days, they were going to die.

Cal hung up the call. Freya had forwarded the email, and they'd taken turns on the phone with Major Haverfeld and Captain Oswald, coming up with a plan. The village was to the south, between Mbandaka and Kinshasa. North of the Kwa River, it was situated on the edge of an unnamed jungle and fed by a tributary of the Kwa.

Remote and isolated, it had been a mining town until the collapse that had killed Cal's grandfather. Nearly two decades later, mining resumed, and two of his aunts and one of his uncles returned to their childhood village, escaping Kinshasa at the same time the population was mushrooming in the decline of Mobutu's reign. They lived there still with their families. Twelve first cousins and three first cousins once removed plus his aunts, uncle, and their spouses all lived in the village, along with over two hundred more men, women, and children he wasn't related to by blood or marriage.

He stared at the map, trying to figure out the best way to protect the village. The original mine, the one that collapsed, had been hard rock. The modern mining operation was an open pit mine. SOCOM was working on getting updated satellite images.

It was obvious why they'd been given two days to get there. This was Congo, and there would be no flying in. Plus Lubanga had no idea where they were, how far they'd have to travel. He'd probably gambled that they were close enough to get there in two days, knowing that if they were in Kisangani or somewhere farther, they'd do whatever it took to get a flight to Kinshasa to reach the village in time.

The man needed the physical USB disk, and once he attacked the village, he'd shot his wad. So he'd given Cal and Freya time to get there—but not so much they'd have backup support from Camp Citron. Those two days also meant Lubanga had time to amass an army to contain the hostages.

It would be impossible for Cal and Freya to arrive more than a few hours early. Not without a helicopter. SOCOM couldn't get that sort of authorization without going up the line, and the CIA was in the way. They couldn't show their hand to the enemy within.

Basically, they were fucked. They had a few hours to plan and prepare and would set out just before dawn.

He thought about his mother, imagined her waking up in her home in Arlington, Virginia. The house where Cal had grown up, the oldest of three rambunctious boys. She would make her coffee, filling a mug his brother had painted when he was eight years old. She'd read the latest headlines on the iPad Cal had given her for Christmas years ago so they could FaceTime from anywhere when he was deployed.

She'd go about her day as if it were the same as any other, unaware her siblings and their children were in danger. Not knowing her oldest son was the cause.

He'd seen the worry lines on her face deepen during the First and Second Congo Wars. He knew the fear she'd felt for her mother and siblings. For their children. For a country she loved. He'd seen her cry when his cousins had been conscripted. He'd been ten and hadn't known then about the rapes, the nightmare his aunt and other cousins had survived.

His mom worried about Cal when he was deployed. All mothers did. He didn't want to think about what she'd go through if Cal failed her now.

He closed the computer and stood. He never considered failing, and now wasn't the time to start.

Freya was cleaning one of the AKs.

Cal picked up a second AK and did the same. He was a weapons sergeant. He knew the ins and outs of weapons better than anyone on his team. "Three AKs aren't enough."

"We have our pistols. Knives. Five blow darts. Two gas pellets," she said. The items were laid out on the coffee table in a neat row.

He studied the pathetic arsenal. "To take on an army."

She shrugged. "We don't know how many we'll face."

He wished they'd stolen guns from the camp last night, but that would have been noticed.

He and Freya discussed their approach. Cal had visited the village with his mother. He knew the layout. They weren't without advantage there. She reminded him of this and channeled his focus, asking questions, pulling memories from his mind with just the right questions.

They came up with a plan to protect the children. It was far from ideal, but better than nothing.

They could do this. He and Freya made a formidable team.

He watched her as she prepped their packs for the coming journey. They had most of a night before they'd set out. Everything needed to finish recharging, and they could go faster if they traveled during the day. They had to take the road—there wasn't enough time to bushwhack their way through the jungle on the bike—and at least during the day, they would blend with other travelers.

They had a few hours.

She tucked a strand of hair behind her ear, something he'd watched her do a thousand times at Camp Citron, and each time, he'd imagined running his fingers through her hair, rubbing a lock between his fingers to see if it was as soft as it looked.

Now he'd had the chance to find out. Her hair was even finer than he'd realized. His fingers had slid through the soft straight strands easily. Like silk.

They had a few hours.

He took a deep breath, then words that had been on the edge of his consciousness for days slipped from his lips. "I love you."

A frisson ran through Freya as she met his gaze. She had no trouble reading him now, and her heart squeezed to see that he meant it. She looked down, taking a deep breath. She'd accepted what she needed to do. He wasn't making this easy.

He scooted across the floor toward her, took the pistol she'd been cleaning from her hand, and set it on the coffee table. He cupped her cheek and lifted her face, making her look at him. "I love you," he repeated.

She smiled and kissed him, repeating his words back to him in her mind. Her kiss was urgent; his was slow and seductive.

She knew exactly what he was thinking. After all, she could read him now. They had time. A few hours at least. Then they would take off on a suicide mission. He planned a night to remember—except they wouldn't live long enough to remember.

But she could make a different choice. One that didn't include him or his family being sacrificed. One in which he would have decades more to live and remember this one night.

She wanted to sink into the seductive softness of his mouth, his touch, but her mind was on a different track, where she wanted to give him all the passion and fire she felt at once. Hard, fast. The intensity of a flash flood.

A month's worth of rain in thirty minutes.

A lifetime's worth of passion in one night.

Her tongue slid against his as her fingers slipped beneath his waistband. She wrapped her hand around his thick erection and stroked. His body quaked at her touch, and he let out a soft groan.

She didn't waste a minute. She unzipped his fly and freed him from his boxer briefs. She scooted down his body and took him in her mouth. As she had in Dar, she lifted her gaze to his, watching him watch her go down on him.

He groaned as she took him deep. His eyes were soft and hot and beautiful brown orbs that she could stare into for hours. His cock was so hard, she let out a soft groan at the feel against her tongue, imagining how good he would feel inside her.

He ran his hand down her belly and under her waistband, into her panties. His fingers found her slick center and he groaned again. "You're so wet for me."

She ran her tongue over his cock and took him deep into her throat as he slid a finger inside her, then withdrew to stroke her clit with a wet fingertip.

She let out her own groan. He felt so good in her mouth while he touched her so intimately. It wouldn't take much for her to come, but this memory needed to last him a lifetime.

She scooted back, moving out of his reach as she continued to go down on him. Then she released him and stood. "Strip," she said as she began to undress herself.

He just lay there, watching, and she smiled, letting him enjoy the show. Naked, she stood before him, then she squeezed a breast, pinching the already erect nipple.

"Mine," he said.

She nodded and squeezed the other one. Then she moved her fingers between her thighs and teased herself there as well.

"Also mine," he said, sitting up and grabbing her ass, bringing her to his mouth.

She really loved this possessive side of him.

His tongue found her clitoris, and she bucked against him at the sharp jolt of pleasure. He slid two fingers inside as he licked her clit. She was so damn close to coming. She stepped back, moving out of his reach. "Strip," she repeated.

This time he obeyed, and a moment later, his beautiful body was bared to her gaze. She drank in the view. All that dark skin and hard muscle. She remembered the hours she'd spent ogling him in the gym on base. "Mine," she said with satisfaction.

He took his cock into his hand and stroked the shaft. "Yours," he said.

She licked her lips. She wanted him in her mouth. She wanted him in her vagina. She just wanted, with an urgency that couldn't be contained.

Cal took control. Rising to his feet, he scooped her up and made a beeline for the wall. His thickness slid deep inside her at the same moment her back pressed against the cool wall. She clenched around him at the raw pleasure of his invasion.

"I can't count how many times I've fantasized about fucking you against a wall." His words were hot and breathy. "In my CLU. In the gym. In your office. Hell, even in SOCOM headquarters."

She'd had the same fantasies. "One time, you gave me a look during a meeting"—she gasped as he thrust deep—"and I completely forgot what your commander was talking about. He asked me a question, and I was fucking *blank*. I was so embarrassed."

He didn't let up on the thrusting even as he laughed. "I felt that way more than once. I had to stop looking at you at meetings."

He gripped her ass and pulled out, then slid deep. His rhythm changed, and she lost the ability to think or speak. She kissed him as he nailed her against the wall. Her eyes were closed when her orgasm pulsed through her, but she forced them open, wanting to see Cal's face as he came with the same intensity.

Hers. He was hers.

His orgasm ended, and he slumped against her, breathing heavily. She kissed his neck, memorizing the feel of his skin against her face. His hard body pressed to hers.

"I love you," he said again, his breath now ragged.

His grip on her tightened as he straightened and then turned, carrying her to the couch. They both stretched out, and she lay drowsily against him. His hand stroked her back, then moved lower to cup her ass. She closed her eyes, letting herself have this one moment. She kissed his neck, rubbing her cheek against the coarse hair of his beard.

She tilted her head back and opened her eyes. Everything she'd ever wanted to see in his gaze was there before her. She kissed him again as she reached behind her to their supplies on the coffee table. Her fingers found what she was looking for, and she released his mouth.

"I love you too," she said, then jabbed him with a tranq dart.

Chapter Thirty-Two

Cal's head throbbed, and his eyelids were heavy. He was disoriented and a little nauseated. His tongue felt thick. Was he sick? He wanted to ask his CLUmate, Pax, if they'd bypassed the two-drink limit at Barely North, except he didn't think he'd been at the club in days. Maybe weeks? He tried to open his eyes.

Tried. And failed.

Opening eyes shouldn't take this much effort. He focused on it. Wanted to use a finger to push the lid up. But he couldn't move his arms.

Sleep paralysis? No. He could move his fingers. Wiggle his toes. He could move his legs, but not separately.

Adrenaline pumped into his system, and he managed to open his eyes. The room was pitch-black. But he could tell from the feel of the space, the quality of the light, he wasn't in his CLU. He took a deep breath, and with the smell of the air—the scent of sex and tropical heat—it all came rushing back.

The hotel in Mbandaka. The threat to his family. Making love to Freya. Her last words before he'd gone lights out.

She must've tranquilized him with one of the fucking darts. He lay on his side, tucked into the couch. He shifted. He needed to go after her.

Fuck. She'd tied him up. His hands were bound in front of him and cinched with rope, elbows to waist. Legs were bound together. And *shit*, she'd tied his hands to his legs.

Dammit! She'd said, *"I love you,"* drugged him, and then trussed him like a pig.

She had to be heading south to deal with Lubanga on her own. Even through the haze of anger, his heart twisted. She was sacrificing herself to protect him. To protect his family.

Motherfucker. She was walking right into the trap with no intention of saving herself.

And tied up as he was, there wasn't a damn thing he could do about it.

He rolled from the couch. She'd meant to delay him, not kill him. He'd be able to get free. Then he'd hunt her down and make her pay for this stunt.

Freya's love affair with Congo was officially over. She was sick of the motorbike. Sick of the rutted, muddy track that passed for a road. Sick of the insects. Sick of the heat.

She would be content to never see another vine or leaf again.

And more than anything, she was sick of the rain, which had destroyed the road, fed the insects, made the heat somehow thicker—more cloying— and the motorbike impossible to maneuver.

A storm rolled in just hours after she'd set out, and the already impossible road turned to soup. She understood why so many rode the barges down the river, when this was the best going by land had to offer.

She had to marvel that Cal had never complained once about driving the bike in similar conditions—with her on the back to boot. She'd think the man was a saint except she knew for a fact he was all too human.

He had to be livid about now. She'd hated leaving him trussed up. Dreaded how much he'd ache when he woke. But at least he would wake. Tonight. Tomorrow, and for many days to come.

He'd live.

His family would live.

That was all that mattered.

The bike dropped into another hole and nearly pitched her over the handlebars. She grunted as she righted herself and twisted the throttle. She should pull over until the rain stopped. But she couldn't stop, not if she wanted to get to the village early, scout out the opposition, and end the standoff before it even began.

At least she'd had the decency to dress him before she tied him up, because if Cal's A-Team had arrived in Mbandaka to find Cal both naked and trussed, he might have to rethink the proposal he had in mind.

As it was, he might not forgive her for the ring of Pax's laughter, or the way Espinosa wiped tears from his eyes after hunching over and making a guffawing sound like a jackass.

Bastian, on the other hand, just stood to the side, smirking.

Cal gave him a look that very clearly said, *Get your ass over here and untie me or I will tell everyone about that night in Naples.*

Not surprisingly, Bastian stepped forward and pulled out his knife. "Bet you could use one of these about now."

Espi started howling again.

Cal glared at the sergeant. "Fuck all of you," he said.

Goldberg pulled out his cell phone. "Wait, Chief. We need a group photo. Everyone gather round."

Ripley, Pax, Bastian, and Espi moved to either side of where Cal lay on the floor. There was nothing to do but smile for the camera. At least if he were smiling, they might not paper the walls of the gym at Fort Campbell with this photo. It only worked for humiliation if he looked miserable.

Goldberg snapped the photo, then Bastian cut the rope that Freya had tied in an intricate knot he hadn't been able to loosen in spite of hours of effort on his part. He'd begun to worry about what he would do, when the door burst open and half his A-Team invaded.

Hands and legs freed at last, he stood and rubbed his wrists. His joints tingled with the flow of blood returning after hours locked in the same position. He idly wondered if Freya was into bondage. If so, he could think of ways to pay her back.

"How the hell did you guys get here so fast?"

"We were already on a transport flight to Brazzaville when you called Captain Oswald about the ransom note," Bastian said. "Funny thing. Kaylea Halpert showed up at SOCOM headquarters, and she and Haverfeld and Oswald and the other officers at the top of the food chain all disappeared in a private meeting. Next thing we knew, they'd signed off on sending half the team to liberate the kids from the mine in an off-the-books sort of way."

"Cap didn't say a word," Cal said.

"He doesn't trust Savvy. He was willing to support the mission, but he didn't want her to know we were coming."

Cal bristled. "She's innocent—"

"Yeah, then where is she?" Ripley asked. His gaze scanned the hotel room. "And where is the USB drive with the money?"

"She left. She's sacrificing herself to save me. Save my family. Save the world." He thought of Fitzsimmons and the end of days and realized he wasn't exactly exaggerating.

"You're sure of that?" Pax asked.

Cal nodded. "My guess is she thinks if she destroys the drive in front of Lubanga, he'll know the money is unrecoverable. He'll have lost."

"And then he'll kill her."

"Yes. But he won't have reason to kill the villagers."

"But he might anyway."

"He might," Cal agreed.

"Kind of a stupid plan," Espi mused, all humor gone from his face.

"Yeah, but it's the only way to make sure he doesn't get the money back that has a chance of sparing the villagers. And sparing me. There were only two of us, and all we had was three AKs and a couple of magazines."

Bastian dropped onto the couch with a sly smile. "Well, now there are six of us, and we've got an Osprey full of M4s, grenades, and other goodies."

Even better than the weapons, Cal had his team: Assistant Detachment Commander Ford, Operations Sergeant Blanchard, Communications Sergeant Ripley, Medical Sergeant Goldberg, and Engineering Sergeant Espinosa. For the first time since reading the ransom demand, true hope bloomed in his chest. "Seven," he said. "There are seven of us. Freya's part of the team."

Chapter Thirty-Three

Freya tucked down behind the rocky outcrop on the hillside above the village. She had about two hours before dawn would light the valley. In eight hours, she was supposed to present herself with the USB drive.

She scanned the valley below with Cal's night vision binoculars. Across the stream, Lubanga's forces were assembling. Dozens of men were visible, and there could be hundreds more in the jungle. She spotted a scout and cataloged his gear. AK-47, camouflage clothing, and…nothing else.

Not even binoculars.

She wouldn't sweat taking down these mercs, except there were hundreds of them. Hundreds of men with AK-47s and no conscience was a formidable force for one person. Even if she did have two AKs. She'd left Cal with the third because it hadn't felt right to leave him unarmed. If he somehow managed to break free in time to get here, he'd need a weapon.

It was rather shitty of her to have taken everything else, even his binoculars.

She'd made sure there was nothing sharp within his reach—trussed as he was—to cut the ropes. A shout for help would get him free eventually, but she'd bet he'd work the knots a good long while before he disturbed the neighbors. Long enough for it to be impossible for him to get here in time, especially when he didn't have the motorbike.

She scanned the valley again, spotting another scout. She turned the binocs back to the village on this side of the stream. All was quiet. The residents had no idea a force had been amassing all night just across the shallow stream.

She tucked the binoculars away and scrambled down the hill. She needed to wake Cal's aunt. He'd drawn a map of the village from memory. It was bound to be off, but she might be able to guess which hut belonged to Aunt Patrice.

According to Cal, Patrice Beya spoke French, Lingala, and English like his mother. Freya knew enough about the family to convince the woman to listen to her. With her help, they'd convince everyone—or at the very least, the children—to hide in the old mine. If she had her way, there would be no one for the rebels to threaten.

Freya would set up her camera to monitor the entrance to the mine. She had her fully charged satellite hotspot and would set it up so the video would upload automatically. If Lubanga's men tried to blow the mine to trap the villagers, BBC and CNN would have the video of the atrocity. The villagers would be rescued, and Lubanga's attack on a peaceful community would be known the world over.

The plan wasn't great, but it was far better than being gunned down in cold blood. Or worse. There was a whole lot that was worse, and the people of Congo knew it. Cal's aunt knew it. One of her sisters had lived it and shared the tale.

The mine had been dug out and reinforced after the collapse that had killed Cal's grandfather. There had been an attempt to resume mining in 2004, but then the company backing the resettlement of the village changed course about a year later, opting for easier, safer, open-pit mining, so the old mine now sat abandoned. The villagers could hide in the reinforced section. They would survive.

Freya, however, would not fare so well. Her ace card was that Lubanga needed her alive to make the transaction. Handing over the USB drive wasn't good enough. Her bitcoin wallet was stored on a key that required two-factor authorization, one of which was her *live* thumbprint. He couldn't simply snip off her thumb and hope a password-cracking program could work out her seventeen-character password.

She would wield that shield to her advantage. She'd destroy the drive that held all forty-eight private keys she'd created in the tunnel under the palace. Without the private key to match to the public key, the money was unrecoverable. Lost forever.

Lubanga would kill her, certainly. But he'd gain nothing by going after the villagers except having his brutality exposed.

She heard an engine in the distance. The road to this village was a mess, but she'd seen trucks maneuvering even worse roads in this country, and trucks delivered supplies to the mining operation and the villagers.

It was insane how resilient the people of Congo were. The way they overloaded their barges and trucks. Even their bicycles. Anytime someone was hauling something somewhere, they carried more than seemed humanly possible.

The engine noise continued, but she couldn't see the vehicle, not even with the night-vision binocs. It was out of her line of sight, under cover of the jungle.

She tucked down and scrambled down the backside of the hill. She needed to check out this truck. Find out who she was dealing with.

If Lubanga sent troops into the village, she was screwed.

Much as Cal wanted to find Freya, first he needed to speak to his aunts and uncle. Ford and Espinosa would search for Freya. They'd seen the tracks of the motorbike coming in. She was here. Tracking her should be easy in the mud—except she was a trained operator, so maybe not.

He approached his aunt's hut from the cover of the jungle that abutted the village. Odds were there were scouts across the river, watching, ready to sound the alarm if they saw an unusual amount of activity in the village.

He paused behind the hut he thought was his aunt's and listened. Muffled words from within. His uncle questioning the engine noise in a sleepy voice. They'd driven as close as they dared to the village, knowing the sound would give them away, but time was a precious commodity and hiking in from miles away would squander the one benefit they had in arriving early. Plus they had supplies in the truck—more than anyone wanted to carry on their back if they didn't need to.

He signaled to Blanchard, Goldberg, and Ripley. Together, they circled around to the front of the hut, stepping quietly so as not to alarm anyone in the village before he had a chance to speak with his family and explain the situation.

Freya crouched low. She'd heard a noise to the right but hadn't seen anyone. It crossed her mind that Green Berets could move like shadows through this kind of vegetation. She'd seen Cal do it a number of times. But it wasn't Cal. She'd know by his scent, or his step, or his breathing, or whatever it was that caused the tingle in her neck whenever he was near.

Whoever had made that noise wasn't Cal.

It had been a fleeting, wishful thought, the idea the engine noise could signal Cal had magically arrived with his team. She dared to rise on her toes to peek through the leaves, when a hand covered her mouth.

Her instinct wasn't to scream. She didn't want to scare the villagers. Instead, she elbowed whoever it was in the ribs. He let out a grunt of pain, but his grip held. She dropped her hand, aiming for his balls.

He blocked and said, "Savvy, stop." The words were a low hiss of sound.

Bastian.

She relaxed. Or at least, she stopped trying to hurt him. He released her, and she turned to face him. "Chief Ford, what are you doing here?"

Maybe magic was real.

"Saving your ass."

She studied him and Espinosa, who materialized by Bastian's side, face covered in jungle-colored paint. "I think Cal wants to talk to you," Espinosa said. "He didn't seem too happy with you when we found him. Tied up. Like an animal."

She covered her face with a hand. "Oh shit."

"Yeah," Bastian said.

"Don't worry. Goldberg snapped a picture with all the guys. For posterity."

"Oh. Fuck."

"Yeah," Bastian said again.

"If you guys don't mind, I'll let you take care of things here and will head back to Camp Citron now."

"Yeah...no." This from Espinosa. "We might not mind, but Cal, he wants to talk to you."

"Oh shit." She was so dead.

"C'mon, Sav," Bastian said. "Time to reunite you with your partner on this op." He took her arm and pulled her toward the road.

There was no escape. Might as well get this over with. "How many of you are here? The whole team?"

"Just half. This isn't entirely...sanctioned. The other half stayed behind to continue the training. SOCOM felt we need to present the front and someone in the CIA might've noticed if there was no one training the Djiboutians."

She would've asked why Haverfeld hadn't told Cal they were en route, but the answer was obvious: because their CO didn't trust her. She could live with that. Trust or not, he'd sent Cal's team. Six Green Berets against an army of rebels? She'd seen them go against worse odds, and her money was on Special Forces, every time.

Guerrilla fighting—a small band versus a much larger traditional force—was what these men did best.

She remembered telling Cal at the start of this mission that there would be no cavalry. It appeared she'd been wrong.

As they moved through the jungle, Bastian mumbled something into his radio. A code word, she guessed. He'd probably told Cal she'd been found. She braced herself to face him.

They stepped into a small clearing, and she spotted the truck. She wondered where they'd gotten it, because it wasn't military. They must've paid a local a hefty sum to "borrow" it for a few days.

Espi leaned against the side panel.

"What happens now?" she asked.

"We wait," Espi said.

"Are you guys babysitting me?" she asked. "Because this is a waste of time. We need to get the villagers inside the mine."

"Cal's talking to his aunt," Bastian said. "He needs a minute before he can see you. We need his aunt and uncle's help in convincing everyone to take cover in the mine."

She resigned herself to waiting for her doom with her two babysitters.

"So…any chance you'd put in a good word for me with Kaylea?" Espinosa asked.

She cocked her head. "Why do you think I have influence there?"

"I don't know," Espi said, "Might have something to do with the way she came tearing into HQ and then had a private conference with Haverfeld and Oswald, and next thing we know, we're scrambling to fly to Congo."

Emotion flooded her. It hadn't been magic that brought the team here, it had been Kaylea, risking everything by talking to SOCOM instead of her superiors at the CIA. She was a better friend than Freya had ever imagined. "Sure, Espi. But she's pretty special."

"Yes, she is."

Espi and the rest of the team were pretty special too. They were here, and she was grateful. "I saw two scouts from the hillside," she said. "They had AKs and nothing else. No idea how many rebels there are across the river."

"Blanchard and Espi will do a recon and get a count." Bastian pulled out a printout of satellite images of the valley and laid it over the hood of the truck. "Where are the scouts?"

She pointed out the location to Espinosa, who nodded. "Thanks."

"How did you get the map?" she asked. "You must've been in the air before the ransom demand. Before we knew we'd be here."

"We were en route to our Forward Operating Base in the Republic of Congo. Major Haverfeld sent the coordinates to the base. They had these printed for us before we landed."

She clasped her hands together. "Please tell me that means you have other supplies, say a shoulder-fired rocket launcher, or some heavy artillery?"

"'Fraid not. No artillery, but we've got guns and grenades."

She pouted. They'd already had guns. "*Big* guns?"

"M4s, some grenade launchers. An M2."

"M2? A fifty-caliber heavy machine gun?" That was big.

"Yeah. And we have Cal's M107."

As the A-Team's senior weapons sergeant, Cal was the technical specialist when it came to firepower. He also had a gift for sniping. Armed with either the fifty-caliber machine gun or the fifty-caliber rifle, he could do some serious damage to the gathering army. "That's more like it."

She studied the map, much larger and higher resolution than the small computer screen she and Cal had as they strategized in their hotel room.

Cal. The hotel room.

She closed her eyes. There was no escaping this. She had to face him. The heat became oppressive as they sat in the stagnant jungle. No wind. No rain. Just thick air as she waited for her doom.

At last she heard footsteps, and her heart began to pound. She'd drugged Cal and tied him up. She couldn't begin to guess how angry he would be.

He stepped into the clearing, flanked by the other three members of his team. At least he couldn't kill her with so many witnesses.

Light from the gibbous moon reached the clearing, revealing his dark features. It was criminal how handsome he was.

And terrifying how much she loved him.

His gaze fixed on her as he crossed the short distance to the truck. He grabbed her shoulders and pushed her back. She bumped against the grill, her body pinned between his and the truck.

His mouth landed on hers, and he kissed her. There was nothing mild or chaste about the kiss. It was hot, deep, and maybe just a little bit angry.

"Yanno, that's not what I expected," Espi whispered. "Who had 'Cal kisses her' in the pool?"

"I did," Pax said. "I win the pot."

"Shit, as his roommate, you had inside info." This from Goldberg.

"No one made you bet."

She lost track of the chatter as Cal's fingers threaded through her hair. Finally, he lifted his head and said, "What was that thing you said right before you tranqued me?"

She caught her breath and ran her fingers over his smooth scalp. "I said I love you."

"Shit. Did anyone put money on 'I love you' from her?" Espi asked.

"I was going to," Bastian said.

"'Going to' doesn't count," Pax said. "The pot is still mine."

Laughter bubbled up in Freya's chest, and Cal wrapped his arms around her as she laughed. When she could speak again, she tilted her head back to meet his gaze. "I was trying to save your life."

"I know," he said. "And if you ever pull shit like that again, I will dump your ass. We're *partners*. But this time, I forgive you."

She brushed her lips against his. "Okay, then. Let's get the civilians into the mine, then kick some *génocidaire* ass."

Cal nodded. "Time to get to work."

Chapter Thirty-Four

Cal's aunts and uncle went from hut to hut to explain why everyone needed to retreat into the old mine. As dawn broke across the sky, the children were tucked inside, clutching blankets and favorite items. The parents did what they could to convince them it was a grand adventure, but even the youngest among them seemed to know something was wrong. After all, the abandoned mine had always been off-limits.

A skeleton crew of miners and mill workers remained in the village. They would go through the motions of starting their workday so the village would look business as usual. They'd retreat into the mine with the others when Cal gave the signal.

Cal's team was assembled in the mill, downriver from the village. The generators were silent for now. A quick inspection showed they had more than enough gasoline and diesel to fuel one part of Cal's plan.

Pax Blanchard and Carlos Espinosa radioed in from their recon mission with the news that at least four hundred soldiers had gathered on the other side of the river. Freya blanched at the number.

"How did Lubanga gather so many soldiers this fast?" Cal asked. "I thought his most loyal men were in the east, near the border."

She frowned. So had she. "He must've been closer to staging the coup than we realized."

They waited for Blanchard and Espinosa to return so they could plan their next move. They wanted to strike before noon, but with only seven against four hundred, they needed to plan carefully.

Both soldiers entered the mill, broad grins on their faces. "Good news," Espi said. "As we were heading back, a vehicle drove up. We snapped some pictures." He held up a digital camera. "This ugly mug look familiar?"

Freya looked at the screen and felt dizzy. Shock. Relief. Vindication. They swirled together. "Lubanga," she said, letting all those reactions show.

She probably looked like some sort of rookie to the A-Team, with her emotions on the surface and making doe eyes at Cal. She wasn't the cool operator she'd always strived to be when she'd worked with SOCOM. But as Cal had said—who knew how many days ago—this mission had gotten personal. How could she be expected to be reserved, cold-hearted Savannah James when Lubanga had threatened Cal's baby cousins?

She'd feared Jean Paul Lubanga wouldn't show. But then, three hundred and fifty million was pretty good motivation. He needed to be certain the transfer went through and couldn't trust a subordinate. The last time he did that, he'd lost the money.

"This army isn't exactly loyal, and their training is for shit," Blanchard said. "They're armed, but they don't have much beyond guns in the way of gear, and I'm pretty sure some of these guys have never held an AK before. We aren't seven against four hundred. I figure we're seven against about fifty. But really, this is more of a chess match. To win, all we need to do is take the king. Lubanga has security, so in all likelihood, we're seven against ten at best."

"Seven *special operators* against ten," Espinosa said.

The soldier earned a nod for including her in his count. She knew the men were aware she was SAD, but that didn't mean they would automatically accept her as an equal. Yet they had. "I can live with those odds," she said.

"I've faced more daunting challenges taking my kids to Chuck E. Cheese," Ripley said.

Everyone laughed.

"We can't completely dismiss the fifty or so decent fighters," Cal said. "Those guys will be *génocidaires*. They've been at war forever and lost their souls years ago. Their only rules of engagement are rape and kill. We can't let them get past us and to the mine."

"We won't let you down, Cal," Ford said.

"No fucking way they'll get past us," Espi said.

Everyone else chimed in with agreement.

"So what's the plan?" Freya asked.

As Assistant Detachment Commander, Chief Warrant Officer Sebastian Ford was technically head of this mission, but no one turned to him. This was Cal's op. "We need a diversion," Cal said, "to get the green troops scrambling."

Ford nodded. "Bring our odds down to seven to fifty."

"The hillside above the troops is loose from the rain," Espi said. "I wish we had C-4. We could cause a mudslide. Bring the hill down on them." Espinosa was the team's senior engineering sergeant. His specialty was building and demolition, which was why he'd been sent with Blanchard on the recon mission.

"The mining operation has explosives," Cal said. "My uncle is the overseer. He can set it up for us. Any risk to the mine if we do this?"

"Nah. Opposite sides of the stream, pretty far apart. The blasting they do in the open pit mine would be more dangerous to the old mine, and that's been going on for years."

"Let's do it, then," Cal said. "You and my uncle can talk about where to set the charges."

"Hot damn," Espi said. "This is gonna work."

"So we freak out the rebels by bringing the hillside down. Then what?" Freya asked.

They had their maps laid out on the table. Cal pointed to various points on the village side of the river. "I want Rip over here with a grenade launcher. He'll have a good angle on troops fleeing in this direction and can cut off the path of anyone trying to slip around to get to the mine."

Ripley nodded.

"Ford, I want you with the M2 over here. You'll have a good angle on the river, and the range is right. No one crosses the river from here south."

"Will do," Ford said.

As weapons sergeant, this was Cal's specialty, selecting where to position munitions and assigning arcs of fire. "I'm going to be up here with the M107." He'd selected a position that overlooked the river and would be armed with his sniper rifle.

"You'll take out Lubanga from there?" she asked.

He nodded. "But not until the army is subdued. Because once the leader is dead, there is no telling what the soldiers will do."

"How do we subdue the rest?" she asked.

He grinned and glanced around the mill. "I think we can improvise a few more weapons with the supplies on hand here. Blanchard and Goldberg, you'll be armed with those."

Espi would be busy with Cal's uncle setting up the explosives. So that left only her without an assigned weapon and role. Was Cal planning to leave her out?

"Blanchard and Goldberg will bring on the firestorm," Cal said. He glanced at her and smiled. "*Vultures will feast.*" He delivered the words with televangelist bombast, then added, "Odds lowered to seven to ten."

"Dibs on the extras. I can take out at least three," Espinosa said.

Goldberg jabbed him in the ribs. "Dude, Savvy's taken. Stop trying to impress her."

She rolled her eyes and looked to Cal. "What about me? Where will I be?"

He grinned and pressed a kiss to her forehead. So not a professional-ops sort of thing, but Goldberg's lame joke practically begged him to stake a claim, and she didn't mind the gesture at all. She'd actually kind of longed to be the touchy-feely type, but had never met a guy she wanted to be touchy-feely with. Who knew it was less about her personality than the relationship itself?

"I need you to draw Lubanga and his best soldiers out," Cal said.

She cocked her head. "Sergeant Callahan, are you saying you want me to be bait?"

"Yes. You up for it?"

She grinned and nodded. "I thought you'd never ask."

Chapter Thirty-Five

The countdown clock was running. They'd agreed to strike ninety minutes before the time Lubanga had set, to let him know exactly who was in control here. In two minutes and twenty-eight seconds, Cal's uncle would blow up the hillside above the encampment. That would keep a good number of the troops busy while Espi set off charges along the perimeter, driving the men toward the river to escape collapsing hillside.

Cal could only hope the rest would play out according to plan.

They'd cut the timing close. It looked like the soldiers were mobilizing to move in on the village. Another ten minutes and they'd be crossing the river en masse to round up their hostages.

Thirty seconds before go time, they each chimed in on the radio, confirming they were ready. Uncle Frederic reported first, Cal last. They were ready.

The countdown reached zero and a blast sounded in the distance. Military timing, delivered by a civilian, giving Cal a fierce surge of family pride.

He zoomed in on the hillside with his high-power binoculars. The hillside shook but didn't collapse, just as Uncle Frederic predicted. The man knew his job, and Espi was no slouch either. A second explosive detonated, and this time, the hill gave way. First came mud, then rocks and trees. The slide gained momentum as uprooted trees rolled down the hillside. Debris flowed like liquid, a massive wave of soft earth, hard rock, and a jagged tangle of vegetation.

Shouts echoed across the river. First in warning, then in fear. From Cal's perch above the river, he could see it all. Some men went to drag their comrades out of harm's way, while others fled left or right, out of the direct path of the mudflow.

Espi's secondary charges went off, redirecting the fleeing men, sending them to the river, in the path of mud and rolling logs that were gaining speed.

On this side of the river, Freya stepped from the cover of jungle and approached the gently sloping bank. Across the water, men screamed and ran toward her.

Lubanga would have given strict orders not to shoot Freya. Without her, he couldn't access the bitcoin key. If she were shot and the key went down the river... Lubanga couldn't risk that. This might be a small, shallow stream here, but it met with a much larger river that flowed into the Congo River. If she dropped the key, it could go all the way to Inga Rapids, forever lost in the world's largest and deadliest whitewater.

That Freya didn't give a damn about the money was another risk for Lubanga. She could watch the USB key disappear without shedding a tear for the lost millions. Lubanga had to tread carefully if he wanted to recover the money, which explained the drastic ultimatum of holding an entire village hostage. And he'd chosen not just any village, but Cal's family.

Cal would have protected any community, anywhere, with the same ferocity. But the fact that this was family, targeted because of him... Yeah. This fucker was going to die.

Freya wore body armor and a Kevlar helmet as she marched toward the river. Cal's heart constricted at seeing her standing so exposed, but he couldn't exactly tell her to sit in the corner while the men did the work. There were a dozen reasons for her to take this role, and only one objection he could think to raise: because he loved her.

But she loved him too, and she wasn't playing that card to tell him to stand down. Her job scared the hell out of him, but his was just as risky. If this relationship was going to work—and it would—he had to accept her work in the same way she accepted his.

So there she stood, in the most vulnerable position, waiting for Lubanga to show his ugly face.

Freya was miked, but he didn't need that to hear the collapsing hillside and screams in French, Lingala, and a half dozen other Congolese languages. "It's her!" a man shouted, and Cal saw a group of men at the river's edge, eyeing Freya.

AKs were lifted and pointed at her, but one man put his hand on the barrel of the man next to him and shoved it down. "Shoot her, and the general will kill us."

So Lubanga had given himself a rank. Not surprising. It was what wannabe dictators did.

Freya lifted the bullhorn they'd gotten from the open-pit mining operation and her voice projected across the valley. "Jean Paul Lubanga, step forward if you want my bitcoin key."

She raised a hand. Dangling from her fingers was quite possibly the most valuable USB drive in the world. They'd toyed with the idea of using a different drive as a decoy, but Freya's key was distinct in that it had a built-in thumbprint reader. Professional grade. Lubanga might be suspicious if he saw a cheap keychain shaped like a comic book character.

Lubanga's men were probably zooming in right now and taking a picture of the drive, noting that it was high-tech and required two-factor authentication.

A man broke apart from the crowd of soldiers and stepped to the riverbank directly across from Freya. Less than thirty feet separated them. His shout carried across the water to her microphone. "Give me the drive, *Savannah*." His voice and the emphasis he put on the name had Cal zooming in with his binocs.

Shock filtered through him. He hadn't thought Seth Olsen would dare show up here. This didn't make sense. He'd exposed himself. There was no going back from this.

Was it possible the CIA was *supporting* this coup?

As if Freya could read Cal's thoughts, she whispered over the radio, "I am *so* fired."

He recognized Ford's laugh. Ripley was slower on the uptake, but then, he couldn't see who stood at the river's edge from his position. "What's going on?"

"Freya's boss is here," Cal answered. "This could mean we're fighting…" *Shit.* "The CIA?"

"What the fuck?" Goldberg chimed in.

"Yeah. The fuck," Blanchard said.

"CIA wants Lubanga?" Ford said. "Did they learn *nothing* from Hussein and Mobutu? And…a dozen other assholes?"

"Frey—" Cal said. It was weird using her first name when he'd slipped into military protocol with everyone else, but he didn't think of her as Lange, and she was no longer James to him either. He hoped she understood he meant no disrespect. "Do you think Evers was assigned the mission so he could deliver a USB drive with CIA money to Lubanga? Could the CIA have been trying to snipe him from Russia?"

"It's possible."

Of course, if that was the case, then why the hell had Olsen told her to kill Lubanga?

What was the real order—copy the hard drive, kill the man, or finance the coup?

"Are there American operators out there?" Ripley asked. "SAD, like James—er Freya?"

"I don't think so," Freya said.

"You got anything more than gut instinct to go on there?" Blanchard asked.

"No."

"It doesn't matter if CIA is involved," Cal said. "We may not have official rules of engagement, but don't forget, these assholes are targeting civilians. Children. Babies. Lubanga brought four hundred soldiers here. If we hadn't struck first, they'd have moved into the village and taken everyone hostage."

"Burn them all," Espi said.

The others echoed the sentiment.

Seth Olsen shouted across the river. "Stand down. The CIA is behind me. Behind the general."

Cal watched as Olsen slowly waded across the river, moving ever closer to Freya.

"The US doesn't support mining uranium to sell to Syria," she responded. She took a step back from the bank, then halted. Cal guessed she realized she was retreating and stopped herself.

The asshole had been manipulating Freya for years and probably believed he had her programmed, his to command. It could take years for her to work through and understand all the ways Seth Olsen had used her. And Cal would be right by her side, holding her hand as she did the hard emotional work.

"The Agency will look the other way," Olsen said, midriver now. "With over twenty trillion up for grabs, they can't afford not to."

"It's not up for grabs. It belongs to Congo."

He shrugged. "The current regime isn't protecting the resources. Up for grabs."

"You talk about the CIA as if it's one person. As if it's *you*. But I know dozens of operators, analysts, and directors who will fight your kind of corruption."

"Those people are leaving the IC in droves. It's so easy to drive the idealists out of the intelligence community. The ones who stay are easily manipulated. All you have to do is tell the trainers to assault them. Take away their control over their bodies." Olsen stood just twenty feet from Freya now, calf deep in the shallow river. "Then you let them cry. But everyone knows a woman who doesn't fight—especially one who's been trained to kill with her hands—can hardly claim she was raped."

She took a step toward him. Cal could see Olsen had rattled her. "I was threatened with losing everything I'd worked for. I'd devoted my entire life to the CIA."

Cal could see Olsen's smirk through his binoculars. "A woman with your strength? You'd have fought. Obviously, you saw the advantage of fucking him but didn't want it known you screwed your way to the top of your training group. So you cried rape. You even had me convinced, until you went after Harry because he could expose your lies."

That must be the story Olsen had given the CIA after he'd backed her with Captain O'Leary at Camp Citron. As they'd suspected, he'd backtracked, changing the narrative to make Harrison Evers the victim.

"Fuck you, Seth," Freya's voice showed annoyance and not the strain Olsen had obviously been attempting to trigger. She'd been sucked in for a moment, going on the defensive, but now his grip on her was gone.

That's my woman. Forged from steel. Harder than a diamond.

"What do you possibly think you can get out of this?" she said. "You're fronting a shitty army of untrained rebels. What did you promise them?" She waved the USB key. "Because without this, no one is getting paid."

"You can't win," Olsen said. "You think we don't know you're on your own here?" He nodded toward the carnage behind him. Dozens of soldiers had made it to the river, but they must've been given orders to stand down while Freya and Olsen negotiated. "Nice fireworks display, but the flash and bang are over. So you got some explosives from the miners. Big deal. There are still only two of you against an entire fucking battalion."

It wasn't surprising Olsen didn't realize she and Cal had backup. Olsen believed he'd smeared her to the degree that SOCOM wouldn't send aid, and in fact, SOCOM had made certain the CIA remained ignorant of Cal's A-Team being dispatched.

Across from Freya, the trained soldiers stood in a line, weapons in hand but pointing up. Ready to attack, while the untrained men fidgeted, holding weapons with lax fingers, or the opposite, stiff as statues, clutching rifle stocks with white-knuckled grips. She snorted in disdain. "It's two against fifty actual soldiers, tops."

"Two against fifty, two against a thousand. You are still only two."

She shifted. Something in her stance changed, subtle but somehow projecting dejection, even as she remained standing tall.

Cal couldn't help but grin. She was giving the right cues to lure Olsen in. Damn, but she was good at this. As she'd said at Camp Citron, she didn't break character. He'd witnessed that multiple times since this mission began, and now he saw another layer of her talent. But then, she knew Seth's triggers as much as her mentor knew hers.

"Did the CIA order Lubanga's assassination?" she asked.

Olsen said nothing.

Not surprising. He wasn't a dumb man. He'd guess she was recording this. Olsen knew she needed proof of his lies. A confession would do nicely.

Finally, he said, "Your orders came from above. If you have an issue with them, raise them with my superiors."

"Somehow, I doubt I'll live that long."

"Frankly, I doubt that too." He held out a hand. "Give me the key, Freya. We can cut a deal."

"Who owns you, Seth? Is it Lubanga or Gorev?"

Cal fixed the binoculars on Olsen's face. No reaction.

"I'm thinking Gorev," Freya continued. "In fact, I think originally you belonged to Drugov. What I can't decide is if you are glad he's dead because I removed your puppet master, or if you decided to frame and kill me because you fear I'll find the truth in Drugov's files."

Olsen's gaze flicked downward. Subtle, but there was a shift. She was on to something with the Drugov connection. This all went back to the oligarch's death in Morocco last month.

If that was the case, then the CIA wasn't backing Lubanga's coup. That was a bluff on Olsen's part.

"No more talking. Give me the drive."

She shook her head. "Only Lubanga gets the drive. You take one step toward me, and it burns." With her free hand, she grabbed the propane torch she'd hooked to her belt at her back and flicked the trigger. They'd adapted the nozzle so it shot a bright puff of orange two feet in the air before settling in to an eight-inch stream of blue flame.

Olsen took a step toward her, and Cal fired a warning shot with his M4—the fifty-caliber M107 was much louder, and they didn't want to tip their hand just yet. The bullet just missed Olsen's shoulder and landed in the stream behind him.

"You've read Cal's file," she said calmly. "You know he doesn't miss unless he wants to."

That was a slight exaggeration. But only slight.

"That was your only warning," she continued. "I'll give the disk to Lubanga, and only Lubanga." She gazed across the river. "Is the big man too chickenshit to face a mere woman?"

A man like Lubanga—one easily manipulated by his ego—wouldn't like that.

"I think I'm in love too," Goldberg said.

"Back off, Goldie, she's mine," Cal responded. "Don't forget, I only miss when I want to."

Ford laughed.

"You sure have her snowed," Blanchard said.

"No one tell her about Mosul," Espi chimed in.

Goddamn, he was so glad his team had his back. How could Freya work alone as she did? No wonder she'd always seemed so unhappy.

"Oh, I know all about Mosul," Freya said, her whisper soft and smooth on the radio. She covered her mouth with one hand so Olsen couldn't read her lips and wouldn't realize she spoke to more than just Cal. "You boys have no idea what kind of info SOCOM gave me access to. And Espi, I wouldn't be quite so smug. One word: Kandahar."

Cal laughed. "I *really* love you."

"I know. Now let's finish these fuckers."

"Yes, ma'am," his team said, practically as one.

"Lubanga," she shouted. "Come to me, or I burn the drive." She fired the torch again.

The mudslide had stopped, caught in a trough before reaching the river. Espinosa and Cal's uncle had predicted that. Less than a hundred soldiers remained, gathered on the thin stretch of land between mudslide and river.

Seven to a hundred. Not bad odds, but these hundred had to be the seasoned men. Soldiers who'd seen action in the east. Some would be the *génocidaires* Lubanga had threatened.

The formation of the soldiers across the stream shifted. It looked like the seasoned fighters were ordering the green troops to circle around.

"Ford, they set one foot in the river on your end, and you lay down a line," Cal said. "They cross it, and you open fire."

"Roger."

"Where did you hide the villagers, *Savannah*?" Olsen made the name a sneer, trying to regain control. "You think we didn't guess you'd hide them in the mine? It will just make it easier to kill them all. You know how many toxins are in the air in that mine? They could already be dead."

The villagers had powered up generators to run fans for just that reason, but the danger remained. This standoff had to end in a few hours, or innocent people could die.

Cal studied the hardened soldiers. It was possible—no matter how finite the odds, it remained possible—he had a cousin near his age in the opposing force. But that didn't change the situation.

The men who hadn't fled the collapsing hillside had stayed to back Lubanga. They were in it for money or ideology, but no matter what, they were threatening unarmed civilians. Children. Even babies. This assault was a war crime.

Freya raised the bullhorn to her mouth and spoke in French, then repeated the words Cal had taught her in Lingala, then said the same in English. "Leave this valley. Lubanga cannot pay you. If you attack this village, you will burn."

Men shouted back, calling her a liar and a whore. She stood there, repeating the phrases in all three languages.

They couldn't claim they hadn't been warned.

Olsen retreated. Freya stood on her side of the river, the queen protecting her domain.

A group of men made a break to the south, wading into the river. Ford laid down a line of fire midstream. The men came to an abrupt stop, looking up in shock at the hillside where Ford was concealed.

Olsen stepped forward again, and this time, Lubanga was behind him, surrounded by his men. Now they knew who the best soldiers were.

"So you managed to get a fifty-caliber machine gun," Olsen said. "Well done, Savannah. But your soldier can't be in two places at once."

"Ford, short burst."

A moment after the machine gun stopped, Cal fired a warning shot from his position. Proof there were at least two of them.

Olsen scanned the hillside, clearly nervous now. "So you trained a local to shoot. Too bad you're wasting your bullets."

Freya fired up the torch again. "I'm tired of fucking around. Jean Paul, you want your money? Come and get it."

Before anyone could respond, an explosion sounded to the north. "Rip, what's going on?" Cal asked.

"Eight men trying to sneak across the stream around the bend. Five are still coming. Fire in the hole."

Another boom sounded. Ripley had the grenade launcher to guard against attempts to cross the stream around the bend, out of sight of the rest of the team. It could fire nearly a quarter of a mile. The effective range might be shorter, but fear would push the untrained troops to the limit, separating them from reinforcements should they attempt to cross.

"Two are retreating," Ripley said.

"The others?" Ford asked.

"Injured. They aren't going anywhere."

Cal fixed his binocs on Lubanga's face. For the first time, the man's expression registered fear. His planned siege wasn't going well. He said something to Olsen, his face contorted with anger.

They couldn't move on Lubanga until the camera they'd set up to record this operation caught something incriminating from the big man. Lubanga had to order the men to attack the village. They needed proof this guy was going after civilians. They had the ransom note, but video was harder to ignore.

Lubanga looked at the shallow river with annoyance. "Come here," he shouted.

Freya's voice was cold and calm. "No."

She wiggled her fingers, flashing the USB drive. "You want your money, you need to come and get it. Bring a computer so I can initiate the transaction."

That, right there, was the rock and the hard place for Lubanga. He needed the money. Three hundred and fifty million dollars could buy him over twenty trillion. But none of this was simple. Freya had tied all the money to her. Two-part authentication. Required thumbprint.

Lubanga had to give if he was going to get. "Your Green Beret will shoot me."

"And risk your army destroying this village? Killing his cousins? You chose this location. You know he won't risk his family."

C'mon, asshole, listen to her. She speaks the truth.

Cal wouldn't risk the village. A hundred—even only fifty—soldiers was too many. But separate Lubanga from his backup, and he was dead.

But. Dammit, there was always a *but*.

Special Forces couldn't strike first. Not without an international incident. Lubanga needed to make a move that was undeniable. The camera needed to capture it. And then all rules of engagement were on—or off, as the case may be.

"Bring the drive to me, and I will spare the villagers. That is our deal."

"The CIA knows why Abel Fitzsimmons is buying uranium. Forget the lies Seth has told you. No one in the CIA will support you knowing you're selling yellowcake to terrorists."

Lubanga shrugged. "America wants Congo's minerals. The only way to get it is through me."

"Did you know Seth sent you a Trojan file on the thumb drive with Drugov's money? The Trojan gave him access to the computer in Gbadolite—so he could steal your money. It's his Trojan that destroyed your backup files—right after he copied everything."

"She lies!" Olsen said.

"He told you it was me, didn't he, Jean Paul?" she asked. "Seth here has been lying to you, setting you up, so he could clean you out once your coup attempt fails."

Cal knew Freya was the one who destroyed Lubanga's files, but her bluff was working, as Olsen's agitation grew, Lubanga's face showed more suspicion.

"Damn, she's good," someone whispered over the radio. Cal couldn't even be sure who. He was too focused on the conversation on the river.

"And you will fail, because without CIA support, you don't stand a chance." She cocked her head. "You really should be more careful in choosing allies, Jean Paul. Some men, they just can't be trusted."

"She lies," Olsen repeated. "I'm here on orders from the DDO."

"Really? Well then, the director will be pleased to see the video that is uploading right now, the one of you standing with a group of militants threatening a peaceful mining village." She hooked the propane torch onto her belt and pulled a small disk from her pocket and held it up. "In fact, he'll be even more pleased to see this tracker's data upload, proof the video he's viewing is streaming in real time and the location is exactly what I said it would be. I sent the entire Directorate of Operations the URL for the video and this tracker thirty minutes ago. I'm guessing everyone at Langley is watching us. If you're really here on orders from the DDO, then this isn't a problem. Smile for the camera, Seth. Make Aunt Kim proud."

Olsen charged across the river, pulling his gun. He aimed at Freya.

Cal pulled the trigger on the M107.

Olsen dropped into the water. Cal guessed he wore body armor, but this was a fifty-caliber bullet. He was done. Cal could probably put his arm through the hole in Olsen's chest.

Lubanga scanned the hillside, looking for Cal. He pointed to Cal's right. "There," he shouted.

A man near Lubanga raised his rifle.

"Take the shot!" Lubanga ordered.

The man fired at the hill.

Lubanga returned his focus to Freya, as if the sniper threat had been taken care of. This guy was no general. What was it with these wannabe dictators who knew nothing about fighting? It was obvious he thought this was all about numbers: show up with a big army and make threatening statements. He had no clue that war was about strategy. The size of the army didn't matter if you didn't know how to use them.

"You're the whore from Gorev's party," Lubanga said. His voice held surprise.

"Seth didn't tell you?"

Lubanga glanced at the body in the river and shrugged. "Give me the key, or my men will charge the river. You can't shoot us all."

"I think we can."

"If you don't give me the key, I will order my men to blow up the mine with everyone inside. We have explosives too."

She jangled the USB drive. "Come and get it. Like the dog you are."

Lubanga signaled to his men to charge her. Four did. Cal and Goldberg shot them.

"You," she said. "Just you."

"You will shoot me too."

"I give you my word as a Spaniard."

Blanchard laughed.

"Inconceivable," Espi said.

Cal watched from his perch, shaking his head at the joke even as sweat poured down his brow. It wouldn't take much to separate the man from his army. Not when he was desperate to fund his coup.

Lubanga spoke to a man by his side then disappeared behind others in the cluster of soldiers.

"I'm getting tired of waiting, Jean Paul," Freya said.

Lubanga had no intention of crossing the water, but he needed a living, breathing, talking Freya to access the bitcoin key.

This was his all-or-nothing moment, and Cal knew exactly what the man would do. He'd send everyone across the river at once, effectively separating him from his security. He was so certain all the firepower would be focused on protecting Freya, no bullets would be spared for him.

As if Cal had written the script, all at once, the hundred men or so who lined the river charged.

"Blanchard, Goldberg, you're up."

The soldiers were positioned to the north and south with hoses connected to high-powered dredging pumps. But instead of pulling water from the river, they'd connected the pumps to tanks filled with a mix of gas and diesel. Both men opened their hoses and lit the stream. Fire shot a hundred feet from each hose, creating a rain of fire that arced the length of the stream. Charging men ran into the flames, then fell and screamed. The soldiers behind them tripped over their fallen comrades and pitched forward into the firestorm.

And behind it all, Lubanga was alone, retreating from the burning river.

They had enough fuel to sustain about thirty seconds of flaming rain before the pump would shut off to prevent air from flowing down the fuel line, which would be dangerous. But it was enough. Cal had Lubanga in his sights and pulled the trigger.

The would-be dictator dropped. A head shot.

The rain of fire stopped, but chaos continued in the river.

Freya lifted the bullhorn to her lips. "Your general is dead. Leave here before UN troops arrive to arrest you."

Slowly, the men withdrew, some dragging others from the stream.

Goldberg would provide medical aid to anyone who surrendered, but she didn't make that offer, as there would likely be too many takers.

"Cover me," Freya said into her radio. "I'm grabbing Seth."

The CIA operator had floated twenty feet downstream before getting caught on something in the shallow water.

"Got you," Ford said.

She reached the body and turned him over, revealing the gaping hole in his chest. She tucked her head down as she worked the body free of whatever had snagged it.

Two soldiers separated from the chaos in the stream and charged Freya. Cal's heart, already beating fast, went into overdrive.

A burst of gunfire rang out, and the men dropped.

Freya looked up, seeing the fallen men just feet from her. "Thanks, Bastian."

Yes, thank you, Bas.

"Anytime," he said smoothly. "You should probably get yourself and that kabillion-dollar key out of sight. Let Blanchard recover the body."

She dropped Seth's arm and backed away. "Roger."

She disappeared from Cal's line of sight, retreating into the jungle that flanked the village.

Cal watched the river and the men retreating, feeling his heartbeat in his fingers. She was safe. And as soon as they got all these men out of the valley, the village would be safe too.

They'd gotten Lubanga and Olsen and decimated an entire battalion.

"Cassius?" Her voice came from behind him, not over the radio.

He got to his feet and turned to her. She was wet from wading in the river, but otherwise absolutely perfect. He pulled her against him and planted his mouth on hers.

"Uh, Freya's mic is still open," Espinosa said. "None of us wants to hear this."

"Please stop," Ripley said.

Cal released her mouth and ripped off his radio headset as Freya pulled off her miked Kevlar helmet.

Her eyes were lit with a warm light. "You did it."

He pulled her to his chest again. "We did it."

"So I want you to know, I lied about one thing when I asked you to do this op with me."

He raised a brow. "What's that?"

"You were absolutely my first choice."

Chapter Thirty-Six

Five days later, Freya sat at her desk in SOCOM headquarters, feeling a little dazed as she stared at her computer screen. There'd been so much to sort through to figure out who was really to blame and who was guilty. This was a job she usually reveled in, but now she had no patience for it. Writing her account of the event with citations had been exhausting.

They'd fished Seth out of the river, and his body had returned to Camp Citron on the Navy Osprey with the rest of the team. Lubanga's body had been dragged off by his soldiers. The official story in Congo was that Jean Paul Lubanga had been raising an army for a coup but had been assassinated by one of his soldiers, a man who was really a spy for the FDLR.

The assault on the village was left unmentioned. Not a single villager had been injured, and arrangements had been made to replace the supplies that had been used in their protection. The Congolese military had sent in several trucks to remove bodies and debris from the jungle across the river, erasing all evidence of the assembled army.

The men who had joined Lubanga's forces were on the run, wanted for treason, the situation in Congo contained.

Freya's situation was also contained...for the most part. The CIA had initially wanted to haul her in to one of their secret prisons for interrogation, but Major Haverfeld—bless the man—went to bat for her and said SOCOM had suspected Olsen of dirty dealing for some time and had asked her to trace the leads found in Drugov's files to look for Olsen's fingerprints.

It wasn't exactly how it happened, but close enough, and it was a springboard for the truth to come out. With SOCOM behind her and the evidence in video, bitcoin, and uranium—which had been recovered from the Central African Republic three days ago—she had been cleared for the most part. A few loose ends remained that would take months to tie at this point, but she wouldn't spend that time in jail as it was sorted out.

She'd learned, to her great relief, that Seth had been operating on his own. The CIA had explored the possibility of supporting Lubanga's bid for power—thanks to intel provided by Seth—but had rejected the Congolese minister as being too volatile. No kill order had been issued. As far as those higher up in the Directorate of Operations knew, Freya's mission was to copy Lubanga's hard drive, which she'd done.

Seth Olsen and Harrison Evers had their own side deal going on, and the answers to why were in Drugov's files. Seth had been owned by Russia for some time. In the midnineties, he'd screwed up an op and revealed the identities of two Americans working undercover in Moscow. The operators had been killed, and that was all the leverage Nikolai Drugov needed to blackmail him.

As far as they'd been able to piece together from Seth's communications, when Drugov died, JJ Prime went running to Radimir Gorev—and brought with him files he'd swiped from Drugov—files that included proof of Drugov's blackmail of Seth. When that happened, Seth gained a new Russian master.

When Freya proposed going after Lubanga's computer, it offered a perfect opportunity for Seth to deliver a payment to his new master while also getting rid of Freya before she uncovered his treason.

The Reverend Abel Fitzsimmons was facing intense questioning by the FBI back home. The day after the showdown by the river—before word could leak that Lubanga was dead—a team of SEALs had descended on the uranium mine and freed the children.

Fitzsimmons was clinging to his story that the money he sent to Drugov and Lubanga had been charitable donations, but given that the former had been attempting genocide and the latter had funded uranium mining, and Freya had copied communications between Fitzsimmons and Lubanga, he wasn't likely to escape justice.

There was still a lot left to sort out, but the picture was becoming clear. The best and brightest at the CIA would do a deep dive into the files she'd gotten from Lubanga and Drugov, along with Seth's communications. The FBI would scrutinize Fitzsimmons. The FBI would also examine Lubanga's intention to dump money into accounts for the US attorney general and a US senator. Freya had managed to find evidence in Drugov's files that he'd actively pursued compromising the attorney general because his Justice Department was aggressively prosecuting Bratva along with investigating Drugov and Prime Energy's oil price fixing. She had already spoken with AG Dominick on the phone and would likely meet him in person in the coming months.

She'd done all she could from here. At this point, she was out. Done. She'd contributed to the takedown of Drugov, Lubanga, and Olsen. Hell, she'd even found dirt on JJ Prime, who was currently being held in Tanzania and awaiting extradition to the US.

She was proud of her work for the CIA and greatly relieved to know they hadn't supported Lubanga, as Seth had claimed, but at the same time, she was done. Burned out. After what she'd gone through as Seth's protégé, she couldn't see going back to the job.

Much as she knew it wasn't the CIA's fault, the fact that he'd been unchecked in his manipulation for so long was disturbing. How could she trust anyone there—except Kaylea—again? How many other women had been victimized by Seth and Harry? So far, one other woman had come forward. Freya suspected there would be more.

She sat at the desk and stared at her computer. A person's life could change in a moment. She'd experienced it at seventeen, when a bomb went off in a market in Greece, and she'd lost her brother, father, and mother. People lost families to car accidents, house fires. Illness. Mass shootings.

She looked up at the picture of the CIA memorial wall and thought of her Uncle James.

There were a million ways to die.

But now it was time for Freya to live. For herself, not for a cause.

She took a deep breath and typed the words she'd been fighting since she'd been assaulted in a motel room in Savannah, Georgia.

Dear Director of the Directorate of Operations,
I quit.
Sincerely,
Freya Lange

She hit Send, not giving herself a moment to dither over wording. To question the wisdom of this action. She had money in savings. She could last a few months.

And Cal and his team were scheduled to fly home at the end of the week. Their deployment was over. Camp Citron wouldn't be the same without the Green Beret who'd caught her attention in her first days on this job.

There was nothing for her here. Not anymore.

She closed her laptop and stood. She snatched the picture of the memorial wall on her way out the door.

Epilogue

Kentucky
One month later

Girls' night out. Freya had enjoyed a few of those in college, but even then, she'd been an outsider. Morgan and Brie, on the other hand, had both perfected the art of girlfriend bonding and were determined to teach her the nuances of female friendship.

It was interesting because the women were so different. Morgan was open and friendly. A blonde bombshell comfortable in her own skin. She didn't view other women as a threat, although Freya could tell she'd been stung in the past by women who took one look at her and cast her as a villain. Or dumb bimbo. But Dr. Morgan Adler was neither of those, and past experience hadn't closed her off to friendship.

Brie was different. A different kind of pretty. A different kind of friendly. Slightly more reserved—but then, Freya knew well why she held herself back from others—but she was skilled at superficial friendship. She knew how to hang with the girls and have fun. She was learning to open up more. Be herself with people.

Freya didn't fit with either of them, but they'd reached out to her in friendship when she'd chosen to move to Kentucky to be with Cassius, and one thing Freya needed in this world was friends.

Tonight, they were at a bar for girls' night, and Freya was enjoying every moment. She'd been this girl once, before her family died. She'd had friends. She'd crushed on boys and dreamed of being Jane Goodall.

She wasn't sure about the Jane Goodall part, but the rest… She could be that girl again. Woman now, but the headspace was similar.

Their waiter delivered their second round of drinks—soda for Brie, beer for Morgan, vodka martini for Freya—when Ripley's wife, Amira, arrived. "Sorry I'm late. The sitter had the wrong date on her calendar and I had to scramble to find another one because *damn* but I need a night out tonight."

The team was off on a multiday overnight training thing, which had been the inspiration for girls' night out, and it had been natural to include

Amira, who'd spent the months the team had been deployed as a single mother to her and Ripley's three children. Their son was eight, and they had two daughters, five and three. The eight-year-old was prone to night terrors—especially when his dad was deployed—and if anyone needed a night out, it was Amira Ripley.

Amira was gorgeous with long, thick dark hair, big brown eyes, ample curves, and warm brown skin. She had a big laugh that made every room feel a little brighter.

The waiter delivered Amira's drink and announced that some guy at the bar had picked up their tab. They declined as a group. They were not here to play a pickup game, but the waiter said it had already been paid.

Freya felt a tingle in the back of her neck. "The guys are here," she said, standing and scanning the room.

"They can't be. They're off playing commando or something," Brie said.

"No. They're definitely here."

The song changed, and Freya recognized the opening drums to the song "Africa" by Toto. She smiled and waited. With the same uncanny ability they had of being invisible in the jungle, the men somehow materialized, stepping from behind and between patrons of the packed nightclub. It was as if they'd been vapor, but now they'd taken human form.

"Wow," Morgan said as Pax stepped up behind her and kissed her neck. "How do you *do* that?"

"It's a skill," he answered.

"Not you. Freya. She knew you all were here."

Freya laughed at Pax's disappointment that Morgan hadn't been impressed by his trick, but she gave an honest answer. "I can always feel when Cal's near. Plus..." She nodded to the speaker in the ceiling. "The song."

"Told you the song would give us away," Bastian said.

"You knew before the song," Brie pointed out at the same time.

Cal grinned down at her, and her heart did that fluttery thing. "Will you dance with me?"

She slid from her stool. They'd never danced before. It was fitting that this song should be the first.

The others followed. They were the only four couples on the dance floor. It wasn't really a dancing sort of place when there wasn't live music playing. But she didn't care. She was in Cal's arms. And it was sweet seeing how Amira glowed as she looked up at her husband of ten years.

Freya returned her attention to the man holding her and knew she was emitting a similar glow. "What are you doing here?" she asked. "I thought you would be gone for another day at least."

"We finished up early. Decided it would be fun to surprise you. But if you want your ladies' night, we can go. I just wanted this one dance."

"Stay. I'm sure the others feel the same." There were plenty of girls' nights in the future, when the men would be deployed again. Now that they were all back from Djibouti, none of them wanted to waste a moment of their time together.

She closed her eyes and enjoyed the feel of being pressed against him. The beat rose, and the chorus swelled, and she was in Cassius's arms, and she still had no idea what she was going to do with her life, but right now, she was in the only place she wanted to be.

The song ended, but they stayed on the dance floor. She held him close and breathed him in. A song by George Michael came on, and Cal said, "Bastian picked that one."

She smiled. "Brie said he got the dates cleared for their wedding. Is the whole team going to get the week off?"

"Yes. Just got it approved today."

"Good." Bastian's grandmother—an Elder in his tribe—was ill and had requested that Bastian and Brie have their wedding early. Initially, they'd intended to get married next spring, but with his grandmother's request, they'd been scrambling to arrange for the wedding to take place in one month. Once they'd decided to marry, when didn't matter.

Most of Brie's friends lived in the Seattle area, and the reservation where the ceremony would be held was on the Olympic Peninsula, so travel wasn't a problem for most of the guests. The main problem had been making sure the team could be there. Bastian had asked Cal to be his best man.

"I can't wait to see you in your dress uniform." She grinned.

"And I can't wait to dance with you at the wedding." He pulled her closer. "When you're ready, I'm going to ask you to marry me."

"I know. And when that happens, I'll say yes." They'd agreed to put off talk of marriage until after she figured out what came next. She had months of sorting through issues with the CIA after more than a decade of classified work. She wanted to be free of all the legal complications before binding him to her.

The song ended, and all four couples returned to their table.

Morgan was practically bouncing with excitement now that Pax was here. She'd been crushed when the multiday training had been announced just as they were settling in at home.

"So…since we're all here," Morgan said, "there's something I wanted to talk to you all about." Morgan had been hinting there was something big in the works. This must be it.

"My dad...he's doing his usual meddling and sent me a request for proposal he happened to notice."

"No," Pax said before she could continue, but he laughed, showing it was a joke.

Everyone knew Morgan had issues with her father. Things were better, but it was a long road to true reconciliation. It would take years and a lot of work to rebuild their relationship.

"Yeah," Morgan said. "You aren't going to like it."

"Then no. For real this time."

She covered his hand with hers and squeezed. "So you know how during World War II, the Army sent out a group of guys to track down and recover art and artifacts stolen by Nazis?"

"No," Pax repeated. "I mean, yes, I know. And no, I don't like where this is going."

"Syria," she continued, "as you all know, has a big problem with antiquities theft. Smuggling. It's all funding terrorism, and the Army—"

"Yeah. Definitely not. You aren't an operator."

Morgan smiled. "But Freya is."

Beside Freya, Cal stiffened, but he didn't voice objections like Pax. Pax's objections *were* valid. Cal's objections, if he had any, would not be.

Morgan shrugged. "Basically, the Army put out a request for proposal for some analysis of what's been stolen, what's been destroyed, who's buying and who's selling. It's similar to the work I've been doing with the professor at William & Mary. My dad thinks I should submit a proposal. They might send some experts in with a team of Delta operators or something as protection, to track the trafficking, identify the dealers. Find the buyers. The sale of antiquities is funding terrorism. If they can stop the money flow, it will weaken the organizations." She looked at Freya. "Isn't that what you were doing in Congo? Interrupting the money flow?"

"You want to go to Syria?" Pax asked, his face lit with horror.

"No. Not me. I'm too noticeable. But my company could do the training necessary for the person who does go. And it's more likely to be Turkey and Iraq." She mumbled both country names, probably knowing Pax wouldn't find it that comforting.

"I'd probably work the European end," she continued. "Many of the artifacts are ending up in the hands of wealthy European collectors. Anyway, I'm thinking of submitting a proposal, but Freya, I'd need you on my team. And Brie, your experience with USAID would be helpful too. They're infiltrating aid organizations. And...the foundation you're starting is likely to be a target of terrorism. Your cause is education for girls…and that's exactly the type of thing ISIS and similar groups wish to stop." She turned to Amira. "I've got a job for you too."

"No," Ripley said, "One of us in a hot zone is enough. The kids—"

"It's right here in Kentucky. I need you for translation work and your mad computer skills."

Amira was fluent in Arabic—her parents were Syrian immigrants—and she worked from home as a software engineer. Freya didn't know when the woman slept with three small kids, a thirty-hour-a-week job, and a husband who'd been deployed for months. Amira leaned forward. "Sounds interesting. How many hours per week?"

"If I get the contract, only a few at the start."

Morgan glanced around the table. "It'll take months for the Army to award the contract, and if I do get it, it could take months more before it really gets going." She looked at Pax. "I have no plans, ever, to go into a war zone. But I can't make the same promise about Freya." She met Freya's gaze. "I need to know if you're interested or if I should find someone else with your unique set of skills. There's no need to answer tonight. I just want you to think about it."

"You want to form a team of Monuments Women?" she asked.

Morgan smiled. "In a sense, yes."

Freya sat back and looked at Cal. She knew her work for the CIA had terrified him. This wouldn't be much better. Worse, actually, because it could involve going undercover in Syria, Turkey, Iraq, Yemen, and who knows where else.

But it wasn't CIA, and it was still work to stop terrorism.

She took Cal's hand and pulled him away from the group so they could talk without everyone listening in. She glanced back and noticed everyone was watching, and pulled him deeper into the crowd.

"What do you think?" she asked.

He cupped her face, staring down at her with a look that turned her to jelly. "I'm scared to death because I know how much you're willing to risk. But I also know you'd be brilliant." He brushed his lips over hers. "I love you, Freya. And I will never hold you back from what you want to do."

Emotion swamped her. "God, I love you." She pulled his head down for a deeper kiss, then pressed her forehead to his chest, feeling the steady beat of his heart through his shirt. His arms wrapped around her, holding her tight.

Finally, she looked up. "You're sure?"

He nodded. "A hundred percent. You'll be amazing."

She kissed him again, then took his hand and pulled him back to the table. Everyone—especially Morgan—looked at them expectantly.

She grinned. "I'm in." She lifted her drink. "To the Monuments Women."

Morgan let out a squeal of excitement, and everyone raised their glasses and said in unison, "To the Monuments Women."

Author's Note

There are many fascinating and heartbreaking books and documentaries available to readers interested in learning more about the Democratic Republic of the Congo. For documentaries, I recommend starting with *Mission Congo* and *When Elephants Fight*. For details on the collapse of Zaire and the First and Second Congo Wars, *Dancing in the Glory of Monsters: The Collapse of the Congo and the Great War of Africa* by Jason Stearns is a comprehensive account. For insight into how nascent governments descend into corruption and kleptocracy, I recommend *Thieves of State: Why Corruption Threatens Global Security* by Sarah Chayes.

The above ground description of Mobutu Sese Seko's palace is based on photos and news reports. While there are accounts of tunnels and a nuclear bunker beneath the palace, the tunnels described in this book are fictional.

The problems of the DRC can feel insurmountable, but that is only true if we turn our backs and give up. If any part of this story has touched you, and if you can afford to give to those in desperate need, please join me in donating to a charity working to aid children in the DRC. Some suggestions are Save the Children, CARE, and Chance for Childhood (working in partnership with Street Child Africa).

Thank you for reading *Firestorm*. I hope you enjoyed it. If you'd like to know when my next book is available, you can sign up for my mailing list at www.Rachel-Grant.net. While there you can find links to follow me on Twitter and Facebook.

Acknowledgements

As always, thank you to Darcy Burke and Elisabeth Naughton for our writing retreats and plotting chats. It is always a joy to have you physically and virtually by my side. For readers who are wondering if the references to Zagreus in this book are a nod to Elisabeth's Eternal Guardians series, the answer is yes.

Thank you to Gwen Hayes and Serena Bell who helped me plot the beginning of this book, which was the jumpstart I needed. And thanks to Toni Anderson, who insisted I write this book next. You were right. You are always right.

Thank you again to Gwen Hernandez, Gwen Hayes, and Toni Anderson for critiquing *Firestorm* and helping me to find the path Savvy and Cal take through Congo. I don't know how to write without you anymore, so never leave me. Okay?

Huge thanks to Lola Famure who read this manuscript with an eye for sensitivity in writing a character with a different ethnic background from myself and set in a country ravaged by colonialism and wars. Any errors, misunderstandings, or misrepresentations in these areas are mine.

To my readers, as always, thank you for the wonderful emails, Tweets, and posts. It means so much to me to know my work brings you joy. Thank you for allowing my characters to enter your world.

Thank you to my children. I love you with all my heart and am so proud to be your mom.

Thank you to my husband for being my partner in this adventure. I love you.

About the Author

Four-time Golden Heart® finalist Rachel Grant worked for over a decade as a professional archaeologist and mines her experiences for storylines and settings, which are as diverse as excavating a cemetery underneath an historic art museum in San Francisco, survey and excavation of many prehistoric Native American sites in the Pacific Northwest, researching an historic concrete house in Virginia, and mapping a seventeenth century Spanish and Dutch fort on the island of Sint Maarten in the Netherlands Antilles.

She lives in the Pacific Northwest with her husband and children and can be found on the web at www.Rachel-Grant.net.